The

Midnight

Rose

THE MIDNIGHT ROSE

ISBN-978-0-6459563-0-6

ISBN-978-0-6459563-2-0

www.catalinaparis.com

The

Midnight

Rose

Catalina Paris

"Dreams are what make the stars sparkle

and the moon shine"

-origin unknown

In dreams of midnight where all things begin

I saw you,

Do you remember me?

Contents

The Midnight Rose

Daughter of shadows and fairest night

Blooms in the darkest hour

Shine with most brilliant light

Doth this bright and most loveliest flower

A popular twelfth century folk song of unknown origin

Prologue

Blue Lightning

December 1525

Under an ink black sky filled with clouds and stars, a single lit room glowed within an ancient tower. Beyond the coloured stained glass, a teenage boy with golden curls that fell around his ears sat studiously copying out notes in a strange script. A mix of Alchemical symbols accompanied the words as he carefully weaved the quill across the page. The candles on the desk and the bookshelves around the room bore a curious mixture of different coloured flames. Outside a raven perched upon the stone window ledge, peering in.

A flash of blue lightning illuminated the sky, casting the objects around the room in shades of cobalt. The boy, Leo, paused and glanced outside the window but the raven had crept to the side, out of view. He resumed his writing. He was dedicated to his work, determined to become a fully-fledged Alchemyst who could serve others and the Alchemical Court. However, at the moment he was just an apprentice.

The symbols fascinated Leo as he copied them across the page, along with the words of Alcheme-the language of the Alchemical Court, a blend of ancient Latin, Greek and Persian. Some seemed traditionally Alchemical in nature, representing the elements, sun, moon, stars and planets. Others seemed to originate in other forms of magic, including some of a more

Celtic design. He had never come across such different symbols in the texts he had studied before. One in particular caught his eye: three leaves or petals, their bases overlapping one another, linked by a circle. His fingers gently caressed the page, tracing the symbol. He wondered what it meant as he copied it down in his Alchemyst's Almanac. Another appeared more like a tree within a circle, its branches extending up towards the edge of the circle while the roots grew down.

A swirl of pink magic suddenly rose in a spiral from the floor where chalk-drawn circles were marked with more Alchemical symbols. Leo's mentor, Lady Vidjaya, appeared in the room dressed in her usual dark pink kaftan. She was a rather beautiful woman in her forties with dark tan skin and almond-shaped eyes. In the months since Leo's master had disappeared mysteriously she had taken over his previous role as his main mentor at the Academy.

'Leo!' she addressed him, and he snapped up from his work, quill poised mid-sentence.

'Lady Vidjaya, what has happened?' he asked immediately. She never interrupted him during his studies unless it was an urgent matter.

She approached him, a look of warning clear in her eyes.

'Leo, you must go! The Alchemical Court is in danger and so are you.'

'What? Why? What do you mean in danger?' Leo stood and went to gather his bow and quiver of arrows from where they rested beside his linen satchel. He slipped the sling of the satchel over his chest, then the quiver of arrows over the top, lastly picking up his bow.

'I can't explain to you right now. Please trust me, Leo.'

She clasped his hands and Leo kissed them. Unlike his other teachers, Lady Vidjaya was like a mother to him, the only mother he had ever known.

'You are the most precious thing in this world to me,' she told him.

She stepped back and peered out the doorway, down the corridor to the left.

'Come, Leo, hurry.'

He approached the doorway, peering into the corridor. He heard the sound of footsteps approaching as he turned around and repeated, 'Danger? What danger?'

Lady Vidjaya answered by grabbing his wrist and pulling him behind her, hurriedly making her way down the corridor, and into another room.

'Lady Vidjaya!' Leo protested. His teacher had never acted like this before.

'Leo, listen to me. Someone is after the talismans,' Lady Vidjaya explained quickly.

'Find the scroll depicting the riddle of Atlantica. Decipher the riddle and find the talismans before he does. He thinks the scroll is here but it is not. Go to the Great Library. You will know which one.'

She glanced anxiously back down the corridor behind them.

'He? Who's he? Who are you talking about, Lady Vidjaya?' Leo asked.

'They call him the Dark Alchemyst. He wants the talismans because they are very powerful. They cannot be allowed to fall into his hands. Leo, you must go!' she insisted.

'Go? Go where?' asked Leo, still confused.

'Anywhere for now. Then find the scroll and return to me. Then we can find the talismans. For now, go! Make a portal. Hurry!'

Leo glanced back down the corridor behind them, then back towards Lady Vidjaya.

'May the Spirit guide you on your journey,' she told him. 'Now go!' she implored and he turned to leave. He would need to make a portal, he thought, recalling the series of circles already drawn upon the floor of the study belonging to one of his other teachers. Master Lumír often left this one open with a portal half complete for such emergencies.

'And remember, Leo,' Lady Vidjaya called out from behind him. 'Find the scroll. Find the talismans. Save the Realm.'

He turned towards her one last time and nodded.

Leo hurried along the labyrinth-like corridors of the Alchemical Court. The detailed carved-stone ceiling cast shadows on the floor as he ran. Flames flickered at intervals along the corridor, which was only protected by a wall on one side, opening up on the right to look upon the courtyard below. Leo turned left and then right, when he suddenly pulled to a stop.

There, at the other end of the corridor, was a group of sorcerers led by a figure in a dark cloak, his face concealed by a hood. His lithe body was muscular and well-formed, and despite being hidden by shadow, he seemed somehow familiar.

The figure turned and looked towards Leo, lowering his hood to reveal his features in the moonlight. Long black hair framed his angular face. Dark blue eyes scanned the corridor, landing on Leo. A brief flare of recognition passed across his eyes and reflected itself in Leo's. Then his expression hardened as he pointed towards Leo and the sorcerers' eyes followed.

Leo spun on his heel, breaking into a run. He sprinted down the corridor towards the main study, where another set of circles had been marked on the floor, a basic portal blueprint. He grabbed a piece of chalk and hurriedly sketched a couple of symbols beside the circles at each of the four directions, including the petalled flower and the tree-like symbol. He muttered the typical incantation, and the edges between the stones hummed and glowed a vivid blue as the portal started to activate.

He returned to the large oak doors on the other side of the enormous room, watching as his pursuers approached. They turned the corner and Leo also turned, sprinting towards the portal. He pulled an arrow as he ran, drawing back his bow. He let the arrow loose over his shoulder as he slid to the ground, the enchanted arrow bursting into lightning-blue fire as he was sucked up by the portal, the flames disappearing behind him.

* * *

Chapter One

The Briar Wood

Roses

love, honour, beauty, passion, devotion, sensuality, intrigue, eternal love

Under the full moon cast rose petals upon the water to attract a lover

Six Months earlier

June 1525

Far away to the east, in a parallel realm, a sixteen-year-old maiden sat in a room on the top floor of an elegant cottage. The intricately laced bodice of her lilac dress contrasted with the simple design of the skirt, long pieces of matching fabric hanging from her arms just below the shoulders. Long red hair fell in waves to the small of her back, and her playful green eyes twinkled beneath long, dark eyelashes as she sat reading by the window. Her long, slender nose was juxtaposed with full, rose-shaped lips that pursed themselves ever so slightly as she read.

The cottage itself, being of strong character, was over a hundred years old, and featured intricate woodwork not unreminiscent of the Tudor era combined with Victorian Gothic design. Pots of green and purple orchids grew upon the windowsill, surrounded by climbing red roses on the outside walls. Inside the maiden gazed out towards the township in the distance, her elbow resting on the ledge as she surveyed the landscape surrounding the cottage, distracting her from her reading. Forest protected the cottage for miles, but far off in the distance she could spy rolling yellow hills and fields of flowers lined with tall, thin cypress trees. The dense forest closest to Rose Cottage had become known over the centuries as the Briar Wood, a mysterious place where magic dwelled.

The Great Library in the opposite direction was like a beacon, calling her, drawing her towards its illustrious spires for as long as she could remember. The great white marble dome was decorated with aquamarine tiles and bronze detail that sparkled in the sun. The Great Library was by far the tallest building in Florencia and could be seen from several miles away.

She sighed and returned to her book, lying back on the antique divan by the window. She dreamed so often of exploring the world beyond Rose Cottage. Of travelling worlds beyond her own, of adventure, of discovering-

A rapid succession of knocks on the front door below interrupted her train of thought, quickly followed by her aunt's voice.

'Flora, could you see who it is, per favore?' Aunt Bellissa called from downstairs. 'I'm getting changed.'

'Mi Dia.' *Oh, Goddess.* Flora pulled herself off the divan and headed downstairs to open the front door. A scrawny messenger boy stood there, barely visible behind a bouquet of massive sunflowers.

'Mi Dia, again,' she muttered to herself quietly. He must have been only a year or so younger than herself, she noted as he struggled to carry the enormous bouquet.

'For the lady of the house,' he said, eagerly handing over the bouquet to Flora. 'Grazia,' she awkwardly thanked him. He gave a small bow and left. Flora took the sunflowers inside, setting them upon the table. She smiled as Aunt Bellissa came down the stairs, adjusting the scarlet feather on her stylish hat, tucking a loose strand of her auburn brown hair behind her ear and back into her bun.

'Oh Aunt Bellissa, they're gorgeous! Who sent them?'

Flora asked as she fetched a blue ceramic vase from the cupboard in the dining salon. She filled it with water from the jug, then placed in the vibrant flowers, adjusting them to form an elegant display. Upon her touch the flowers became more alive, moving their heads and leaves in her direction.

She has always had an otherworldly way with flowers, Aunt Bellissa thought with a small smile that she swiftly masked.

'I am not sure, Flora,' she said elusively, feigning interest in some letters. Flora saw right through her aunt's pretence.

'I must know. Tell me!' she insisted, then her eyes lit up as she remembered.

'What does the card say?'

The two of them looked towards the card left in the bouquet. Aunt Bellissa reached for it but Flora snatched it out of her hand.

'Ooohl, an admirer!' She raced off with the card, well out of her aunt's reach.

'Flora!' Aunt Bellissa chastised, following her as she wandered around the ground floor of the cottage. Flora came to a stop in front of the window where she stood in a shaft of sunlight. She held up the card to the light and read the elegant script.

'A bloom of sunflowers for Senorita Bellissa, Lady DuPoitoires, mi belladonna. *My beautiful lady,*' Flora translated. She looked up at Aunt Bellissa. The card had addressed her as senorita, her title in the language of the South.

'They're from him, are they not? Felippe, I believe his name is,' she teased gently.

Aunt Bellissa pouted. Flora clasped her aunt's hands and kissed her on the cheek.

'Aunt Bellissa. You are a wonderful, successful business-woman. You are bound to have admirers.'

Aunt Bellissa walked away, readjusting her hat in the mirror so it was tilted at a more fashionable angle. She was much shorter than Flora, who had been taller than her aunt since the age of eleven, having inherited her father's height.

'Yes,' she admitted. 'I suppose I must be off, sweet girl, though I do hate to leave you alone like this.' Aunt Bellissa placed her gloved hands upon the sides of Flora's face and kissed both cheeks, before hugging her.

'I will return in a fortnight, darling.' She picked up her bag and headed for the door, where a horseless carriage had pulled up on the road, pulled by a technology involving the air that Flora could not explain. Fuschia was quite sophisticated for a kingdom without magic.

'Farewell, Aunt Bellissa. Have a safe journey,' said Flora, standing on tip toes in the doorway of the cottage.

'Farewell. I shall see you soon,' Aunt Bellissa turned and waved before stepping into the coach. Flora waved in return, watching as the coach sped away.

She turned around and closed the cottage door behind her, resting her back against it. She had the cottage to herself for the first time since . . . Well, since forever. She rested there for a moment, soaking in her newfound independence. For years her days had been spent either studying the various languages of the realms or assisting her aunt's tailoring business. Whether it was stitching embroidery, sewing feathers onto hats, or making sleeves for dresses, Flora could have easily found work as a seamstress if that was what she desired.

But she loved her dear Aunt Bellissa, who had raised her since she was a baby. Her grandfather, Stefan DuPoitoires, had also lived with them until his death when Flora was five. Bellissa and her mother had grown up in Rose Cottage themselves. Flora's grandfather had been a fabrics merchant and jeweller who had emigrated from the Western Kingdom of Brittainnia. He had supplied the ladies and gentlemen of the court and kingdom with fashionable fabrics and clothes and jewellery, all with a genuine smile and keen eye for which colour suited each person who sought his services.

After he died, Bellissa had taken over the business, expanding it to become the most successful across the realms, even making an impression upon the renowned Australis Empire of the east. She had always had a keen interest in fashion and the skill and diplomacy to match, making her a rare successful businesswoman. Flora admired her confidence and determination.

She raced up the stairs, her hand casing the railing, heading to the third floor and then to the attic where she went to an old wooden wardrobe and opened the door. She bent down and pulled out a wooden chest in fine condition, lifting the lid to reveal the contents within. From among various necklaces and jewellery, she retrieved a large old book.

The Book of Moon's purple cover was adorned in silver calligraphy along with a silver crescent symbolising the moon. Flora placed the book on the floor and opened it. Elegant scripts decorated the ancient pages, describing various spells in silvery ink. She had found the Spellbooke three months before, when she had first come across the chest among her mother's things before her sixteenth birthday. The chest itself had been hidden in her mother's old wardrobe, which was covered by a tapestry in the attic.

Flora had quickly realised that her mother had been a witch and, upon trying some of the spells in the book, found that she too had the ability to weave magic. She had kept the Spellbooke secret from Aunt Bellissa. She was unsure how her aunt would react to witchcraft —, after all, the book and her mother's things had been hidden. Besides, Aunt Bellissa had never mentioned magic.

Flora stood up and opened the other door of the wardrobe to reveal a collection of magnificent dresses. She stepped forward and examined them, fingering the soft material. She had never known her mother. All she knew was that her name had been Arianna.

Her fingers rested on the red dress. It was one of her favourites, and yet she desired to add some finishing touches of her own. With a wave of her hand, the chosen dress floated out of the wardrobe, enchanted. Flora began to use her magic on the dress, bewitching the fabric, making alterations that would normally take hours of sewing: cutting the sleeves open, transforming them into a lighter material, lowering the neckline to reveal the shoulders in the fashion of the Southern Kingdom. Her spell made quickwork of the task at hand, a spell she had practised the last few months on parts of other dresses for her aunt's business, bringing her designs to fruition. Gold embroidery now decorated the scarlet fabric along the low neckline, with a matching golden belt and tassel around the waist.

Flora stepped behind the changing screen, where she changed into the red dress. She adjusted a pair of ruby earrings as she emerged, sweeping her hair over her shoulder before examining her appearance in the mirror. She pulled back the upper strands of the sides of her hair, tying them in an elegant pair of knots to which she added a pair of green orchids.

Finally she brought out an emerald necklace. Its rectangular-cut oval green gemstones were dispersed between two chains of pearls worn close to the neck. The central gemstone depicted a phoenix carved into the emerald, its wings spread mid-flight as it rose into the air. Below this was a pearl and a single rectangular green bead.

Flora placed the necklace upon her neck and reassessed her appearance in the mirror. Satisfied, she carried the book downstairs and fetched her lavender cloak and her wicker basket, in which she placed the book before striding back to her dresser in her own room, opening a drawer to retrieve her bejewelled dagger. Peridot and emerald gems decorated the hilt in an intricate design, the largest matching the necklace.

Where her mother had gotten such things, she knew not. Part of her wondered if her mother had become a pirate maiden and stolen them. She also wondered if they were possibly heirlooms of her father's family, whoever he may be. A knight, perhaps?

Flora placed the dagger in the basket and slid up her hood before she set off for her destination.

* * *

The stars had already started to come out as she set off for the forest under the cover of night. The silver crescent moon shone blue in the sky as Flora stopped in the Briar Wood to collect certain leaves and berries from the bushes in the moonlight. She continued along the narrow trail through the forest, the trees becoming denser and deeper, until she came to a shimmering pool beneath an old rowan tree. Its majestic branches stretched proudly towards the sky, and the shimmering surface of the pool below reflected the moon.

Flora knelt beside the pool and set aside her basket. She retrieved her Spellbooke, opening it to a particular page before setting it aside on the ground. She lifted her hood, raised her head to the skies and sang to the moon. She sang a lover's charm, casting crimson pink rose petals in a circle upon the pool.

'May his eyes meet mine

And with this charm of mine

Let him fall under my spell

Thy noble prince, Mikhail.'

As soon as she finished casting the spell the petals rose up, spiralling in a swirl through the air, floating towards the moon. Flora untied her cloak and placed it over the book. She stood, her red dress shining indigo in the moonlight. Retrieving a branch of rowan, she gazed into the pool's myriad depths and slowly traced a circle, silently wishing to encounter the worlds beyond this one.

'Let the enchanting rowan speak

As I cast my ancient spell

To see before my eyes

Visions of the world beyond

The Kingdom of the Midnight Sun I do seek

Where divine magics doth dwell

Deep in starlit skies

A world of light and song'

As she finished casting the words to open the portal, the water rippled and the edges of the pool began to glow a luminescent light blue. The water's surface shimmered to reveal an image of a glamourous palace of sapphire-blue towers with golden orb-shaped domes beneath a starry sky.

Flora glanced up at the stars in her own sky, then glanced down toward the pool as determinedly, she stepped in.

* * *

Leo woke in a forest.

Sunlight illuminated the branches. He propped himself up on his elbows, realising he was lying on the ground. Leaves, small pebbles and dirt covered the forest floor. His head ached a little, but most of the fall had been softened by the leaves.

He remembered falling, almost as if through a void as he was sucked in by the portal, his pursuers left staring as it closed after him, leaving no trace, no clue as to where he had gone. He gazed up at the dense forest blocking out the sky. It was as though if he were in an underworld of branches and trees. They seemed to stretch high for miles.

A male faerie stood beside the door, dressed in tights and a forest green tunic decorated with an emblem of a leaf edged with gold thread. Long vines entwined with tendrils of leaves at the edges around the large wooden doors. *Are those actual living vines acting as hinges?* Leo wondered as he stood up, his attention drawn to the thick biomass that weaved itself in and out. He had little time to pursue the thought as the curtains of vines parted and the door opened.

'The Lady Lisandre,' the male faerie announced, and the Alchemyst found his eyes drawn to another faerie who appeared in the doorway: a young maiden with long dark hair streaming past her shoulders. She wore a sleeveless cream coloured dress with a decorated bodice, the collar lined with crystals. Her lips were bright cherry-red and her eyes were orbs of brilliant amber. Her nose was sharp and well-formed but pleasing. A glint of reflected light drew his attention to tiny crystals woven into her hair. Her figure was gentle yet strong, and the way she held herself with such grace, yet there was something distinct about her, quite unlike the other maidens he had met so far in his travels. And then there were her wings. They shimmered, reflecting the light as if they too were made of crystal.

The young Alchemyst gently bowed his head in respect and Lady Lisandre nodded subtly in return. Leo had read about many of the other beings and realms in his studies at the Alchemical Court, and remembered that the fey were known for valuing respect.

Then she spoke.

'The faerie queen wishes to welcome you to our realm, strange traveller,' she greeted him earnestly. 'She cannot see you at present as she is attending other matters but she hopes that you will accept her invitation to be our honoured guest this evening. You are also welcome to stay for the Winter Solstice Ball if you wish,' she added, her gaze gently examining him.

'Thank you. I feel most welcome,' Leo said and Lady Lisandre blushed.

'Where am I, may I ask?'

'Na Foraise Síorai,' she answered. *The Eternal Forest,* the spell translated in his head while his mind recalled from his textbooks that it was another name for the Realm of the Fey.

'Would you care for some refreshment? Or perhaps some berries? Are you not tired after your journey?' Lisandre questioned while Leo stared at her wings. Before that night he had never even seen a member of the fey in the flesh, only drawings of them in the books at the Alchemical Court.

Lady Lisandre suddenly became self-conscious as she realised he was staring. Then her expression quickly changed to surprise.

'You can see my wings?' she asked, and he nodded. 'How?'

'I am an Alchemyst,' he answered.

She appeared puzzled.

'You can transform metal into gold . . . ?' she enquired, a hint of curiosity in her voice. Leo clasped his hands behind his back.

'Among other things. I am still learning.'

'Some water would be nice, thank you,' he added and Lisandre gave a small smile.

'Follow me.' She turned to guide him through the archway into the room beyond, passing through the veil of vines and vanishing from the room. Leo glanced around, but the other fey seemed disinterested, unfazed by Lisandre's disappearance.

He followed her through, emerging in a hall with a ceiling that was easily a hundred feet high. Golden carvings of leaves decorated the trim of the cream walls and ceiling. An enormous long table filled the hall that could comfortably fill a hundred guests. Plates of nuts as well as overfilled bowls of different coloured and shaped fruit and berries lined the centre of the table, along with various raw cakes.

Leo sat down at the end of the table closest to them, presumably the opposite side from the queen, given the ornate chair at the other end. There were twelve similarly decorated chairs, six on each side of the queen, he noted, wondering who they were for.

Each chair's carvings depicted different leaves; some featured berries or small flowers, while others did not.

Lisandre soon returned, holding a pitcher and a pair of cups. She sat on the bench beside him before pouring them each a glass and offering one to Leo.

'Thank you,' he said, taking a sip.

'What is this?'

Lisandre panicked. *What if mortals . . .*

Still marvelling at the water, Leo noticed Lisandre's worried expression. 'Are you alright?' he asked concerned.

'I'm sorry, I did not realise . . . Are mortals able to consume our water? Does it affect you differently?' she said.

'I have never tasted water so pure, so refreshing . . .' He paused for a moment as he searched for the right word to describe the feeling. 'So *good.*'

Lisandre relaxed. 'It's crystal water,' she explained. 'It comes naturally filtered by the springs in the crystal caves below us. Those from other realms are generally not used to it,' she warned him.

'It's delicious,' he reassured her, drinking the whole cup.

Lady Lisandre did the same, albeit a bit more slowly, then helped himself to some strawberries.

'What is the cake?' Leo enquired.

'Berry cashewcake,' she answered, 'We use nuts and berries, sweetened with tree nectar.'

'May I try some?'

'Of course.' Lisandre stood and cut them each a slice. She placed each one a small plate of silver, then added a fork and passed a plate to him.

Leo picked up the fork and took a bite. *This is amazing,* he thought, he would stay down here for the food alone. None of the other realms he had travelled to had such nice food. He voiced his admiration to Lisandre.

'I know,' she answered, her eyes sparkling as she watched him with curious interest. The Central Forest received few visitors from other parts of the realm in her years, and none of them had reacted as he did. 'What is your name?' she asked at last, after a lengthy silence.

He paused, then looked at her as he answered. 'Leo.'

'Leo,' Lisandre echoed, tasting the name in her musical tongue.

'What are you, Leo? What exactly is an Alchemyst?' She leaned her elbow on the table, her head resting on her hand. 'Are you another kind of magician?' she teased.

Leo smiled. 'Yes and no,' he answered, amused. 'We study Alchemy, which is both science and magic. We learn about elements, yes, as well as transforming them and activating portals among other things. We also study the movements of the stars and planets.'

'How interesting,' she replied, eager to know more.

Leo watched her. She was so beautiful, not just aesthetically, but also in her general demeanour and her personality, from the little that he knew so far. He remembered stories, myths even, of the fair folk, and fair they were in appearance as well of character. He had read that they lived for thousands of years while mere mortals perished. Leo couldn't help but stare at Lisandre's youthful face, wondering how old she really was beneath her glowing appearance. The thought saddened him. She probably could not relate to him at all, just like the nymphs.

The silence between them was beginning to become awkward when another young female faerie with long dark hair and a tan complexion entered the room. She appeared about seventeen and wore a dress with strands of ivy woven across from one shoulder down to the opposite thigh.

'Lady Lisandre,' she acknowledged his host, then turned to him. 'Honoured guest. The queen requests your presence now in the Grand Atrium,' she informed them.

'Thank you, Lady Alaïa,' Lisandre replied. 'We shall be there soon.'

Alaïa curtseyed before exiting the room.

Lisandre turned to face Leo. 'Are you sufficiently nourished?' He nodded. 'Then I hope you do not mind if we attend to the Queen at once. Queen Ivana does not like to be kept waiting.'

Leo stood. 'Then we shall not keep her.'

Lisandre led him through a wandering maze of hallways from the Grand Hall to what she informed him was called the Grand Atrium. The trees grew in and out of the halls, forming many of the walls themselves. Balconies several stories high surrounded the centre, filled with many members of the fey gazing down.

Lisandre approached the figure sitting upon the throne in the centre at the other end of the room. The young woman sitting upon the throne bore a slight resemblance to Lisandre, her sweeping dark raven hair framed by sharp cheekbones and piercing dark eyes. *Perhaps they were cousins,* Leo thought. The queen was dressed in what appeared to be a silk-like fabric enriched with dark purple and silver. Her wings were purple, edged with black and were of a more gothic style yet still elegant. Sparkling silver dust decorated around her eyes.

She appeared a few years older than Lisandre, yet looked as though she had not aged past nineteen. As for how old she truly was, Leo could hardly tell. In fact, every faerie he had met or seen down here seemed no older than twenty-five.

'My queen.' Lisandre dipped lightly into a curtsey and took her place on the throne's right-hand side along with three other ladies, leaving Leo in the middle of the room.

Alone, he bowed. An awkward silence hung in the air for several minutes as she examined him.

'Strange traveller,' Queen Ivana finally addressed him. 'Dromaga nu Na Foraise Síorai. We welcome thee to the Eternal Forest, our realm and ancient home.' She paused, resting her chin on her hand curiously. 'How may I ask, did you arrive here? Few venture into our realm. Even fewer venture out.'

The last bit made him shudder. What did she mean by that? He made a mental note to ask Lady Lisandre about that later if he got the chance.

He clasped his hands behind his back and took a deep breath before answering.

'I created a portal, fairest one.'

Having thought about it that was the conclusion he had reached about what had happened. He'd meant to open an existing portal, but he must have drawn one of the symbols wrong or pronounced a word incorrectly. Somehow, he, a lowly yet dedicated apprentice, had created the first new portal in over a century, at least according to the histoires he had studied at the Alchemical Court. Perhaps there were larger forces at work.

He had used the title *fairest one,* as those he had read about addressed the sovereign of the fey in books. The queen did not comment on it. Instead, she seemed confused.

'It was an accident, really. I apologise. I was trying to get to —' His hands fumbled together as he nervously tried to explain. Where was he trying to get to, exactly? He tried to remember.

'An accident? Unlikely . . .' The queen peered at him with a focused gaze that seemed to cut right through him. 'A portal? How intriguing.'

'Yes. Do the fey not use them?' Leo asked.

'Of course not,' Queen Ivana replied. 'Our realm has been isolated for a hundred years to protect ourselves from races such as your own. Though I admit we have rarely had the odd traveller stumble across us during that time, always by a natural portal they had found. Not by one they had created. Indeed I have not seen visitors enter our realm in twenty years.'

It was true, then: he really had created a portal to another realm. He wondered if he could do it to others, and more importantly, if he could do it to get back to his own realm . . . The Alchemical Court was in trouble, he recalled. He hoped Lady Vidjaya was safe.

'I think it is safe to assume you are not a mortal, then,' Queen Ivana stated.

'No, I am not,' Leo admitted. *Mortals* was the term used by magic-users to define those who could not wield magic. Though Lisandre had incorrectly assumed he was one, understandably.

'He is an Alchemyst, my queen,' spoke Lady Lisandre now. 'He goes by the name of Leo.'

The Queen listened attentively, then returned her gaze to Leo. The Queen seemed to hold a high regard for Lisandre, Leo observed.

'An Alchemyst. How interesting . . .' said Queen Ivana. Her eyes focused upon him as she asked, 'Do others know how you created this portal?' She spoke as if she despised the very topic.

'No, fairest one,' Leo answered, only now noticing the banners and circular stained glass artworks hanging from the trees behind her. They each depicted a yellow rose in all its glory upon a green background.

'Good.' Leo noticed a hint of relief belying her composed manner. 'Do you have a way to return home, young Alchemyst?' Queen Ivana questioned.

'Not yet. I shall need access to your library, if you have one. After some calculations and redesigns, I think I shall be able to create a portal to my realm,' he answered confidently.

'Very well.' Queen Ivana gestured to Lisandre, who walked over to stand beside her. 'Lisandre, you are to be this Alchemyst's guide while he is here in our realm. See to it that our *honourable* guest is comfortable,' she instructed her.

'Yes, fairest one.' Lisandre curtseyed politely and joined Leo in the centre of the room.

'If you would follow me,' she instructed Leo, who glanced to the queen.

'Good day, strange traveller,' she said, and dismissed him, watching intently as Leo followed Lisandre out of the Atrium.

* * *

Chapter Two

The Midnight Court

Orchids

love, exotic beauty, luxury, enchantment

Entwine a pair of orchids to enchant a lover

S he emerged from the pool into a world of light and sound.

The beautiful interior of the palace radiated grandeur and extravagance, from the gold-lined walls to the jewel-encrusted fountain in the centre of the room. As she stepped out of the fountain, Flora glanced up at the clear glass dome that revealed the night sky. She paused, studying the positions of the stars and constellations — constellations that were different from her own.

Flora muttered a quick spell to dry the hem of her dress, the only part that had somehow gotten wet, it seemed, from her journey through the portal. She glanced around, taking note of what appeared to be the circular entrance hall of the Midnight Palace. The dark blue walls were adorned with various life-size portraits. One depicted a middle-aged man with black hair and a thick beard and moustache. He stood proudly, wearing a golden tunic. King Cesaire, she recalled from a book she had read on Alyssrian history. He was the present ruler of Alyssria, the Kingdom of the Midnight Sun.

Another portrait showed an impressive lady around the same age, dressed in purple with long dark brown hair. Queen Katya, also a powerful sorceress. The last Safarov princess, they had called her in her youth. The only survivor, apart from her grandmother, during the failed uprising of 1498, when she had been just thirteen. She defied both the court and her grandmother when she married the lowly jewelsmith upon becoming queen at eighteen.

The third portrait was of a handsome man of around twenty-one with dark brown hair and stubble. His thick eyebrows were matched with sparkling blue eyes and a bright smile, and he was dressed in a smart scarlet red tunic. Flora recognised him as the crown prince, Mikhail. She wondered if he was as handsome in person as his portrait suggested.

The next portrait featured a younger man with blond hair wearing an orange tunic. He wasn't smiling; his face seemed to be fixed with an unreadable frown. Prince Aleksandr. The middle son. Flora did not know much about him. She had read about each of the Alyssrian princes, Mikhail, Aleksandr and Lucien, but the court gossip usually focused on Mikhail, as he was the crown prince.

She found herself startled as her eyes were drawn to the next portrait. Flora had dreamed of this portrait. In her dreams she sometimes saw a young man, also with dark hair, but his face was always obscured by shadow.

She read the name underneath the portrait. *His* name. *Lucien.*

The youngest of the Alyssrian princes, he was also the closest to her own age, with lengthy black hair and startling blue eyes that spoke unto her soul. He seemed somewhat familiar, though she could not explain why. She brushed the feeling aside.

Flora glanced at her reflection in the fountain and tucked a loose strand of hair behind her ear. Now all that was missing was a fan. A red rosebush standing in a detailed ceramic pot nearby caught her eye. Flora picked off a rose with a long stem. With a flourish of her hand, the flower transformed into an elegant fan with folded edges of soft rose petals. She fluttered the fan and raised her other hand to her head. *Yes, perfect.*

Music was emanating from somewhere further inside the palace. Listening to the tune, Flora followed the sound of flutes and violins, her footsteps echoing upon the shiny marble floor. She soon found the hall where the courtiers had gathered. Their fine clothes were reminiscent of jewels, with metallic hues of blue, green, red and purple that dominated the fabrics. Upon further inspection, Flora noticed tiny jewels had been sewn into the material. Here, heavy layers and puffy shoulder sleeves seemed to be the height of fashion, in contrast to the low necklines and often bare shoulders of the fashions of Fuschia and its neighbour, the Southern Kingdom of Castelle. This divergence in style seemed to reflect as much a difference in culture as well as in climate.

Flora paused and looked around. The crowd of people cast her the occasional stare as she passed calmly by them. She was truly a beauty, and she knew it. She could probably dance with any of the many handsome eligible young men in attendance. But tonight she had a mission and she couldn't afford to be distracted. She needed to blend in, yet also make a good impression.

She stood at the edge of a throng of gossiping ladies, reminding herself that she was playing a role . . . To observers she must seem a frivolous young girl, despite the wit concealed beyond her exterior. The ladies ignored her as she likewise hurriedly waved her fan to cool herself. Nervously, she laughed, glancing as a figure walked by. Their eyes met, causing her breath to catch.

There was a gleam in the prince's sapphire-blue eyes that reflected her own. There was something else as well, something that made her feel like falling into an abyss, something dangerous and somehow inviting.

Then he strode away and was gone. Her eyes followed him as he stood at the edge of the court beside his brother.

One of the ladies beside her introduced herself, but Flora found herself distracted as she watched the two brothers converse among themselves. The other ladies also curtly introduced themselves, enquiring as to who she was. She provided them with her chosen identity and, satisfied she was no threat to them, they left her alone and resumed ignoring her. Much of their attention seemed to be centred upon a young lady wearing a black-and-red dress with puffy, ruby-coloured diamond sleeves, standing in the middle of the group. Unlike most of the others, she dared to reveal the bare skin between the end of the sleeve and the start of the forearms, from which point she wore ruby-red gloves. Black lace decorated the rounded skirt of her dress. A pair of teardrop ruby earrings hung from her ears and her light blonde hair was neatly pulled back into a bun, revealing her pleasing round face. She waved her fan anxiously as her hazel eyes scoured the court.

'I'm sure he will be here soon Eleanora,' one of the ladies reassured her, touching her arm.

Eleanora ignored her, her face remaining taut as she stared straight ahead. Flora observed as the other ladies resumed chatting amongst themselves, ending in an eruption of giggles behind fans. Nervously, she also laughed.

She noticed babushka figurines on top of the cabinet along the wall on one side of the room, recognising them from when her aunt had received one from Felippe on one of his travels. Flora wandered over to admire them. Each piece of wood had been delicately hand-crafted and decorated. Small gemstones upon them glittered in the light. The prized craftsmanship of Alyssria. The kingdom was known for its ability to mine precious gemstones, which were used in magic.

'Good evening, beautiful creature,' a male voice spoke in Alyssrian behind her, and she turned around to see Crown Prince Mikhail standing before her in his elegant red tunic.

She replied in Alyssrian in return, albeit with a Southern accent. 'Добрый квечер.'

Good evening, Your Grace.

Flora felt the eyes of the court fall upon her as he knelt and kissed her hand, much to the other ladies' dismay. Her spell had worked better than she had thought.

'May I have this dance?' he asked, gazing up at her.

Flora smiled flirtatiously. 'I would be honoured, Your Grace.' She blushed as she waved her fan, attempting to cool her face. Flicking the fan away, she interlaced her arm with his as he led her out onto the dancefloor. His hand slid along her back, resting upon her waist as the music started again and he began to move with her across the dancefloor.

Under the domed glass ceiling, she gazed up at the midnight sky above, at the beauty of the stars and constellations so different from the ones she knew back home. She caught glances of the other dancers, as well as the spectators who stood in a circle around the dancefloor. She was a bit thrown when she caught Eleanora staring at her with eyes that absolutely despised her. Mikhail seemed to sense this and smiled reassuringly at her. She smiled gently in return.

* * *

On the other side of the court, Lucien watched the dancers beside his brother.

'And who is this bewitching beauty?' he asked Aleksandr as he watched Mikhail lift Flora off the ground, her dress sweeping the tiles.

Aleksandr's eyes followed Lucien's. 'The Countess de Roselle.' He took a sip from his goblet. 'She has recently come of age. She claims to be from the mysterious Southern Kingdom,' he informed him.

'Claims?' Lucien turned to his brother with a dubious eye.

'Is any maiden all that she seems?' replied Aleksandr.

Lucien sighed and leaned back against the wall. 'Isn't that true?' he replied, pensive. 'Besides our brother appears quite captivated by her for the moment, does he not?' he added as they watched Mikhail lead her off the dancefloor and down a corridor away from the grand ballroom.

A tall lady dressed in green with golden blonde hair beckoned Aleksandr from the other side of the room.

'You'll have to excuse me, brother. It appears I have business to attend to.' Aleksandr swept his hand through his hair and hastily excused himself, downing the rest of his berry drink before he left.

Lucien swirled the contents of his own bejewelled goblet; the crimson rose petals floating on the surface of the red liquid. He looked up over towards where, only moments ago, his brother had been in the centre of the dancefloor with the new beauty, dancing. Her red dress, most assuredly of the Southern fashions, reminded him of rose petals. From a distance she cast a certain allure, unlike any other lady of the court ever had. Perhaps it was because she was a foreigner? No. He had met other foreign ladies at the court many times, and none had this effect on his brother. It was usually the other way around, with his brother's charms instantly winning the ladies over at first sight. No, there was something more to this mysterious beauty, he thought. Who was this new jewel of the Midnight Court?

He became determined to find out.

* * *

'And where is the map room?' Flora asked, glancing up at Mikhail as he led her, wrapped around his arm, on a tour through another grand corridor of the Midnight Palace.

Mikhail paused and sighed. 'Dearest countess . . .' He kissed her hand. 'You have already seen the library, the conservatory, the astronomy tower, the grand galleria, the musé, the grand ballroom, the little ballroom, the pianonata, almost everywhere besides my bedchamber. Surely you are not that intrigued by Alyssrian architecture that you insist on exploring the entire palace?'

'So what if I am? What is so wrong with that?' she flirted, placing her fingertips on his chest. 'Alyssrian architecture is so different to the Southern kingdom. Surely as crown prince you would indulge a young lady such as myself a grand tour?'

'Very well,' he acquiesced, and nodded to the door behind her. 'The map room is through there. Shall we?'

Flora swung from his arm to the enormous large golden doorknob in the centre of the maroon coloured door. She turned it and the door opened, revealing the room beyond. Flora rushed back to Mikhail's side, pulling him inside.

A huge incompleted map of the realms encompassed an enormous table in the centre of the room. Flora bent over slightly to peer at it, intrigued by its contents. The kingdom of Alyssria lay at the heart of the realm while several more familiar kingdoms were depicted to the south. Other smaller maps covered the corners of the table, some depicting constellations and stars. Many scrolls sat in shelves along the far wall. Glowing crystals hung from the high domed ceiling above, while an intricate astronomical clock within an elegantly carved wooden frame rested on top of the shelves.

Flora's fingers trailed the map table as she examined the names of kingdoms she had never traversed before: Brittannia, Ægyptia, the Alchemical Court, the Australis Empire . . .

She was so captivated by the map's contents she didn't even notice Mikhail sneak up behind her until he wrapped his fingers around her waist and kissed her neck. Flora's head shot up as she glanced at the clock. It was late — very late. She would have to return another night.

'I must go, Your Grace,' she said, and he withdrew as she turned around to face him.

Mikhail bowed and kissed her hand. 'Until next time countess,' he whispered.

* * *

His brother had informed him that the countess would not return until the next ball in two weeks. On the July evening in question Lucien wandered the halls of the Midnight Palace. Many of the guests had arrived by now; surely so had she. He paused at the end of a corridor to address a footman.

'Excuse me, do you know where I may find the Countess de Roselle?' he enquired politely.

'I believe she is on the balcony overlooking the South Terrace, Your Grace,' the elderly man answered.

'Thank you.'

Lucien headed toward the South Terrace. The sun was now setting, casting glowing hues of blue, orange and pink across the sky as the court gathered for the evening's activities. The faint scent of gardenias filled the air as he approached a figure in a familiar red dress, facing away from him as she gazed at the gardens below. The first thing he noticed were the flowers she wore braided atop of head. The green orchids stood out in contrast to her long red hair. Lucien paused midstride, taken aback. It was as he had dreamed, except in his visions the flowers had been green roses, and it had been night-time as she gazed fondly at the moonlight.

He stepped behind a nearby pillar, crossed his arms and watched her from a distance as she admired the myriad gardens of the Midnight Palace. Here she was, the mysterious Countess de Roselle, leaning her elbows on the sandstone balcony between two classical-styled columns as he watched her from a side-on angle, just outside of her periphery. Up close she was even more beautiful than at a distance, with a long, heart-shaped face, wide, sensuous eyes and seductive lips. He was certain he had seen that face before, somewhere aside from his more recent dreams, but where, he could not remember.

'Excuse me, Your Grace.' He felt a soft tap on the shoulder as a voice whispered to him. Lucien turned to see one of the older courtiers peering at him, his fingertips neatly poised together. He was of short stature with large, owl-like eyes, grey hair and a bushy moustache. A single diamond hung from the lobe of his right ear.

'Åsmund!' Lucien greeted the man before encouraging him to walk back down the corridor with him away from the countess. 'Are you well? How may I be of service?'

'I am very well, my prince, thank you. Your brothers have requested your presence in the map room,' Åsmund informed him. 'The crown prince said there was a particularly urgent matter to attend to.'

'Something urgent?' Lucien inquired, intrigued.

Åsmund shrugged. 'Something very important I suppose.'

'Very well. Lead the way.' Lucien threw one last glance back towards the countess before turning to follow Åsmund down the hall. As he did he could have sworn he saw her turn and cast a glance at him in return.

* * *

The hallway bustled with the chatters and murmurs of curious guests as the gathering courtiers moved out of the way. Lucien strode past, quickly arriving at the map room. He entered and shut the door behind him.

'What is it, Mikhail?' He strode to join the others as they stood around the map table, placing his hands behind his back.

Mikhail looked up to greet him. 'Ah, Lucien. At last,' he clapped his younger brother on the back.

'I came soon as I could, brother.'

'Good, very good,' said Mikhail. Aleksandr watched on in silence, his arms crossed as he stood with his back against the wall.

Mikhail returned to his previous discussion. 'There have been rumours Arianna the Magnificent has returned and has placed a spy within the Midnight Court,' he said, his tone serious.

'Are you sure? For all we know Arianna started these rumours herself,' proposed Aleksandr, unconvinced.

'I considered that but we found this.' Mikhail presented a handkerchief. Upon the fabric, embroidered in dark purple thread, was an iris.

'Her token,' he explained. 'One of the ladies found it after the Summer Ball.'

'I will find this traitor,' Aleksandr vowed passionately. 'I will find them and bring them to justice.'

'No, thank you, Aleksandr. I entrust Lucien with this most sensitive matter.'

Mikhail placed his palms upon Lucien's shoulders. 'Discover their identity and bring them to me. Apprehend them, whomever they may be and prove your loyalty to your House and future king. Find them, Lucien. Find the traitor.'

* * *

The game had started one evening when she had been waiting for Mikhail and had come across Lucien, the youngest brother, instead.

'Forgive me, prince, but I was looking for your brother. He asked me to meet him here,' she courteously explained, turning to leave.

'Stay. I am sure he will be here shortly. Matters of state and such.' Lucien reassured her. Restless, she paced up and down the chamber as Lucien's gaze followed her curiously. What was taking Mikhail so long? He had never been so unpunctual with her before. She turned and looked out the window towards the nearby city of Safir, wondering where he could be.

'Do you play chess?' Lucien asked after a while, breaking the silence.

'Actually, yes.' Flora turned, surprised. 'My grandfather taught me before he died.' She sat down on the sapphire-blue chaise cushion opposite him. 'He always said a lady should know three things: how to dress, how to impress and how to play chess.'

'He sounds like an interesting man. I am sorry for your loss.'

'So am I,' she admitted. An awkward silence passed between them before Lucien spoke again.

'My name is Lucien but you are probably already aware of that,' he said quietly as he set up the pieces.

'I am,' she remarked nonchalantly. The game began.

'And you are?' Lucien asked.

'Flora. Rhymes with "Oh, how I *adore* her!"' she said, extending her hand to her forehead with a dramatic flourish.

Lucien cracked a half-smile. Then his mask returned. 'My brother . . . indeed half the court finds you utmost amusing. Where is it you are from, exactly?' he enquired, moving a chess piece forward.

'Amusing? We shall see about that. Here I was aiming for fascinating,' she replied playfully, raising an eyebrow. Lucien remained silent. 'The Provence of Roselle, the answer to your question. In the Southern Kingdom.' Flora moved a piece forward confidently.

'I hear the Southern Kingdom is famous for its music, particularly its singers. Tell me, do you sing countess?' Lucien asked with his eyes firmly upon her as he moved one of his in turn.

What was he playing at?

'A little, Your Grace,' Flora admitted. 'Are you offering an invitation?' She raised an eyebrow again and smiled one of her enchanting smiles, laughing. *Goddess*, she reprimanded herself. *Why am I flirting with him?* Here he was playing inquisitor and the best she could do was match wits while batting her eyelashes! If she wasn't careful . . .

But part of her also wanted to be caught. To be caught in his embrace, to have someone in whom to confide her secret . . .

She quickly changed the subject. 'Tell me, prince. Have you ever been to the Southern Kingdom?' She leaned forward and rested her chin upon her hands. 'The ladies here say you are a great sorcerer.'

'And do you believe them?' he asked.

'Well I said "I don't know about great . . ."' she teased.

'Well, yes. I have,' he answered.

'Do you ever dance, great prince?' she asked.

'No,' he firmly answered.

She moved another chess piece. 'Is that because you cannot or do not know how?'

'Neither. I just haven't found someone to dance with,' he replied, moving his knight cleverly.

Flora responded with a clever move of her own, surprising him.

'I win,' she declared triumphantly.

'I wouldn't be so sure of that,' Lucien replied, and in a swift calculated move, won the game.

'Though I must say I do enjoy the challenge,' he remarked truthfully.

'We shall see about that,' she replied.

'Play again?' he requested, and Flora smiled.

* * *

'If you come this way, Leo, I can show you to your rooms,' offered Lisandre as they left the Atrium. Leo nodded and she took the lead, heading through a maze of circular corridors lit by golden orbs.

'Lady Lisandre, tell me, when is this Winter Solstice Ball you mentioned earlier?' the Alchemyst asked as they walked.

'Oh . . .' Lady Lisandre glanced over her shoulder. 'On the evening of the solstice, in three days.' She came to a stop outside another door covered with dark green leaves. 'It is held every year, not only to mark the solstice and the start of a new year, but to also rejuvenate the energy of the Crystal Tree at the heart of this realm. Which is much needed sadly.'

Leo reminded himself to ask her more about this Crystal Tree later. Now did not seem an appropriate time. 'Will you be there?' he asked her instead.

Lisandre caught his eye, then quickly looked away as she blushed. 'Of course,' she said giving him a small smile that vanished as quickly as it had come. 'The guest chambers are beyond that door. I hope you shall find them comfortable,' she said and placed in his hands a small golden key decorated with a diamond-shaped crystal on the handle. 'If you need anything call my name three times with intention,' she told him, then gently bowed and walked away.

After she had turned the corner, Leo placed the key in the lock and turned it. The lock clicked and disappeared in a flutter of sparkles as the leaves withdrew from the door, revealing the golden panel underneath. The door swung open.

A giant tree stood in the centre of the room. Large cream ceramic tiles lined the floor around an enormous pool-sized bath built into the ground. On the other side of the room was a large four-poster bed with green sheets and thin pale green curtains. Glowing orbs illuminated the space beneath the expansive canopy of trees. Leo looked up into the branches, which seemed to reach endlessly towards the sky. It was like living in a tree, he imagined. Vines of jasmine flowers fell from the ceiling, their sweet scent filling the air.

Leo sat down on the green sofa beneath the trunk of the gigantic tree, closing his eyes as he breathed in the calming, reinvigorating scent. After a while he opened them and went to draw a bath. It took him a while to figure out how to turn the strange taps on.

He undressed and sank into the warm circular pool of water. *What a strange yet wondrous world this is!* he thought, admiring the architecture — if that was what it could be called. To be immersed in nature and such beauty was truly a gift.

He covered himself hastily in surprise as a beautiful doe strolled up to the bath. White spots dotted her tawny fur. She approached the edge, her eyes meeting Leo's, and he felt a connection, as he did with all creatures. They watched one another for a few moments before the doe turned away and left him to bathe in peace.

* * *

Later that afternoon, Lisandre returned, knocking at the door before letting herself in at Leo's request.

'Leo,' she called as he emerged from one of the adjoining rooms, now dressed in the clean clothes left on his bed by the fey: a pair of leafy green tights and a slightly darker tunic over a cream linen shirt with long, loose sleeves. As he had glanced in the mirror after trying them on, he'd felt almost like one of the fey.

'My Lady,' he greeted her, and Lisandre blushed again. She was unsure if it was because of her not being used to the title she had only inherited three months on her birthday before, or because of another reason altogether.

'I thought perhaps you might like to spend the rest of the afternoon outside of your chambers. I could give you a tour of

'—Leo caught something in a Celtic-like language that translated instantly to his native tongue as *grand tree home* —'and afterwards we could share an evening meal,' she offered.

'I would be honoured, my lady,' Leo answered, and he followed her into the corridor outside. 'A doe appeared in my chambers as I was taking a bath earlier. Is that to be expected here?'

Lisandre's smile quickly turned into barely concealed giggles, her hand flying to her mouth. Her laughter was like water gushing over a bubbling brook, a pleasant, delightful sound.

'Oh no!' She removed the hand from her mouth. 'I do apologise, Leo. That must have been Desideira, she is my —' Again, she used her native language to convey a concept that meant something similar to *familiar*. 'She is very curious and friendly. I hope she did not scare you.'

'Not at all,' he said, 'I was only surprised, that is all.'

'I am glad to hear it,' Lisandre replied, glancing at the ground with a smile still on her face. There was a momentary pause before she looked up again. 'Before we begin, please tell me. Is there any place that would be of particular interest to you?'

'Tell me, do the fey have a library?' he enquired. He had been wondering ever since he had arrived.

'We have an extensive collection of literature, but I must warn you, much of it is in the Ancient Script,' she informed him.

'Can you show it to me?' he asked anyway.

'Of course.' Lisandre led him downstairs and along a few more corridors until they reached a pair of large oak doors almost completely covered with vines. 'This is the Hall of Knowledge,' she said as they entered. 'Also known as the Hall of the Yellow Rose.'

They passed an assortment of large books on a long rectangular table in the centre of the room. Roses grew in elegant spirals around the columns. Scrolls depicting a Celtic-like script hung like banners amidst a background of dark green walls that consisted, Leo saw as he looked closer, of vines and leaves. The entire faerie palace seemed to be alive, a living structure, he realised as he glanced at the other end of the hall and out of an open window decorated with curtain-like vines. There was little to distinguish the boundaries of where the forest ended and the palace began; indeed, the edges of the two seemed seamless.

Endless forest filled the landscape outside the window. It was unnerving to Leo, so different to the Alchemical Court where he had been raised. The home of his childhood had only sparse trees which decorated the courtyards behind the stone walls of the Academy, though there had been forests in the distance, further along the river's course.

His focus then returned to Lisandre as she explained, 'Here we keep the archives of our race as well as our studies of nature and magic, which we consider one and the same. We call it Nádúr.'

'Nádúr . .' he repeated after her. *What a beautiful word. Why have I never heard of it before ? Even in the archives of the Alchemical Court . . .*

Lisandre seemed to pick up on his thoughts. 'The fey like to keep such things to ourselves; we believe knowledge is precious and should be given only to those who can be trusted.'

'But why have I never seen nor heard of a faerie outside old textbooks on matters of history and consequence?' Leo pressed his palms into the central table. It too seemed to be living, with leaves growing healthily from its legs. Another mystery of the fey.

Lisandre seemed slightly taken aback. 'We dare not venture too far from the borders of our realm,' she answered, stoically repeating the line the previous queen, Queen Arsinoë, had given her years ago when she, as a young girl, had asked of the worlds that lay beyond their realm.

Leo seemed unsatisfied. 'Why is that?' he pressed further, and Lisandre realised she did not know. She remained silent as she pondered the issue. Was it for their protection? Or for some other reason? Regardless, of the reason she needed to seek the queen's response on this particular issue.

'I know not,' she admitted, and Leo reluctantly dropped the topic as Lisandre carried on with the rest of the tour.

She led him across much of the rest of the palace, showing him the dining hall again, as well as the crystal gardens where crystals grew like flowers, and the quiet gardens where the fey came to meditate beside the calming clear streams. She even took him to the kitchens, where, upon his request he spoke with the faerie chefs, whose profession was valued — as indeed all were in the Realm of the Fey.

'Each is encouraged to follow their heart's calling from an early age,' Lisandre explained while Leo enquired about this over a slice of raw pumpkin pie. 'It is for the greatest benefit of the whole to have each specialise in their passion, as we value what each contributes. The queen is merely our leader from whom we seek guidance and wisdom, individually and as a whole for our race. She has twelve advisors; together they make thirteen, and they are the innermost court, one each representing a sacred tree in their title. Queen Ivana is known as the Holly Queen; you may have noticed the berries woven to create her crown. The others are called Lord or Lady. For example, my dearest friend Lady Alaïa's title is Lady Ivy, and I am-'

'Lady of the Vines,' Leo interrupted suddenly.

'Yes, but how do you know that?' she asked cautiously.

'I overheard another member of court refer to you as such,' he admitted. 'Does that mean your father was Lord of the Vines?'

'Actually, no, he was Lord Hawthorn. It does not work like that. A title such as Lord or Lady can be passed from parent to child, but the sacred tree of that title depends upon the month of the child's birth. If the tree is already taken the title of Silver is added to their name. It is said that the court is most harmonious when each of the thirteen trees are represented,' she told him.

'The thirteen trees are birch, rowan, ash, alder, willow, hawthorn, oak, holly, hazel, vine, ivy, reed and elder. Each tree has their own influence upon Nádúr,' Lisandre explained as they returned to his rooms. 'I hope I have answered all of your questions. It seems only fair that you answer one of mine.'

'Very well, my lady,' said Leo as they stood outside the door to his chamber.

Lisandre glanced at him curiously. 'How is it you can understand our language? Did you study it?'

'A little, yes, but the Academy has few books on the subject. Mostly it is a spell taught in Alchemy so we can understand any language. Alchemy of the tongue, so to speak. Alchemysts speak Alcheme, which is also the language we use for spells. It is descended from three of the Ancient Languages, Latin, Greek and Persian.'

'And what do Alchemysts study? What is Alchemy?' Lisandre appeared puzzled, yet intrigued.

'Alchemy?' Leo studied her carefully before answering. He glanced toward one of the rosebuds growing upon the door. Alchemy is the art of transformation,' he said, and as he spoke, his hand merely inches above the rosebud, it transformed, blossoming into a golden yellow rose. 'Of working with the elements and studying the alignments of the heavens to calculate the movements and locations of portals. It can be applied in many practical ways. Alchemy is considered the science of magic. Alchemysts often travel to other realms and kingdoms to act as ambassadors or peacekeepers, or to collect information.'

'Like spies?' she asked.

The unexpected accusation cut him though he attempted to hide it. He knew she meant no ill will by it. 'Not exactly . . .'

Lisandre glanced anxiously at the low rays of moonlight upon the corridor floor. It was now well into the evening. 'I must go,' she informed him. 'I have other duties, including studies of my own, to attend to.' She stood tall and bowed slightly, lowering her eyes in respect. 'I shall return tomorrow. Fare thee well, Leo.'

'Good night, Lady Lisandre.'

She looked up at him once more before she turned and walked back along the corridor. As Leo watched her leave he wondered just what it was that the fey studied.

* * *

Chapter Three

The Witch of the Forest

Ivy

Fortitude, resiliency, determination and strength in the face of adversity and difficult challenges

Hang a wreath of Ivy to guard against negative influence

The sun was rising as Flora closed the picket gate behind her and walked along the path beside the herb garden of Rose Cottage. Lavish herbs grew abundantly here, particularly rosemary and sage.

Basket in hand, she went inside and headed straight to bed. She awoke later in the warm summer afternoon. She stretched, then slowly emerged from under the fine linen sheets and went to open the shutters, letting the sunshine in and airing the room from the stifling heat. Flora liked Fuschian summers. The days were long and warm and sunny, and the air was thick with the perfume of flowers that had bloomed in spring. The kingdom was known for its trade of abundant flowers and blossoms, used as decorations and made into teas and perfumes by the people of the Australis Empire to the east.

She washed with the jug and basin on the washstand before dressing in her favourite lilac dress, tying a dark purple ribbon in her hair as she sang to herself. Her hand trailed the wooden balustrade as she headed downstairs, where she picked up her basket and headed towards the village.

Though Rose Cottage lay on the edge of the Fuschian border with the mysterious Southern Kingdom as well as the *Grande Foresta*, the Great Forest, the nearby village was undoubtedly Fuschian in character and design, with terracotta roofs and cream-coloured buildings. Villagers gossiped rumours of a witch of the forest, especially within the Briar Wood. Flora ignored them as she walked past.

Last night she had been unsuccessful at the Midnight Palace, unable to get even near the map room. Guards had stood outside it for hours as the princes remained suspiciously absent from the ball. Flora had spent half the dances checking by pretending to go for a walk to the nearby conservatory. After a while, the huge doors had opened, and she'd heard Mikhail say 'If you must' as he left.

She sang to the flowers as she gathered herbs for her spells in the Briar Wood. Later, Flora returned to the cottage, where she sat curled up by the window, reading *The Book of Moon*. She found the chapter on Dream Magic particularly fascinating . . .

In the early evening she heard a carriage pull up to the road in front of Rose Cottage. Out stepped a familiar figure dressed fashionably in blue.

'Aunt Bellissa!' Flora rushed outside to greet her aunt, wrapping her in a hug.

'Flora! I bring news of the realm,' said Aunt Bellissa. She stroked Flora's cheek. 'How are you dearest?'

'Oh, I'm fine, Aunt Bellissa. How was your trip to Castelle?' Flora answered, pleased her aunt was finally home.

'Wonderful! Allende is a beautiful city — and the music! The music there is so beautiful,' said Aunt Bellissa, then added, 'It is too early to tell but I think it will indeed be a success.'

Flora returned her smile.

'I shall have to travel again in two weeks,' Aunt Bellissa remembered, reaching forward to cup Flora's chin. 'I'm so sorry. Perhaps one day I shall be able to take you with me.'

'Why don't you?' Flora asked, her arms laced behind her back. 'Take me with you?'

Aunt Bellissa wore a pained expression. 'I'm sorry. I can't . . . Not yet. You are so young. And I worry . . .'

Flora was confused. 'I'm sixteen. I'm old enough to be presented at court,' she insisted.

'I know. However, I cannot discuss the matter more at this time.'

Aunt Bellissa headed upstairs, leaving Flora with even more questions.

* * *

Lucien trudged up the steps of the dark tower, a remnant of the Ancient Castle overlooking the lake. Across the water he could see the shining golden orbs of the Midnight Palace. Its outer walls were light blue, like the sky on a clear sunny day.

Inside the tower, violet purple flames licked the base of the cauldron which his mother stood behind in the centre of the room. Queen Katya had always been of impressive height. This, combined with her solid build, immaculate posture and piercing eyes, made her an intimidating presence at court, even if one did not take into account her impressive knowledge of sorcery. She wore a dark purple dress with sleeves that split at the elbows, flowing down to trail along the ground. A silver diadem with a crescent moon at its centre rested upon her dark brown hair, which she wore loose in long waves to her waist.

Lucien stood opposite her as she concentrated on the spell she was working on. Purple smoke and an overwhelming smell of sage poured out from the cauldron, filling the room as she finished the spell before turning her attention to him.

'Lucien,' she greeted her youngest son, opening her eyes. She had a mystic atmosphere of otherworldly power around her, which intimidated even the other sorcerers of the Midnight Court.

'I don't know why, mother.' Lucien began pacing the room with his arms crossed. He paused, leaning back against the ancient stonework as Katya's eyes followed him. 'Why does she keep appearing in my visions?'

'It could be for many reasons, Lucien. Could she be the traitor you seek?' she asked, glancing back down at the contents of the cauldron while she stirred.

'Perhaps,' he admitted, 'But I am not sure.'

Katya looked up at him. 'Then become sure,' she told him. 'Let your intuition guide you, my son, in this and all things.'

* * *

On his next morning in Na Foraise Síorai, Leo got up early and dressed, ready for a full day of study. He had just finished breakfast — bowls of fresh fruit and nuts had been laid out on the table earlier before he had risen — when he heard a knocking at the door. He opened it, expecting to see Lady Lisandre, only to be met with another faerie: taller, though vaguely similar in looks, except with skin the colour of honey and shapely eyes of a more exotic nature. She wore a long dress of shimmering green, which matched her emerald wings.

'Alchemyst,' she greeted him, dropping her gaze as she performed a small curtsey.

'It's Leo, actually,' he informed her politely.

'Do you remember me, Leo?'

He tried to recall the name of the fairy who had interrupted them. 'You are a friend of Lady Lisandre, I believe. I'm sorry, I cannot recall who you are,' he replied honestly. He hoped she would not be too offended.

'Lady Ivy. You may call me Lady Alaïa.' She smiled cryptically at him. 'I will be your guide for today.'

'Forgive me,' Leo apologised, shutting the door to his chamber behind him as they left. 'I was under the impression that the Lady Lisandre would be my guide.'

'Lady Lisandre is . . . otherwise occupied with her duties, as I am sure you can understand. I am to escort you in her absence,' said Lady Alaïa. She offered him her hand. 'Shall we?'

Leo glanced down the corridor along which Lisandre had retreated yesterday evening, as if simply wishing would draw her presence to him. Lady Alaïa watched him, curious. He took her hand and together walked down the hall.

'Forgive me but you seem quite young to be a lady, even for a faerie. As does Lady Lisandre,' Leo commented as they walked.

'It is true, Lady Lisandre and I are by far the youngest members of the Sacred Council, myself having only turned seventeen just two moons past. Lady Ash was my mother. She died when I was born. I almost died along with her.' She paused and glanced back at Leo. 'Did you know that the ivy plant is known as the survivor? They say my title is well-named for that is what I am: a survivor.'

Leo could not help but notice there was a sharpness to Lady Alaïa that he could not quite place. Was she warning him, perhaps? Or threatening him?

'And your father?' he asked, undeterred.

'He is not of one of our royal houses,' said Lady Alaïa as they arrived at the entrance to the Hall of the Yellow Rose. 'I was raised by my uncle instead. I grew up split between the clan of the purple rose and the Court of the Fey, much like Lisandre except her clan was from the mountain garden.'

'Was it always called such?' Leo asked, gazing up at the golden archway adorned with yellow roses coiled around the columns. 'The Hall of the Yellow Rose?'

'You have a keen mind, Alchemyst.' Lady Alaïa gave a sly smile. 'No, previously it was the Hall of Duirrose, and before that, the Hall of Oak. It is named after the ruling house. Why do you ask?'

'Just curious,' he said, shrugging his shoulders.

'I trust you can manage from here.' She clasped his hands. 'Summon me if you have need of anything, Leo.'

'Of course. Thank you.'

Alaïa turned and left, returning back down the long corridor. Leo watched her briefly, then entered within.

No Alchemyst had stepped inside these archives in possibly hundreds of years, or at least from what he knew. He wandered past many shelves of scrolls and books, occasionally passing members of the fey also browsing various tomes. He saw books on every subject of study imaginable. He saw scrolls detailing Crystal Magic, books discussing Tree Lore, others on healing spells.

As he continued his search for astrological calendars and star maps, Leo soon became distracted by his curiosity. He found himself drawn to a red-covered volume in particular, opening the pages to a chapter titled the Oak King.

The Oak King

Also called the Green Sorcerer, Lord of the Forest. The Oak King is a master of metamorphosis and eternal youth. He represents the light defeating the Holly Queene each Winter Solstice, when the days begin to become longer and brighter again.

He closed the book, returning it to the shelf and continuing to browse the scrolls on history. He quickly found a scroll titled *A History of the Houses,* which he then unfurled down to the most recent entry at the bottom.

The House of Glen Eire

Beneath the illustration of the yellow rose were the words 𝕰𝖛𝖊𝖓𝖎𝖓𝖌 𝕲𝖑𝖔𝖗𝖞, their other name for the flower.

Symbol for the House of Glen Eire, The Evening Glory flower is so named for it blooms in the night.

The entry was accompanied by a diagram of the family tree, featuring two prominent branches: the House of Glen Eire and the House of Duirrose. Leo noticed Alaïa was the daughter of Lady Yaesmin, also known as Lady Ash, cousin to the previous Queen Arsinoë I, and from an entirely different house to Ivana, the current queen. He also noticed that Ivana was an only child.

Leo continued reading until his eyes reached the bottom of the page, where he came across that symbol again:

The same symbol he had seen in his master's notes, was here. In another realm.

Stunned, Leo hurriedly rolled up the scroll, adding it to the pile, hoping he could present his findings to Lady Lisandre. Perhaps she could help him find some answers. With the assistance of one of the male librarian fey, he brought the growing gargantuan pile of scrolls back to his chamber, where he consequently poured over them until the evening meal.

* * *

Leo spent the next day in his bedchamber, scribbling over the tiles with chalk and in the notebooks provided by the fey, lost in his thoughts as he wondered: what did the symbol mean? Perhaps it was some clue as to his master's disappearance?

He returned his attention to creating a portal, considering the elements needed. *And then there were the astrological calculations to consider . . .*

Leo's thoughts were interrupted by a knock at the door behind him. He paused his musings and went to answer, opening the door to find Lady Lisandre with her hands clasped around a gold cup containing a pink liquid.

'I brought you some berry tea,' she greeted him cheerily.

'Lady Lisandre. Please do come in.' He stepped aside, allowing her to enter the chamber.

'You are well this morning I hope? Do you have everything you need?' she asked, setting the tea down upon the table and turning to face him.

'Er, yes, thank you.' He shut the door and came to join her. 'I thought — I rather hoped — yesterday that you would be the one escorting me,' Leo explained.

Lisandre appeared rather downcast at that. 'I am sorry, I was occupied by my studies,' she said. It was a half-truth; Lisandre had found it difficult to concentrate after yet another night of strange dreams disturbing her sleep. 'I trust that you found the Hall of the Yellow Rose?' she asked.

'Yes. As you can see, I had some help. Lady Alaïa helped me find the Hall, and then another faerie helped me carry all these back to my chambers.' Leo glanced at the piles of scrolls and open books on the table and around the room. 'She seemed to know you quite well,' Leo commented as Lisandre examined the titles he had selected.

'Hmm, who?' she asked without looking up.

'Lady Alaïa,' he answered.

Lisandre paused. 'We grew up at court together. It is rare to know another faerie close to my own age,' Lisandre explained. 'She is the closest living relative to the queen. However, she is of another house, House Duirrose. The house that ruled before House Glen Eire, the house of the yellow rose. House Duirrose is represented by the purple rose beneath the oak tree. Before the previous queen, there was a dispute between the houses that led to a civil war. The Willow Queen lived an exceptionally long life; her reign lasted five thousand years. So long that she had outlived her children and the fey had become divided among the heirs, especially her two granddaughters, Princess Arsinoë of Glen Eire and Princess Yaesmin of Duirrose — Lady Alaïa's mother. Well I guess you know how that turned out.'

Lisandre glanced at some of the open notebooks upon the table, intrigued by the strange symbols.

'What are these markings?' she inquired, drawing Leo's attention.

'Symbols, for Alchemy. They represent the elements, planets and much more,' Leo explained.

'This is different from Nádúr — from our magic.' Lisandre caressed the page, noting the symbols with interest. She turned to look at him. 'Can you teach me any?'

'Yes, yes of course,' Leo replied, turning the page. 'See these ones here.' He pointed to a group of symbols representing the four elements: Fire, Air, Water and Earth. He taught her their names in Alcheme: Pyros, Aeris, Aqua, Tellus.

They talked for hours. First he taught her the basics of

Alchemy, then Lisandre assisted him in his work as together they sorted through the piles of scrolls and books, astrological calendars and star maps, looking for anything that could give Leo an idea of the location of the Great Library.

After a while Lisandre asked him, 'Why the Great Library? What exactly are you looking for?'

'I'm looking for a scroll,' Leo answered without looking up from the pile of scrolls he was reading intently.

'We have many scrolls here in our archives. Perhaps the one you seek is among them,' Lisandre suggested.

'No. She told me to go to the Great Library. She said I would know which one . . . The Great Library . . . The Great Library of Florencia perhaps?' Leo mused.

'Florencia?' she pronounced the strange word carefully.

'It's a city in Fuschia, another kingdom in my realm,' Leo explained.

'Oh. Your realm. What is it like?' Lisandre asked shyly.

'Well, it depends on which part you go to.'

'Tell me about the part you come from then.'

'The Alchemical Court? Well, it is in the mountains at the centre of the realm.' Leo opened his Almanac, turning the pages to find a map to show her when something else again caught his attention. 'Here. Look at this,' he pointed at the symbol.

The strange symbol leapt out at Lisandre. 'What is that?' she asked curiously.

'I don't know,' Leo admitted. 'I was hoping perhaps the fey might have some answers.'

'What happened? The day you arrived. You were running from something, or someone?' she asked perceptively. 'It's why you messed up the portal isn't it? It was some kind of accident . . .?' She seemed almost unsure of her own words. 'I've seen your work; it is meticulous and precise,' she then asserted, gesturing towards his notes scattered across the table.

'Or perhaps it was another reason,' said Leo.

'Such as?'

He turned to face Lisandre, stepping closer towards her. 'Maybe it was destiny. Or fate,' he told her, his eyes meeting hers.

'Fate?' Lisandre questioned.

'Surely faeries believe in fate?' he gently teased.

'Perhaps,' she answered, her gaze shy. 'Tell me more about your realm,' she went on as she looked away, changing the subject.

Leo's eyes followed her as she wandered the room. 'Well in some parts there aren't quite so many trees.'

'You mock me.' She sounded offended.

'No! Not at all, my lady,' he apologised hurriedly. 'Just an observation. You did ask me what it was like.' He sighed. 'I wish there were some way to show you. Perhaps one day I could take you there.'

Lisandre looked up at him, eyes sparkling with curiosity. No one had ever spoken to her that way before. Due to her young age she was often in the shadow of the older, wiser faeries of the court. But she did her duties as best she could, and continued her studies in Nádúr and crystal magics as requested.

But something in his words spoke to a hidden part of her, a part that longed to travel and have adventures and explore the worlds outside her own.

Leo looked up at her as she placed her hand on his.

'I would like that,' she said.

* * *

'Rumours are that the Kingdom of the Midnight Sun is ripe for revolution,' spoke the young male faerie who stood before Queen Ivana as she sat on the throne in the Grand Atrium.

'You are well aware that I do not concern myself with such rumours, Lord Rowan,' Queen Ivana responded tersely.

'Then perhaps you will be more interested in other rumours

circling the court, fairest one,' he continued. 'The Lady Lisandre grows more beautiful each day, and some cannot deny a certain resemblance to Queen Arsinoë . . .'

'Silence!' Ivana warned. 'Now go and speak no more on this matter.'

Lord Rowan bowed and retreated. Once he had gone, Ivana raised her hand to her head as she sat alone in the silence. No more than a moment had passed when she was interrupted by a knock at the door.

Ivana composed herself as Lisandre gently pressed open the door. 'You wish to speak to me, Lady Lisandre?'

'Yes, fairest one. There is something I don't understand,' Lisandre said, cautiously stepping forward. 'There are other realms out there, realms aside from The Eternal Forest, filled with creatures like us. Should we not become better acquainted with them and offer our friendship? Instead of hiding in the trees?'

Ivana spun swiftly around, turning on Lisandre. 'It is in the best interests of our people to remain hidden, and for you to stay in the shadows, Lady Lisandre. Do not forget that,' she warned.

Lisandre backed towards the door and hurried out of the room as fast she could.

* * *

She walked down the Grand Atrium in the moonlight, passing under the corridor of trees. The Crystal Tree was calling her, singing softly in the breeze, the secrets it held for her written in its chimes. Its ornate silver branches were adorned with luminous amber leaves, like three-pointed stars. A hollow cavity rested within the centre of the tree trunk where the heart should be. Standing proudly at the heart of the Realm of the Fey, the tree seemed to have fewer and fewer leaves and more bare branches each year.

Dark green vines coiled around a crown at the base of the Crystal Tree.

Lisandre glanced up.

Beware the snake that lies beneath the Oak Tree, a voice called.

Lisandre looked down to find the vines had been replaced with a pair of emerald-green snakes. They hissed at her as she stumbled backwards before they were absorbed in a burst of green flames. Lisandre fell towards the ground . . .

* * *

She woke in the morning bolt upright in her bed. Yet another dream. Her head filled with thoughts from the strange scene, she needed to clear her head. She got up and dressed, tying her purple cloak on top of her dress. Grabbing her bow and sling of arrows, she placed them over her shoulder and quietly left her chamber.

She headed downstairs in the quiet morning, unseen except by the occasional faerie attending their duties. She passed along the grand corridor towards the edge of the palace, then through the detailed archway and outside.

Outside being a relative term, Lisandre thought as she set up in the forest gardens for archery practice. The sunlight filtered through the treetops even here. The thick trees protected the entire realm, it seemed.

She drew an arrow and aimed at the straw-filled target square. She released the arrow and it flew through the air, landing successfully on the target centre with a resounding *thud*. She drew again, and again and again, each time releasing a little more of her frustration. She liked practising archery; it focused her mind.

'Lady Lisandre?'

A familiar voice broke her focus and the arrow whistled through the air, landing in the grass well to the side of the target. She turned to see Leo walking towards her from the entrance to the clearing.

'Leo! What are you doing here?' she asked.

'I was told I could find you here.' Leo noticed the abundance of arrows resting squarely at the heart of the target. Her uninterrupted aim was perfect. 'May I join you? I hope I have not disturbed you,' he added.

'Not at all—I mean yes. Oh, I'm so sorry. I was trying to clear my head. Yes, you may join me, Leo.' She noticed he had brought his bow.

'You have excellent aim,' Leo noted.

'Thank you.' Lisandre turned back towards the target.

Leo sighed, drawing her attention once again. He had not yet lifted his own bow. He had decided to tell her about the talismans and their importance.

'When I left the Alchemical Court . . . when I came here, I was sent to find a scroll believed to be hidden in a great library. A scroll that will help me find the lost talismans, or the Dark Alchemyst, if he gets his hands on it first. The scroll was the reason the Alchemical Court was attacked in the first place. It is possible the fey have knowledge on this matter. With the power of the talismans, the Dark Alchemyst could destroy or enslave both our realms if he wanted to. It is imperative that we find them before he does.'

'Why are you telling me this? Surely it would be better to ask the queen,' Lisandre pointed out once he had finished.

'Queen Ivana seems quite reluctant to tell me much about anything. I think that she would not tell me even if she knew.' Leo paused. 'I trust you.'

Her eyes met his then looked away. 'I'm sorry but I have never heard of such talismans. But I will help you as best as I can to find them,' she reassured him.

* * *

Leo returned to his chambers to find Lady Alaïa pouring over the makeshift drawings in his Almanac.

'My lady?' he asked tentatively.

She glanced up. 'Interesting sketches,' she remarked, as if she had been expecting him.

'Your Alchemy intrigues me,' she added, her fingers casually tracing the designs.

'What are you doing here?' Leo asked.

'I was sent to inform you the Holly Queen requests that you attend dinner tomorrow evening with the Court of the Fey as our honoured guest. And you have also been invited to our Winter Solstice Ball, which will take place the following evening, followed by three nights of celebration. The winter solstice is one of our grandest celebrations of the year. Few outsiders have borne witness to it. Congratulations, Alchemyst. You shall have to save a dance for me,' she smiled and left before Leo could say a word.

The Winter Solstice ball. He remembered Lady Lisandre mentioning it before to him. He made another note to himself to ask her more about it.

* * *

The following evening Leo put his Alchemical jacket on top of his fresh white linen shirt and headed off to dinner. The court was already bustling as he entered the Grand Atrium. Observing the variety of courtiers in their fine clothing, he noticed that all the female fey seemed to wear dresses of a timeless, ancient style and the faerie men wore long coloured tunics over hose.

His eyes scoured the room for a sign of Lady Lisandre, wandering through the crowd until he spotted her. She was standing alone in a corner, pondering as she held with a golden apple with both hands, wearing a dress of buttercup yellow. Like all her dresses it was sleeveless and elegant. She reminded Leo of a Greek goddess the way she always stood so perfectly poised. A habit of the fey, perhaps?

'Lady Lisandre.'

She looked up and bowed as he approached her. 'Greetings Leo,' she smiled.

Leo brought forth a sprig of jasmine. He had noticed Lisandre admiring them previously.

Out of the corner of her eye Queen Ivana watched as he then offered the white star-shaped flower to Lisandre.

She blushed, her face lighting up with happiness at the gift. 'Jasmine. My favourite.'

Ivana's eyes remained fixed upon the pair as Leo gently tucked the flower behind her ear.

'Ahem . . . Fairest one?'

Queen Ivana turned to see a male faerie addressing her. 'Yes?' she inquired, a hint of annoyance in her tone.

'Dinner is served,' he informed her.

'Thank you. You may address the others,' she instructed, and the faerie left to inform the crowd, who then made their way over to sit down at the banquet table.

Queen Ivana sat at the centre of the table. Leo observed Lisandre sitting tensely on her left. Throughout the course of the meal, Lisandre spoke even less than usual, and when she did respond to Ivana's occasional questions, she did so in a taut, tight-lipped tone.

After dinner, Lisandre joined a group of musicians as she played her crystal flute. Another fey played the harp, and others performed using a variety of classical instruments.

After they finished playing, Leo offered Lisandre her refilled silver goblet as she returned to their table. Tonight the fey were drinking blackcurrant and apple juice. She graciously took the cup of purple liquid and thanked him, sitting back down.

'Beautifully played, Lady of the Vines,' Queen Ivana immediately addressed Lisandre, who simply nodded shyly and turned excitedly to Leo.

'How is the portal work going?' Lisandre enquired. 'How go the scribbles?' she gently teased with a smile.

'You will be leaving soon I trust?' Queen Ivana interrupted as Leo opened his mouth to answer.

'I shall need a few more days, fairest one, but yes, the portal is almost ready,' he replied. He glanced over to observe Lisandre's reaction to such news, but she hid her emotion behind a mask of intense thought.

'May I be excused?' she asked, and Ivana reluctantly nodded. 'Goodnight, Leo. Goodnight, fairest one.' Lisandre left for her chambers.

Perhaps he would get a better chance to talk with her alone tomorrow at the ball, away from the constant watchful eye of the faerie queen.

'I think I will retire early as well. Goodnight.' Leo promptly stood up, bowed towards Ivana and left in the opposite direction, returning to his chambers. At least he could get some work done instead of lingering in this awkward silence with the Holly Queen.

* * *

The Grand Atrium had been transformed into a winter paradise when Leo entered the next evening. Enormous pine trees dusted with snow stood around the edges of the room, interspersed with white birch and golden maple. Baskets of pinecones rested upon the tables, along with decorations of holly berries and leaves. In some kingdoms at this time of year they would celebrate Yule, he remembered —

And that was when his attention was captured by Lady Lisandre emerging in a spectacular golden dress.

Like a magnificent golden butterfly, she stood out from the crowd with her beauty and elegance. The colour of her dress contrasted perfectly with her dark hair. A headdress of hanging pearls and crystals rested upon her hair, the two chains crisscrossed in a band around the crown of her head. Three rectangular pearls hung like tears from a large golden circle upon from each lobe.

Her eyes met his and she walked over to greet him.

'Salutem, Leander,' she said.

'Salutem — good evening, my lady.' Leo bowed. 'Leander?' he asked.

Lisandre tilted her head to the side and smiled. 'Your faerie name.'

'I see. I mean no disrespect, my lady, but my name is Leopold. Leopold De La Fontaine. I prefer Leo.'

'Leo,' she repeated. 'Very well. I apologise. But tonight you must call me only Lisandre.'

'Of course. Now. Would you allow me the honour of a dance?' Leo asked her, offering his hand.

'Dance? Do you think that would be appropriate?' she questioned hesitantly.

Leo glanced around. 'We are at a ball. I can think of nothing more appropriate,' he reassured her kindly.

'You know what I mean,' she said as she slid her arm over his and allowed him to escort her out onto the dancefloor. He placed his arm around her waist and they started to dance.

They danced for what seemed like hours. Snowflakes began to fall from the ceiling causing Lisandre to glance up and smile.

After a while, she spoke. 'You are not like us,' she observed quietly.

'Is that such a bad thing?' he replied.

'Not at all,' she answered as he twirled her in a circle.

* * *

'At least Queen Ivana appears to be in a much happier mood,' Leo noted a short while later, glancing over towards where the Holly Queen sat on her throne. Queen Ivana wore a more decorative crown this evening, woven from holly leaves and berries. She contrasted heavily with Lisandre in her gown of dark purple.

'She is still displeased with me,' Lisandre replied as they continued the dance. She caught several members of the fey staring at them, the Alchemyst and the faerie, Lady Ivy among them.

* * *

'May I offer you a refreshment, my lady?'

Lady Alaïa's attention was diverted as she turned to find Lord Rowan offering her a drink.

'Very well,' she replied drolly, accepting the goblet of sweet berry juice as he sat down beside her. 'The winter solstice is her holiday after all,' she remarked with considerable sass.

'My dear Lady Ivy, it appears that you have grown into quite the beautiful faerie after all,' he flirted as she drank.

'If I am so beautiful, why is the Alchemyst over there talking to her and not me?' Her gaze drifted towards Leo and Lady Lisandre.

'Because the young Alchemyst is an idiot,' Lord Rowan whispered into her ear. He poured more sweet berry juice into her goblet and tucked her hair behind her ear. At just over one hundred years old, Lord Rowan was one of the younger fey, and despite his age appeared no older than nineteen. 'You are quite clearly the fairest of them all,' he continued.

'Careful not to let Queen Ivana overhear you say that,' Alaïa warned.

'Why not? Because it is true nonetheless,' he persisted.

She snapped her head back to look at him. 'You know why,' she said bluntly. 'One cannot say such things. Not if you wish to keep your title, Lord Rowan.'

'She's only queen because of what Arsinoë did. Otherwise you would be queen by now,' he stated simply.

She leaned toward him and replied, in a low voice only he could hear, 'If all goes well, I still will be.'

* * *

'I'm afraid that I do not know this dance,' Leo admitted shyly as the next song began with a rather different tune to the others, and the fey around them began the unfamiliar dance.

'Then I will teach you.' Lisandre took his arm, pulling him into the crowd as the dancers formed a large circle.

Leo followed her lead. As their palms met, their feet crisscrossed in time with the music. Lisandre seemed happy whenever he snuck a glance in her direction.

The circle parted as the song ended and the dance came to a close. Leo spun Lisandre around and then back towards him until her back was against his chest, their hands still joined. He caught Ivana's disapproving glare towards them.

'Is there somewhere we can talk for a while?' Leo asked, eager to get away from the queen's watchful eye.

'Yes, but not here,' she told him. 'I know of a place where we will not be overheard.'

She took his hand and led him out of the Grand Hall, then along a small corridor to an archway covered with cascading lilac blossoms. Lisandre swept the blossoms aside and together they stepped into the daylight, entering a charming woodland. Bluebells blossomed beneath the shade and comfort of the oak trees.

Leo realised he was still holding one of the pinecones he had picked up as they left.

'Why are there so many pinecones at the feast? Surely you do not eat them?' Leo suddenly spoke aloud, lost in thought.

'We give pinecones for luck,' Lisandre explained as he examined the pinecone. Leo offered it to her.

'Máith anise,' she thanked him, holding the cone with both hands. She sat down on the grass and Leo sat beside her. A pair of young bunnies watched them with interest from nearby.

'Lisandre is a beautiful name. What does it mean?' he asked her.

'Joyful one,' she answered. 'And Leo? Does your name mean something as well? What does Leo mean in your language?' she asked inquisitively.

'You don't know — it means Lion' he quickly explained.

'What's a lion?'

'Oh — well it's like a big cat with . . .'

He quickly realised she was teasing him as he caught her smiling.

'Lady Lisandre, may I ask? Have you always been a part of their court?'

'I have been fortunate,' stated Lisandre, her tone turning serious. 'Queen Ivana has always been rather kind to me,' she reflected. 'I knew her before she was the Holly Queen.' Her eyes were lost in memory. 'When I was growing up, we played like sisters, though she is truthfully much older than me. My father often left me at court under the guardianship of the Hazel Queen as he travelled the realm, fulfilling his duties,' Lisandre recalled wistfully.

'Forgive me my lady, for I cannot help but wonder. How old are you?' Leo asked.

'Nine-twelfths of one cycle old, or 198 moons,' she answered, then upon seeing his confusion added, 'Fifteen of your years, I believe.'

'What about Queen Ivana?'

'She is nearly six hundred of your years older than I. But you are correct to assume that many of us are far older than we look. Many of the members of the court are centuries old.'

'Have they always called you Lady of the Vines?' Leo questioned further, intrigued.

'I inherited the title from my father, Lord Gwennaël. He was Lord Hawthorn and the previous queen's most trusted advisor, and her closest friend,' explained Lisandre.

'I am sorry to hear of his passing,' said Leo.

She glanced up at him. 'Thank you Leo. I loved him very much,' she said. 'He died when I was ten of your years old.'

'And your mother?' he inquired gently.

'I never knew my mother — she died when I was born — but my father and I were very close.'

At that moment Desideira entered the clearing, approaching Lisandre who gave her an affectionate pat before draping her arms around her neck.

'Desideira is often my only companion since Ivana became Queen.' She turned her attention to Leo. 'Do you have a family?'

'I have a mother, but she is not my birth mother. She adopted me. Her name is Lady Vidjaya. She is a teacher and a member of the Alchemical Council. I was told she found me abandoned by the fountain on the steps of the Alchemical Court. It was generally assumed that I am the son of lowborn Western travellers, given the blanket I was wrapped in. Nonetheless, Lady Vidjaya persisted, persuading the Alchemical Court to take me in, despite their difficult relationship with the Western Kingdom. I was just a child, after all. So they trained me to become an Alchemyst. She said I was very talented.

'In the realm I come from . . .' he went on, then started again. 'In a different realm to this one, there are three different kingdoms and an empire, each with their own culture, language and leaders. Some professions are valued more than others, even at the Alchemical Court; some of the older Alchemysts considered themselves to be above the cooks and the librarians because of their chosen field of study. They thought Alchemy to be a noble pursuit only a select few could comprehend.'

'Such arrogance does not add to their character, nor their study,' declared Lisandre.

'No, it does not,' he agreed. 'Not only that, but some kingdoms such as Brittannia, the Western Kingdom, maintain a difficult relationship with the Alchemical Court because of their differences. You see the Western kingdom is largely comprised of mortals, mortals with the potential to learn magic — to tap into their own natural abilities and heal others among other things — whereas the Alchemical Court is a small municipality of Alchemysts formed only less than one thousand years ago, by those who have devoted themselves to the study of

Alchemy. The mortals of Brittannia, especially their rulers, have long feared magic and hang witches and wizards, which are different to Alchemysts, though they used to return Alchemysts to the Alchemical Court sometimes for a price.

'Their relationship has somewhat improved with the Alchemical Court—now they do not prosecute Alchemysts, provided they leave the land or are there visiting as ambassadors for the Alchemical Court. As such, the Alchemical Council, which is the head of the Alchemical Court, is not overly fond of Brittannians. My birth family were from the Western kingdom, so I didn't really fit in at the Academy. I guessed they were worried that I'd learn all their secrets and turn on them, but I would never do that. Lady Vidjaya gave me a family and a home, and I would never do anything to hurt her. She adopted me much against the advisement of the Alchemical Council.'

'They thought I would never understand magic,' he added. 'Even Lady Vidjaya was surprised by my ability.'

'And look how you proved them wrong,' she told him. 'You created a portal to a forgotten realm no one has visited in possibly a hundred years.'

They sat and talked for a while, eventually deciding to return to the ball before anyone noticed Lisandre was missing. They had just entered the Grand Atrium when something swiftly caught Leo's eye.

'Lisandre look out!'

He pushed her aside and placed himself in front of her, his arms outstretched as he urgently performed a transformation spell, turning the arrow into a rose mid-flight. It landed on the ground to her right.

Lisandre's hand remained on Leo's chest as he and Ivana looked directly to where the arrow appeared to have come from, within the shadows somewhere up upon the balcony. The queen's normally composed expression was furious as she stood in front of the throne. Whoever it was, the culprit had managed to disappear into the shadows of the trees and was likely long gone, but Ivana sent up her guards to investigate anyway.

'Go to your chambers,' she instructed Lisandre who nodded faintly and left.

Ivana looked ready to kill. Leo sensed that she somehow thought the attack was all his fault.

'And you,' she addressed him. 'You will leave as soon as it is possible to do so.'

As she left, she added coldly over her shoulder, 'Which cannot be soon enough.'

* * *

Three more days of celebrations passed, but Leo was barely present at any of them. Lady Lisandre had been forbidden to attend, and when she did try to leave her chambers, she quickly found that Ivana had placed two guards in front of her door.

Ivana had come later that first evening to explain that they were for her protection, and so she had remained inside. But by the third day she was starting to feel very bored and trapped indeed. So when she heard someone knock at the door, her heart rose and she became rather excited, grabbing her bow and arrows as she rushed to answer the door to find . . .

'Leo!' She greeted him with a gratuitous smile. 'I was hoping we could spend some time in the forest today —' she began eagerly.

'Actually, I came to say goodbye,' he interrupted.

Lisandre's face fell. 'I understand.' She cast her eyes down, fingering the arrow fletching, a soft olive-green feather.

Leo noticed the golden headpiece in her dark hair as she stood with her bow slung over her shoulder. 'I wanted to see you, at least speak with you once before I go,' he said, though it pained him to say so.

He reached into his satchel and presented her with a golden

pinecone. He had transformed one of the pinecones from the feast during the past few days in his chambers as he had thought about Lisandre. A truly unique gift for a truly unique faerie.

He took a step forward. 'Come away with me,' he said quietly.

Lisandre looked up. 'What?'

'Come with me,' he offered again in a whisper. 'Don't you want to see the world?'

He could tell she was curious about his realm.

'Of course,' she started to answer, not looking into his eyes, 'if my queen permits —'

'You are the queen of your own life, aren't you?' he challenged her. 'Surely she cannot keep you locked away forever?'

In her mind Lisandre raised her eyebrow and thought, *Well she can.*

'What does your heart say?' he pressed.

There was tense silence for a moment between them. Then Lisandre looked up into Leo's eyes and gently placed her hand in his.

There was a knock at the door, causing them to jump apart.

'Breakfast!' a very enthusiastic young male faerie announced, entering with a crystal tray laden with bowls of berries and leaves. 'Oh!' he stammered as he glanced between the pair, noticing Lisandre's blush. 'Forgive me, my lady,' he apologised hastily, backing out of the room.

'I must go,' Lisandre said suddenly, and left.

She walked swiftly along the corridor, then broke into a run, her rich purple dress sweeping the circular staircase as she raced downstairs to the ground floor and then outside — *if it can be called outside.* As she ran into the familiar comfort of the trees, the guards followed her, but quickly became lost in the thick branches as she headed deeper into the forest.

She kept running until she reached a clearing where twelve large trees stood in a circle, noticeably different to the rest. The Trees of Wisdom. Exhausted, Lisandre collapsed to the ground.

* * *

'The attempt on Lady Lisandre's life came from within the court,' Leo argued passionately as they stood in the Grand Atrium the next day. 'She is not safe here — surely you see that.'

'Lady Lisandre will remain here, Alchemyst,' Queen Ivana commanded in a warning tone. 'She is safer with her kin than anywhere else.'

'Lady Lisandre should decide for herself,' asserted Leo fiercely, glancing at Lisandre as she stood between him and Queen Ivana.

'Enough!' Queen Ivana rose to her feet. 'I will not be advised on these matters, especially not by one so foreign to our court,' she declared.

Lady Lisandre glanced uncertainly at Leo as he gave a small bow and left.

* * *

For the remainder of his stay, the attempt at the ball played over and over in his mind. Leo felt haunted by the same question. *Who would want to harm Lady Lisandre?*

After a while he got up and decided to visit the Hall of Knowledge. *Perhaps the trees could help answer my question,* he thought as he passed by the doors to Lisandre's chambers.

In the Hall of Knowledge he wandered past the many shelves as he pondered, letting his intuition guide him. He meandered deeper into the centre of the archives, where the trees grew denser, more protective of their contents. Few visited this part of the hall, it seemed, for the branches and their lush foliage seemed largely untouched.

Leo reached out to touch one of the branches. The vines around it moved to reveal a large golden book that had been hidden away in the shadows beneath. He removed the book, examining the title on the cover, deciphering the unique script of the fey.

Historium à lë Fey, it read.

As one of the few Alchemysts who enjoyed studying languages, Leo knew enough of the language of the fey that he could read the basics, though he had been taught it was a dead language. *So much for that,* he thought. He carried the book back to one of the reading tables, where he placed it down and began reading.

He soon came across the name Lord Gwennaël again. Lisandre's father. A finely sketched portrait accompanied the page. He was a handsome faerie with tawny brown hair and a pale complexion similar to Lisandre; the long slightly pointed ears featured by all the fey; and large emerald green wings. On the page opposite was a portrait of another faerie with dark hair. Leo scanned the information below the portrait and quickly deduced she had been Lord Gwennaël's wife.

As he continued, something he read suddenly caught his attention, his eyes devouring the words and widening in disbelief. He slammed the book shut and hurried out of the hall to the surprise of the few around.

* * *

Leo had never used magic to summon anyone before; that kind of magic belonged to sorcery, not Alchemy — or so he had thought. The fey appeared to have their own special kind of magic, one that was intrinsically linked with nature. *Nádúr,* Lisandre had called it. In the morning light, he decided to try it.

'Lisandre, Lisandre, Lisandre,' he called out loud quietly but with intention. He waited, then he heard a sound like the soft twinkling of chimes combined with the trickle of a waterfall.

Lisandre appeared like an angel in a vision, her wings sparkling as they reflected the sunlight.

'Leo, what is it?' Queen Ivana had as good as ordered her not to see him anymore. Whatever it was must be important for him to summon her in such a way.

He approached her. 'Lady Lisandre. There is something I must show you.'

Lisandre's brows drew together in confusion.

'Something very important.' He clasped her hands. 'I hope I am not keeping you from anything, but I think you will want to know what I am going to show you.'

'No, tell me, Leo,' Lisandre persisted. 'What is this matter of importance of which you speak?'

'I found something while I was reading in the archives –' he began.

'The archives? What were you doing there?' she asked, releasing his hands and turning away.

'Never mind that. You will be very interested to see what I found. I promise you,' he assured her.

Lisandre glanced around, unsure. She was still wary of trusting him. He was a foreigner. He had only come into her life a few days ago, and yet he had always been truthful with her, as far as she could tell.

There was also something else about him. She pondered the matter, then curiosity won her over.

'Show me,' she instructed him, offering her hand.

Leo gracefully took it and led the way.

* * *

Together they entered the Hall of Knowledge. Yellow roses grew everywhere, and silver lanterns hung from the trees, their magical flames glowing bright. Leo led Lisandre to the book he had found.

'You need to see this,' he told her as she sat down beside him. 'You told me that your mother died when you were born, did you not?'

'Yes. I do not remember her, and my father never spoke of her. He said that although she is gone, we must do our best to serve our fellow fey. Why do you ask?'

Leo opened the book to the page about Lady Elina and showed it to Lisandre, who started reading.

'No. It cannot be. Someone has made an error,' she exclaimed. 'It says here that my mother died in the year of the Silver Oak . . .'

'1509'

'A year before I was born.' She turned to him. 'Where did you find such lies? How dare you come to me with this!' she demanded, hurt shining in her eyes.

'I have examined this book thoroughly to the best of my abilities,' Leo replied calmly. 'This is a historical record, Lisandre. A record kept hidden on purpose.'

'But, why would anyone do that?' Lisandre said. 'What would they gain? To achieve what purpose? The queen . . .' She trailed off, lost in her thoughts.

Leo sensed what she was thinking and placed his hand on hers. 'She deceived you Lisandre and for that, I am truly sorry.'

Lisandre looked up and met his eyes. He spoke of betrayal as if he knew it himself, and she wondered: who had betrayed him?

She stood, adjusting her wings. 'There is no need for you to apologise for that which you are not responsible, Alchemyst,' she said.

'I am sorry you were deceived, nonetheless,' Leo said. What else was there to say in such a situation? Words could express so little and yet so much, it seemed.

Lisandre glanced at him over her shoulder before she suddenly took his hand.

'Máith anise,' she thanked him in her native tongue, but her thoughts drifted quickly elsewhere as she left.

If her father's wife had not given birth to her then who was her mother? Why had this knowledge been kept hidden from her? Why had her father decided to keep such a secret? Endless questions floated around in her head, all leading back to the same tangent. Surely the Queen of the Fey knew something about this. As queen she was informed of all faerie births. And yet Ivana had said nothing. But Lisandre doubted she would even get a truthful answer about this if she tried.

She glanced up at the night sky through the trees. Was her mother even a faerie? If so, then who was she?

* * *

'I win,' Flora declared, triumphantly knocking over Lucien's chess piece during another nightly visit in the Midnight Palace a few weeks later.

'Perhaps in this, but not in other matters,' Lucien replied cryptically.

'Speak plainly, prince.' Flora spoke carefully while inside, her thoughts raced. Was the love spell wearing off already? She did not have the ingredients to make another until the next full moon. No — Mikhail was enchanted by her, surely . . .

Like a soothsayer, Lucien continued, 'His interest in you will wane as swiftly as the moon, my lady. Mikhail likes to flirt but if a lady resists his charms for too long he quickly moves on . . '

'And now you are an expert in his affections?' she countered. 'The Dark Prince, he who always remains in the shadows of his brothers.'

'For good reason.' He stood to leave. 'Do not say I did not warn you, countess . . .'

'And what of you, Lucien? Will you ever marry?'

She surprised him with her prodding. 'Perhaps. But know this. She will be my equal, my bride to be. Whoever she is.'

Behind him Flora saw Åsmund enter. 'Then let me warn you in return, fair prince. Do not tell me what to do.'

She left for the ballroom through the opposite end of the hall.

* * *

'Fairest one, she is gone. We cannot find the Lady Lisandre,' Lord Rowan informed the Holly Queen the following evening.

Ivana's nails dug into the throne as she clenched her hands. The rest of her body radiated anger despite appearing deadly calm. Lord Rowan had never seen her so tense. He stood there, timid as a rabbit, subtly backing away lest she prematurely unleash her wrath.

She finally spoke, her words as clear and cold as ice. 'What do you mean?'

'Pardon, your majesty?' This was not off to a good start.

'What do you mean you cannot find a young faerie in the halls of our realm? If you are incapable of completing such a simple task, perhaps you should be removed from your post on the council.' Her words dripped with evident disdain.

'Fairest one, no! Please, I beg you. I cannot bring such shame to my family.' Alistair fell to his knees.

'Then I ask you to do your duty, Lord Rowan. I need you to find her. Find Lisandre.'

* * *

Lisandre turned to face Leo. 'I'm coming with you,' she proclaimed, surprising him. 'Together we can find the scroll and the talismans. Just let me get my things. I'll meet you by the stairs.'

She turned to leave, but Leo reached for her wrist.

'Wait. Are you sure?'

'I am sure,' she told him. 'The queen hid the truth about my identity and my family. I may not know who my mother is, but I can no longer trust her to protect my safety.'

Leo nodded and released her hand, and she hurried towards her chambers.

Once inside, Lisandre hurriedly tied her purple cloak over her dress. She retrieved her wand; she had been training with the beautifully carved apple wood, a gift from the Hazel Queen before she had died. She placed it inside its wooden box and put it in her knapsack. She then picked up the drawstring bag, her bow and arrows, slinging them over her shoulder.

Outside her chambers, Leo created a distraction with his magic, drawing the guards away to the other end of the corridor while Lisandre snuck past. She met Leo by the stairs closest to his chamber.

The portal in Leo's chambers was glowing, ready. Distinct blue light emanated from the stonework where he had marked the stone carefully with chalk.

Leo held out his hand. Lisandre accepted it, and together they leapt into the portal which disappeared behind them.

* * *

They had landed among the grass in a clearing of some sorts. Lisandre stood and listened as she observed her surroundings. *So this was another realm . . .* she thought with wonder. She could hear the trickle of a stream somewhere nearby.

Leo stood as well, surveying the clearing and the forest that surrounded them. The trees were different here, with darker trunks even though they grew less densely. He glanced up at the sky overhead through the branches of the tall trees. It was early evening and the sun was setting, painting a vivid mix of orange and purple across the blue sky. He started to listen too: to the sound of water rushing downstream, the music of the little birds tweeting and chirping merrily in the woods, and to something else . . .

A girl was singing captivatingly — a young maiden to be precise.

He then looked towards Lisandre. 'Your wings. We should conceal them. The people in this realm are not accustomed to such things.' Her wings were beautiful, but would easily draw too much attention.

Leo stepped towards her, outstretched his hand and began casting a spell in Alcheme. As he spoke the ancient words, her wings became invisible before their very eyes. Lisandre turned and glanced over her now bare shoulder, examining the space where they had been.

They stood near an ancient fountain in the centre of the clearing. Dark green vines coiled around the weathered stonework. Around the edge of the clearing was a ring of trees entwined with dark branches. Nearby, Lisandre felt the presence of an elder tree, and looked up to see a large old Rowan tree before a moonpool.

She glanced over at Leo when vines suddenly wrapped around them, lifting them off the ground and into the trees. They curled around Lisandre's waist as she glanced to the ground below, where a stranger was now standing before them.

The figure lifted the hood of her light green cloak to reveal long tresses of red hair that almost reached her waist. Silver embroidery decorated her lilac bodice over her full chest. Her dress was cut in such a fashion to reveal her bare shoulders, its short sleeves starting just beneath her shoulders and ending in a diamond cut across her elbows. Long, thin material fell from each elbow, draping towards the ground. She was also quite beautiful and alluring, with green eyes that seemed to laugh in an enchanting kind of way.

'Let us go!' Leo called down to her.

The maiden held a basket of herbs and flowers over one arm, lazily pointing at them with a wand in the other. A long, thin piece of carved rosewood, Lisandre surmised, by its reddish-brown appearance. The maiden waved the wand in circles before crossing her arms.

'If you wish me to help you . . .' She spoke the words playfully on her tongue as her eyes sparkled in the sunlight. 'You could at least answer my question.'

'And what question is that?' Leo asked warily, keeping his eyes on the strange maiden.

'What *are* an Alchemyst and a faerie doing in the Briar Wood, anyway?' she asked confirming Leo's suspicions.

'How can she see my wings?' Lisandre whispered nervously to Leo. 'I thought you concealed them.'

Leo kept her eyes locked on the maiden as he answered. 'I did. She can see through the enchantment because you're a witch.' In one swift motion raised his bow and drew an arrow, pointing it at the maiden.

'Very good.' She lifted an eyebrow, smiling at Leo. That smile was a little unnerving, he thought. 'Now lower your bow, *Alchemyst*, before you become fertiliser for my plants.'

'Release us from your enchanted vines, witch!' Leo tensed, preparing to shoot the arrow, blue flames flickering warningly at the tip.

'Leo, no do not! Leo!' Lisandre cried, reaching out and placing her hand on his shoulder.

Leo slowly turned his head to face her.

'Witches are daughters of earth, and are our friends,' she said and Leo suddenly remembered a poem Lady Vidjaya had taught him at the Alchemical Court as a young child:

Faerie of the Air

Witches and Wizards of the Earth

Alchemysts and Warlocks are of Fire

Nymphs and Mer of the Water

Friend, Daughter

Son, Brother

Bound to all are one Another

The witch smiled as if she found his reaction a mixture of strange and somehow amusing. 'The faerie is right. We can be friends,' she decided. 'That is, of course if you can keep a secret,' she warned them, narrowing her eyes. 'In return, I can guide you to wherever it is you are going. You do seem quite lost, if I do say so myself.'

'Of course.' Leo put his bow and arrow away and the witch gave a quick wave to the vines wrapped around them, which lowered Leo and Lisandre and drew back into the undergrowth of the bushes.

Lisandre stepped forward, in awe of her magical ability. 'What is your name?'

'Flora,' the witch answered proudly. 'And yours?'

'I am Lady Lisandre of the fey, and this is Leo.'

'Enchanting to meet you,' Flora greeted them in return.

'We shall need a place to stay for the night,' Leo noted. 'Perhaps you could direct us to the nearest inn?' he suggested.

'Not dressed like that I won't!' Flora replied. 'You two would stand out for miles around here. The mortals would drag you in front of the King of Fuschia! You can stay with me,' she decided. 'Come, I'll show you the way.'

Flora left in the direction of the cottage on the edge of the forest. Lisandre glanced questioningly at Leo, and the pair started walking after her.

'You are far prettier than I expected a witch to be,' Leo commented, the brambles scratching his leg as he walked.

Flora guided them through the forest as the sun set quickly behind them. 'Pfft! The Alchemical Court has a lot to answer for. What did they teach you, anyway? Never mind. They probably told you witches are all old, ugly-looking creatures with warts and green skin. Witches, like all creatures, can be beautiful too. Even without the use of magic,' she added, seeing Leo's sceptical glance. 'Although I'm sure that for some people, a little beauty spell every now and again does help.' She patted her cheek.

Flora held the silver lantern high as they wandered through the trees to the forest's edge. It was dark now that night had fallen, stars beginning to twinkle in the sky overhead.

'Welcome to Rose Cottage,' she told Leo and Lisandre as they gazed up at the cottage in the moonlight.

'My aunt is busy travelling, overseeing the family business for two weeks,' Flora explained as she led them along the garden path.

'Is she a witch too?' Leo asked suspiciously, eying the assortment of plants within the garden as he shut the picket gate.

Flora swivelled around from where she stood in the doorway and tilted her head thoughtfully. 'No. Not that I know of,' she admitted.

She entered the cottage, Lisandre and Leo following after. They each copied Flora, taking off their cloaks and hanging them on assigned hooks within an alcove inside the doorway.

'So where are you going?' Flora asked, retrieving a teapot and filling it with water before placing it over the fire. Drying bunches of flowers hung from the ceiling, including an abundance of lavender and rosemary. Leo noted a wreath of ivy hanging upon the mantel.

Leo and Lisandre sat down on the old wooden chairs, watching Flora as she pulled out small pots of dried herbs and poured them into the tea pot. She whispered some words to it, causing the water to boil and bubble. Leo recognised a smattering of the words as Latinacaec, the language the witches and wizards used for spells.

He and Lisandre looked at each other, a silent conversation passing between them before Leo answered.

'We ... er ... I ...That is, we are currently unsure where we are going. I'm not even sure where we are now. If I had to guess, I would say by your accent, clothes and the architecture of this cottage, that we are in Fuschia, near the forest that runs along the border with the Southern Kingdom.'

'Well done,' said Flora, pouring them each a cup of steaming-hot tea. 'Now that you know where you are, perhaps you could tell me where you are from?'

Leo and Lisandre glanced at each other again before Lisandre decided to tell her the truth.

'We came from the Eternal Forest, the Realm of the Fey,' she said, her hands wrapped around the sides of the steaming cup.

'Na Foraise Síorai!' Flora exclaimed, surprising both Leo and Lisandre. 'I have only read about it. What was it like? Is it as beautiful as they say?'

'More so,' Leo told her.

'Also, may I ask — how is it you can understand Fuschian?' Flora enquired.

'Alchemy. It's an Alchemical languages spell,' explained Leo.

'Ah!' said Flora. 'I am still curious, though . . . *Why* are you here?'

Leo and Lisandre glanced anxiously at one another again.

'Trust me. I am the only non-mortal around here for miles. And I am offering you shelter out of the goodness of my heart.' She clasped her fingers together and rested her arms upon the table. 'Whatever it is. Perhaps I can help you.'

'We're looking for a scroll,' Lisandre said eagerly. 'In the Great Library of Florencia.'

'I see. Well, the Great Library is rumoured to hold such manuscripts. Indeed, it is said to be the largest reservoir of books and artefacts outside the Alchemical Court. However, not just anyone is allowed to browse those particular collections. Foreigners would need to ask the permission of the king to access such scrolls. However, as an Alchemyst, he may just grant it,' Flora noted thoughtfully.

'So we will need to meet the King of Fuschia, then?' Leo asked.

'Yes. But, Alchemyst or not, strangers aren't just invited into the palace. If you wish to see the king, though, there might be another way . . .' Flora said, aware the Alchemyst and faerie were hanging onto her every word. 'The King is having an end-of-year masquerade ball to celebrate the new year. Perhaps we could attend?'

'Masquerade?' asked Lisandre, her accent showing.

'The Fuschian court is known for its masquerades and dances,' explained Flora. 'It would be the best opportunity to ask, and should anything not go our way, it is easier to slip away when there is a crowd such as will be present at the ball.'

'Good point,' remarked Leo. 'Wait, one more thing. What is the Briar Wood?'

Flora began dramatically, showcasing her storytelling voice. 'The Briar Wood is an ancient part of the wood, where creatures such as faeries and elves are said to exist and witches dwell with large cauldrons over fires, brewing their potions and weaving spells and enchantments . . . It's the part of the wood where I found you,' she added simply at the sight of their blank expressions. 'Okay. Well then, we best get some rest.'

Leo and Lisandre followed Flora up the wooden staircase, trailing behind her before she paused on the landing. She ducked into a room where she retrieved pillows and blankets from a large chest.

'We have a few days before the celebrations to prepare,' Flora noted, shoving the bedding into Leo's hands. 'Your room is through there.' She gestured to the door at the end of the hall upstairs. 'Bonna nuite,' she wished them goodnight and promptly retreated to her room, closing the door behind her.

Lisandre chose a blanket and pillow from Leo and started heading upstairs. As he followed her, Leo noticed the banner tapestry draping the wall behind him. The design on the scarlet background could not help but remind him of the symbol that seemed to keep following him everywhere since the night he had seen it in his master's notes. The purple iris was not unlike that mysterious symbol.

Leo continued to ponder what it all meant long after he went to bed.

* * *

Chapter Four

The Golden Apple

Apples

Beauty, knowledge, divination

A wand made from wood of the apple tree enhances a love spell

*A*nd she was back in his arms, dancing under the falling snow . . .

Snowflakes, enchanted, fell from the cloudless ceiling.

The ballroom walls featured trees with golden leaves covered with frost.

The fountain water frozen in a mid-air display. Crystal chandeliers hung from the canopy.

The Crystal Tree sparkled with delight as she picked one of the golden apples.

She held it in her hands, pondering. Should she go, with Leo?

Or should she stay?

'Lisandre. Lisandre, wake up.'

Leo's voice called her from her sleep. It had been a week, and yet it felt like the Solstice Ball had only been a few nights before. They had seven days to prepare for the New Year's Ball.

The morning after they had arrived, Flora took their measurements and had begun working on finding and altering clothes for them. She perused her wardrobe for a suitable dress for Lisandre. The first she chose Lisandre was a white dress edged with lacework across the shoulders and a Fuschian cut neckline revealing Lisandre's bare shoulders.

'This is for everyday wear,' Flora explained, handing her the dress to change into. She rummaged through a couple of chests upstairs, where she found another day dress and a nightdress, as well as some extra clothes for Leo as well.

'In the meantime, it is probably best not to wander too far and always wear a cloak if you go out,' she informed them.

The week passed quickly. During the day Lisandre practised Nádúr with her wand underneath the apple tree. Connecting with the tree spirits strengthened her magic as she rehearsed the movements with her wand as described in her book. The motions were like a dance, and she directed the energy with the help of her wand.

Meanwhile, inside, Flora prepared for the masquerade, creating masks for each of them, and Leo helped around the cottage, collecting firewood and tending the vegetable garden. In the evenings they read books and played puzzles, and some nights Flora would even sing for them. During this time they got to know one another well, and Flora quickly became the closest friend Lisandre had ever known. Flora, too, seemed delighted to have made such friends.

Soon the last day of the year arrived. As evening fell, Flora noticed from the second floor that Leo was checking no one was watching as Lisandre came in from the trees below. He seemed paranoid someone would spot her from the road to the village.

Catching her watching him, Leo quickly explained, 'No one can know either of us are here, especially Lisandre.'

Flora stepped closer so she was standing beside him in front of the windows.

'Well, obviously. She is fey.' Her tone turned more serious. 'But there is more to it than that, isn't there?'

Leo didn't answer. At that moment they heard Lisandre enter the cottage.

Flora turned to confront Leo dead on. 'Who are you? Is someone after you?'

'Yes. I cannot say more than that. I'm sorry, but for now some matters must remain secret,' Leo insisted as Lisandre appeared in the doorway. 'I hope you can understand.'

'Of course. I understand,' she said, more so to herself as she stepped back, her expression thoughtful. 'And we all have our secrets.'

Her words were followed by silence.

She brightened up as she turned towards Lisandre. 'And our talents! Speaking of which I have just the right dress for you.'

Flora hurried off into another room. She returned with a light purple dress featuring fitted sleeves and a bodice that had lilac ribbon lacing at the front and back.

'Go on, try it on!' Flora encouraged her.

Lisandre remained hesitant but took the dress from Flora, who showed her to a dressing screen. Once alone, she took off her white day dress, pulled on the lavender gown and glanced at herself in the mirror. Mortal dresses were so vexing in comparison to the loose soft clothing of the fey. Why couldn't mortals let their women just breathe? The long lilac laces were in a mess, hanging down her bodice at the front and back. She fiddled with them, uncertain where they should go.

'Uh, Flora?' Lisandre called from behind the screen.

'Si?' Flora answered.

'Could you help with this dress, please? I am having some trouble.'

'Are you covered?'

'Yes.'

'I'm coming in.'

Flora stepped behind the screen as Leo stood waiting at the other end of the room. She took the ribbons, and with a wave of her other hand they rose up and started lacing themselves.

'There you are,' Flora said with a smile, tying them up effortlessly at the ends in little bows.

'Are you dressed?' Leo asked, ignoring the urge to turn around and catch a glimpse of Lisandre's elegant form.

Lisandre and Flora stepped out from behind the screen. 'Is this less conspicuous?' Lisandre asked him, pulling at the ends of the tight sleeves. *The fey never wore sleeves like this.*

Leo's mouth formed a small 'o', which she caught a glimpse of as she looked up. He recomposed himself. 'Ah, yes . . .'

'You will be once I find you your mask,' Flora remarked as she rummaged through a trunk across the room. 'Here.' She handed Lisandre a gold mask with a dark purple rose adorning the edge. She then turned to Leo. 'Now for you, signor . . .'

Flora stepped towards him and started to remove his Alchemical jacket, startling Leo.

'The gold brocade and black fabric are simply much too conspicuous. The palazzo guards would spot you by your glittering jacket a mile away,' she apologised. She carefully placed his jacket over the chair in the corner, and then went over to another wardrobe, where she retrieved a red jacket instead. 'Put that on,' she commanded.

'Isn't this rather bold?' he questioned, warily examining the jacket before putting it on over his white linen shirt.

'Not in Fuschia it isn't,' she told him firmly. 'Here, you will blend in.'

Flora went behind a screen to change into her own dress. Dark purple ribbons laced the corset and the underside of the long scarlet sleeves, whose fabric matched the skirt. The dress had been cut straight across to reveal her bare shoulders, as per the Fuschian style.

She emerged from behind the screen and her eyes fell upon the red-and-gold mask on her dressing table, quickly moving to the red camellia-like rose beside it. Her eyes remained focused on the mask as she sat down in front of the dresser mirror to put on her jewellery. First her mother's amethyst iris necklace, the symbol for the House DuPoitoires. Next, a circle of miniature roses in her hair. The tiny green leaves contrasted with the red of the roses and her dress.

She felt her eyes once again drawn to the strange flower. Her mind was transported once again to the magical world of the Midnight Court, to a time of flirtation and innocence. His breath on her neck, her skin tingling, her soul on fire. His hand on her lower back as he guided her along the Great Hall to the waiting room . . .

* * *

'My brother will be present shortly. There are some chocolates you may enjoy while you wait,' Lucien said, releasing Flora. She wandered across the room. Alyssrian chocolates were a well-known delicacy.

'Here I was hoping that you would dance with me,' she remarked half sarcastically as she lounged on the sofa. She was wearing her favourite crimson red dress with the elegant gold trim and girdle.

Lucien smiled behind her back as Flora chose a chocolate infused with rose oil.

'You were, weren't you?' he replied.

The sound of the door opening provided Lucien with the

excuse to leave, and he turned around as Mikhail appeared at the other entrance. As he walked down the lengthy corridor, he glanced over his shoulder and saw Mikhail raise his hand to cup Flora's cheek, gently kissing her before escorting her out into the ballroom to dance.

Once they were gone, he glanced down to the object he had removed from the folds of his tunic. Clasped in his hands was a particular silver-and-gold dagger with a peridot-jewelled handle . . .

* * *

'The Countess de Roselle shall now sing for us,' announced Mikhail as Flora saw Lucien appear at the back of the room. She glanced uncertainly at the king.

'Would you do us the honour, my dear?' asked King Cesaire from where he sat on his golden throne. The symbol of the Kingdom of the Midnight Sun, a crescent moon combined with a smiling sun, was carved into the high back of the throne, surrounded by a pattern of arches and stars. Beside the king, a nearly identical throne of silver sat empty, and Flora wondered where the queen was. She had overheard rumours that Queen Katya was more than just a witch, but a powerful sorceress to be reckoned with.

'Where do you think Her Magnificence is off to?' Flora recalled Lady Lilia asking one evening, as the group of ladies watched the queen leave the ballroom in a hurry.

'Off to brew one of her potions or spells,' scoffed Eleanora, tipping back her glass of scarlet cherry juice.

'What do you mean?' asked one of the other ladies in blue, curious.

'I heard Queen Katya is a powerful sorceress — but then again every second person in Alyssria has *some* magical ability,' Eleanora remarked.

'That's right. You come from a long line of silvercasters don't you, Eleanora?' the maiden beside her gushed excitedly.

'Shh, Lilia! Not everyone at court need know of my heritage,' Eleanora hushed her as her gaze swept over to Flora, who stood at the other side of the ballroom. She watched as Mikhail approached and began talking to Flora, clearly enchanted with her. 'Besides, they will know soon enough,' she added, taking another sip as she peered over the edge of the glass at Flora who turned and addressed the king. 'It would be my pleasure, Your Magnificence,' she curtseyed and walked to the front of the room under the watchful gaze of the three princes. The eyes of the court fell upon this mysterious midnight beauty, a southern countess.

She took a deep breath in an attempt to calm her nerves and looked up, her eyes meeting Lucien's curious gaze. The musicians started to play, and Flora began to sing beautiful high notes along to the sweet sounds of the flute and deep tones of the violin.

'There are stars within your eyes

Spells like jewels fall from your tongue

Beneath blue midnight skies

I know you are the only one

There are stars within your eyes

And endless worlds around you

There is a sparkle within your eye

And a name on your lips like desire

Your very gaze turns my heart to fire . . .'

She had been worried, but she bloomed, the words blossoming like flowers with every note of the song.

At the end she curtseyed as they all clapped in appreciation — including Lucien, Flora noticed, surprised. He rarely displayed appreciation for any of the other court artisans. Mikhail rushed to greet her as she left the stage, offering her his arm. Her eyes glanced once more towards Lucien as she accepted, letting Mikhail lead her to the king, who complimented her singing voice.

'Excellent, my dear. You have an exquisite gift for the art of music,' he noted fondly.

'Thank you, Your Magnificence. You are very kind.' Flora curtseyed again. She was turning to leave when King Cesaire continued.

'Indeed, I have never heard such a beautiful voice, so full of character and charm.' He smiled broadly, and Flora heard Lucien mutter under his breath. Her eyes darted towards him, shooting him a warning glance. How dare he be so rude!

Focus Flora! There are more important matters at stake than the manners of some prince, she thought and turned around to graciously face the king.

'Thank you,' she said, taking her eyes off Lucien, 'but if you would excuse me Your Magnificence, I would very much like to get some air.'

'Of course.' The king waved his hand, dismissing her.

Mikhail started to follow her, but Lucien clasped his arm. 'Let her go.'

Mikhail shook him off and met his eyes, a silent

understanding passing between them. Gazing once more at Flora's retreating form, Mikhail turned the other way and left.

* * *

Lucien soon excused himself and retired to his chambers, where he sat twirling a blade at his desk. He had spent the past fortnight between the countess' visits examining the blade, enquiring with the forgers and skilled craftsmen of Safir, and spending many hours researching in the Libraire about the mysterious crest carved in the golden peridot-set handle. The crest depicted a magnificent bird, a phoenix perhaps, with its wings spread as if in flight, hovering in the air in its glory.

The craftsman in the city told him what he already knew: that the dagger was high-quality (no surprise for a countess, he supposed). The hilt was either southern or Fuschian in design, and impossible for them to tell which. They could tell him it was old, an heirloom, perhaps from the 13th century, well taken care of. But none of them recognised the strange bird upon its pommel.

Tired and disappointed again, Lucien had returned to his chambers sometime later and sat down in front of his desk. Again, he'd found himself drawn to the dagger . . .

The elaborate golden hilt was beautiful, as was the peridot embedded in the handle. Lucien found himself captivated by the gemstone, gazing into its endless depths, and soon he felt himself falling into the familiar depths of sleep . . .

* * *

She stood at the end of the corridor, by the balcony in the blue moonlight. Like a vision, she was hauntingly beautiful. Her elegant figure cast a shadow on the stone as she held a red rose, long lilac sleeves blowing in the gentle breeze.

'Flora?' He slowly approached her, almost stumbling upon the stone tiles.

Her head rose and she turned her gaze upon him.

'You want me.'

The words fell from her lips, then she vanished, reappearing beside his other ear. The look in her eyes turned forlorn.

'But you can never have me.'

She moved behind the column and vanished completely.

Lucien woke up, covered in sweat.

* * *

Flora woke to moonlight pouring in through the window. She got up, dressed and raced downstairs and through the forest, where she knelt by the moonpool. She pulled out the amethyst iris necklace from beneath her bodice, glancing up at the moon overhead as she set her lantern on a branch of the tree and knelt again.

Rays of silver moonlight shimmered on the surface of the pool as she cast the spell. The waters began to glow and churn. Closing her eyes, she stepped into the portal.

Flora lifted her eyes and found herself staring at the glass ceiling toward the starry night sky beyond. She stood up, assessing her surroundings. She was in the Midnight Palace, with its familiar gold-and-blue coloured tiles and crystal lamps. Gently brushing off the hem of her dress, she listened for the sound of music, luring her to the ballroom.

Her dress this evening she imitated the style of the Midnight Court, with her own alterations: a lowered neckline to reveal her bare shoulders; loose sleeves cut open in a V-shape beneath the puff; midnight-blue fabric matched with swatches of sapphire, woven in tightly together to form a corset and a lighter blue material peeking out beneath her skirts. The entire dress seemed to sparkle and shimmer. She wore a matching band of sapphires in her hair, and the emerald-and-pearl necklace around her neck.

She stood on the edge of the Midnight Court, watching the dancers below from a second-floor balcony. Flora watched as the partners lifted their ladies each in time to the music, one after the other. Their metallic skirts swept the ground in a grand symphony of colours. She watched, searching for the one she had come to see. Then a familiar figure caught her eye: the crown prince, Mikhail, dancing with a blonde girl in a light green gown with a white lace frill collar.

Eleanora. Her thoughts raced at the sight. Was Lucien right? Had Mikhail moved on so quickly? She had only flirted with him to gain access to the Midnight Court, only played the game, and yet part of her ego was hurt by seeing him move on so swiftly. What about her reputation? Her status at court? Part of her had even dared daydream half-heartedly about becoming his fiancée. But the spell had worn off; Mikhail didn't seem interested in her anymore.

'Flora.'

A shiver ran up her spine as he called her name. She turned to see Lucien approach her. Perhaps he had taken pity upon her?

Flora raised her chin. 'Come to gloat, my prince?' she asked sombrely.

His expression changed as his eyes met hers. 'No', he told her sincerely. 'I seek no pleasure from your pain, countess. Not tonight.'

A bemused smile crossed her face. She seemed surprised, he thought. He took her by the hand.

'Come with me.'

'Where are we going?' Flora asked.

'I have someplace to show you. The portal opens at Midnight,' he said cryptically.

Lucien led her out of the palace, through the gardens, then beyond the trees, into the forest. They passed through between two aligning trees, their branches curved to form an archway. Flora felt them pass through a ripple in the air as they crossed into another realm. The stars sparkled above as they swept through the tall, dark trees before coming to a stop in a clearing. Glowing flowers were abloom here, growing scattered among the ground surrounding them, their petals vibrant in the moon's gaze.

They were in the Dreamworld now.

'The Midnight Forest,' Flora breathed, suddenly engulfed by a memory. She remembered coming here alone nearly six months before, in the months after she had discovered her mother's Spellbooke. She remembered how she'd stood watching in the crowd as a familiar figure approached. She thought it had been a dream . . .

'They say he is a prince of the night . . .' one said.

'The Dark Prince . . .' whispered another.

'A prince in his own realm, wherever that is,' another guest muttered.

Their eyes met as he walked past, his gaze lingering for a brief moment on hers. *Did he remember?* she wondered. *That night last Spring . . .*

'I think I have been here before,' she told him as she walked forward, admiring their surroundings.

'I know you have.'

She swivelled around to find Lucien's eyes on her.

'You do?' she asked innocently.

'Walk with me,' he said, and she saw the longing written in his sapphire eyes mirrored perfectly in her own. He offered her his arm and she accepted, entwining her arm around his as they strolled amongst the luminescent flowers. 'I'm sorry about Mikhail by the way,' Lucien said.

'Don't be. It was never meant to be,' she replied, looking away.

They walked and talked intimately, Lucien speaking of his experiences growing up in the Midnight Court as the youngest brother and Flora listening intently. They paused as they heard music coming from within the forest.

'I believe that you owe me a dance,' Lucien said.

A sly smile flashed across Flora's lips. 'I'm not sure that I do,' she spoke over her shoulder with a twinkle in her eyes.

'Fine. Flora, may I have this dance?' he asked, offering his hand.

'You may,' she answered, placing her hand in his; his other hand slid around her waist.

Although she had never seen Lucien dance at the Midnight Court, Flora was relieved to find that he was actually an excellent dancer. Together they moved in time with the music, dancing along the edges of the lake. Their movements balanced one another perfectly, their hands always finding each other. Lucien held her form gracefully as they spun and twirled downstream, their silhouettes mirrored beautifully in the waters of the lake below.

A while later they sat by the lake, watching the dancers in the distance across the water as they listened to the music.

'Wait, one more thing,' Lucien said.

'What are you doing?' Flora asked.

He appeared to be concentrating, his hands raised in front of him. A purple blanket suddenly appeared beneath them. A crystal fire appeared before them also, the magical flames trickling and dancing around the violet branches of the crystal.

'So you are a sorcerer,' she noted, intrigued and also somewhat impressed.

He smiled. 'Yes.'

'You know they already call you the Dark Prince,' she quipped.

'You did call me something like that the last time we spoke, I believe,' he remarked.

'Yes.' She smiled. 'Originally I thought it was because of your hair, but now I suspect it is because of your reputation for sorcery,' she teased and Lucien smiled.

'Tell me of your family, countess. Are they like mine? Do you have brothers? Sisters, perhaps?' he inquired curiously.

Flora paused. She did not want to deceive him any further than necessary.

'My mother died in childbirth giving birth to me,' she finally confessed, her eyes cast down. 'I am an only child. I was raised by my aunt.'

'And your father?' Lucien asked.

'I never knew him,' she admitted truthfully.

She leant her head against his shoulder as they sat and watched the stars.

'I never got to ask you before. Why you were there, at the Midnight Forest? When I first saw you last spring,' Flora asked after a while.

'I used to come here often, to get away from the Midnight Court and my brothers. Here in the Dreamworld I am just *a* prince, not a Safarov. Here I can be something more, here I can be —'

'Yourself,' she finished.

'Exactly.' He met her eyes and saw that she understood.

They sat together under the midnight sky, listening to the music in the distance, watching the silhouettes of the dancers in comfortable silence. The songs reminded Flora of something else she had been meaning to ask him.

'Do you sing Lucien?'

'No, never if I can help it. I prefer other pursuits.' Blue magic suddenly swirled in the air around his hand. Lucien opened his palm, having conjured a red camellia-like rose. He presented it to her.

Flora looked at him questionably. She recognised this particular flower only from books of myths and legends. Did he truly know the meaning of such a gift? She let him place the fragrant flower in her hair.

> *'Daughter of shadows and fairest night*
>
> *Blooms within the darkest hour*
>
> *Shine with most brilliant light*
>
> *Doth this bright and most loveliest flower'*

He recited the words of the ancient song as he gently tucked the stem between the strands of her hair.

'The Midnight Rose,' he explained, nodding to the flower.

How fitting, Flora wanted to say but suddenly she didn't feel like joking anymore.

'Of course, it is just a replica. No one seems to know where *that* particular flower is or if it even exists, or even what colour it is,' he explained, rambling. 'That flower is so named because it blossoms in the moonlight,' he recalled from his books. 'But I suppose it is the thought that counts.'

Flora knew the song of myth and legend well. Indeed, it was one of her favourites. But he did not know that.

'It's beautiful.'

She wondered if he wanted to kiss her. His eyes traced the arch of her lips. Then his hand reached out, touching the side of her face, and he leaned forward, gently pressing her lips to his, before kissing her passionately. She returned the kiss with equal fervour.

In that moment time to seemed to race and somehow seem endless all at once. Out of the corner of her eye Flora saw a shooting star pass overhead. Even without the star, this moment was truly magical.

A few moments later, Lucien stood up and offered her his hand.

'Come. You must meet my mother. If anyone can help find your family, it is the most powerful sorceress of the realm.'

He led her back to the palace, her skirts floating across the floor through the old section that had been part of the original castle. The ancient stone had held for centuries.

As they walked along the crystal lit corridors of the Midnight Palace, Flora suddenly felt a strong pull as if they had walked together here before, once upon a dream.

What a strange feeling, she thought as Lucien led her up the circular stairs of a narrow tower in the older section of the palace. This part looked extraordinarily ancient, Flora observed as she noticed the crumbling brickwork.

At last they reached the top of the tower, where a tall, imposing figure stood waiting at the top of the stairs.

'Mother.' Lucien bowed, still holding Flora's hand.

She felt butterflies within at the mere thought of meeting the princes' mother again. As she glanced around the tower, she noticed an assortment of rather exotic plants, many used in witchcraft. A cupboard also featured shelves full of crystals and glass bottles of different coloured liquids. A collection of different types of mosses, mushrooms and strange barks were also present.

The figure turned and moved toward them, into the light emanating from a crystal lamp glowing in the corner.

Queen Katya was a tall, impressive woman of strong build. Anyone who had studied the history of Alyssria knew true power lied with the elusive queen. King Cesaire was of a low born but skilled family of jewellers and had even gone so far as to take Katya's family name, Safarov. Katya, however, had been born an Alyssrian princess. The last surviving Alyssrian princess, to be precise, after the tragic rebellion of 1498. At the tender age of thirteen, the queen had lost her older brother, Paul, and her parents, barely escaping the same fate herself. Katya had become heir and was raised by her grandmother until the age of eighteen, when she was deemed old enough to rule. The young queen soon married the royal jewelsmith, much against her grandmother and many advisors' wishes, but they were in love. A year later Mikhail was born, and things seemed somewhat peaceful in the kingdom for a while again.

A silver tiara with a crescent moon in the centre rested upon Queen Katya's long, dark brown hair. She was dressed in her signature deep purple with very long sleeves that trailed from her elbows. Her presence was somewhat intimidating, with her long hair framing elegant features and strong cheekbones. Upon realising that she was in the presence of Katya Safarov, renowned sorceress and one of the most powerful witches she had ever heard of, Flora immediately fell to her knees, her eyes cast towards the ground.

'Good evening, Your Magnificence. It is an honour to be in your presence,' Flora said, keeping her gaze down.

Katya turned to Lucien. 'You may leave us.'

Lucien glanced over his shoulder at Flora as he left. Once they'd heard his footsteps descend the tower steps, Katya addressed Flora.

'Come, sit.' She sat down before a table beside the fireplace. Flora sat in the chair closest to the fire. 'It is an honour to finally meet you, countess. Though I suspect that is not entirely what you are.'

Unsure how to respond, Flora remained silent, but being in the presence of a witch as knowledgeable and powerful as the queen, she soon could not help but ask, 'How do you know so much about magic?'

'Such a simple question, with a simple answer: I studied it. I come from a long line of powerful witches — as do you,' Katya stated, surprising Flora. For a moment she feared Katya knew she was a Fuschian as well. 'I can sense your power,' the queen continued. 'Though you hide it well, I must admit.'

'Will you tell him?' Flora asked quietly.

'That you are a witch? Heavens, no. But Flora, he will know soon enough,' she warned. 'What I don't understand is why you feel the need to hide your magic from my son at all. Castelle may not have half as many magicians as the Midnight Court, but here most are magicians of one kind or another. Micha and Aleksandr can do minor magics. It was Lucien who chose to develop his gifts and study the ancient art of sorcery,' the queen told her proudly.

Flora carefully hid her relief.

'Lucien is a sorcerer himself; he even studies Alchemy. He would probably be delighted to learn of your power,' Katya continued then paused in the middle of adding more dried plants to a potion. 'Unless that is not all you are hiding . . .'

Flora's heartrate rose again.

'Witches are not so . . . *accepted* in my kingdom as they are here, nor some of the other places I have travelled. I thought it best to be cautious,' she explained carefully.

'I see,' said Katya. 'You have quite enchanted him, you know,' she added.

Flora was surprised. 'I have?'

'I have never seen him like this. Truly happy,' Katya said, and Flora glanced down nervously as she blushed. Katya continued stirring the potion, her long sleeves draping across the ground. 'I hope you will not break his heart,' she warned harshly. 'Countess or not, it would end very badly for you.'

'Do not worry, for I do not intend to,' Flora answered. Perhaps asking Queen Katya about her family was not such a good idea after all. What if they were her enemies?

'Not all do,' remarked Katya, returning her attention to the potion.

Flora rose and curtseyed again. 'I am sorry, but I really must leave now.'

'Of course. Feel free to come and speak with me again, Flora.' Flora backed away and hurriedly returned downstairs, leaving the witch queen in her tower.

* * *

She returned to the Midnight Court a fortnight later, Lucien sending her enchanted notes in between. He had given her the first note as she had returned from the tower, just before she'd left. He had hurriedly informed her she could reply simply by writing on the back of the paper with her quill.

From her conversations with Lucien, it was unclear whether he had told anyone, even his brothers, about their new attachment. Flora thought at least Mikhail deserved to know from her, and so she had sought him out upon arriving early for the evening dances.

'Mikhail. I, uh, need to speak with you.' Her nervousness dissipated somewhat upon seeing a warm smile appear on his face.

'No need, countess.' He took her hand and clasped it with both of his. 'Trust me, I understand,' he assured her.

'You do?' Flora was confused. 'Mikhail, I'm sorry —'

'I'm not. It is truly all for the best, it seems.' He released her hand as Lucien entered from the opposite end of the room behind her. 'Brother,' Mikhail greeted him warmly, and took Lucien's hand.

A confused expression also fell across Lucien's face. Mikhail then placed Flora's hand in Lucien's. They fit together perfectly.

'Now, I'd better be off. Eleanora is choosing flowers for the wedding today —'

'Wedding?' Lucien almost choked.

'My wedding, not yours. Though I wouldn't be surprised if the two of you did consider it.' Micha winked at them. 'Anyway, Eleanora is choosing them and she insists *I* be there. So, dobrey dien.' He smiled cheerily as he wished them good luck, and swiftly exited the ballroom, leaving the pair of them alone, her hand still clasped in his.

* * *

A few days later, in early October, Flora visited the halls of Alyssria once again, her fingers gently touching the precious stones that encrusted the intricately decorated walls of the Midnight Palace as she passed by. Alyssria was as known for its magic as for its precious stones, whereas Fuschia was known for its magnificent flowers and gardens, as well as its heavenly perfumes. Flora picked up an exotic silver star-shaped fruit, tossing it playfully in the palms of her hands as she walked down the hall.

'Good evening, my lady,' Aleksandr greeted her without stopping as he passed her by.

'Good evening, Your Grace,' she answered, wondering where he was off to. Aleksandr had never been fond of her, even when she had courted Mikhail. Now he was casually exchanging pleasantries with her?

Intrigued, she set down the fruit by a nearby vase and turned to follow him. Aleksandr then headed downstairs, and down again, turning left into one of the many rooms along the corridor as Flora snuck carefully behind. She hid behind the doorway, close enough to overhear Aleksandr and whomever he had gone to meet beyond the ruby-curtained arch.

'I don't care how you go about it, just get rid of her. She could ruin everything,' a familiar female voice almost shrieked. Eleanora's voice, Flora realised with shock. She had never suspected Eleanora to be plotting with Aleksandr.

'I agree, she is quite a nuisance,' he replied, thoughtfully.

'*Nuisance?!* She had Mikhail distracted for weeks! I never want to see that countess again!'

Flora heard shoes squeak upon the wooden floor as Eleanora paced the room. She listened intently as Aleksandr stepped towards Eleanora.

'Trust me, Eleanora, my dear. When this is all done and over, that *jenta* will wish she had never stepped foot in the Midnight Court,' he told her assuredly.

Eleanora turned to leave.

'Just remember your role in this and it will all be taken care of,' Aleksandr reminded her coldly.

'See that it is,' she told him.

Hearing her footsteps approach, Flora rushed to hide behind the nearest curtain, her back to the window. She held her breath as Eleanora walked past her, along the corridor and back upstairs. Aleksandr then left in the opposite direction. Once certain she was alone again, Flora crept out from behind the scarlet curtain and headed back upstairs, hoping to find Lucien and warn him about what his brother may be involved in scheming.

First, she found King Cesaire. 'Evening?' she heard the king scoff as she entered the main ballroom. 'It is barely five past noon!'

Seeing Flora approach, the king dismissed the courtier with whom had been discussing plans for the evening.

'Ah, my dear!' He reached out for her, clasping her hands in his. He then wrapped her arm around his own and started walking with her around the ballroom.

'Your Magnificence?' she asked cautiously.

'I have been hoping you would entertain us this evening — that is, if you do not mind of course. You have a splendid voice, if I do say so myself. Magnus, our court maestro, has some new music he wishes to perform for tonight's audience and is looking for a singer.'

Out of the corner of her eye Flora noticed Lucien enter from the other end of the ballroom. He paused, watching her admiringly, overhearing their conversation with subtle amusement as Cesaire continued.

'Eleanora offered, of course, but have you *heard* the young lady sing? Cats howling would be easier to listen to. Aye, you would be doing the court a favour, really. So what do you say, my dear?' The king looked at her hopefully.

'I would be glad to, Your Magnificence,' she reassured him. 'If I could meet this maestro, I'm sure we can prepare a performance for this evening.'

'Perhaps Lucien would be able to escort you, give you a tour of our magnificent city?' the king said encouragingly. He turned around at just the right time to see Lucien approach to save Flora from his enthusiasm. 'Ah, Lucien! Excellent! Please escort the Countess de Roselle to Maestro Magnus Wolfe. Tell him I have found his songstress for the evening. Very well, my dear. Good day.' He left her and Lucien alone in the empty ballroom.

As they exited, walking side by side along the grand corridor to the foyer Flora questioned Lucien, her eyes cast downward as she spoke. 'I did not see you attend last night's dances. Where were you? I missed you.' She focused on her sleeve as they descended the stairs.

Lucien took her by the hand, pulling her into the nearest alcove. He began kissing her urgently, his hand sliding down to come to rest on her hip. They were lost in one another's embrace for a moment before at last coming up for air.

'I'm sorry. It wasn't about you—I had to travel to the Alchemical Court to study. I left a note for you. Did you not receive it?' he asked, concerned.

'No, I did not,' Flora answered. 'I thought you were a

sorcerer—why do you need to study Alchemy?' she asked.

'I may not be a king but I aim to be proficient in all areas of magic someday. It is my passion, and the best way I can contribute to my brother's kingdom in the future—' Lucien explained, then had an idea. 'Come.'

He started to lead Flora down the steps, but paused in the doorway and glanced at her elegant red dress.

'Do you have something just a *little* less formal?' he asked, staring at her dress.

'Yes, in my invisible travelling box!' answered Flora sarcastically, and he gave her a look. 'No! Of course not!' she protested. 'I came for a ball, remember.'

'Here.' Lucien used his magic to summon a pair of cloaks, which appeared over his elbow. He took one and placed it carefully around Flora's shoulders. The dark blue fabric was covered with silver stars and swirls on almost every inch, contrasting perfectly with her red hair. He gently tucked a loose strand behind her shoulder.

'Where are we going?' she asked as he guided her through the courtyard and down the steps in front of the palace. 'I promised the king to meet with the maestro, remember?'

'And you shall. His house is in another part of the city. I thought I would we could spend some time together first. I'm not letting the maestro have you all day,' Lucien told her, grinning.

They passed through the gardens and palace gates. Soon they entered the town centre of Safir.

'My mother often goes to the city by herself. She has oft been gone of late,' Lucien commented as they entered the heart of the city: the marketplace.

'Lucien, wait. I am concerned about something. I overheard your brother, Aleksandr. He was with Eleanora. They were talking. They want me gone,' she told him, becoming more and more distressed with each word. 'She resents me, Lucien. I don't know what they were planning – '

Lucien turned her towards him. 'Listen to me,' he said. 'It doesn't matter what they are planning because I will protect you. Aleksandr is a novice in comparison to my magic. However, I will have a word with him about this. Remind him not to touch what is not his.'

Flora paused for a moment, taking in his words.

'Does this mean I am yours and you are mine?' she hinted playfully.

Lucien smiled as he pulled her closer and kissed her.

* * *

They wandered the market together, the young prince and his mystery young lady passing by largely unnoticed. Few concerned themselves with the youngest brother. After all, it was Mikhail who was destined to be king.

One of the most famous in the realm, the Safir market was known for its fine and often magical wares brought in from flying ships that travelled all across the world. It was a welcome change from the markets of Florencia, which although sold many books and flowers, herbs and perfumes, books whose contents were on magic were strictly forbidden. As such, the markets of Alyssria were a welcome change for a witch like Flora, even though she could not indulge herself too much lest Lucien become suspicious. She wasn't ready to reveal her abilities just yet – for things to change between them when she was so happy just as they were. So she continued to wander the market with him as a songstress instead, quietly browsing some of the magic books with mild curiosity.

They came to one such bookseller, where they examined a table of rare Alchemy books, which Flora found herself intrigued by. She knew very little about Alchemy other than it being a branch of magic Lucien studied. She picked up the volume, examining the yellowed pages written in a mixture of Alyssrian and Alcheme. She saw various symbols representing the elements and planets, a description illustrating how to create a portal, not just when and how to open pre-existing ones like the Spellbooke had shown her. She wanted to know more . . .

And then she remembered who she was, where she was and who she was pretending to be. She could not show such interest in magic here unfortunately. She set the book reluctantly back down and found Lucien absorbed in reading another. Noticing her attention wandering elsewhere, he returned his own attention to her, following her as they then wandered to the part of the market where many strange fruits were on display, as well as exotic flowers and various herbs.

Flora enjoyed seeing the unusual Alyssrian flowers and Lucien indulged her interest, watching as she examined them in wonder, admiring their colours and scents. They must be so different to those in the Southern Kingdom due to the difference in climate. His mother grew flowers from all across the realm in her conservatory — *conservatorio,* Flora had called it. . .

Odd. He was sure the word was pronounced *conservatoria* in Castelleani, the language of the south. A simple mistake in translation, perhaps? Anyway, he would show her his mother's flowers when they returned. He was sure she would appreciate them.

After that they passed a display piled with fresh dark red cherries, which immediately drew Flora's interest. Cherries grew in many kingdoms, but the ones she had found in Alyssria had an unusual flavour to them. Due to the cold winters they were more tart, yet still sweet and every visit to the Midnight Court she could not stop herself sampling them. Eying a rather brightly coloured one in particular, Flora picked up the cherry, drawing it playfully to her lips as Lucien watched. She liked to tease him. He was intrigued by her and she found him equally fascinating in turn.

They spent much of the day touring the city together, taking twice as long to do so as Lucien kept pulling her away into the nearby gardens to kiss her.

'Are you sure you are not a witch?' he asked her after one such escapade.

'Why? Are you not sure that you are a sorcerer?' she asked coyly in return.

'Because you are absolutely enchanting,' he said earnestly, 'and I cannot stop thinking about you . . . and I do not wish to try.'

She blushed and he smiled.

'How long until you return to the Academy again for your studies?' she asked him, remembering the students usually began the new year of study this month.

'I return next week,' he answered. 'But we can still see each other, I promise. And perhaps we can still write to each other.'

'I will not be a distraction to your studies?' she responded, tilting her head to the side.

'A welcome one, I assure you.'

'And what else do princes study?' she asked playfully. 'Do you learn swordplay perhaps?'

Lucien performed a summoning spell and a dagger appeared in his hands, only slightly bigger than Flora's own. A series of small, beautiful sapphires decorated the detailed silver hilt, in a pattern like stars, a constellation. Unusual markings had been engraved upon the top half of the blade as if written in liquid sapphire. She examined them, noticing the design of symbols looked almost Ægyptian.

'My father imbued spells into the sapphire,' Lucien explained, watching her.

'It's beautiful,' she breathed. She knew about the Alyssrian practice of casting spells into jewels and metals, most often silver. Silvercasting was a prized skill among the people of Alyssria, a practice that could be traced back to the near-mythical civilisation of Atlantica that predated them all.

'At the Academy I was the best, or at least one of the top two students,' Lucien explained. 'We were both excellent students, I suppose, but my friend was better at some areas of study and I others. One of which was the art of the sword. I always beat everyone at that.' He smiled.

Flora glanced up at him mischievously. 'Until now, perhaps,' she told him, a hint of teasing in her voice.

'I am sorry, but I would not want to disrespect a lady with such a humiliating defeat,' he responded stoically, his arms crossed across his chest.

'The only way you would be disrespecting me is not to accept my challenge,' she replied, pointing the dagger at him.

'Fine. I accept. But I did warn you.'

'Very well, my prince.' Flora handed him back the dagger and continued walking ahead as he put it away. She added over her shoulder, 'And you will lose.'

He hurried to keep up with her. 'And what about you? Do you suppose to remain a songstress?' he asked as they walked.

She thought about it. 'I suppose I do . . .' If Aunt Bellissa would take her, then perhaps she could perform for the Court of Fuschia, which like the Midnight Court of Alyssria was also known for its arts, fashions and dances. She had often daydreamed of performing in her own kingdom, and yet somehow she had ended up entertaining the people of another.

'It's a shame you don't have any magical ability, then,' Lucien noted suddenly, drawing Flora's attention.

'And why is that?' she said, a curious smile forming on her lips.

'Because then you could become a songcaster. You've already

enchanted half the court,' he said proudly, 'With a little magic, you would be . . . unstoppable.'

Flora's eyes subtly widened. Did he know?

Queen Katya's words echoed in her mind. *He will know soon enough . . .*

She had the sudden desire to flee, to run, before it was too late. She had bewitched his brother — what if he thought she had done the same to him too?

'Where are you going?'

Lucien's voice brought her back to reality; Flora quickly realised she had already taken two steps away from him. She recovered herself and swiftly replied, 'To find a birthday gift worthy of a prince.'

It was true — she had been hoping since earlier in the day she could find something for his upcoming birthday, which was only a few days away.

Lucien stepped forward until he was again standing close to her. 'I know the perfect gift but it requires we abandon today's itinerary and return to my chambers,' he whispered in her ear, touching her arm.

Flora hid her smile with a blush. 'Another time perhaps. Such an offer is very . . . tempting,' she assured him with a kiss. 'Wait here. I want my gift to be a surprise.' Flora turned to wander the market alone.

She wandered among the different stalls, passing more books on magic, as well as a variety of unusual plants, crystals and gemstones, candles, babushka dolls and more. It would be Lucien's birthday in a few days on the seventh. *Perhaps he would like a book on magic?* she thought. *But he has so many already.* She wanted to give him something a little more unique.

A new dagger, perhaps? No, nothing she could afford would match those already in Safarovs' possession, anyway. Where was her own dagger, now that she thought of it? It was not on her person . . . perhaps she had left it at the cottage? As she drifted further along the stalls, she reminded herself to look when she returned later.

She was a long way from the palace end of the city now. The sound of voices drew her attention; many people had gathered at the other end of the square, on the steps of Parliament.

'The mines are empty!'

'Children are hungry!'

'We demand answers!'

'Come and face us legendary Safarovs! Face your people now!'

Flora stood at the edge of the crowd with her cloak's hood turned upward, watching as the guards chased people away and tried to disperse the crowds. There was a loud noise — an explosion. She looked up. A pair of broken windows on the second floor drew her attention and she watched as a gigantic fire erupted from within the Parliament.

Lucien found her as she watched, transfixed by the blaze. 'Flora, we must leave! Come on!'

He pulled her away from the scene, heading quickly for the palace.

Once inside, Lucien pulled her aside into an alcove, away from the prying eyes and ears of the guards. 'Are you alright? Are you hurt?' he asked her, concern evident within his voice.

'I'm fine, I'm fine,' she answered, still processing what she had seen. Then, regaining her composure, her eyes resolutely met his. 'What is it, Lucien? What is truly going on? Is it the Fuschians?' *Is my cover blown?* she thought in the back of her mind.

Lucien sighed. 'There have been rumours. I cannot say more,' he answered coldly. Then, noticing the concern in her eyes, he added, 'Do not fear, Flora, you are safe here, with us.'

'Cannot say or do not want to say?' she asked warily.

Lucien remained silent. She pulled off his cloak and tossed it back at him.

'I see. Very well. Farewell, Dark Prince.'

'Flora . . . ' Lucien stepped forward, but she had already slipped out of reach. He placed his hand to his forehead and groaned before he turned back to follow her, spotting her retreating figure at the other end of the corridor.

'Flora, wait. I'm sorry –' he called, but Mikhail's voice interrupted from an adjacent corridor.

'Countess de Roselle.'

Flora turned around to find Mikhail's gaze upon her as he approached.

'Micha,' she greeted him with a small smile.

'Countess,' he returned. 'Brother,' he addressed Lucien, who had caught up with them both.

'Micha,' Lucien replied.

'I'm afraid that I need to relieve you of my brother, countess. An important matter of some urgency has arisen,' Mikhail explained.

'Very well, Your Grace. I was just leaving anyway.' Flora cast a glare at Lucien as she left.

The two brothers watched her walk away towards the fountain, where others often waited for a carriage. Many of the few mortal guests of the Midnight Court would often take carriages into the city to one of three designated portals to return to the other realm.

Lucien still had his eyes on her as Mikhail leant over and whispered into his ear.

'There have been rumblings of a rebellion in the north,' he told Lucien as the third brother, Aleksandr, joined them.

'And there's more. I found these,' Aleksandr retrieved large, crumbled pieces of paper from within his pocket. He unrolled them to show his brothers. 'Pages from *The Book of Crests.*

Valuable information on the noble families of our realm and our closest allies and enemies. In other words, we have a spy at court and at last a clue as to what their purpose might be. Most likely they are from one of our neighbouring kingdoms or realms. Probably the Fuschians.'

'Or the Empire,' added Lucien.

'Or the Empire,' Aleksandr repeated, yet his tone indicated it was very unlikely.

'Perhaps it is someone closer than we think.' He cast his eyes in Flora's direction.

Lucien's gaze followed. Was he accusing Flora? His mind began an unstoppable chain of thoughts as he started to wonder . . .

He turned to his brother. 'How did you come across this treachery, Aleksandr?'

'I intercepted a messenger smuggling these out of the palace,' explained Aleksandr.

'Can the messenger describe this spy?' Mikhail asked, his intense focus falling upon his brother. Aleksandr looked away before he answered grimly, 'Only that they spoke Alyssrian with a southern accent.'

* * *

Flora stood at the opposite end of the promenade, watching as the three princes conversed in serious, hushed tones. Lucien glanced in her direction as she wondered how much longer their conversation would take. Truthfully, she had not needed to come to the Midnight Court for her mission for many weeks now. She had already found the information she had been seeking in the highly guarded *Book of Crests* weeks ago. Not that it had truly helped much—her father's identity remained as elusive as ever. She remembered how, only a few fortnights ago, she had dragged Mikhail around on a tour of the palace.

It had been a hot August summer evening . . .

* * *

'And is this your Libraire? The famous library of Cesaire the Great?' she had asked as they stood in front of the elaborate doors.

'Indeed it is, countess,' Mikhail answered, watching as her eyes marvelled at the lavishly decorated marble doorway and carved wooden double doors before returning to him.

'Can we go inside?' she requested.

'Of course.'

He was opening the lock with a quick password spell when Lucien turned the corner and approached them, quickly ruining Flora's plans.

'Brother, my lady,' he greeted them. 'What are you doing in this part of the palace?' he enquired suspiciously.

'Well — actually, what *are* we doing in this part of the palace?' Mikhail asked, puzzled, and Flora laughed. Lucien appeared doubtful as he glanced at his brother, then Flora.

'What an excellent question! Micha was giving me the grand tour when I became hopelessly lost until he found me.' She clung to his arm, her eyes daring Lucien to question her.

'Uhh . . . yes,' Mikhail answered, as he glanced at Flora questioningly.

'Yes,' Flora agreed, steering him away from Lucien, 'And now he was just going to show me . . . the conservatorio,' she said, accidentally slipping into her native tongue.

'Conservatorio?' Lucien asked, still a little confused and suspicious.

'I mean the gardens,' she hastily corrected herself. Perhaps she wasn't as fluent in this language as she thought. She glanced quickly at Lucien, who was watching her curiously, then continued to drag away Mikhail down the corridor. She would have to find another opportunity to ascertain the knowledge she sought.

* * *

Lucien returned to his bedchambers, where he took off his doublet, revealing a simple linen shirt underneath. He waved his fingers over the candle, which burst into flame, creating a soft glow. He then waved at the glass orb in the centre of the ceiling and the crystal started to glow brightly as well. Lucien gathered the books he had been reading on sorcery and lay comfortably on his bed. Magic was a great and much-needed distraction and so he delved into his favourite subject, leaving the troubles of the Midnight Court behind.

* * *

Flora pulled the jewelled hairpin out from her hair. Tumbling tresses of her hair fell to her shoulders as she picked the lock. It clicked, and she gently pushed the door open, entering the room.

The Libraire was dimly lit, with shelves of books from the floor to the ceiling. In the centre was a series of ginormous maps of the five realms, covering a large wooden table. Encompassing the top portion of the map was Alyssria, Kingdom of the Midnight Sun. In another, her home realm, the Eastern Kingdom of Fuschia, to the south was the Southern Kingdom of Castelle and to the west, the Kingdom of Brittannia. At its centre lay the Alchemical Court within its circular domain. Others were realms she had only heard of in folklore — the Eternal Forest, the land of the Fey; Labassia, the City of the Mer; and so on.

She drew herself away from the map to browse the shelves, her fingers lightly dusting the titles before at last pulling out a particular volume, *The Book of Crests,* with its elaborate gothic lettering in glittering gold ink. Only the royal families in each kingdom seemed to keep a copy of the collections of symbols used by the noble houses. Flora had first tried the largest library in Fuschia, the Great Library in the city of her namesake,

Florencia, but had come up empty, despite her efforts.. If the King of Fuschia possessed such a book, it was well-hidden. Her goal now was to travel to each of the kingdoms and search until she found information on the one that matched her father's.

Flora placed the heavy tome on the map table, opening the first page to a list of contents written in Alyssrian, detailing names of noble families. She started to flick through the pages one by one. Each depicted a crest and other smaller symbols for that house, as well as details about the family, including the family tree and place of residence. But none resembled the mysterious bird that featured on the signet ring she had found in her mother's jewellery box.

She had just closed the large book when she heard footsteps approach the door.

Flora's eyes glanced up as she dropped what she was doing and reached for her dagger — only to find it was not there.

'Dia!' she cursed and looked around for a makeshift weapon, quickly deciding upon a letter opener she had spied on the desk earlier, tucking it behind her back with one hand. She also had her magic if she couldn't somehow talk her way out of this one, though that might blow her cover.

The door creaked open and Flora was surprised to find not a guard, but Lucien, casually dressed in his linen shirt and tights. His usually neat hair was messy and he appeared engrossed in his book as he entered. Flora kept still as a statue. Perhaps the prince would not notice her.

She wondered what he was reading as he approached the shelves. His back was turned to her as he browsed, and she started to move.

He turned around.

Goddess! She cursed in her head. She had been hoping to sneak out when he wasn't looking. *Lucien notices everything.*

'Flora? . . . what are you doing here?' he asked, surprised.

She glanced towards the shelves, spying a book she knew well. 'I was . . . er . . . looking for some books on poetry for Mikhail,' she said hastily, approaching the shelves behind him and picking out a book she'd seen before.

He turned and set down his book on the shelf behind her, his arm brushing closely past her.

'Poetry?' Lucien clasped his hands behind the small of his back. 'I was not aware that Mikhail appreciated the art form of the written word. May I ask what *kind* of poetry you were looking for in particular?'

'No, you may not. Now if you will excuse me—'

'So Mikhail sent you here? And left you unaccompanied? That's not like him,' Lucien pointed out.

Dangerous questions. Was he on to her?

'Yes, Mikhail *trusts* me to choose a book of poetry, but seeing as I am clearly in your way, perhaps I should go.' Flora curtseyed before turning to leave.

'Wait. Your hair,' he noticed. 'Was it not up before?'

She glanced at him over her shoulder. 'Yes, and now I want it down,' she rambled, keeping her distance as she fumbled her way around the map table towards the door. She attempted to smile through inside her heart was pounding. 'Much more comfortable!'

And distracting, Lucien thought.

'Well, it was, uh, interesting talking to you again, my prince, but I really must go, so goodnight.' Flora shut the door rapidly behind her, heading outside to the nearest portal in the fountain in the gardens.

After she left, Lucien turned around to examine the book she had left open on the map table, but it was gone, returned to its proper place on the shelves—almost as if by magic . . .

* * *

Chapter Five

The Alyssrian Revolution

Lilies

Humility, devotion, innocence, death, majesty, passion, love

Place a white calla lily in the magick circle to lift the veil and communicate with the dead

*D*usk was falling outside the windows of Palazzo Fuschia. The days were short in winter, yet despite the chill night airs, it never snowed. Inside the ivy-covered stone walls, the King of Fuschia sat within his parlour, in his chair in front of the fireplace, where a roaring fire was glowing. Garlands of red winter roses and branches of silver fir and holly decorated the parlour and palazzo stairs throughout the castle. Five white candles stood in a candelabra on the table.

Orlando glanced at the empty chair opposite him, his face bathed in the candlelight. In his outstretched hand was a golden locket.

Tomorrow began another year, another year without her. He glanced down at the miniature portrait in the open locket. Delicate brushstrokes depicted a young woman with a heart-shaped face, high cheekbones and a pointed chin. Her illustrious dark auburn brown hair reached the waist of her exquisite scarlet dress.

'Arianna . . .' he sighed wistfully.

Sixteen years since his beloved wife had died in childbirth. Oh, what a fool he had been when she was alive. . .

* * *

Elegant rose bushes lined the gravel pathway, their leaves shimmering in the warm glow of the torchlight. Flora, Lisandre and Leo paused to admire the wonderous sight before approaching the Palazzo together. The red roses bloomed as Flora trailed past to none but Leo's notice as he followed along behind them. The music of violins drew them closer to the Palazzo Fuschia, followed by the sounds of laughter and merriment.

Purple and pink fuschias grew in abundance everywhere, hanging from baskets underneath the stone balconies. The symbol of Fuschia, they featured on the flags and banners of the palazzo, with their deep pink cover petals and dark purple underpetals against a vibrant orange background.

They moved through the courtyard and along a corridor, passing servants and an increasing number of guests as they approached the centre of the celebrations. Leo and Lisandre caught a glimpse of the king as he entered, while Flora examined the many surrounding guests — only to lock eyes with one rather unexpected one.

Lucien.

His presence spelled trouble for their plans, she was sure of it. She would have to find a way to get rid of him, or at the very least distract him while Leo and Lisandre approached the king. He was wearing a mask over his eyes, like many of the other guests, except his was made of black cloth and decorated with silver. Leo and Lisandre had not seemed to notice him yet either. Nor would they, she reminded herself. They did not know each other.

He stood in front of a fountain near a tall lilac tree, the moonlight reflecting off the tree's empty branches. He wore a matching elegant tunic of black embroidered with silver thread. *Even as a dark sorcerer he couldn't help but dress like a prince,* she thought wistfully, remembering his loyalty to the Dark Alchemyst.

'Given the number of guests I think the best approach is to. . .' she heard Leo' s voice fade into in the background. 'Flora?' he called.

She turned away, only to see Leo and Lisandre staring back at her.

'Are you alright? You seem startled,' Lisandre asked, clearly concerned.

Flora swiftly mustered a smile. 'I'm fine,' she reassured them. 'You go ahead.'

Leo and Lisandre glanced at her curiously before heading across the room. Flora turned to look behind her, only to find Lucien was gone. He had slipped away . . .

'You certainly have cast quite an impression, *witch,*' a familiar voice whispered in her ear.

'I don't know what you are talking about.' She pretended to ignore him as he stood beside her.

'*Oh* my lady.'

In one swift movement she turned around. '*Don't* call me *my lady,*' she warned Lucien from behind her mask.

'Well, what can I call you? You aren't exactly a countess anymore,' Lucien said.

'And I hear you aren't exactly a sorcerer either. What is the term they use nowadays?' She tapped her finger to her chin as if thinking. 'Ah, yes.' Her eyes lowered as she removed her mask, 'Warlock. What exactly did you do to earn that distinguished title Lucien? Kill another?'

Lucien's face went cold.

'I brought my mother back from the dead.'

Flora kept her eyes level with his. 'I see.'

'Do you?'

* * *

The autumn winds of October came swiftly, and with them the winds of change upon Alyssria. Meanwhile, in Fuschia, Flora sat before her window in Rose Cottage, overlooking the countryside, the city of Florencia in the distance. All week she had tried to distract herself by helping Aunt Bellissa as much as she could, to no avail. Her mind always wondered back to Lucien and the Midnight Court. Things had seemed so uncertain when she had left.

After seven days of endlessly sewing dresses, she had had enough. All week, each time Aunt Bellissa visited the village, she returned with some report or other from the city that the situation in Alyssria was descending even further into chaos. Flora needed to know he was alright. And Micha and Queen Katya and the rest of his family as well.

She went upstairs into the attic and opened her mother's chest, where she retrieved a crystal ball. She had only used it a couple of times before. Scrying was tricky, but she had to make it work somehow.

'Crystal of the light

Crystal of the night

Reveal to me

All I wish to see

Show me the city of Safir

So mote it be

Verum revelare.'

The vision within the crystal suddenly became cloudy, before growing clearer. The clouds soon parted to reveal the familiar gold-domed spirals of the Midnight Palace. The vision then moved to focus upon the immense gathering crowd outside the Parliament.

'Down with the Safarovs!' a man holding a blazing torch shouted, and the crowd roared in agreement.

'To the Palace!' another cried, brandishing a sword, and the crowd turned and set its sights on the Midnight Palace, beginning to make their way down the avenue like an encroaching, unstoppable wave.

Flora recoiled, knocking the crystal ball over before leaping to catch it in her arms. The vision gone, she carefully placed the ball back in her mother's chest and crept downstairs, checking from Aunt Bellissa's breathing that she was well and truly asleep before she headed outside to the moonpool.

Summoning the portal, she cast the familiar spell. The waters churned and started to glow, and she plunged into their endless depths.

* * *

Stepping out of the fountain, she emerged in the familiar interior of the Midnight Palace, heading straight upstairs along the familiar route to Lucien's chambers. She found Lucien within, standing to one side of the balcony by himself. He stood with his back to her, one arm across his chest, the other resting upon his cheek as he watched the scene below helplessly.

Smoke rose from where the Parliament was on fire at the other end of the Grand Avenue, opposite the palace. Below, people were charging at the palace gates as the guards pushed them back.

'I hope you do not mind . . .'

Lucien turned swiftly at the sound of her voice.

'The servants let me in,' she continued cautiously.

Lie. But easier to explain than the truth.

'Flora!' He snapped out of his misery and rushed to her side. 'What are you doing here? It's not safe. You need to go home. Now,' he instructed. 'It is safer in your realm right now.'

'And leave you? What will happen to you Lucien? Are you alright? I was so worried.' She refused to back away.

'Flora, I'm sorry — I should not have kept this from you. I don't know who to trust,' he told her. 'None of us do.'

'You can trust me,' she reassured him. As she said the words, the thought crossed her mind. *How could he, when he does not know who I truly am?* No more countess. No more hiding. She was a Fuschian witch, nothing more. Hopefully he would understand . . .

'Can I?' Lucien snarked bitterly in response. Flora felt taken aback. 'I'm sorry. Someone at court has betrayed us,' he told her, observing her reaction. She seemed off guard, he noticed. Whether her secret was that she was guilty or not, he had yet to decipher.

Flora watched him carefully in turn. She was not responsible for the situation Lucien's family now found themselves in. But she was Fuschian and that would probably be enough reason to blame her in some part anyway. But the truth needed to be said. Lucien deserved to know it. And so she looked within and found her courage.

Well, here goes nothing.

'Lucien . . .' She took a deep breath and exhaled. 'There's

something I need to tell you, something you should know.'

He looked up at her warily, meeting her eyes. 'What is it? You can tell me,' he coaxed her.

She opened her mouth to speak . . . and Mikhail burst into the chamber.

'Lucien. It's Mother,' he blurted out, clearly distressed. 'She was . . . she was stabbed.'

Lucien turned his head sharply towards the door. 'When?'

'A few hours ago.' Mikhail's hand came to rest upon Lucien's shoulder, already sensing Lucien's thoughts. 'The healers already tried everything . . . Lucien, I'm sorry, it's too late.'

'No,' Lucien muttered to himself quietly as Mikhail and Flora watched him, concerned. 'No!'

Lucien pushed past him and raced upstairs to Queen Katya's bedchamber, where she lay lifeless on the enormous bed, her hands clasped over her waist, still wearing her elegant purple dress. Flora and Mikhail had followed; Flora watched as Lucien knelt and placed his hands over his mother's and wept, unable to hold back his emotions any longer. Aleksandr stood in the corner, looking sombre, while Eleanora wept openly into a handkerchief beside him. Mikhail waved his hand, and a bouquet of Alyssrian blue lilies appeared in Katya's hands.

'Whoever has done this shall pay with their own blood,' Lucien cursed as King Cesaire placed his hand on Lucien's shoulder, a tear shedding from his eye.

Lucien stood and took Flora's hand, and they stood solemnly opposite Mikhail and Eleanora. Queen Katya was the first witch other than herself Flora had ever known. She had barely known Lucien's mother, and yet she still felt her loss. She was more concerned for Lucien, however. He had been the very close to Katya, as the two of them shared a bond in magic. She glanced at him, but he seemed distant, wrapped in his thoughts.

After a while, Mikhail finally spoke.

'Revolution is upon us,' he said seriously. 'Upon Alyssria. Things will never be the same again. We may have to leave if we do not resolve this. But these are our people and so despite the clear infiltrating and agitating of our enemies, we will try to come to a solution that benefits Alyssria.'

Lucien led Flora by the hand out of the room. Once they had passed the Sun and Moon tapestry, he turned her around to face him.

'Go home, Flora.'

'What? Now? Surely you cannot be serious.'

'Go.' He turned his head and looked away. 'I need to fix this.' There was a cold note of determination underlying his voice. He would not even look at her, so lost was he in his resolve.

Something in his energy unnerved Flora. She left, glancing back over her shoulder as she walked down the corridor and back down the spiral stairs.

* * *

Each night Flora checked on Lucien with the help of the crystal ball. Usually she only saw him with his brothers or with their father as they tried to figure out what they should do. The city guard was still defending the palace, but as each day wore on, fewer and fewer guards continued to do so. It was only a matter of time.

At first Cesaire tried to save his son by ordering Lucien to go to the Alchemical Court but he refused to leave his family. He would retire to his chambers late at night, exhausted as he poured over an endless pile of books on Alchemy, only to go out again a short while later. Flora worried. Where could he possibly be going? Of the princes, he had been the closest with the queen, and her absence in the palace was deafening.

Some nights he was still not in his rooms when she checked, and so she would scry the different rooms of the palace, searching for him. First the courtyard, then the Libraire, the portrait hall, even the conservatory. But tonight, he was nowhere to be found. Flora decided to scry the kitchens next. It was a long chance, but she had once come across him there, making himself some hot chocolate before returning upstairs. Only a handful of servants still worked once the revolution had broken out. Many had chosen to return home to their families, and others had fled.

But this time Lucien was not in the kitchens. Instead, an obscured figure stood in the doorway.

'And remember three drops in the king's soup. No more, no less. Then we shall deal with the princes,' he told the servant who simply nodded as he accepted the drawstring bag. Inside was an assortment of large enspelled gemstones of many colours and fine quality.

'You will be rewarded,' the male voice said ominously and Flora realised something about it was familiar, but she could not quite place it. Perhaps they were disguising their voice with an accent? Or a glamour spell? She was not sure, but she needed to warn the king. Whoever had killed the queen planned to strike again, and soon, it seemed.

She rushed to put the crystal ball away in the chest. Throwing her cloak over her lilac Fuschian dress, not caring what Lucien saw her dressed in now, she headed downstairs and into the forest, to the rowan tree, where she cast the spell that opened the portal and dove straight into the moonpool.

* * *

She arrived in the Midnight Court just before sundown. She needed to find the king, but the court was empty. The last tendrils of sunlight streamed through the domed windows overhead.

A few minutes after she emerged in the familiar foyer, a note materialised in her pocket.

Meet me in the Libraire. I need your help. Micha

Odd. Mikhail had never signed their letters. Perhaps it was about Lucien. She hoped they were both alright. Perhaps Mikhail had also somehow come across the poisoner's nefarious plans?

She set off for the Libraire as night fell quickly and the cloudy sky outside darkened. The palace seemed even darker than usual, and somewhat foreboding; some of the crystal lamps were now missing, and enormous shadows fell across the room from those remaining. Flora continued down the empty corridor, fast approaching the familiar doors of the Libraire beneath the detailed archway. Through the already open doors she could see *The Book of Crests* was out upon the bookstand. Her suspicions rose.

'Micha?' she called amongst the books as she slowly, cautiously stepped closer. Once close enough to examine the book, she noticed several pages were missing, having been carefully cut out. Her suspicions began to rise even more, and she turned to leave.

Footsteps echoed through the Libraire.

Lucien walked towards her from the other end of the room.

'Countess.' He pronounced her title with evident sarcasm.

'Sorcerer,' she returned, smiling sweetly at him.

'Witch,' he retorted, and her eyes narrowed. How did he *know*?

Her mind raced and her eyes darted back and forth between Lucien and the wall behind him, searching for an escape route.

'Yes, I know your secret.' He took a step closer. 'There never really was any Countess de Roselle, was there?'

Flora reached for her dagger, forgetting it was not there. She looked up towards Lucien to see the bejewelled dagger appear magically in the palm of his hand.

'Looking for this?'

'Lucien, please . . . '

She tried to remain strong. It was the first time she had spoken his name since that night she was going to tell him who she really was and now he knew anyway. Flora fought back tears.

'You could say I borrowed it. The design is definitely Fuschian, and high-quality at that,' he marvelled bitterly.

Flora outstretched her hand. 'Return it to me.' Her eyes and her tone now dared him to defy her.

'No. I don't think you *can* actually explain yourself, but I'd like to see you try.'

'That is not why I came here tonight. Lucien, please. Someone is planning to poison the king—'

'Well, that is the preferred method,' Lucien commented, half sarcastically, half bitterly.

Flora persisted.

'I was unsure how to tell you, whether it would be safe to send you a message. Whether it would reach you in time. *Please,* we must hurry!'

'Of course. And how long have you been reporting to the Fuschian king, Flora? Were you here on *his* orders the entire time?' Lucien accused. 'You deceived us all, I bet *your* mother isn't even dead.'

Flora took a step back in shock.

'You think I am a spy,' she breathed. She couldn't believe this.

'You wouldn't be the first,' he replied harshly, without looking at her.

'This is ridiculous! Lucien—'

'Ridiculous?' he cut her off, 'My father is dead! The Fuschians are probably behind this revolution to finish us off.'

'What?' Flora raised a hand to cover her mouth. She had come too late. The king was already dead. Lucien had lost his mother and now his father. She feared for him, feared for his and Mikhail's safety. 'I assure you I had no hand in his death. I swear by the Goddess, I would never wish him dead. I knew how much he meant to you.'

She slowly placed her hand on his. He turned to look at her.

'It is true, I am no countess. But I am still in every way worthy of you and your brothers. I assumed the role of countess so that I would gain access to important records in the Libraire so that I can find my father. The dagger was his, given to my mother. I came hoping to find my true family, and so that I could escape . . . ' Tears started forming in her eyes. 'My day-to-day life as a seamstress bored me to no end, and then I came here, to the Midnight Court and I met you — found another world that I longed for, full of beauty and life. But I am sorry that my deception hurt you.' Her voice fell to a whisper. 'I am so sorry.'

Silence enveloped the gigantic room. Lucien stood in shock. After a moment, he spoke.

'Come.' He offered her his arm. 'Follow me.'

She glanced at him hesitantly, then accepted. 'Where are we going?'

The doors suddenly opened and Aleksandr entered, followed by Mikhail and a legion of palace guards dressed in their blue uniforms.

'There she is! There is the Fuschian assassin!' Aleksandr pointed directly at Flora, and the guards quickly surrounded her with Lucien quietly stepping back to join his brothers. Beside him, Mikhail wore a plain expression of disappointment while Lucien's remained unreadable. A quick smirk danced across Aleksandr's face as Flora glanced between the three of them.

Now she knew who was truly behind this. Aleksandr was using the ancient rivalry between the Alyssrians and Fuschians to his own advantage as part of his play for the throne. It made sense now. The jealous middle child, who envied his older brother's position and his younger brother's talents, was using her as the perfect scapegoat to manipulate Lucien into joining him in whatever plans he had for Mikhail.

'Thank goodness I found you just in time, Lucien,' Aleksandr said. 'Don't you see? She must have been sent here by the King of Fuschia to get close to you brother. Only to strike once she had made you fall under her love spell. First the queen – she would never have seen it coming. Then the king . . . Then you.'

Flora could only watch as Aleksandr saw his opportunity and seized it. 'Lucien, no! I would never –' she protested, but Aleksandr continued.

'She has stolen even more pages from the Book of Crests! Search her! Do it!'

Lucien performed a spell, moving his finger up and then down in a straight line, examining her. The note levitated from the pocket of her dress, floating into the palm of his hand. As he unfolded the piece of paper, Flora saw it was no longer a note from Micha asking her to meet in the Libraire, but one of the missing pages from *The Book of Crests*, with its illuminated inks.

Disappointment grew on Lucien's face. 'Where are the others?' he asked coldly.

'She must have hidden them,' accused Aleksandr. 'You witch!'

'It was not – it was a note! From Micha . . . I don't understand!' Flora couldn't stop the tears now. Aleksandr had set her up, and now Lucien hated her, thought she had betrayed him.

'She is the one you have been hunting – don't you see, brother? She was using you all along, and Mikhail, like the Fuschian traitor she is. She never loved you,' Aleksandr spoke the poisonous words into his brother's ear before he turned to the guards. 'Take her to the dungeons.'

Lucien stood examining the torn page, his face full of despair and shock.

'Lucien! No! Don't listen to him! He's lying!'

Flora resisted pointlessly as the guards pulled her away.

* * *

A lavish golden tent stood inside the courtyard of the palazzo. Leo and Lisandre had surmised that perhaps the King of Fuschia would be found within, and so they had wandered past the other guests standing around the gardens, slipping past the curtain into the surprisingly empty space. A pair of beautifully carved wooden chairs and various pastel orange, blue and purple detailed cushions featured in the sparsely decorated tent. A vase near the entrance held a few unused coloured fireworks.

'Lost, are you?' a low voice growled from somewhere behind them. They spun back around to see King of Fuschia enter at the other end of the tent, his sharp eyes set upon the pair of them.

Leo cautiously stepped forward. 'I am here on behalf of the Alchemical Court,' he announced. 'That is—we are,' he corrected himself.

The king continued to eye them warily. 'You say you are an Alchemyst yet you are not dressed like one. Even *I* know all of them, even their apprentices, wear black and gold,' Orlando remarked as he sat casually on one of the chairs.

'We thought it best not to draw too much attention. Allow me to introduce us. My name is Leo De La Fontaine, and this is . . .' Leo berated himself for not deciding earlier upon a cover identity to explain Lisandre's appearance. Panicking, he turned and glanced at the flowers in Lisandre's hair, having found an answer. '. . . Jasmine.'

'Why are you here, then, Alchemysts?' the king asked, clearly disinterested.

'I need access to your collections in the Great Library. We need to find a particular scroll before the Dark Alchemyst does,' Leo said urgently.

The king's eyes flitted up at the mention of that particular name. 'The same Dark Alchemyst rumoured to have recently attacked the Alchemical Court?' Orlando questioned.

'Yes, but how did you know about that?' Leo asked.

'Everyone knows. Lady Vidjaya sent out a distress message to each of the three kingdoms,' explained Orlando.

'So you know he was after the scroll?' Leo said.

'Which scroll?' Orlando asked, now intrigued.

'I don't know what it's called. But it's an ancient scroll. The scroll details the locations of the Talismans of Atlantica,' Leo explained. 'Please, we will know it when we see it.'

'What talismans?' asked the king, now with a tone of obvious disbelief.

'The Dark Alchemyst is after them. He has already attacked the Alchemical Court looking for the scroll.'

'I take it the scroll was not there?'

'No,' admitted Leo. 'But we cannot allow him to find the talismans first. I have strong reason to believe that he has sinister intentions for them, for the realm. He was willing to attack the Alchemical Court just to find the scroll. We must find them before he does.'

'There's just one problem,' Orlando announced, his eyes meeting theirs. 'I don't believe you. Magic is a curse, best left untouched,' he warned them. 'Leave, now and I will forget you were ever here.'

Leo glanced at Lisandre and Orlando followed his gaze, looking at her properly for the first time as the pair turned to leave.

'Wait,' he commanded, and they paused, slowly turning back around, quietly hoping he had changed his mind. 'Another message was sent out to each of the five realms. A message from the faerie queen, looking for a young faerie.'

Leo's expression hardened as Lisandre became evidently

worried.

'A Lady of the Vines had abandoned her post on their Sacred Council and has gone rogue, it said. She ran away with the assistance of a handsome young *Alchemyst*.' Orlando emphasised each of the last three words slowly.

He suddenly stood up, walked quickly over to Lisandre and pushed her hair back behind her ear, revealing the pointed tip — the distinguishing feature of a faerie.

'He may have placed a glamour over your wings but your ears give you away my dear.' Orlando stepped back and turned his attention directly towards Leo. 'If I send her back Queen Ivana promises to leave me and my kingdom alone.'

Leo moved to stand between him and Lisandre. 'You will do no such thing.'

'Give her to me and I will grant you permission to enter the Great Library so you can look for this precious scroll that you so desire,' Orlando offered, sitting back down in his chair. Lisandre watched him warily from behind Leo.

'No,' Leo immediately answered. 'I cannot. Lady Lisandre is under my protection.'

'Then I have no choice but to arrest you both.'

Orlando clicked his fingers over his head. Two pairs of guards dressed in emerald-green tunics at the edge of the palazzo garden turned their heads towards the king.

Orlando then addressed Leo. 'And you, boy — once the fey collect Lady Lisandre, you can go and send a message back to your Alchemical Council. Let them know that *Alchemysts* are no longer welcome in Fuschia.'

Lisandre looked to Leo. They were surrounded.

Spying the nearby fountain just outside the tent, he had an idea.

Leo outstretched his hand towards the fountain. '*Aquem volari!*'

A column of water shot up into the air. He used his hands to guide the energy, the water following his movements. The water moved like a snake out of the fountain onto the path between them and the guards. With a flick of the wrists, the water suddenly froze and the guards slipped onto the ice, falling into one another.

Orlando watched with barely concealed contempt at the display of magic. Unable to prevent them from leaving, he signalled for more guards. Leo grabbed Lisandre's hand, and with his other hand sent a burst of energy toward the collection of fireworks by the door, igniting them. Orlando and the guards saw this and immediately evacuated the tent as they started to go off.

Leo and Lisandre had already ran out the other side of the tent. Together they continued in the other direction, running through the moonlit gardens, past several surprised courtiers and guests, under the eruption of colours and starlight.

* * *

As she sat in the dungeons for hours, Flora plotted her escape. She stood up and paced the length of the cell. She examined the door to the cell once again, only to confirm her frustrations.

'Enchanted locks!' she cursed under her breath. Aleksandr had taken no chances. The Kingdom of Alyssria was known for its magicians, after all.

Hands behind her back, her eyes quickly surveying the gardens outside her window, Flora had an idea.

She waited and watched, checking the guards as they passed the corridor outside. Once they'd gone, she started to sing softly to the vines, summoning them toward her. The vines slipped through the bars of the ceiling-high window and floated through the cell, then dropped and crawled across the floor, through the bars on the other side of the room and out into the corridor. Their slithering green tendrils found their way down the corridor towards the door.

Carefully, she charmed the vines to examine the lock, and after a few moments a vine transformed itself into the shape of a key, which, under her guidance, inserted itself into the lock. The lock had just clicked when she suddenly heard footsteps coming back along the corridor. Hurriedly, she instructed the vines to recede out the window, dropping the key as they did so. Flora bent down, retrieving and slipping the key down the front of her dress, then stood up, turning around just in time to see —

Lucien.

She did not expect to see him, not ever again.

He stared at her, examining her thoroughly. For the first time he noticed something strangely familiar about her necklace, something about the arrangement of emeralds and pearls. Where had he seen it before, other than on her? In his studies, perhaps? It was not a common Fuschian design.

'Are you mad that I didn't tell you I was a witch or that I bested you?' she asked.

'Both,' he admitted.

'Then let me go,' she implored, and he fell silent.

For a moment he continued to stare at her, as if he were examining every depth of her soul. It felt like the longest moment of her life as she stood there under his gaze. Lucien then suddenly made up his mind, producing his own key from the air. The door swung open and Flora found herself stepping forward warily.

'Why are you doing this?' she asked.

'I know you are innocent, therefore I cannot let you die,' he said simply.

She arched an eyebrow suspiciously. 'How can you be so sure of that?'

He glanced down as he shrugged. 'I cast a spell upon the page found on your person. It revealed the note had been glamoured twice. First to appear in my brother Mikhail's handwriting then as one of the missing pages from *The Book of Crests*. I also thought it strange for a Fuschian king to hire a witch.'

'Is that all?' she asked, one hand on the open cell door.

'I will deal with Aleksandr,' Lucien told her. 'But he is my brother, and you are still Fuschian, and you deceived us.'

'For what it is worth, I am sorry,' she said, but Lucien remained silent, his expression unreadable.

Flora brushed past him and he remained still, taut and icy cold. She glanced back at him over her shoulder, then followed the torchlight leading out of the dungeons, trying to make sense of the twisting maze of corridors. Further along, she heard more footsteps echoing, and so she hitched up her skirts, hastening her pace.

* * *

'What are you doing here?' Lucien asked as they stood near the fountain, beneath the lilac tree. He seemed every bit as surprised as Flora was.

'What are *you*?' she swiftly retorted. 'Playing it a bit dangerous, aren't you? Being here, in the heart of Fuschia?' she questioned, 'What if the king recognises you? What could possibly be worth risking your life?'

'You didn't answer my question,' he contended.

'You didn't answer mine,' she replied.

Their heads then both turned at the sound of a series of explosions coming from the direction of the king's tent. Colourful fireworks zoomed in and out, drawing the attention of the crowd.

Flora turned back only to find Lucien had slipped away into the crowd.

Dia! What is he up to? Will I ever find out?

* * *

Autumn leaves were blowing in the wind past the window as Flora sat waiting for Aunt Bellissa to return from her walk to the village. Outside the air was brisk, and the dark grey clouds overhead appeared ready to rain upon the gardens of Fuschia. Inside Rose Cottage, Flora sat curled upon the sofa beneath the window, close to the fire, watching the maple leaves fall past the glass. A small pot of vegetable soup hung over the flickering flames.

She soon spotted a figure in a beautiful red cloak with a familiar straw basket over her arm, walking along the road and up the garden path towards the cottage. Her aunt had returned from the nearby village, hopefully with news.

The door opened and Aunt Bellissa entered, her normally pale cheeks flushed red from the chill wind. She shut the door behind her, then settled the basket, which Flora now discreetly saw held a bouquet of red roses, upon the table. Lowering her scarlet hood, Aunt Bellissa untied the ribbon fastenings of her cloak, taking it off and placing it upon the hook.

'Flora?' she called, expecting her to be upstairs.

'They're from him again, aren't they?' Flora emerged from the parlour and began examining the flowers.

Aunt Bellissa shifted uncomfortably. 'Yes.'

'Things are getting quite serious, aren't they?' Flora enquired, peering over the roses.

'He has asked me to marry him,' Aunt Bellissa revealed, becoming visibly distressed. She could feel a headache starting to come on.

Flora turned and looked at her aunt. 'And did you accept?'

'I want him to meet you first,' Aunt Bellissa answered as she sat down.

'Oh. When is he coming?' Flora asked sweetly, her arms wrapped behind her back.

'Tonight. For dinner. So be on your best behaviour, per

favore. I do hope the two of you will get along.'

'Very well. And what news of the realm?' Flora asked carefully.

Aunt Bellissa retrieved a piece of parchment from within the basket and began reading aloud while Flora listened absentmindedly, quickly becoming lost in her thoughts again. The Midnight Court was gone, the Kingdom of Alyssria too, she was sure of that. Aunt Bellissa continued reading until one article in particular grabbed Flora's attention.

'Prince Lucien Safarov has used sorcery to break one of the old laws . . . the people of Alyssria have formed the Alyssrian Republic . . . the Dark Alchemyst strikes again . . .' Aunt Bellissa continued, but Flora was no longer listening.

She brought her hand to her mouth in shock. *So it is true, then. Now he is truly a warlock . . .*

Warlock was the title given to a wizard who had broken their oath and performed forbidden spells. Part of her wondered if it was because of her — because Lucien felt she had betrayed him when she had deceived him only a few months ago. That, combined with the loss of his mother and father in the Alyssrian Revolution, had made him vulnerable in her eyes, easily manipulated and seduced by those with promises of power and revenge . . .

* * *

'Come on Flora!'

Her thoughts returned to the present as she felt Leo grabbing her arm and dragging her away through the city. Flora felt the cobblestones beneath their feet as they quickly raced along the street towards the edge of Florencia. The road curved around the side of the hill as it came to meet the fountain and they stopped to catch their breath around the corner of a shop.

'The Fuschians sure know how to party,' remarked Leo as more colourful fireworks were set off in the distance. 'Happy new year. 1526,' he said wistfully, gazing off into the distance at the spectacular display.

'Happy new year,' Lisandre replied, even though for the fey the new year had already started over a week ago with the solstice.

The trio did not rest for long; the city guard quickly caught up with them. Lisandre peered carefully around the corner of the wall as they saw them approach.

'Hey, Flora — you know those vines of yours?' Leo whispered.

'I'll handle it,' she answered quickly, as if reading his mind.

With her back to the brick wall, Flora muttered the spell, making flowing hand gestures inciting growth. Instantly, vines of ivy rose from the ground, creeping upward and covering the wall as Leo and Lisandre watched. Flora peeked out around the side of the wall, watching the aftermath of her handiwork.

From the high vantage point on the other side of the wall opposite, Lucien stood, watching it all unfold.

'There they are,' he pointed out as he caught a glimpse of Flora's ever-familiar red hair retreat behind the brick wall.

The guards swivelled in their direction.

Damn it, Lucien's trying to divert attention from himself.

With a flick of Flora's wrists, the vines leaped out and wound around the guard's legs, ensnared them. Out of the corner of her eye she saw Lucien watching, then slipping away.

Not so fast, she thought.

She waved her hand and another vine tore through the ground and wrapped itself around Lucien, reaching around his torso, becoming ensnared by the vines. At first he struggled — then after a few seconds, he transformed into a raven, the vines falling away from his changed form. He took off into the dizzying heights of the sky, flying on the high winds towards the forest.

They ran the rest of the way back through the forest, their cloaks and dresses catching on the brambles so they had to keep reaching down to unhitch them from the thorns. They kept running until they reached the outskirts of the village, from where they walked for half an hour back to Rose Cottage. The lantern light was still glowing, waiting in the window.

Inside, they took off their cloaks and rested their backs against the door, trying to catch their breath. Flora clasped her hands behind her and closed her eyes as she sighed in relief.

'You're home. Where have you been?'

Aunt Bellissa's critical voice drew her back to the present. Her eyes flashed open.

She saw Felippe sitting at the table. Aunt Bellissa was now standing, addressing her with a questioning glare.

Flora reflexively placed a clenched hand to her stomach. 'Aunt Bellissa, I thought you would not return for weeks. And Felippe is with you . . . how grand.' Flora waved in return as Felippe held up a hand in greeting from the parlour table.

Bellissa shot a warning look to each of them. 'Flora . . .'

'Yes, introductions. These are my friends, Leo and Lisandre. May I introduce my Aunt, Lady Bellissa DuPoitoires.'

Aunt Bellissa politely extended her hand and Leo gently kissed it.

'Pleasure. An Alchemyst and a faerie,' she stated calmly, and spun to face Flora. 'You know.'

Flora froze.

'How long have you known? *How?*' Aunt Bellissa seemed sure she had kept *that* secret.

'About that . . You see . . Um, nearly a year,' Flora awkwardly confessed.

'Dia!' Aunt Bellissa cursed. 'I should have known you would eventually find your mother's things. That or you would stumble across magic on your own.'

Flora's gaze suddenly caught the new diamond ring on her aunt's finger.

'Oh my! You're engaged!' she exclaimed.

'Not now, Flora!' Aunt Bellissa chastised her for changing the topic.

'Congratulations,' Leo added, to Aunt Bellissa's annoyance.

'Thank you,' she replied, then returned her sharp gaze directly to her niece. 'Now, where were you tonight? You were supposed to stay home.'

'Well, you see . . . About that, . . . We were at the Palazzo Fuschia . . .' Flora admitted evasively, casually touching the back of the empty chair beside Felippe as she retreated.

'Amora la Dia!' Aunt Bellissa cried. 'Why were you at the Palazzo Fuschia? You were not invited by the king!' She seemed overly concerned about the matter to Leo.

'We were at the end-of-year masquerade, except not really,' Flora explained. 'Leo and Lisandre needed to see the king, and it was the only way to get them an audience.'

'And did you?' Aunt Bellissa turned to the two guests, raising an eyebrow.

'Our conversation was not what we had hoped,' Leo revealed.

'And you, Flora—you did not meet the king?' Bellissa questioned carefully.

'No,' she answered, wondering why her aunt was so focused upon that particular detail.

'Very well. Let us all sit in the parlour and our guests can tell us more about why they are here.'

She beckoned Leo and Lisandre to sit at the table. They glanced at one another before choosing to sit down opposite Felippe.

'May I ask why an Alchemyst and a faerie are here? It has been many years since anyone in Fuschia has seen a member of the fey,' noted Aunt Bellissa.

Flora glanced at Leo, who decided to speak up.

'The Alchemical Court has been attacked by the Dark Alchemyst. He was looking for the ancient Talismans of Atlantica, or rather, a way to find them.'

'There were rumours of an attack, but no one knew by whom, and why. These talismans—do you know how to find them?' Felippe asked in response.

'We need to find the scroll detailing the riddle of the talismans,' replied Leo. 'My teacher believes this scroll is being kept in the Great Library of Florencia.'

'That's why you were at the ball. You were hoping the king would grant permission,' said Aunt Bellissa.

'Yes,' Leo confirmed.

'And he denied it but the three of you intend to go to the Great Library anyway?' Aunt Bellissa questioned.

'The Dark Alchemyst is after the scroll as well. He may be sending somebody else to find the scroll as we speak. We need to find it and the talismans before he does,' explained Leo. 'They cannot be allowed to fall into his hands. The results would be unimaginable.'

The gravity of the situation cast a heaviness across the room felt by each of them.

Aunt Bellissa broke the silence. 'Even though, as you say, the matter is urgent, may I offer a suggestion? That you wait a week, or better yet, a fortnight, before the three of you try anything? At least then I will be out of the country for your next shenanigans. I am a lady, after all.'

'I should not be hearing this,' Felippe muttered, realising their plans. He retreated into Aunt Bellissa's rooms at the other end of the cottage, shutting the door behind him.

'You are not forbidding us from breaking into the Great Library?' Flora asked her aunt, surprised.

'Entering without permission the greatest collection of knowledge in this country, perhaps the entire realm, is not ideal, but I see no other choice. The Dark Alchemyst seems to be finally enacting his plans and he must be stopped. I would help you myself, but any change in my current schedule would draw too much attention. The court would quickly notice my absence, word would swiftly reach the king, and he would become suspicious.' Aunt Bellissa turned to address Leo and Lisandre. 'For the time being, you may stay here.'

'Thank you, my lady, for your kind hospitality,' Leo replied.

'Need I remind the three of the you that breaking into the Great Library is actually quite dangerous, so you shall need to prepare and study appropriately beforehand,' warned Aunt Bellissa.

'Of course,' replied Flora confidently, and Aunt Bellissa gave her a grim look. Leo and Lisandre shared a glance that conveyed their unspoken thoughts : *It is a library – how dangerous could it be?*

'Please excuse us, Lady Bellissa, but Lisandre and I need to rest. Bonna nuite, Flora,' Leo interrupted, and he wished her goodnight in Fuschian before retreating from his chair.

'Bonna nuite,' Lisandre repeated, leaving with Leo to return upstairs.

'Bonna nuite,' Lady Bellissa and Flora each replied in chorus.

Flora could hear snippets of the pair whispering among themselves on the landing before the door to the attic shut with its noticeable creak.

'I think I should go to bed as well.' Flora rose from the chair and left the parlour, but paused at the bottom of the stairs. She turned around, her hand still resting on the balustrade. 'Aunt Bellissa?'

Aunt Bellissa looked up. 'Yes, my darling?'

Flora stared curiously at her aunt. '*Are* you a witch?' she

141

finally asked.

A moment's silence passed between them. Aunt Bellissa's face was half-hidden in shadows cast by the soft light of the candles.

'Yes,' Aunt Bellissa answered matter-of-factly. 'But I vowed only to use my gift to help others.'

'It is okay . . . that I learn magic, isn't it? We are witches,' Flora continued cautiously.

'Well, I suppose I cannot stop you. You are so much like your mother that way. But please, be careful. There have always been those who envy our power, and those who seek to use magic for their own gain, no matter the cost to others,' Aunt Bellissa warned.

'Could Grandpapa use magic?' Flora asked.

'No, he was mortal. Your mother's and my abilities were passed down through our mother,' Aunt Bellissa explained. 'I can use magic a little, but I didn't study it to the extent Arianna did. I suppose I was frightened because of what they did to our mother. But also, I wanted to succeed on my own talent, not because of magic. But when we were young I'd use little spells to help people. Arianna called me "the good witch".'

Aunt Bellissa smiled at the memory. She looked up at Flora, who could feel that she recognised some resemblance to her mother. The ghost of a woman she could never live up to; someone she did not know.

'Now off to bed,' her aunt instructed and Flora silently began to retreat upstairs, lost in her thoughts.

Did that make my mother the bad witch?

* * *

Upstairs in the attic, Lisandre changed into the nightdress Flora had provided. She wrapped her purple cloak around herself and stepped out in front of the screen.

'Thank you,' she told Leo. 'For not betraying me.'

'I told you, you are under my protection, Lisandre,' he replied sincerely. 'And I will keep that promise.'

For a moment they stood there in the calm silence, lost in one another's gaze. Leo began to take a step towards Lisandre, when all of a sudden the door burst open and Flora entered.

'I hope you don't mind, but I forgot . . .' she said absent-mindedly as she looked around, not noticing Leo and Lisandre stepping away from one another and out of her way. 'There it is,' Flora remarked, and retrieved a purple blanket from one of the wooden chests. It was still the middle of Winter in Fuschia and the nights had turned rather chilly.

She stood up and glanced curiously at Leo and Lisandre.

'Is everything alright here?'

'Yes, thank you, Flora,' Lisandre answered politely.

Flora looked between them once again, then left.

Lisandre let go of the breath she had been holding in once Flora had shut the door. She then turned back towards Leo, rejoining him by the window in the light of the stars.

'Happy birthday, Leo,' Lisandre said, now that they were alone again. His seventeenth.

'You remembered.' He was caught off guard, then smiled at her warmly. 'Thank you.'

'You're welcome,' she replied, and they lay down to go to sleep. 'And you will see Lady Vidjaya again soon. I am sure of it,' Lisandre added in the silence.

It was difficult to sleep after all the excitement of the evening, and so for a while they simply lay there, awake under the blankets.

'Leo?' Lisandre asked in the quiet hours of the night, trying to somehow find the courage to voice the suspicions that had stayed in her mind ever since Leo's research had brought them to light.

'Yes, Lisandre?'

'You think my mother was the queen, don't you?' she asked tentatively.

Leo paused, then sighed. Lisandre seemed to be able to intuitively pick up on his thoughts. 'I don't know what to think. I am not as familiar with faerie custom . . . with your ways, your history as you are . . . but yes, I suspect so, yes,' he admitted. 'What do you know of her?' he asked as together they stared out the window into the starry moonlit sky.

Lisandre paused, taking a deep breath then spoke.

'They called her the Hazel Queen, Queen Arsinoë I. She died when I was . . . thirteen,' she said, after quickly calculating her age in the years of his realm. 'After my father died, she took me under her wing, and made me her ward. She took care of me. She was already like a mother to me,' she explained. 'But if I am a princess, it would mean I would be heir, even above Lady Alaïa, and it would cause much strife amongst the Sacred Council. I do not wish for that.'

'You did not ask for this, I know. But you cannot help who you are, Lisandre,' Leo said.

'And Queen Ivana is still looking for us,' Lisandre replied.

'For you. She doesn't really care about me,' Leo pointed out.

'Perhaps I should have stayed in my own realm. Perhaps then you would not be in so much danger –' Her worries seemed to pour out of her.

'Lisandre, no. You were not safe there, remember?' Leo reminded her.

'Do you think it will ever be safe to return to Na Foraise Síorai?' she wondered aloud, solemnfully watching the clouds pass over the silver moon outside.

'One day, yes, I think it will. Things will get better,' he reassured her. 'But for now, we must find the talismans.'

With the help of his calm presence, Lisandre started to relax. Her breathing settled and she soon drifted towards sleep.

'Goodnight, Lisandre,' he whispered and she replied softly in return.

'Goodnight, Leo.'

* * *

Chapter Six

The Book of Moon

Vines

Connection, eternity, diversity, regeneration, continuation,
opportunity, growth, renewal

Vines entwine our love for eternity

early three weeks later, they rose at daylight. Things in the city had finally settled somewhat, Aunt Bellissa had informed them after returning from her weekly trip into Florencia. When she had visited the city just days after the New Year's Masquerade, she had quickly found *Wanted* posters for both Lisandre and Leo. And none for Flora, she had noticed with a sigh, pulling them down when no one was looking and hiding them in her basket underneath the bundles of cloth.

That morning they dressed in simple Fuschian attire, with Flora donning her usual lilac dress, lacing up the corset herself with a wave of her fingers. Leo wore a white linen shirt beneath his simple Fuschian orange jacket. Lisandre wore a dress of sunshine yellow in the Fuschian style with long, loose sleeves below her bare shoulders. She stood behind the screen as she laced up the white ribboned corset.

'Amora la Dia, please be careful!' Aunt Bellissa had told Flora only a few days before when she and Felippe had left for an extended trip to Castelle to meet her fiancée's family. Her scarlet gloved hands wrapped around Flora's bare ones as she wished them farewell.

Now, after a light breakfast, they put on their cloaks and set off along the road towards the city. Florencia was a vibrant, bustling place during the daylight hours, and even more so once inside the city walls. As they walked, Lisandre and Leo observed the unfamiliar city and its inhabitants. They saw craftsmen and women, fashioned colourful glasses; painters and artists; florists on the corner of every block, their tables abundant with many different types and colours of flowers. The townspeople spoke Fuschian, yet Lisandre found herself understanding every word because of Leo's spell. She found it interesting to listen to the fluidity of the language; Fuschian had a different kind of musicality compared to her native language of the fey. All the words in Fuschian seemed to end in 'ah', 'o' and 'chi'.

The other thing she noticed was their dress. The everyday wear of the people was similar in style to the fashions she had seen at the masquerade ball, simpler in design yet still distinctly colourful. Most of their fabrics did not sparkle as those of the fey did. Those that did often featured silver or gold embroidery much like Flora's, leading her to speculate they were pieces of her aunt's work, which Flora sometimes helped with herself.

Leo and Lisandre followed Flora as she led them into the heart of the city, where they soon approached the Great Library. The impressive structure was easily the centrepiece of Florencia and the most iconic building in all of Fuschia. The metallic panels sparkled in the sunlight, their dazzling beauty easily seen from many miles away. The building itself was very grand

and tall, with doors easily fourteen feet high.

'I don't understand,' Leo said, watching as they stood across the plaza. 'Why are there no guards? Lady Bellissa said entering would be dangerous.'

'Because everyone knows the real traps are *inside* the library,' Flora explained confidently. 'The Great Library was built in the late 13th century at the request of King Maximillan the Wise. He designed it so those who do not know the way out would encounter many traps and obstacles, as a way of deterring thieves. They were so famous that many scholars across the kingdoms began to choose the library to guard their works. That is how, over time, the Great Library became one of the greatest collections of knowledge in all the realms. Except, of course, for that of the fey.'

'Then how will we get out?' Leo asked.

'I know a way. I have been inside the Great Library before,' Flora revealed.

'You have?' Leo questioned, surprised.

'Yes. Last year. I didn't find what I was searching for, but I did manage to find a guard inside and followed him out. It is designed like a labyrinth in there, so you shall have to follow me. If the scroll is there, it should be in the ancient document collection.'

'So we cannot create a portal to go in because of the possibility of it coinciding with one of the traps. I understand that,' said Leo. 'Then why don't I draw a portal for us to go out?'

'Alright then. That actually sounds like a better plan,' Flora admitted.

'There are guards on the inside?' asked Lisandre suddenly, visibly concerned.

'Yes, but it's the traps that are the real problem,' Flora told her. 'So, remember to stick close with me and we should be alright.'

'Alright. Let's go, then,' said Leo and they headed across the crowded plaza to the enormous bronze doors.

Glancing cautiously around, Flora pulled upon the large brass handle, opening the door, and they slipped inside.

Inside the Great Library was a large entrance hall, with stairs leading to the upper floors. Three levels wandered off from the ground in a hexagonal structure. Additionally, three corridors run underneath the stairs in front of them. The cavernous high ceiling and detailed architecture filled them with an unexpected wonder, for the library's interior was just as impressive as the exterior in its detail. Exquisite quartz flowers decorated the tops of the columns on each side of the corridors. Vines had been carved into the marble into the columns and the borders of the walls. Beautiful mosaic tiles decorated the floor with fantastic designs and murals depicting the native flora and fauna of Fuschia.

'Now which way do we go?' Leo asked Flora.

'This way.' She indicated the right-hand path. 'Come on, let's go, before the guards come back,' she whispered urgently, and hurried over to the third corridor.

Leo and Lisandre swiftly followed, heading down the dark corridor, navigating its twists and turns. Some of the corridors were lit by torches, others by reflected sunlight through the corridors above. About midway through the building, Leo guessed, they approached another set of stairs, which they ascended to the second floor. Flora led them along even more corridors before they saw an expanse of light drawing them at the other end of the hallway.

The three stepped out into an immense room filled with seemingly endless high shelves of scrolls and books. Some were even preserved in glass cabinets in the centre of the room. The Great Library.

Stairs led to the floors below and above, which were also

filled with similar sized shelves. A large globe and several telescopes stood at one end of the expansive space. The library's magnificent dome towered above them.

Lisandre marvelled at them as they stood on the balcony at the top of the stairs. She was in awe of the Great Library. So many books and scrolls that she had never seen before. Indeed, it was certainly a collection almost to rival that of the fey.

'Lisandre. Lisandre?'

Leo's voice called her attention and she returned to the present. Their mission was of utmost importance and they had little time to spare.

'Where do we look first?' Leo asked Flora.

'This way,' she replied, pointing towards one of the shelves above, where a sign written in gold read *Antiquo*.

'*Ancient* in Fuschian,' Leo noted thoughtfully. They followed Flora deeper into the shelves.

'There are thousands of scrolls. How will we know what to look for?' asked Lisandre as they passed between the enormous shelves.

'The scroll should be titled *The Riddle of Atlantica*, or something similar,' Leo answered.

They split up amongst the three different walls of shelves, spending many hours investigating the thousands of scrolls for any mention of the talismans. There were a couple of instances when Leo or Flora thought they had found something, only to realise it was something else upon further examination. They came across scrolls on a number of mysterious and intriguing topics, some very old indeed. Some described forgotten magics, strange creatures and ways to access the Dreamworld few knew about. Some had even come from the ancient civilisation of Atlantica. But none so far mentioned the talismans.

'Perhaps it is not here,' Flora suggested late into the afternoon as they took a moment to rest. They had searched much of the

Ancient section; the sun would be setting soon and they would have to return to Rose Cottage.

'Lady Vidjaya seemed quite certain it was,' Leo said, and so they kept looking. By this point, Lisandre had commenced exploring the upper shelves, assisted by one of the Great Library's ladders. She searched through the various documents and scrolls she found up there, before pausing, having almost missed one scroll up the back. Hidden behind many others, this scroll drew her attention for a couple of reasons. First, it was wrapped in a piece of purple parchment, and second, it bore a particular symbol inscribed in gold.

She paused. She recognised that symbol from Leo's Almanac. The three petals within the circle. Sensing its importance, she brought the scroll down from the shelves, examining it further. Stepping down off the ladder, Lisandre unfurled the long vertical piece of paper, holding one end with each of her hands. The sunlight seemed to reflect straight down from the windows above and onto the page. The scroll itself was written with gold ink in Alcheme, and yet thanks to Leo's spell she was able to understand it. Reading the inscription, she quickly realised the importance of what she had found.

'I think I found something,' she called to the others without looking up from the page, entranced by its contents. Leo and Flora dropped the scrolls they were perusing and rushed to her side as she began reading aloud from the piece of paper rolled around the outside of the document.

'"*Herein lies a copy of the ancient poem The Talismans of Atlantica*", *as written in Ancient Atlantican*,' she read aloud. '*Transcribed from an ancient tablet, the poem describes the potential locations of the five talismans that originated in Atlantica, an ancient city rumoured to be buried beneath the city of Labassia and the sea . . .*'

Lisandre paused and raised her head. 'Labassia? Where is that?' she asked Leo.

'The City of the Mer, beneath the star also known as *Labassia*,' spoke a casual male voice behind them.

Leo tensed, as did Flora, Lisandre noticed. In a matter of seconds Leo withdrew his dagger and swiftly turned around to face the newcomer, pinning him to the wall.

'What are you doing here?' he demanded.

The young man laughed. 'It's good to see you too, Trystan,' he remarked.

'Trystan? I thought your name was Leopold,' Lisandre asked, confused.

Leo threw her a sideways glance. 'I go by many names' he said, before returning his focus to the stranger. 'I ask you again: what are you doing here?'

The young man glanced directly at Flora, who had subtly reached for her dagger behind her back.

'Put that away and I may just tell you,' he told Leo, yet he glanced over at Flora, his eyes lingering on hers before returning back to Leo.

'Let us hear what he has to say,' suggested Lisandre nobly.

Flora visibly pouted, but put the dagger back in its sheath, Lucien's eyes never straying from her the whole time. 'This should be interesting,' she muttered under her breath.

'Leo . . .' Lisandre said.

Leo continued to stare the prince down, then reluctantly withdrew. Lucien stood straight and readjusted his long, elegant dark blue tunic.

'May I introduce myself?' he asked Leo.

'I know who you are,' Leo quickly replied and Lucien tilted his head, disappointed.

'Yes, but . . .' He turned to Flora, who raised an eyebrow and gave him a silent warning look. He glanced over and met Lisandre's curious gaze. '*They* don't,' he finished.

'Very well, then,' Leo replied.

'Thank you.' Lucien addressed Flora and Lisandre. 'I am Lucien Safarov, I attended the Academy at the Alchemical Court alongside Leo up until a few months ago. And you are?' he asked politely.

'Flora,' she answered, remaining tight-lipped.

'Pleasure. And you, my lady?' Lucien asked, turning to Lisandre.

'Lady Lisandre of the fey,' Lisandre introduced herself somewhat warily.

'Nice to meet you both.' Lucien bowed lightly. 'I came to help. The Dark Alchemyst knows about that little scroll and the talismans. Once I knew what it was, I realised it is far too important to fall into his hands.'

'How can we trust you? Last time I saw you, you were carrying out orders for the Dark Alchemyst against the Alchemical Court!' Leo accused bitterly.

'You can trust me,' Lucien said calmly.

Flora also seemed unconvinced, her arms crossed.

'Because I have turned against him,' Lucien declared, redirecting his attention to Leo.

A thundering boom suddenly echoed throughout the Great Library.

'What was that?!' Flora cried, looking around for the source of the noise. She glared at Lucien. 'Was that you?'

'We must have triggered the defence mechanism. I suggest we leave, now,' stated Lucien, still calm.

'We?' Leo and Flora exclaimed at once.

'Leo, look!' Lisandre pointed to the end of the library. The main doors had sealed themselves shut.

'You there! Halt!' a voice implored from the end of the corridor.

They all turned to see a man wearing a suit of spectacular golden armour, his gloved hand outstretched, pointing directly towards them.

'Told you the King of Fuschia doesn't let just anyone into his collections,' Flora hissed as they set off into a run, splitting up into pairs as they ran along the corridors. Leo and Lisandre headed west while Lucien and Flora headed east, following the corridor as it circled around the corner.

As soon as they were out of earshot, Lucien leaned close and whispered in her ear, 'Flora, please. I need your help.'

She snapped back her head from peering around the corner and glared at him.

'And why should I help you, *warlock*?' Flora pulled up her hood and started walking along the empty corridor, Lucien beside her, struggling to keep up with her quick pace.

'Well, I did help you escape prison . . .' Lucien shrugged and pulled up his own hood.

'*You* were the one who helped put me there!' she exclaimed. 'Besides I would have escaped eventually.'

Lucien grabbed Flora's hand and a shot of electricity passed between them. In one swift move she removed her dagger and had its tip pressed up against his chest.

'Please, Flora. I can help you find your mother,' Lucien told her.

'Don't make false promises, *warlock*,' she warned him. 'Besides, my mother is dead. You know that.'

'Yes.' He looked down. 'About that. You once told me her name was Arianna, correct?'

Flora glanced away. 'All I know is that her name was Arianna DuPoitoires.' She met Lucien's eyes once more. 'And that she was like me, a witch. Perquoi? Do you have a lead, warlock? What is in this for you, Lucien? Why do you care?'

'I care,' he said, and took her hand. He noticed she did not instantly swat him away or outright refuse his advance as he'd been wary she might. 'Because I know what it is like to lose someone you love. And if I can bring my mother back, so can you,' he promised her.

'What you did is forbidden,' Flora told him quietly.

'We find ourselves will go to many great lengths for those we love,' he stated simply, and Flora found herself becoming distracted by his words, by his touch as his other hand reached for hers.

A glimpse of gold flashed across the corner of her eye. She turned and caught a glance of the suit of golden armour as it raced across the balcony above.

She turned to face Lucien. 'And now the Leone di Fuschia is after us!'

* * *

They broke into a run at the end of the hall, turning into the next corridor.

'Who?' Lucien asked her as they ran.

'The Leone di Fuschia? He is only the king's most elite knight,' Flora answered over her shoulder. 'However, his true identity remains unknown. This way.' She suddenly turned sharply left, and they ascended the stairs — only to find the man in golden armour waiting for them at the other end of the room, standing resolutely in front of the doors.

Even from this distance, Lucien could see the detailed floral engravings upon the golden metal. Flora glanced towards the helmet, and her eyes met the knight's. They held one another's gaze intently for a moment before she quickly looked away. The energy behind the mask unnerved her, like something familiar.

She raced back down the stairs, Lucien following swiftly behind.

'He was expecting us?' How?' he asked once they had turned the corner at the bottom of the stairs.

'How do you expect me to know the answer to that!' Flora replied as she tried to remain calm and find another way out.

Their best bet would be to figure out a way through the traps in the corridors and return to the Main Entrance, hopefully before more guards arrived. Leo could at least draw a portal for he and Lisandre to escape. *If Lucien had not chosen to become a warlock, he could have done the same*, she thought wistfully.

They hurried to the end of the corridor, which suddenly split into three more. Flora hastily chose one, only to see a pair of closing doors at the other end of the room.

'Come on! We can make it,' she told Lucien, but he sensed something was amiss. It seemed too easy. There appeared to be no obstacle between them and the rapidly closing doors.

He glanced at the floor. The blue-and-white tile pattern . . . Something about it seemed familiar. He recognised it just as Flora rushed ahead.

'Wait. Flora, no!' He reached for her hand as she continued running forward. Her shoe made contact with the particular tile whose design was slightly different from the others in the pattern and the floor fell away, revealing the cavern underneath.

Flora clung to the edge, staring at the thirty-foot drop into the dark below. A trap to catch thieves — one she had fallen into unawares, she realised.

Lucien slid to her aid, reaching for her, and pulling her up onto the remaining ground. 'Maybe next time you will listen to me,' he remarked.

Flora looked up at the sealed door on the other side of the chasm. Lucien helped her stand and she brushed the crumbling tile dust off the hem of her dress.

'Now what do we do?' she asked him.

'We find another way out of here. Come on.' He pulled her by the sleeve as they returned to the set of three corridors. This time Lucien chose the central one and Flora followed closely behind.

The corridor was dark and dimly lit by a few sparse torches, prompting Lucien to summon fire within the palm of his hand. Flora then cast a spell for light, creating a glowing orb that floated along the air in front of them. They saw the door at the end of the tunnel was well lit with candles on each side. They paused and glanced at one another. Again, it seemed too easy. Surely there had to be some kind of trap here too?

Lucien cautiously stepped forward, ducking swiftly as an arrow shot past his ear, alerted to its presence only moments before by a distinct whistling sound as it shot through the air.

He stepped back and they both watched as the arrows continued to fly forth across the corridor at regular intervals. Their whistling grew stronger as another set of arrows began a few steps ahead, and then another beyond that, shooting from somewhere behind the stone walls.

Lucien glanced at Flora, who seemed to have the same idea as she returned his gaze, raising her hands, ready to cast her spell.

'A transformation spell?' she suggested, and he nodded. '*Mutatio formae.*' She spoke the Latinacaec incantation as she waved her hands in a pattern like a dance.

Lucien spoke a pair of similar words in Alcheme as he gestured with his hands towards the arrows, which froze and crumbled into tiny pieces of stone, falling to the ground like dust.

'No match for a sorcerer and a witch,' Lucien remarked afterwards as they walked side by side along the now empty corridor.

'Warlock,' she corrected him, and he grinned.

They passed through the door, returning to the main entrance hall, where only hours ago they had come in.

'It would seem our troubles are not over yet,' Flora warned him as they stood upon the balcony of the second floor, observing the scene below.

Fading rays of sunlight drifted in through the large decorative coloured glass windows as the sky outside turned purple with the beginning of twilight. The Leone di Fuschia was already waiting for them, standing defiantly outside the front doors, and he had since gathered a platoon of a dozen guards in emerald tunics and silver armour, who stood in two neat rows alongside him.

Flora and Lucien exchanged a look, silently communicating with one another before attacking in unison.

Lucien began chanting something in Alcheme and moving his hands, and suddenly the carved marble vines broke free of their entrapment, emerging as living plants and moving towards Flora, who raised her arms and, in one swift movement, directed the vines towards the line of guards. The vines wrapped themselves around guards' feet, pulling them to the ground before dragging them away down the nearest corridors.

Some of the guards managed to cut themselves free of the vines with their swords and resumed their position by the doors. Soon, nine remained beside the Leone di Fuschia. They were quite outnumbered.

'Try disintegrating their swords?' Flora suggested, remembering the Alchemical spell Lucien had performed upon the arrows a short while earlier. He raised his hands slightly and spoke the words in Alcheme, casting the spell towards the guards, but their swords remained curiously intact, the spell deflecting off them. Flora tried as well, only to find the same result before retreating behind the pillar again.

They heard the Leone di Fuschia address the guards in Fuschian. 'Arresto ani.' *Arrest them.* The sound of heavy footsteps quickly followed as the guards ascended the stairs.

'Got any brilliant plans yet?' Flora asked Lucien, who was

thinking up strategies to escape.

He spied an ornate candelabra standing behind them. The flames flickered above the candles with the subtle movement of the air. Watching them, he had an idea and spun towards Flora. 'Do witches know how to levitate?' he asked her hurriedly.

'A levitation spell? Why? We cannot fly our way out,' she pointed out, glancing up at the elaborate mural-decorated ceiling above them.

'I don't intend to. Thought that could be a good backup plan someday,' he replied.

Flora was still clearly confused.

'Levitate their swords and that will be our leverage,' he informed her.

'But the other spell didn't work! What makes you think this one will?' she exclaimed.

'I'm not sure but I suspect it depends on whatever charm was imbued into the swords. There's no time to explain. Just cast the spell already!' he urged her.

Flora turned around to see the guards drawing closer, their swords raised. They were only twelve feet away now. Outstretching her hand towards them, she drew upon her magic and cast the incantation.

'*Levitato!*'

The swords suddenly floated upwards, before becoming suspended mid-air, out of the guards' grasp. Flora concentrated, directing the spell with her mind as Lucien watched beside her. The swords swiftly swung around and pointed themselves at their masters, catching them by surprise.

The guards threw their hands up, crying, 'Stepepo! Stepepo!' *Stop! Stop!*

Flora held them back by pointing their swords just under their chins as they retreated, stepping backwards along the balcony. She glanced towards where the Leone di Fuschia stood below, only to find he too had retreated, disappearing without a trace.

Lucien and Flora walked quickly past the guards and descended the stairs, hurrying towards the large doors at the entrance. As Lucien opened them, Flora swiftly sent the swords flying through the air up into the wall, where, one by one, they landed like darts in a circle, in the stone wall, high above the guards' reach. Half the guards remained where they were, frozen in fear and wary of such magic. The others had already fled. She followed Lucien through the doors, exiting the Great Library.

Outside, the plaza was nearly empty, with most of the nearby market stalls already closed and packed away for the night. Flora glanced towards the edge of the city.

'Look. The city walls,' she observed quietly. 'They've shut the gates. We're too late.'

'I know a better way,' Lucien said, pulling her aside. 'Few people know this, but the Grand Fountain was built on a moonpool as were four others. We were taught this at the Academy.'

Darkness was falling as the sun quickly set behind them. The moon soon appeared as together Lucien and Flora began chanting the spell to open the portal.

'Witchcraft!' a Fuschian lady cried, pointing towards them from the other side of the plaza. But it was too late. The fountain's dark blue water began to churn and glow a luminescent turquoise, and the shallow base disappeared, replaced by enchanting, endless depths.

Lucien and Flora exchanged a quick glance before leaping into the mysterious waters.

* * *

Lisandre instinctively pulled her cloak over her head as she and Leo ran together along the corridor, heading towards the western part of the library. She paused beside one of the columns and turned to Leo.

'Wait. Without Flora, how will we find our way out?'

'We will just have to defeat whatever traps are set for us and evade the guards until we find somewhere I can make a portal' answered Leo, glancing at where the room branched off into three corridors ahead.

He chose the left, and they carefully walked along it until reaching a room from which another pair of corridors continued. The floor was not tiled like the others; instead it was a dark red-brown, looking almost like dirt.

Not dirt, Leo realised. The floor was covered in sand.

Quicksand. Simple but effective.

He glanced at Lisandre. 'Or perhaps not . . . Your wings. You can fly us across.'

'But I don't know how to fly. I never learned,' Lisandre protested. 'In the Central Forest none of the fey fly unless they are going to other remote regions of Na Foraise Síorai. And of course, Ivana kept my duties near.'

They fell silent for a few moments as they thought through other solutions to the problem.

'Perhaps you can turn the sand into glass?' Lisandre suggested.

'An Alchemical solution. Yes, I do believe that would work. Thank you Lisandre.'

Leo began to gently rub his hands together as he closed his eyes, concentrating. Blue sparks emerged around his hands as the energy increased, building a dark blue aura around them. He pushed his hands out towards the floor of quicksand.

'*Crystellaisi.*'

Lisandre watched as the sands began to swirl around in a spiral, before hardening with a sudden distinct snap. Leo opened his eyes and dropped his hands. The sands had transformed into solid glass with an aquamarine hue.

'Come on,' he said, and together he and Lisandre hurried across the glass. As they did, Lisandre glanced down. Through the glass she could see into the corridor below.

At the end of the hallway, Leo tried to open the door, only to find it was locked. Lisandre examined the padlock before Leo silently instructed her to step back. He placed his palms together, joining them at the wrist before outstretching them like a clam facing towards the lock.

'*Aperati.*'

The padlock clicked open and dropped to the floor by itself. They passed through the door and entered the next chamber, shutting the door behind them. The corridor continued ahead, but Leo remained where he was, examining the ground instead. Satisfied it was safe, he then pulled out a piece of chalk and began circling the tiles as Lisandre kept watch, holding tightly onto the scroll. Leo added a diamond shape encompassing the circles before inscribing various symbols within them.

'Hurry, Leo,' Lisandre whispered, peering ahead, where she saw a pair of guards pass along the adjacent corridor, currently unaware of their presence.

'Almost . . . ready! Let's go.'

The portal started to hum and the markings on the stones began to glow. Leo held out his hand, which Lisandre cautiously accepted, and together they leapt into the portal.

* * *

They emerged, landing upon the grass under an oak tree just outside the city walls. The noise generated by their arrival caught the attention of the guard at the gate, who looked in their direction.

'Go!' Leo urged her, and Lisandre ran ahead through the forest in the general direction of the village. For a moment Leo lost sight of her, and he began calling her name.

He soon found her as she stood with one hand resting upon

a tree, catching her breath. He paused as he did the same. Lisandre straightened up, removing her hand from the tree.

'I don't understand. Who are you?' she blurted out. 'He called you Trystan. Is that your true name?'

Leo paused and ran his hand through his hair.

'Look . . . my name is Leopold De La Fontaine. My mother, my adopted mother, named me Leopold Trystan after two famous Alchemysts, Leopold Wittenberg and Trystan Blackwood. Alchemysts often use their middle names as codenames. Trystan is the name I used sometimes on missions.'

'Missions?' she questioned.

'For the Alchemical Court. Tasks. Quests.'

'Did you steal for them? Break laws?' asked Lisandre quietly.

'Sometimes. Though I do question some the things he asked of us now,' Leo admitted.

He . . . Lisandre noticed. His missing teacher.

'How can I trust you?' she asked.

Leo met her gaze and reached for her hand. 'Because I am still Leo, and you are still Lisandre,' he reassured her.

They continued walking along the road back towards Rose Cottage.

'I know. I know that is true,' she conceded, 'but what about Lucien?'

Leo seemed unsure how to answer.

Lisandre paused in the middle of the path. 'Leo, how long have you known Lucien?'

Leo looked away for a moment then answered. 'A long time. We have known each other since we were children. We were like brothers once . . . '

He remembered when he had first met Lucien at the Academy. He'd been ten years old at the time, practising archery in the Academy gardens. The gardens were bordered by a six-foot-high plastered wall and a fountain ran in the centre where the paths met. The clock tower of the Alchemical Court towered above them.

He remembered Lady Vidjaya praising him for his skill of the bow and arrow. She smiled and clapped proudly as yet another arrow hit the mark.

'Well done, Leo!' she congratulated him in her familiar, smooth, richly accented voice. Lady Vidjaya had come to the Alchemical Court many years before from a small faraway kingdom now under the control of the Australis Empire in the distant east.

One of his other teachers, who had been lurking in the background, stepped forward, interrupting the scene. Beside him was another boy, the same age as Leo, with fair skin and sleek, shiny black hair. Duvalle, the teacher, stood with his hand resting on the boy's shoulder.

'Leopold,' he formally addressed Leo. 'This is Lucien, a wizard prince from the Kingdom of the Midnight Sun. He has come to study Alchemy with us. I hope you can show him the ways of the Academy.'

The boys quickly became friends after that. As mischievous teenagers, they ran around the Alchemical Court together, weaving through the worn limestone pillars around the castle. They were the top two students of their class. Granted, the classes at the Academy had always been small, usually no more than ten, but their teachers were impressed with the level of skill and talent the two boys possessed.

When they were both fifteen, they fell out over a girl they both liked. She wasn't interested in either of them as she was involved with an older boy, but at the time they didn't speak to each other for a month.

They studied and lived at the Academy together, often competing against each other in their classes. At fifteen they also each officially began their apprenticeship, being sent on missions, often together, including some more secretive ones for their master, Duvalle. While on mission they went by their codenames, which were in fact also their middle names, Trystan and Tobias.

'I'm sorry . . .' Lisandre's gentle voice brought him back to the present.

They walked along the road in silence, returning to Rose Cottage, where vibrant red roses bloomed in the twilight air along the arch. As they wandered through the garden, Lisandre paused.

'Do you trust him?' she enquired sincerely.

'I trust that the only one Lucien is loyal to himself,' Leo answered resolutely, and together they headed inside the cottage.

* * *

Twenty minutes earlier, Lucien and Flora had arrived in the moonpool within the Briar Wood. They had quickly pulled themselves out of the water, returning to Rose Cottage.

As they entered the attic, Lucien trailing behind Flora, he noticed a pair of white calla lilies in the centre of a white pentagram within a circle of salt upon a small table. His eyes swept over the chest of her mother's things, and he browsed the many titles on the bookshelf, which contained books on languages, history and music.

His attention was drawn to a pair of matching portraits hanging on the wall beside one of the wardrobes. The one on the left featured a young man with a friendly smile, brown hair and blue eyes, dressed in an older-style blue tunic with noticeable larger sleeves. The portrait on the right was of a young woman with petite, delicate features and long raven hair. She wore a scarlet dress in the Brittannian style with puffed shoulders and long, tight sleeves. A scarlet-and-gold headband decorated her beautiful hair, and her heart-shaped lips revealed a hint of a smile — the same smile he had seen before, on Flora . . .

Flora.

He turned around as she caught him staring at the portrait.

'Who are they?' he enquired gently.

'My grandparents,' Flora explained quietly. 'Stefan and Tatiana DuPoitoires. My grandpapa came here from Brittannia with my mother and aunt after she died. I never met her. She died when my Aunt Bellissa was a young girl.'

She then wandered away from him, returning to the other side of the room. He turned and noticed a chess set on a square table beside the wall. Flora glanced back at him, and he gestured towards the board with its beautifully carved pieces.

'Perhaps we could play a game later,' he teased invitingly, his eyes twinkling with a touch of mischief.

She smiled, then turned away again. Lucien glanced once more at the portraits, then his attention was drawn towards the bookshelf and its mysterious titles. Perhaps he would get an opportunity to browse some of them later.

Flora was now standing before the bookstand, having removed a large book from the chest and placing it open upon the stand. Lucien's eyes widened, and soon became fixed upon the tome as if it were a precious jewel that had been lost for centuries. The ageless white pages of the book were bound beneath a magnificent purple cover with a silver crescent moon symbol and ornate silver lettering in Latinacaec, the language of the witches.

'*The Book of Moon,*' Flora told him as he came and stood beside her, enraptured. She opened the book. Handwritten on the first page was an inscription:

A & B DuPoitoires

'Arianna and Bellissa,' she whispered their names, her long

lilac sleeves gently draping the cover. 'It was my mother's.'

'May I?' Lucien asked. Flora gently nodded her permission. He reached forward and turned the page. The next was blank. He turned to the next, which was also blank, and then the next and the next, flipping halfway through the entire book.

'They're blank? Why are they all blank? What kind of witchcraft is this?' he asked in surprise.

Flora wore a bemused smile while watching him. 'The ink has special properties. This book can only be read under moonlight.'

She took his hand and he turned back to face her. His eyes met hers and he saw the longing written in her eyes as she looked up at him over her shoulder.

'Come with me tonight, and I'll show you.' Flora spoke captivatingly, yet she seemed a little unsure he would go with her.

'Tonight, then,' he confirmed in a low whisper, holding her gaze.

Their shoulders were touching one another now, her back resting against his chest.

Footsteps upon the squeaky wooden stairs suddenly caught their attention, and the pair quickly pulled away from one another just as Leo and Lisandre walked in.

'There you two are,' Lisandre addressed them as Leo entered behind her, both oblivious to what they had just interrupted.

Leo quickly noticed Lucien's presence. 'What are doing here? Did you follow her here?' he accused.

'It's alright, Leo, he can stay,' Flora said, and Leo appeared visibly perplexed.

'He helped me escape the king's guards at the Great Library,' she told him by way of explanation.

'Very well,' Leo replied brusquely, throwing Lucien a suspicious glare, which he ignored.

'Do you still have the scroll?' Lucien asked.

'It's in a safe place,' Leo answered firmly, still wary of his former classmate. 'We can discuss the scroll later.'

'After some dinner perhaps? I am starving,' Lucien commented, changing the subject.

'Come, Leo,' Lisandre said. 'Let us get dinner started.' She gently guided Leo away back downstairs.

Lucien's attention was drawn back to the lilies. This time he noticed the white candle at the centre of the pentagram. He recognised that particular spell. He had seen his mother use it many times. He looked to Flora, concerned.

'I tried summoning her spirit, just to talk to her,' she said with an embarrassed shrug. 'But the spell doesn't work.'

Perhaps I am not as skilled at witchcraft as I thought, she worried as Lucien continued to stare at the candle, perplexed.

'Come on.' Flora's voice suddenly broke him out of his trance. 'Let us make sure they don't ruin dinner.' At least she could do simple spells to cook. She had no idea if the Alchemyst and faerie were even capable of cooking.

Lucien glanced once more at the book and lilies, then followed her downstairs.

* * *

It turned out Lisandre was surprisingly resourceful when it came to making dinner. She and Leo had picked some apples from the garden earlier—a lot of apples, actually. In the three weeks the pair had been staying at Rose Cottage, she and Aunt Bellissa had somehow managed to keep the Alchemyst and faerie out of the kitchen; a mistake, Flora learned, since they were revealed to be more than adequate chefs, especially Lisandre. And faerie cuisine was a welcome change from Fuschian vegetable soup and Aunt Bellissa's famous herb and garlic pasta.

Lisandre soon began experimenting a bit, creating a range of dishes featuring apples, her favourite fruit. Their crisp scent soon filled the cottage. She made raw apple cake, raw apple pie, raw apple tart and a variety of exotic salads, using what herbs, vegetables and berries she also found in the garden. Salads and fruits were largely a staple of faerie cuisine, Flora soon learned. The fey did not cook their food, she also observed, preferring to keep it closer to its original form than other species. Perhaps their diet was what helped them live so long, she wondered briefly as Lisandre arranged the dishes upon the parlour table.

After dinner, Lisandre and Flora returned upstairs to change into their nightgowns before rejoining Leo and Lucien in the parlour, sitting in armchairs around the fire. The boys had similarly loosened their jackets. Lisandre was shivering as she came downstairs, but at least she felt more comfortable, no longer wearing her Fuschian day-dress. Noticing this, Leo got up and offered her his blanket upstairs, and so she followed him back to the landing.

'Leo, has Lucien met Flora before?' Lisandre asked him once they were alone.

Leo paused. The thought had not crossed his mind before. 'No,' he answered. 'At least not that I am aware of.'

He kept the thought close in his mind, however. Lisandre seemed to have a knack of picking up on things with her heightened intuition, he had noticed.

She waited outside the room as Leo retrieved his blanket. He wrapped it gently around her shoulders, Lisandre acutely aware of his closeness as he stood in front of her, and his gentle touch. Together they then returned downstairs, Lisandre sitting down in one of the armchairs closest to the fire.

'I've never met a member of the fey before,' Lucien suddenly remarked casually. 'You are taller than I expected.'

Lisandre thought it an odd, almost rude remark to make, but said nothing of it.

'Actually, many of the fey are taller than most mortals,' Leo commented in response, sensing Lisandre's irritation.

'Indeed,' Lucien replied. 'Can I see the scroll now?' he asked.

Leo conceded, leaving the parlour to retrieve the scroll from where he had hidden it upstairs. He laid it carefully upon the parlour table for all of them to see.

Flora examined the scroll opposite him, fascinated. The ancient runes of Atlantica were unlike any language she had ever seen before, except perhaps the symbols of Ægyptia, but different again.

'Can't Leo use his Alchemical spell to decipher it?' Flora asked as she perused the scroll's strange symbols.

'The spell was designed for more current languages. These runes are far too old for it to have the desired effect,' Leo explained. 'It would only be able to correctly translate perhaps half the words at best. The others would be mismatched errors . . .'

'I think I can read it,' Lisandre spoke up from behind them.

The other three turned around to give her their full attention, all of them surprised by her claim.

'I don't know why, but I can. Indeed, they are quite similar to the language of the fey,' she said, stepping forward so that she stood in the middle of them before the scroll. '*The Talismans of Atlantica*,' Lisandre read aloud.

'Do go on,' Lucien said, and she gave him a look, quietly warning him not to interrupt her again before continuing to read the riddle aloud.

The Talismans of Atlantica

Beneath ancient springs that ne'er grow old

The Midnight Rose

Lies a gem of flowers of which tales are told

A gem of light this tree doth hold

Glistening with sap of liquid gold

Hidden where all of mortal eye may admire

Behold that which tis scarlet jewel doth inspire

Crafted from heavenly aquamarine waters

Beware for this jewel of the sea be guarded by Neptune's

daughters

Veiled in dreams most powerful

Against poison this stone protects the faithful

Five talismans together are the key

Called upon from beneath the sacred tree

The power of the elements bestowed upon thee

To rule them all for eternity

The four of them sat down upon the chairs in silence as Lisandre finished reading the inscription, pondering the ancient poem. Lisandre rolled the scroll away, holding it in her lap.

'May I?' Leo asked, gesturing toward the scroll a few moments later. Lisandre handed it to Leo, who unrolled it and placed it again upon the parlour table so they could all reread the lines of script.

One pair of lines immediately caught Lisandre's attention, igniting her suspicions.

'*A gem of light this tree doth hold* . . .' she repeated aloud, quickly becoming lost in her own train of thought.

'*Glistening with sap of liquid gold* . . . amber is a golden colour. The Amber Talisman is within a tree?' Lucien mused opposite her.

'It's the Crystal Tree,' she realised aloud. She turned to face Leo. 'The Amber Talisman must be in the Realm of the Fey.'

Leo recognised the difficulty this posed, as did Lisandre. 'What about the scarlet jewel? That must be referencing the Ruby Talisman,' he suggested, and he and Lisandre soon were in deep in conversation, trying to decipher the other possible locations of the talismans.

Neither of them really noticed when Lucien decided to slip back upstairs. Or that Flora waited quietly, sipping her tea a while before going to find him.

As she'd sipped the warm scented liquid, her thoughts had drifted to Lucien. Ever since that *warlock* had turned up again, he had been a constant distraction. Could they even trust him with such an important subject as the talismans? Even Leo, who seemed to know him perhaps almost as well as she did, didn't fully trust him. The pair also seemed to have a past, she'd noticed. Something she would have to probe Lucien about discreetly one day.

She glanced over at the fire, gazing into the dancing flames as she finished the last of her tea and set down her cup before she too returned upstairs, unnoticed. Or so she thought — Lisandre watched her climb the stairs out of the corner of her eye.

Upstairs Flora found Lucien standing by the open window, arms crossed, looking up at the stars. Perhaps he was admiring the constellations. He did not seem bothered by the cold — typical Alyssrian.

'What are you thinking?' she asked gently, coming to stand beside him.

Lucien turned to her. They were alone again. He looked back at the sky.

'I was just studying the constellations — they're different here,' he observed.

'So far from home,' Flora noted.

He then pointed at a particularly bright sparkling star. 'There it is. This is where I am from,' he said. The star Alyssria burned as bright as ever in the midnight-blue sky. The world of the Midnight Court seemed almost a lifetime ago, like a dream they had both woken up from.

Flora turned to Lucien. The loose strands of her hair hung down, hiding part of her face as she fumbled with her hands and gazed towards the ground.

'I've been meaning to ask you . . .' she began. This was not an easy subject to broach.

'Yes?' he said softly.

'The Alyssrian Revolution . . . how *did* you escape?' she finally asked. She wasn't sure he would answer.

Lucien was overwhelmed with emotion as he turned away. 'You do not seem surprised that I did,' he said, trying to distract her.

'I knew you would find a way,' she professed, her eyes still cast down as she fingered the sleeve of her dress. 'Or rather, I hoped.' She glanced back up at him.

Lucien crossed his arms nervously. 'Åsmund helped me escape through an old portal,' he admitted.

'And Micha? Aleksandr? Your brothers?' she dared ask. There had only been rumours about what had happened to the princes after the formation of the Alyssrian Republic.

'Micha . . . Mikhail . . .' Lucien's voice broke into a sob and he collapsed to the ground. Flora fell with him, kneeling beside him, wrapping her arms around him.

'Mikhail, . . . Mikhail didn't make it, and Aleksandr . . .' His tone changed sharply at the mention of his other brother. 'Aleksandr was a traitor.' Lucien spoke bitterly, tears finally pouring down his face. He slowly turned to face her. 'Do you know they say Mikhail and Eleanora were found together, lying in each other's arms? And — and Aleksandr was betrayed by one of his own, stabbed and left to die in the streets of Safir.'

This confirmed the rumours Flora had heard. 'I'm so sorry.' She held him, comforted him as they then sat in silence together.

Lucien had not planned to open up to her quite as much as he did, but part of him was glad to still have someone to confide in.

'And your mother, Queen Katya? Where is she now?' Flora then asked quietly.

'Safe in exile for now. As am I, minus the safe part,' Lucien noted before he looked directly at her.

'All of them are gone, Flora, except for my mother.' He reached for her hand. 'And you.'

* * *

'Neptune's daughters . . . that could mean anywhere in the ocean, or even an island,' Leo mused. They were still speculating when Lucien and Flora later returned downstairs.

'The Disappearing Island?' Lisandre suggested. The island was a well-known myth, even among the fey, it seemed.

'Perhaps—' Leo looked up suddenly as he noticed Lucien return. The pair joined them in the remaining chairs, Lucien sitting opposite Flora.

'Apologies, I needed some air. It's been a long day,' Lucien told Leo, who nodded in understanding.

'We were just discussing the lines about the Sapphire Talisman. Perhaps you have some ideas?' Leo asked him.

'Sounds like you will have to ask the Mer, not me,' he replied.

Lisandre stifled a yawn and Flora glanced at the candle burning low. She stood up.

'Well. I think that's enough discussion for one night. Time for bed.' She began to lead them back upstairs. 'Lisandre will stay in my room and you two *ragazzi* can learn to share,' Flora instructed them firmly over her shoulder.

'Good idea,' agreed Leo, then formally bid Lisandre and Flora goodnight.

Lisandre slipped shyly into Flora's room as Leo entered the room opposite, leaving Lucien and Flora in the hall for a moment to themselves. Their eyes quickly finding one another's, but Flora swiftly retreated and closed the door behind her before anything more could transpire between them.

* * *

The next few days passed quickly as they continued researching and discussing the riddle of the scroll. A few nights later, Lucien returned upstairs one evening to unexpectedly find Flora waiting for him.

'Come.' She outstretched her hand. He placed his hand in hers and allowed her to lead him outside, *The Book of Moon* in her other hand and they walked together into the Briar Wood.

'I was thinking before,' she said as they approached the rowan tree, 'that maybe the book might have a finding spell that could help with the talismans.'

'Those were my thoughts as well,' said Lucien. '*The Book of Moon* is after all, not just any Spellbooke. It is one of the most coveted books of the witches, and it contains some of their oldest spells.'

Flora revealed the book under the moonlight. 'How do you know that?' she asked him curiously.

'My mother told me,' Lucien answered. 'Your mother must have been a very powerful witch to acquire it, at least equal to my mother,' he added, sounding rather impressed.

They sat together under the rowan tree and the soft glow of crescent moon hanging in the sky above. Flora opened the book. Words and symbols were drawn in silvery ink, which shimmered as they came to the surface, appearing upon the page. The book was written in Latinacaec, the ancient language of the witches.

'Vines entwine our love for eternity,' Lucien read aloud. 'A love spell?'

'You read Latinacaec?' she asked, staring at him.

'My mother taught me,' he explained.

'Of course,' Flora replied. 'And no, that one is not a typical love spell. It's more of an amplification spell, really. It can only enhance something that is already there.'

'Sometimes I wonder if it was all just a spell—that maybe whatever magic you intended for Micha found its way to me instead,' Lucien told her as he looked into the surrounding trees.

'That's not how the spell works,' she reassured him, then looked away. 'Besides, the spell on Micha faded . . .'

He took her hand again. 'Why did it fade?'

Flora turned back to look at him, meeting his eyes. 'You know why,' she told him quietly.

It was then he noticed the flowers. Rose vines blossoming

around them in a circle, the red flowers blooming in the darkness.

'Are you doing that?' Flora asked, uncertain.

Lucien appeared as unnerved as her. 'No, are you?'

'I don't know,' she replied. *Perhaps it was another of the forest's tricks. The Briar Wood is known for a magic of its own,* she thought.

Once the circle was complete, the vines stopped their movements and Lucien and Flora slowly began to relax again. They stayed in the circle of roses, not wanting to leave each other's company now they had been reunited. But they could not hide in the wood forever, and so, as the moon began to descend, they returned to Rose Cottage, still holding hands.

They silently headed upstairs, careful not to wake the others, coming to stand in front of the door to Flora's room once again. She turned to wish him goodnight, her dreamy eyes gazing upon his handsome face. Lucien gently leaned forward and kissed her forehead.

'Bonna nuite,' he whispered in her native tongue before he pulled away.

She responded in kind whispering an alluring *goodnight* in Alyssrian. They remained lost in one another's eyes, hands still entwined. The air held the lingering promise of a kiss.

He suddenly brought her hand to his lips, planting her soft skin with a lengthy kiss before retreating to the opposite room, leaving Flora pleasantly surprised. She paused in the doorway, slightly stunned by his gesture, briefly reflecting upon her feelings before turning and going inside, closing the door behind her.

* * *

In the two weeks that had passed since Lucien had arrived and they had successfully acquired the scroll, Leo attempted to contact the Alchemical Court about their discovery three times to no answer. The lack of response left him increasingly concerned. It had been over six weeks since the attack on the Alchemical Court and still no word from Lady Vidjaya.

'I shall try to contact Lady Vidjaya again tonight,' he informed the others the morning of the full moon, shortly after breakfast. He had read that scrying was a practice that worked best during the full moon. Perhaps that was why his earlier attempts had been unsuccessful. 'I shall need to borrow a large bowl,' he added, then suddenly spied something better behind Flora. 'Actually, your cauldron.'

'Why?' Flora asked the Alchemyst, immediately wary. No mortal had ever requested to use her witch's cauldron before, not even an Alchemyst.

'I need a pool of water for scrying,' Leo explained.

'Alchemysts study the art of scrying? I was not aware of that,' she noted with caution.

'We study many forms of magic,' Lucien told her.

'Very well.' She returned her attention to Leo. 'You may borrow it. But I expect it back clean and in the condition you found it,' she warned him, handing him the cauldron.

'Agreed,' answered Leo with an eager smile.

* * *

That night they met in the parlour as the full moon rose outside. Leo had filled the cauldron with water from the moonpool and returned to the cottage, where the three of them gathered around him. He set the cauldron down upon the wooden table and waited for the moon to reach its peak before performing the summoning spell in Alcheme upon the water. The surface of the water turned to mist as the spell took effect.

'Lady Vidjaya,' he called cautiously into the water. 'Lady Vidjaya?'

After the second time he looked at Lucien, silently asking what he knew. Lucien's face remained unreadable.

'Lady Vidjaya, can you hear me?' Leo called again, and this

178

time there was a response.

'Leo? Is that you?' Lady Vidjaya's voice come through. A face then gradually appeared in the water.

'Lady Vidjaya! Are you alright?'' Leo asked her, relieved to see his teacher again.

'Oh Leo! Yes. It has been so long. Are you alright Leo? Where are you?' she asked eagerly, also relieved to see Leo was okay. 'Did you find the scroll?'

'Yes. And I'm fine. Should we return to the Alchemical Court?'

'We?' Lady Vidjaya enquired, confused.

Leo beckoned to Lisandre, who joined in front of the cauldron. 'Lady Vidjaya, this is Lady Lisandre of the fey.'

'Fey? She is a faerie?' Lady Vidjaya questioned carefully. True, the girl had a somewhat air of otherworldly beauty about her, but the fey had wings — quite large ones at that, from what she had learned.

'I concealed her wings with a glamour,' Leo promptly explained. 'It is better people do not know who we are here.'

'And where is here?' asked Lady Vidjaya, growing more concerned.

'Fuschia. We found the scroll in the Great Library, as you suspected,' explained Leo.

'Excellent work, Leo!' she exclaimed, clasping her hands together with joy.

'Well, it wasn't just me. I had some help.'

'Thank you all the same,' she said. 'I hope to see you at the Alchemical Court within the next few days. The repairs are almost complete and classes at the Academy will resume shortly. In the meantime, keep the scroll protected. I am sure the Dark Alchemyst will stop at nothing to get at it, and who knows who else is working with him? These days alliances are not so clear as they used to be,' she warned.

Leo paused. He had never seen Lady Vidjaya speak like this. She seemed concerned that even among the Alchemical Court, there could be more accomplices than just Lucien.

'We'll see you in a couple of days, then, once we have made all our arrangements here,' said Leo. 'See you soon, Lady Vidjaya.'

'Take care, Leo,' she replied, and the mist evaporated as Leo ended the spell with a wave of his hand over the water.

'You're returning to the Alchemical Court. What about the Amber Talisman?' asked Lucien.

'Lisandre and I can't go—they're looking for us. It has to be you two.' Leo turned towards Flora. 'Do you think you can keep an eye on him?'

'I think I can manage that,' Flora answered Leo, then smiled slyly in Lucien's direction.

'I'm right here, you know,' Lucien muttered loudly, his arms crossed.

Leo brought forth a small red drawstring bag. Pulling upon the cords, he tipped its contents into his hand, revealing a pair of rings with green and purple gemstones.

'Here.' He tossed one of the rings to Flora, shooting a quick glance at Lucien.

'What is this?' she demanded, examining it. A large green gemstone was set in a detailed golden ring. Upon the gem's surface was a strange Alchemical symbol.

'To communicate. Talk into the gemstone,' Leo explained. 'First call very clearly and directly, "Leo". The enchantment will then cause this one' —he held up a similar ring featuring an amethyst—'to glow and burn with heat. If I call for you, yours will do the same. It will stop producing heat once you answer with my name.'

Flora glanced up at Leo. 'Did you make this?' Alchemical magic was sometimes peculiar to her.

'Yes.'

'An Alchemical trick they teach us first year,' Lucien muttered behind Flora.

'Wait — how will we get there?' Flora asked.

'Remember where you found us? The portal can be used to go both ways,' Leo answered. 'I should be able to reopen it and reverse the connection.'

'But that was nearly two months ago. Are you sure the portal will still be there?' Flora asked, unsure how exactly the portals created by the Alchemysts worked in this realm.

'It should be,' Leo replied. 'But we can check the ground tomorrow and know for sure.'

* * *

In the morning they went outside to inspect the ground where Leo and Lisandre had appeared last December. A ring of bluebells had started growing in the two months since they had emerged from the Realm of the Fey, marking the spot precisely. The circle of bluebells reminded Lucien and Flora of the roses of the Briar Wood from a few nights before, and suddenly Lucien had a thought that hadn't occurred to him before. Something he would need to ask his mother before drawing any further conclusions.

'Interesting,' remarked Leo as he knelt and inspected the flowers. He hadn't expected them.

'And?' asked Flora expectantly as she stood with the others behind him.

Leo stood up and turned back towards them. 'Yes', he told them confidently with a note of quiet determination. 'I think this can work.'

* * *

Part Two

Chapter Seven

The Amber Talisman

Holly

Protection, vigilance, victory, dreams and the subconscious

Place a pair of twig of holly crossed in a circle to repel lightning

February 1526

L ucien waited until dusk before heading downstairs and outside to the Briar Wood, back to the moonpool underneath the rowan tree. His head was full of doubts as he left Rose Cottage and sought solace in the forest air. He muttered the words of the ancient spell used to activate such portals, casting his intentions for his destination with a few altered words added to the end of the spell. The waters immediately began to churn and glow once again, a mesmerising, vivid blue. Lucien waited a few moments, then leapt into their endless depths.

He emerged in icy waters of a similarly sized pool in the distant ice caves far north of Alyssria. His mother had first shown him the caves as a child. The picturesque crystallic caverns had been decorated with elaborate ice sculptures she had created with magic, like furniture carved from the ice.

At the other end of the cave, his mother sat on her familiar carved ice chair, undisturbed by the cold. She studied amethyst runes on the table before her, examining the various symbols marked on the gemstones in silver before the light of a single silver candle. Lucien stood with his arms crossed as he leaned back and watched. She finished her reading, setting the runes aside, and Lucien stepped forward.

'Mother.'

Katya looked up. 'Lucien. You have returned sooner than I expected,' she noted. 'All is well?'

'More or less,' Lucien replied casually. 'Of what do your runes speak?'

Katya traced a rune with her finger. 'They tell me of the prophecy of the Midnight Rose,' she answered, then traced the symbol in the snow. 'Also called The Sorcerer's Rose. The prophecy speaks of an ancient rose with mystical properties, healing powers—essentially, it offers immortality to the one who finds it and captures its heart.' She stood up suddenly. 'That is what the Dark Alchemyst truly seeks.'

'I thought the Dark Alchemyst had already achieved immortality,' Lucien stated, intrigued.

'Temporary immortality—he can only extend his life with the elixir so many times,' Katya reminded him. 'And if my calculations are correct, he has few remaining. The Midnight Rose offers a much more permanent solution.'

'Do roses have hearts?' Lucien questioned thoughtfully, observing the runes from a distance.

'That is part of the mystery. Does the rose even exist? Is it even a flower? So much knowledge about it has been kept secret or lost since the fall of the sacred city of Atlantica. So much so the Midnight Rose has become little more than a myth, a popular folk song . . . but I have been seeking answers.' Katya walked across the cavern to retrieve a crystal ball from one of the shelves in the ice, then returned to the chair and placed it upon the table.

'And?' Lucien asked, eager to know more.

'There are two in my visions.' Katya's eyes glossed over and became distant as she spoke. 'Neither mortal. Daughters born in shadow. One of earth, one of air. The fates divide . . .'

Lucien was used to his mother speaking cryptically of her visions. 'Ravenna and Ismae? Ravenna's curse?' Lucien guessed. The two witch princesses of Alyssria were well-known figures of history entwined with legend. However, their gifts had been to master fire and water.

'No. Others,' she said. 'And I saw a strange red rose.'

'The rose—did you see where it is?' he pressed.

Katya's eyes returned to normal. 'No,' she answered. 'But the two are the key. I shall have to meditate further upon this, and solve this mystery.'

'I must leave before they notice my absence,' Lucien stated abruptly, interrupting her thoughts.

'Then go,' Katya instructed him. 'And be careful.'

'Take care, mother,' Lucien replied, and she bade him farewell before he exited the caves through the moonpool back into the forest.

* * *

The next day was uneventful as Leo and Lisandre informed Lucien and Flora about the ways and customs of the fey. Lisandre then disappeared upstairs with Flora to help her create an outfit that would pass as one of faerie design. Leo also cast a new Alchemical languages spell specifically for Alcainn, the language of the fey, upon Lucien and Flora.

Once satisfied with their knowledge, Leo began making the preparations for himself and Lisandre to return to the Alchemical Court. After packing their things, they joined

Lucien and Flora downstairs for dinner. They ate quietly, a simple meal of blueberries and pears.

As they ate, Lisandre's thoughts wandered. She would miss Flora. She had enjoyed her friendship the past two months, as had Flora. Flora had never had a true friend such as Lisandre. All the girls in the village were wary of her since she had found her powers, and had been jealous of her beauty and singing voice long before that. It was supposed to be only three days before they were to see one another again, but with the uncertainty that hung in the air, who knew if their plans would come to pass and if they would see each other at all?

That evening Leo drew the portal for the Alchemical Court on the stone floor of the parlour, sketching the familiar symbols he had drawn many times before. He drew the symbols for the elements of air and earth and spirit, as well as a couple of the stars and planets to narrow down the coordinates. And of course, the symbol for fire in the centre, a key aspect of Alchemy.

He looked up at Flora and Lucien. 'Remember, meet us at the Alchemical Court in three days.' Leo glanced over toward Lucien. 'I trust you remember how to activate the portal?'

'Of course, Leo. I could draw such a thing in my sleep,' Lucien replied, his arms firmly crossed.

'Good. Also, before we go—Lucien, may I have a word?' Leo asked.

'Very well,' Lucien replied, following him out of the room.

Once they were out of earshot, Leo asked him directly, his face stern, 'What are you doing?'

'Following you. What do you think I'm doing?' Lucien answered, unimpressed.

'No, with Flora. I've seen the way the two of you look at one another. What happened with you two?'

'Whatever is or isn't happening is strictly between me and

her.'

'Maybe,' Leo admitted, 'But she is my friend, and I do not want to see her hurt.'

'*I* am also your friend, Leo,' Lucien reminded him, 'and I am telling you I do not intend to hurt her, alright?'

'Doesn't mean you won't,' replied Leo sharply, and he went to rejoin the others.

* * *

After they had exchanged their farewells, Leo uttered the incantation to activate the portal and from the lines of chalk rose blue flames that glowed vividly. Lucien and Flora watched as Leo offered Lisandre his hand, which she gladly partook, and together they stepped forward and disappeared, the portal soon closing behind them.

Flora replaced the enormous circular red rug over the centre of the parlour, covering the spot where the portal had been. As she stood up, she asked Lucien, 'That trap with the tiles, in the Great Library — I have been wondering . . . how did you know?'

Lucien glanced at her with an unreadable expression. 'Åsmund,' he answered. 'He was also our tutor. He taught us about Fuschian art and strategies and such things.'

Lucien remembered a time not long ago when Fuschia had been the enemy. He wondered if his tutor had even escaped the revolution himself. He had been more than just their teacher; he was their friend, like an uncle to each of them.

'The pattern was all wrong. Fuschians like their patterns, for their art to be beautiful, And pleasing to the eye.' He glanced at Flora as he said that last part.

Yes, we do, she thought, then spotted the rising moon through the window. Realising the time, she turned back to Lucien. 'Perhaps we should change our attire? Before we attend the Faerie Court?'

'Yes. I suppose now we should.'

They returned upstairs side by side, Flora lifting the hem of her dress as they climbed the stairs. She retreated behind the folding screen where she had left the dress she had altered earlier with Lisandre's help. Lucien gathered the clothes chosen for him by Lisandre and returned to the hall, closing the door as they each dressed.

He returned to the room a few minutes later. As Flora stepped out from behind the folding screen, Lucien couldn't help but stare, marvelling at her beauty. Lisandre had chosen an enchanting peridot-green dress, which had been altered to resemble the style of the fey with long, transparent sleeves that hung loosely from the shoulders. Around the crown of her head was a diadem bearing a teardrop-shaped peridot gem that perfectly accentuated her beautiful, wide green eyes. Her long red hair was down and reached the small of her back. Reaching for her tresses, Flora tossed them over one shoulder, inadvertently revealing the crisscrossing laces of the back of her dress.

She felt Lucien's eyes on her and suddenly became self-conscious again. She then noticed the faerie clothes he was wearing: a long, elegant emerald-green tunic over olive tights. The sleeves of his white linen shirt were visible under the tunic, which featured fine detailed embroidery of vines and leaves. She had never seen him wear green before, she realised. It suited him almost as much as the dark blue tunics she had seen him wear at the Midnight Court.

'Now for the most important details,' he told her then began performing sorcery with his outstretched hand. She watched as Lucien weaved his magic, reciting the necessary incantation in Alcheme as he directed the emerging cobalt-blue energy with his hands, before guiding it towards her.

A pair of large wings appeared, forming at Flora's back, expanding and uncurling outwards like a flower.

'They're beautiful,' Flora said in amazement, admiring her wings over her shoulder once they had fully appeared. The illusion complete with wings of a wonderous, translucent, luminous leaf-green, she now looked like a member of the fey. A small smile tugged at Lucien's lips as he watched her admire his spellwork.

He performed the incantation upon himself as Flora wandered over to stand in front of the mirror. The same spell that had given her the illusion of wings had also pointed the tips of her ears, she noticed, carefully observing her reflection.

'What about faerie names?' she asked, gazing dreamily into the mirror.

Lucien came to stand behind her. 'Tobias and Yvette.'

She turned around. 'Yvette . . . My middle name. You remembered.'

'How could I forget?' he said, and silence fell as something else passed between them. Their eyes met. The tips of his fingers brushed her hand. She wondered if his lips would meet hers again, if his hands would pull her closer . . .

And then, as swiftly as it had come, the moment was gone. Awkwardly, they turned away from one another.

'Wait. One more thing,' Lucien said, and she turned back around as he produced her peridot-jewelled dagger and presented it to her.

Flora carefully placed her hands upon the familiar steel and gold-and-silver handle.

'My dagger. . . You finally returned it.' She raised an eyebrow up at him.

'Finally?' he questioned, raising an eyebrow in return.

She sheathed the dagger, tying the sheath around her leg under her dress.

'Shall we?' Lucien said, and they left the cottage.

* * *

Before the bluebells he spoke the strange words she had heard Leo recite before, and a glowing mist emerged as the portal took shape within the circle of flowers. Mysterious, glowing blue energy formed a series of patterned circles, which depicted a mixture of symbols Flora had never seen before and some she had. She could feel the energy emanating from the portal once again. *Strange power these Alchemysts have to create such things,* she thought, remembering this was one of Leo's creation.

Lucien turned to her and took her hand, and together they leapt forth into the glowing ring of bluebells.

They fell. It felt like the portal Lucien had opened in the Grand Fountain in front of the Great Library, as they fell through the dimensions, through space and time, before being birthed into the bright light of another realm. They emerged, falling onto the leaves and dirt. Flora recognised the birch trees by their unusual white and brown trunks. Behind them seemed to be other trees, oak and beech, that stretched towards the sky, where their branches joined and entwined, forming the overarching canopy. She and Lucien stood up and began to examine their surroundings.

So this was the mysterious Realm of the Fey, Lucien thought as he observed the impressive trees. He had never seen so many; they seemed to be endless in all directions. Neither so many nor so tall, not even in the wild forests of Alyssria. *And this palace? Seemed to be made of, or rather* with, *them.*

Flora seemed equally impressed as she looked around in awe of the beautiful trees. It seemed so peaceful here.

They found a door concealed by a cascade of ivy. Together they passed through the burdensome strands, lifting the vines and emerging in the next room. They wandered the nearby halls, looking for the Crystal Tree.

Soon they approached the Grand Atrium where many of

the fey were gathered. The trees were enormously tall here, like a cathedral of nature, and at the far end, on a raised section of dirt, stood the Crystal Tree. Once a magnificent and large tree almost as wide as the Atrium itself, some of its once-brilliant silver branches were now dull and wilted, bare of the famous luminescent amber leaves legend spoke of — for although the outside world had forgotten the fey, some details of their realm lived on in myth and legend, including those of a particular Crystal Tree. Both Lucien and Flora had read about such legends, except in the texts the authors had always spoken of the tree being as healthy as the fey themselves, blessed with near immortality and everlasting abundant life.

Others must have noted the confusion apparent on Flora's face, for soon a faerie dared approach them.

'You . . . You remind me of someone,' the faerie said. Dressed in blue with long, golden hair, as beautiful as any princess in any realm, she appeared only around twenty, but Flora sensed that she was much older.

'I think you have mistaken —' Flora started to say, but to her surprise, the faerie continued.

'Yes, I remember it now: the witch, Arianna DuPoitoires,' she spoke, now quite certainly.

'She is known in some circles as *Arianna the Magnificent*,' added a male faerie, sipping blackcurrant juice from a goblet. If Flora had glanced behind her, she would have seen Lucien grow pale.

'You have heard of my mother?' Flora was desperate to know more as the fey gathered around her. She frantically searched amongst their faces. Lucien watched with growing concern, for Flora had unknowingly revealed herself to them as a witch.

Another faerie gentleman nearly dropped his goblet as he trembled at the witch's name. 'She who serves the Dark

Alchemyst,' he muttered aloud so all could hear.

Flora was stunned. 'No, it cannot be. You must be mistaken!' she insisted to the surrounding fey, who ignored her as the circle around her suddenly parted.

Murmurs of 'My Lady' and 'Lady Ivy' could be heard as a faerie who appeared the same age as Lucien appeared at the entrance to the corridor. If Leo had been there, he would have immediately recognised her as Lady Alaïa.

'There they are. There is the witch and her companion,' pointed another female faerie with long blonde hair and orange wings. Her accusation drew the attention of Lady Alaïa, who turned her head and walked towards them.

'Companion? I am a warlock and sorcerer thank you very much!' Lucien protested.

'Take them to the Holly Queen immediately,' Lady Aläia instructed emotionlessly.

A pair of faerie guards came to flank Lucien and Flora. They had begun to escort the foreigners to the Atrium when Lady Alaïa raised her hand, commanding them to stop.

'But first, you will remove your glamour. Such deceptions are not permitted.'

Lucien humbly muttered a counter-spell. Their wings promptly disappeared, and the tips of their ears resumed their natural shape, removing all trace of their deception.

'Very well,' Lady Alaïa declared with a sly smile, evidently satisfied. 'Now you may be taken to our fair queen.'

* * *

'Tell me, how do a wizard and witch enter our realm?' Ivana asked with intense interest as she lounged on the throne in the Grand Atrium. This was the second such instance of strange travellers they had had in just as many months. Her calm tone barely covered her seething disapproval.

Lucien and Flora stood in front of the mysterious Queen of

the Fey, pairs of faerie guards on either side of them. The Holly Queen was certainly beautiful, as were all the fey. And she possessed a distinct aura of intimidating intellect as she carefully scrutinised them. Upon her carefully styled raven hair, she wore a crown of holly leaves and berries, and her wings were an intriguing mix of black and purple.

'Sorcerer-Alchemyst and witch,' Lucien finally corrected her, clasping his hands together in front of him.

Flora gave him a glare that explicitly said, *Don't make things worse.* Which he explicitly ignored.

'Technically I am a warlock,' he added, and Flora rolled her eyes toward the Atrium's canopic ceiling.

Another Alchemyst? Ivana thought, pursing her lips in annoyance. 'Why are you here?' she asked bluntly.

'We came for the Amber Talisman,' answered Lucien, boldly stepping forward.

'The realm is in danger,' Flora added behind him. 'We need to find and protect all the talismans before the Dark Alchemyst does.'

'It would appear you are far too late. The talisman was stolen — some years ago I might add,' said Ivana coldly.

'Oh? Very well. If you don't mind us, we'll be on our way,' Lucien replied, turning on his heel to leave.

'Wait — who stole the talisman?' Flora spoke up. She needed to know the truth no matter how uncomfortable it may be. She needed to confirm if her suspicions were indeed correct.

Ivana could not believe the situation she found herself in. That such a situation would arise again in just twenty-five years. She observed the pair in front of her as Lucien turned around to face her again.

'An Alchemyst and witch,' she stated irately, then gave Lucien a demure smile, a cunning play in motion. 'A sorcerer, you said? What are your skills, sorcerer? Can you perform

Dreammagic? I have read it something only taught in sorcery.'

'Yes . . . but it can be tricky . . . and dangerous, if used incorrectly. I really don't recommend it,' said Lucien, uncomfortably.

'Humor me, warlock,' Ivana demanded curtly. 'Or *she* will never leave this realm again.'

Lucien glanced at Flora, who was hoping he had the ability to do what he had been asked. He nodded toward the Holly Queen.

'Excellent. Let us test your skills. We'll start small, shall we?' the queen suggested coyly. 'Show us the past. Show me the Hazel Queen. Show me . . . my mother.'

Lucien raised his hands, beginning the incantation to perform high sorcery. He recalled how Duvalle had taught him to access the Dreamworld through his mind. As he concentrated, clouds gathered in the high ceiling of the Atrium, increasing in density. The room soon fell into darkness as they blocked out the light.

Lightning flashed forth and thunder rumbled in the clouds above before a vision appeared in the sky above. Mist-covered clouds presented a blurry scene as the court awaited eagerly below. Then a face slowly emerged in the mist. A tall figure with long, shiny raven hair and an olive-tan complexion. She wore a long scarlet dress and in her hair rested a crown of golden hazel branches, leaves and a trio of hazel nuts.

Beautiful Arsinoë I. They had called her fairest of them all. Fair of heart, body and mind. The fey stood admiring her, their beloved queen. The once-princess who had ended the civil war and united them all. Ivana's mother.

The scene showed a celebration day, Ivana noticed as she observed the vision, with candles and pinecones abundantly decorating the tables. And then she saw herself enter, wearing her fine dark purple dress, jewels hanging from her hair and across her forehead.

Graceful whispers of 'Princess Ivana' and 'the Summer Princess' sounded while others exchanged kind greetings of 'Merry solstice.'

From across the room she saw Lord Gwennaël standing nearby, unofficially guarding her mother, just an arm's length away from her. Lisandre, still a young child, was hiding behind her father's legs. Her petite crystalline wings sparkled bright.

Is that Lisandre? Flora and even Lucien thought in surprise.

Ivana's eyes suddenly became misty. It was a time she remembered well. She had been happy and content. It was before Lord Gwennaël had died and everything had changed. Before Arsinoë too had died, and she became the Holly Queen . . .

She abruptly raised her hand.

'Enough,' she cried. 'Show us the witch who stole from us.'

Lucien glanced uncomfortably at Flora, who seemed rather confused. He looked down at his hands and sighed to himself before he raising his head. Spreading his arms outward, he performed a kind of sweeping motion, bringing them together once again, all the while performing another incantation in Alcheme. As the energy in the room increased, he set his hands apart again, releasing the spell.

More lightning flashed and danced across the clouds, and thunder rumbled above them once again as he conquered up visions of the past from deep within the dreamworld.

'Show me the summer of 1501,' Queen Ivana compelled him in a determined voice, and Lucien closed his eyes as he concentrated on the spell further. He continued with his eyes closed, moving only his hands as he concentrated. Swirls of magic fog formed again and purple lightning flashed, dancing between the clouds above as he worked the spell.

An image began to form in the mist once again as Flora and

the court watched intently. The vision revealed a rather short petite girl of seventeen with long, dark auburn hair that fell in soft curls to her waist. Around her neck was an amethyst iris necklace, and she wore a dress of dark blue — so dark, like ink, that it appeared to be black. Over her shoulders was a cloak of fine deep purple cloth, from amongst the best in the realm. The fashion was only slightly different to that of modern-day Fuschia, Flora noticed, with the favoured square necklines of the late 1400s.

She had seen that woman before, Flora realised, frozen in shock. Only in portraits but now, through the Dreamworld, she was seeing for the first time her mother in her youth. Arianna DuPoitoires.

Her beau meanwhile appeared to be in his late twenties. He was tall and handsome, with short, kempt dark brown hair. He was dressed in fine black clothes and well-crafted boots under a long, elegant black cloak embroidered with gold. He wore an unconcerned expression, as if even the mighty unrivalled power of the fey was no match for him.

The court watched, intrigued, as the pair was brought before the faerie queen. Alchemyst and witch.

'Queen Arsinoë,' a male faerie standing to the side announced proudly. 'The Hazel Queen.'

The vision turned to reveal Queen Arsinoë again, sitting upon the throne, while dressed in scarlet. Upon closer examination, some of her facial features reminded Flora of Lisandre. Standing beside her was the same male faerie as before, with tawny brown hair and an intense stoic expression on his face as he watched the pair standing below. Lisandre's father. He seemed to be the personal guard of the Hazel Queen, who was indeed fair in beauty as many had claimed.

Queen Arsinoë regarded them carefully from her throne, leaning on her elbow, her hand resting gently against her chin.

'Every twenty-five of your years, the celestial bodies align and the portal to our realm opens,' began the Hazel Queen calmly. At over nine hundred years old, she had seen the portal open many times, yet no one had come through for the past century. 'Welcome to our realm. Who are you?' Arsinoë turning towards the young woman first. 'What is your name, child?'

The young witch raised her chin, her dark eyes staring defiantly ahead, directly challenging the queen's gaze.

'I am not a child, Your Fairness,' she asserted rebelliously. Her alluring voice took on a somewhat husky tone as she continued. 'And my name is Arianna, Arianna the Magnificent.'

* * *

Flora froze in disbelief. In her own realm she had grown up hearing tales of the notorious witch who called herself Arianna the Magnificent. Many had heard of Arianna and her meddling magic, like a legend whispered around the fires at night. None had ever seen her face, and yet her reputation as a powerful witch was known throughout all of Fuschia and the neighbouring kingdoms. There were even rumours that she had been the lover of the Dark Alchemyst, Flora recalled, reeling with shock and lost in their implications as they swirled torturously in her mind.

The tense scene continued as the audience watched, enthralled.

'And you are?' the Hazel Queen asked the young man.

'Richard Duvalle. I am an Alchemyst.' He spoke confidently with a rich, smooth voice that captivated all who heard it.

'An Alchemyst? I have not seen one of your kind in centuries,' noted Arsinoë curiously as she regarded him carefully.

'Many of the Alchemysts believe the fey to have become extinct, your race finished, your language dead and your realm forgotten,' Duvalle explained assertively. 'But I know better.'

'Why do they think that?' the Hazel Queen asked, clearly concerned. 'How have they forgotten us so quickly?'

'Mortals' minds are feeble, their memories short, and they have seen none of you in several generations,' said Duvalle. 'And these days many Alchemysts are also descended from mortal blood. This began two centuries ago, and now we are seeing the results.'

'Then why are you here?' she asked.

'To confirm our knowledge of your realm is true and accurate,' he replied, deceptively.

Arsinoë glanced toward her advisors, the other members of the Sacred Council. Some openly disapproved, while others remained as they were. However, the decision was up to her, and she sought peace between the realms.

'You may stay three nights,' declared Arsinoë, returning her attention to the two travellers. 'After which I request that you return to your realm and share your knowledge of your experience. Remind them of our power. Let the fey be more than just a memory.'

Duvalle bowed his head in agreement.

The vision then changed to show Duvalle and Arianna standing beneath the Crystal Tree. Its golden amber leaves were abundant and bright, even in the darkness of night. The diamond-shaped piece of amber that rested in the heart of its trunk reflecting their faces in its depths as it shone and glimmered.

'Go on. Take it,' Richard urged Arianna over her shoulder as he stood behind her.

'The Amber Talisman. It is said to grant wishes . . .' Arianna was fixated upon the gem. She turned back over her shoulder towards Richard. 'It looks as if it could fit inside the palm of my hand. Yet legend states the whole tree grew from this. And now it shall be mine.'

She cast out her hand towards the pool of amber.

'*Aperi venitati*,' she whispered gleefully, and the diamond-shaped piece of amber broke crudely forth from the amber filled cavity of the tree and floated towards her, falling directly into her hand. She clasped her fingers around the talisman, feeling its power radiate through her as she smiled.

'Allow me,' Richard said.

He reached forth, summoning a piece of vine from the nearby trees. As he performed the incantation in Alcheme, the floating vine transformed itself into string, which he directed towards the gem in Arianna's hand. It wrapped itself several times around the piece of amber before lifting it up. He guided the gem through the air, placing the newly formed necklace around her neck.

'Tell me what you want, Arianna,' Duvalle whispered seductively, his hand firmly placed upon her shoulder. 'What do you desire?'

'I want to become queen.' She smiled and turned around to face him. 'And then all those who mistreated my sister and me, and our kind, will have to bow before my feet and grovel for my forgiveness.'

Richard smiled at her boldness. Her hand reached for the Amber Talisman, twisted the crystal, gazing at her reflection in its golden depths.

'And queen you will be,' Richard said, pressing her hand to his lips as he admired her, staring deeply into her eyes.

They turned at the sound of footsteps approaching as a series of guards emerged from the hall that led toward the Atrium. Richard hurriedly muttered a series of words in Alcheme, meanwhile rapidly making gestures towards a series of chalk circles that had been drawn earlier upon the ground nearby. A swirl of energy rose from the chalk, activating the portal.

Duvalle turned to Arianna. 'My love.' He offered her his hand, and together they ran towards the portal, making a dramatic escape as the fey hurried behind them.

Once they had leapt, disappearing into its mesmerising depths, the portal disintegrated. The faerie guards arrived at the base of the Crystal Tree, out of breath, Lord Hawthorn among them.

'They have gone, my lord,' one of the guards said, turning back towards him. 'What do we do now?'

'We shall have to report this to the queen,' replied Lord Gwennaël grimly and the vision suddenly dissolved.

Lucien opened his eyes, immediately searching for Flora, who he could see was holding back tears.

'You may leave. Return to wherever you came,' Ivana spoke, but Lucien barely heard her.

'Flora . . .' he tried, but she ignored him as they walked down the hall of the fey back to the portal.

The fading golden sunlight descended through the trees of the main hall as Lucien rushed to catch up to her.

'Flora?' He grabbed her by the arm and pulled her towards him. 'Flora!'

Her fiery eyes dared him to speak. What could he possibly say? The words were lost on him as he faced her.

'You knew that vision would show my mother. You knew!' she cried. 'That's why you promised me . . .'

'Yes,' he cut in, confirming what she was alluding to.

'My mother worked with the Dark Alchemyst. How long have you known, Lucien?'

He did not answer.

'Very well,' Flora said, and he activated the portal.

They returned to Rose Cottage in silence. Flora went into her room and closed the door, leaving Lucien alone in the hallway. He slunk away into the other room, unleashing his anger upon the wall. He was angry at himself, really, at this situation—all of it.

Night fell quickly. The haunting call of the forest owls outside were the only noise as Lucien got up and got dressed some hours later, his blue tunic appearing almost black in the darkness. He slipped into Flora's room, presumably unnoticed.

Flora had been keeping *The Book of Moon* in her room ever since the night he had first came to stay at the cottage. His eyes scoured the room for the large tome as she slept in the canopy bed. His gaze was drawn to her sleeping form. He could never help but admire her beauty. A small smile fell from his lips as he paused and watched her for a moment, listening to the rise and fall of her breath, her long red hair spread across the white pillow. The sleeping beauty.

Then the moment passed, and he remembered why he had come.

'I'm so sorry, Flora.' Lucien knelt beside her and gently kissed her hand. 'Please forgive me,' he whispered.

He stood and turned back to where the book sat on top of the chest at the end of the bed. Lucien picked up *The Book of Moon* and left under the darkness of night.

* * *

Hours later, in the soft light of morning, Flora awoke. She threw on her white robe over her nightdress and went to find Lucien. She didn't know what to say, but she had to talk to him.

'Lucien?' she called as she descended to the parlour. The entire cottage seemed strangely silent. A cruel thought suddenly occurred to her, and she rushed back upstairs to check her things.

She was right. *The Book of Moon* was gone.

Her hand rushed to cover her mouth as she began to sob. Part of her wanted to scream. He had betrayed them, betrayed her, again. Despair threatened to overwhelm her. She would make sure it wouldn't happen a third time. For now though, she needed to contact Leo and Lisandre and warn them.

Taking out the ring, she called upon the pair, whispering Leo's name into the green gemstone.

Somewhere inside the Alchemical Court, a similar gold ring with a purple gemstone around Lisandre's finger started to glow, pulsating and drawing her attention with its sudden warmth. 'Leo, is that?' she took the ring off her finger and held it between them.

'Yes,' Leo answered her with visible concern. He had told Flora only to use the ring if something dire had happened.

'Flora? Is that you?' Lisandre's kind, familiar voice could be heard once the gem started to glow. Flora looked up at the sound of her friend's voice, then through the window towards the forest outside.

'It's Lucien. He is gone,' she informed them, heartbroken. He has taken the scroll and the book . . . He serves the Dark Alchemyst.'

And so did her mother. But things must have changed, she realised, or else she would never have been born . . .

A horrifying thought occurred to her.

Perhaps her father *was* the Dark Alchemyst.

* * *

Chapter Eight

The Alchemy of Roses

Ash

Resurrection, enchantment, destiny, intensity, prophecy, harmony, strength

A wand made from the ash tree can perform powerful magic

A few hours earlier

Leo and Lisandre appeared on the end of a long stone bridge. A row of statues lined each side, depicting famous Alchemysts. Before them, an imposing castle sat upon a large hill in the distance. Multicoloured stained glass windows decorated the renowned home of the Alchemical Court.

'Is that it? The Alchemical Court?' Lisandre looked up in wonder at the impressive structure. The glamour removed, her wings were now visible.

Leo nodded. He was busy examining the castle's sparse torchlit windows before he turned and noticed Lisandre shivering.

The chill air was notably cooler than Fuschia; mountains bordered the valley they were now in, their icy peaks seemingly guarding the Alchemical Court from the surrounding kingdoms.

'We could not arrive in your chambers directly?' Lisandre asked. From what she could tell, they appeared to be standing at the edge of the grounds.

'No, unfortunately. Castle policy,' he answered grimly. 'There are warding spells placed around the Alchemical Court to prevent anyone from entering in such a manner. We can only create portals from within the castle.'

Leo took her hand.

'Come,' he said, and together they headed towards the castle.

* * *

Flora didn't bother to change into her daydress before heading straight towards the chest of her mother's things. She had to know. Surely there was *some* clue as to her father's identity, something she had somehow missed. Something more than an old signet ring of a bird she could not identify.

She took out the smaller wooden chest in which she had found her mother's jewellery last year, holding it upside down, but nothing came out. Then she heard something click as, all of a sudden, one of the wooden sides opened. A secret compartment.

She lifted the box, turning it to the side, only to find various sheets of paper neatly folded beneath. Curious, she picked up one and gently unfolded it.

Dearest A,

Long has it been since I have seen you and yet you remain in my thoughts every day . . .

She continued, quickly reading the letter's contents. She picked up another and another, lost within their words as she followed their courtship before coming upon the final letter at the bottom of the pile.

Dearest A,

It has only been a fortnight since you honoured me by accepting my proposal .

. .

Dearest A. Arianna; her mother.
She glanced at the end of the letter.

Forever yours,

Leone di Fuschia

The Lion of Fuschia.

Flora went back and checked the other side of the letters. All had been marked with a golden ink crest at the bottom of the page, depicting a magnificent golden lion standing on his hind legs, paws raised and mouth open mid-roar.

She wondered if her father possessed any skill with magic, like her mother.

She glanced again at his signatures.

The Leone di Fuschia, the Lion of Fuschia, *her father* . . . but who was *he*?

* * *

The Alchemical Court was quiet as Leo stood upon the outer terrace with Lisandre by his side. With Leo having quickly recast the glamour, Lisandre pulled her cloak close over her shoulders and raised the hood. Leo raised his palm and began muttering the appropriate words in Alcheme, using magic to open the enormous wooden door, leading Lisandre quietly inside behind him.

He snuck her through the castle, leading her discreetly upstairs to his chambers. Once they were inside, Leo waved his hand, closing the door behind him. Then, with another wave of his hand, the crystal lamps began to glow around them in the darkness.

Lisandre had been standing in the centre of the room, but she found herself drawn towards the windows. A faint curtain of snow began falling outside the diamond-patterned glass. She watched, enchanted, as the snowflakes fell past the glass into the chasm below. It never snowed in the Central Forest, only the mountains where her father's family were; she had visited them as a child.

She felt Leo's eyes upon her and blushed as she turned around to see him watching her. She then noticed the violin in the corner and wondered if he played, sharing her own love for music.

'I shall go see if I can find Lady Vidjaya. We'll then approach the Alchemical Council in the morning. Don't wait up for me. You can get ready for bed if you like.'

Lisandre's hopes dropped. She would have to ask him another time it seemed.

'But where will you sleep?' she asked instead, confused.

'I have a sofa. It will do,' Leo answered, shrugging his shoulders.

'Thank you for your kindness,' Lisandre replied genuinely.

Leo went to the side of the room and knelt down by what appeared to be an empty fireplace devoid of wood. He waved his hands, one over the top of the other, as he muttered an incantation in Alcheme. Violet flames burst from the stone, instantly adding warmth and a certain cosiness to the room.

'There,' he said, standing up again. 'I'll be back later.'

Lisandre nodded, and he left to go find Lady Vidjaya.

After closing the door to his chambers, Leo cast a lock spell upon the doors to protect Lisandre from any unwelcome guests. He pulled up his hood and begun exploring the castle for any sign of his mentor. He wandered the hallways and corridors, heading towards the eastern tower, where he knocked upon the door to Lady Vidjaya's study. There was no answer. He paused and listened, but his ears were met with naught but the sound of the night-time winds outside.

Odd. Lady Vidjaya was normally in her rooms at this hour each night. He wandered around the castle a bit more, but most members of the court had retired to their rooms, it seemed. Nor was she in the Alchemical Library, where a couple elderly Alchemysts were still conversing with one another, oblivious to Leo's presence as he wandered by.

The hour was now late according to the setting moon outside, and so he returned to his chambers at last, where he found Lisandre already sound asleep.

* * *

In the morning they woke and dressed, helping themselves to some of the fruit Leo had returned with from the kitchens the night before. He then led her to the Great Hall, in which the Alchemical Council gathered each Tuesday morning, seated around a table at its centre.

Lisandre glanced across the crowded hall, observing every detail around her. Alchemysts of every height, shape and colour had gathered, meeting beneath the beautiful colourful stained glass windows. Everyone was dressed head to toe in black and with embroidered details of gold in ornate patterns like those found on Leo's jacket. Lisandre immediately felt out of place and underdressed as they stared at her walking past behind him. Her sleeveless cream-coloured dress suddenly felt see-through in comparison as she followed Leo towards the centre of the large room.

Without the help of Leo's concealment spell, her wings were now on full display, capturing the many curious eyes of the crowd. The exoticness of the fey, combined with Lisandre's natural beauty and unusually calm energy, left many spellbound by her presence. Indeed, it was the first time any of them had encountered a creature such as her.

Leo came to a stop before the council table. He paused and turned, noticing Lady Vidjaya was still not present as he gazed around the crowded room, only increasing his concern for his teacher. Composing himself, he returned his attention forward, formally addressing the nine members of the Alchemical Council.

'May I present Lady Lisandre of the fey, also known as Lady of the Vines.'

'Welcome to the Alchemical Court, my dear,' one of the Alchemysts said. 'Also known as the Court of Black and Gold.'

'It has been many years since a member of the fey has walked the halls of the Alchemical Court, perhaps centuries,' an elderly male Alchemyst said.

'We are honoured to have you here,' a middle-aged woman beside him added. 'We Alchemysts seek to maintain peace between the realms and the kingdoms within them, as well as to preserve our ancient knowledge.'

'Thank you, my lady. I am honoured to be here as well,' answered Lisandre gracefully.

'I do not see Lady Vidjaya present among you. May I ask where she is?' enquired Leo.

The members of the council seemed almost agitated by his questioning.

'She has been called away on duty, it seems, young apprentice,' answered the male Alchemyst, who he recognised as Master Lumír; he had been a member of the council as long as Leo had been at the Academy, which was all his life. Master Lumír turned and muttered something to the members of the council beside him. He then turned and addressed Leo.

'Apprentice Leopold De La Fontaine. As you are aware, the Alchemical Court was attacked two months ago. Many Alchemysts fled into hiding as a result, though many have now returned to help with the repairs. Rest assured that classes will resume shortly, and I apologise for the disruption to your studies. If Lady Vidjaya does not return soon we shall continue your apprenticeship under another teacher.' He gestured to the female Alchemyst with copper hair seated beside him.

'Lady Genevieve has kindly volunteered for this position. You remain one of our best students the Academy has ever had the privilege to teach, Leo. We will not dare let your training go to waste.'

The female Alchemyst opened her mouth to speak.

'One thing first, Lady Genevieve,' interrupted Leo, catching the Alchemysts by surprise.

'Yes, Apprentice De La Fontaine?' she asked, disapprovingly.

'Lady Lisandre requires our protection. An attempt to harm her was instigated at the Court of the Fey and she left their realm under my protection. She may be in danger from the faerie queen,' Leo stated, to the evident shock of the Alchemical Court.

'And why would that be?' Lady Genevieve enquired, confused.

'We have strong reason to think she is the daughter of the previous queen and thus the Holly Queen may see her as a potential rival for the throne,' Leo explained.

'Think? You do not know?' Lady Genevieve replied sceptically.

'We had to leave before I could confirm our suspicions, unfortunately,' admitted Leo.

'How convenient,' another more elderly male Alchemyst remarked, unimpressed.

'And what if it is true? What if she is in danger?' Leo launched forth passionately. 'Someone tried to harm Lady Lisandre at the Court of the Fey — it is why she accompanied me when I left! What if they keep coming after her? Will you still deny her your protection then?'

Master Lumír put up his hands in exasperation. 'Fine, fine. The Lady of the Vines shall remain under the protection of the Alchemical Court for now,' he declared, albeit reluctantly.

'Do I have your word?' Leo insisted, well aware of this master's fickle nature.

'Very well. You have my word: the Lady Lisandre is now under the protection of the Alchemical Court,' Master Lumír agreed, lowering his hands.

'Apprentice De La Fontaine,' another member of the council addressed Leo. One of his former teachers. Lady Selina was tall and slender with her long dark hair worn up in a neat yet stylish fashion, piled high upon her head. Her sharp eyes focused on him behind blue half-moon spectacles. She had taught Leo in his early years at the Academy but had since been assigned the post of librarian, which was considered a great honour after many years of teaching students the basics of Alchemy and subjects such as astronomy.

'Remember, Leo, you shall be her guide and guardian, since it is you who brought her to us,' Lady Selina informed him.

Leo nodded. 'Of course. Thank you all,' he replied graciously, then turned to exit the chamber, Lisandre following closely by his side.

* * *

Leo quickly resumed his studies by himself, reading his textbooks and writing notes in his chambers, until Lady Vidjaya returned unexpectantly a few days later. Classes resumed at the Academy a couple weeks afterward, in late February.

Lady Vidjaya quickly explained to Leo that she had been sent off on some strange mission. If anything, it seemed to Leo that someone on the Alchemical Council wanted her away from the Alchemical Court the past few weeks.

Spring soon arrived at the Court, little pink cherry blossoms forming on the branches outside Leo's window and the sun shining a little brighter each morning. In the month since Lucien's betrayal, Flora had remained in Fuschia, awaiting the return of her aunt, while Lisandre remained in hiding at the Alchemical Court.

Spring in Fuschia was the busiest time of the year in the kingdom with its harvests and festivals, the abundance of flowers colouring the landscape with their beauty and the air with their scent for miles around. It was often a busy time for Aunt Bellissa's tailoring business too, with many ladies from all walks of life desiring new dresses for the springtime dances. And so, Aunt Bellissa and Felippe had of course returned from Castelle the first week of Spring. Not long after that they were married, before her workload increased too much.

It was a small wedding in the Fuschian countryside on the fifth of March. Aunt Bellissa wore a beautiful dress of fine scarlet velvet with a more traditional neckline from the turn of the century, square-cut, like the portraits Flora had seen of her and her mother in their youth. She also wore a lace veil and matching red hood. She held a bouquet of red roses as she walked along the aisle towards where Felippe stood waiting beside the ancient wishing well, opposite Flora and the other ladies dressed in their Fuschian white dresses with minimal lace decorations.

Her aunt was visibly overwhelmed with joy, yet unlike the other bridesmaids, Flora struggled behind the small smile she managed to mask her sadness. Lucien had betrayed her, had betrayed all of them. And for what? For power? Or was it out of some twisted kind of loyalty to the Dark Alchemyst? Why did he inspire such devotion from him and not her? She had thought he had been devoted to her once . . .

After the ceremony, she stood alone on the hillside, still holding the bouquet of purple wildflowers. Aunt Bellissa and Felippe had already left for their honeymoon in the south after exchanging their farewells. The other guests had dispersed and wandered back to the village as Flora stood alone in the wind, wondering if things could have been different somehow, wondering where Lucien was now. It started to make her mad again. How could he do this? To them? To her?

She threw the flowers away, watching them be caught and carried by the wind. Flora then returned to Rose Cottage, where she changed into her green travelling dress. After packing a small bag, she headed downstairs. With a wave of her hand, she removed the rug, sending it flying to the side, where it landed against the wall, revealing the chalk markings Leo had left a month before. Outstretching her other hand, she summoned her magic, casting the spell.

'*Astarte divinum portae magicinae.*'

The portal was easy to restart, as Leo had said. Glowing lines of blue energy reignited along the stones, forming the familiar pattern of geometric shapes around the symbols. The hum of magic filled the air, soon informing her that the portal was ready. Fastening the strap of her bag over her shoulder, she stepped forward, letting herself be engulfed by the portal's magic.

* * *

Once Flora had let them know she was coming, Leo and Lisandre had agreed to meet her in the portrait gallery on the second floor to avoid any confusion. If anyone asked what they were doing unsupervised outside the teachers' studies, Leo would simply explain he was showing Lady Lisandre the portraits of the many great Alchemysts.

As they waited for Flora, Leo and Lisandre found themselves standing beneath one particular portrait depicting a man with intense eyes who wore a grim expression as he stared boldly into the distance.

'Leo, who is that?' Lisandre asked, mesmerised by the painting.

Leo followed her gaze and looked up at the portrait as well. 'That is Master Duvalle, he was my mentor and teacher.'

'The one you said has been missing?' she asked, glancing sideways at him.

'Yes,' Leo answered. 'He has been gone for several months, almost a year now. The night he left, the ash staff went missing as well.' He gestured toward the empty case of glass at the other end of the corridor. 'Duvalle taught us . . .'

Leo found himself lost in another memory, this time of his lessons in the Academy courtyard, the impressive clocktower looming in the background.

He and Lucien were about fifteen, locked in another one of their regular duels. 'For practice,' Duvalle had said, but Lucien was easily superior when it came to blades. Leo preferred archery, the skill of bow and arrow over swordsmanship any day.

'Come on, at least make it a challenge,' Lucien taunted him, caught up in the thrill of the game. He usually won; he didn't even have to try at all though, Leo noted as he watched Lucien casually flipping the daggers in his hands.

Duvalle watched with obvious pleasure as his two top apprentices circled one another before Lucien suddenly lounged forward and Leo dodged to the right, beginning the fight.

'Yes! That's it! Remember your training, boys,' Duvalle instructed eagerly.

They fought for several minutes, dodging and striking towards one another as they moved around the circle of chalk drawn upon the ground. Leo managed to tap Lucien across the shoulder with his dagger; he recoiled, dodging to the right as Leo tried to keep up.

A few moves later and Lucien held the daggers crossed at Leo's throat, both of them panting from exhaustion. The fight was done.

'Well done, Leo. An excellent match,' Duvalle declared.

'No matter what I do, you are undoubtedly his favourite,' Lucien remarked bitterly afterwards as they headed to their next class.

Leo's mind returned to the present as he remembered Lisandre's words.

'You think Duvalle is the Dark Alchemyst?' He finally spoke aloud the idea that had been rumbling around his mind for months.

'I don't know what to think, Leo,' she answered truthfully.

'You suspect it, then.'

She turned to face him. 'So do you,' she said, merely pointing out what was already on his mind. 'His absence is conspicuously timed. It would also explain Lucien's loyalty to him,' Lisandre continued as Leo pondered the accusation in silence.

She was right, of course. It was a definite possibility. A possibility that, if true, meant his master, the one under whom he had started his apprenticeship under loyally, had betrayed the Alchemical Court, corrupting Alchemy itself for his own dark, selfish purpose.

A familiar melodic female voice with a Fuschian accent suddenly caught their attention, and they looked up to see none other than Flora rapidly approaching them from the other end of the hallway.

'There you are! This place is a maze! I have been looking everywhere—'

'Flora!' Lisandre exclaimed happily, instantly rushing to greet her friend with a warm, welcome embrace. Flora returned it, closing her eyes as she smiled over Lisandre's shoulder, glad to be reunited with her friend again.

Lisandre then noticed Flora was wearing a dress she had never seen before. It was dark green with sleeves that flared from the elbows, edged with black lace trim. Another Fuschian design, it too was cut across the shoulders. The forepart of the skirt split open to reveal a black kirtle underneath. A pair of string of pearls also decorated her red hair.

'Welcome to the Alchemical Court,' Leo said with a warm smile as Flora turned to greet him. He too was glad to see her return.

Flora smiled once again. *It was nice to be back among friends,* she thought happily. She suddenly paused as she caught a glimpse of the portrait they stood under, recognising its subject instantly.

'Duvalle . . .' she said in a low whisper. 'Leo, do you remember how you said no one had visited the Realm of the Fey in possibly over a hundred years?'

Leo nodded. Flora arched an eyebrow theatrically as she continued.

'Well, it turns out someone did visit. Twenty-five years ago. My mother . . .'

She looked up at the portrait, then turned back to face them. 'And him.'

'What? How?' Lisandre asked, surprised. Leo looked similarly astonished at this revelation.

Flora drew in a breath and continued. 'When Lucien and I were at the Court of the Fey, we saw a vision of the past. We saw when the portal was last open. It showed my mother, Arianna . . .' She glanced up again at the portrait. 'And this man, Duvalle. He looked *exactly* the same age as in that portrait, maybe a little younger. We watched them steal the Amber Talisman.'

The mention of Lucien reminded them all of his recent betrayal, and a sudden silence fell over them.

'I'm so sorry, Flora,' Lisandre told her again, reaching out to touch her arm.

'Well, I am glad that you took the scroll with you, or else I am sure he would have run off to his master with that as well,' Flora replied bitterly. 'Where *is* the scroll?'

Leo opened his mouth to reply when suddenly they heard Lady Vidjaya's voice.

'Leo! There you are!'

The three of them spun around to see her approaching.

'You'll be late for Master Brandenberg's class if you tarry,' Lady Vidjaya cautioned Leo as she joined them beneath Master Duvalle's portrait. 'Who is this?' she asked warily, glancing toward the unfamiliar young red-haired maiden.

'May I present Flora DuPoitoires, of Fuschia, a witch. Flora, this is my teacher and mentor, Lady Vidjaya.'

Flora curtseyed and Lady Vidjaya took her hand. 'Pleased to meet you.'

Flora nodded. 'Likewise.'

'Flora helped us find the scroll at the Great Library,' Leo elaborated, and Lady Vidjaya smiled.

'Of course. Thank you, my dear,' she said, her tone suddenly becoming more welcoming.

'She has come to help us decipher the scroll and find the talismans,' continued Leo. 'The sooner we find them, the less likely they will fall into the hands of the Dark Alchemyst.'

Flora glanced up again at the portrait of Richard Duvalle. '*He* is the Dark Alchemyst,' she noted with quiet certainty.

'Duvalle? You are quite sure?' questioned Lady Vidjaya. Although he had been among her suspicions for some time, she was still surprised to see him accused with such clarity. 'I have suspected as much, but my colleagues do not share my suspicions. Indeed, you would be wise to keep such speculations amongst yourselves, until we know who to trust,' she instructed. 'Duvalle still has many supporters, even among the Academy and inside the Alchemical Court. Are you sure it was him that you saw?'

'Yes. He was there — the Dreamworld showed it,' explained Flora. 'He helped steal the Amber Talisman, along with my mother.'

Lady Vidjaya's expression turned serious. 'Come. This is more important than your studies.' She turned on her heel and gestured quietly for them to follow her towards her private study rooms in the tower.

Lisandre and Flora followed Leo as he walked behind Lady Vidjaya up the circular stairs. The view from the windows beside the stairs as they ascended was spectacular. Flora could see the various mountains that surrounded them and glimpses of the valleys that lay beyond them. Mist gathered around one level of the windows, making it seem like they had passed through into the domain above the clouds.

At the top of the stairs was a door, at which Lady Vidjaya spoke the enchanted password, *draconi volantis*, and led them into her study. Inside the circular room, the stone walls were covered with bookshelves that stretched toward the cone-shaped ceiling. Detailed colourful stained glass windows decorated the room in all the cardinal directions. A series of stairs led away through a narrow archway to the floor below, where her private living quarters resided. And upon the desk in the centre rested a familiar item: the scroll.

Upon seeing it, Flora threw her hands across her chest. 'Oh, Dia! Thank the Goddess,' she sighed with relief.

'Do not worry. The scroll is safe here,' Lady Vidjaya reassured her as she went and rearranged the objects on the desk, creating room to open the scroll. 'There is a certain irony that the scroll he destroyed part of the Alchemical Court for is now in fact here,' she noted to herself more so than the others. 'Come, now sit.'

She gestured to three chairs that suddenly appeared behind each of them with a few movements of her hand, startling Flora as she glanced behind.

'Now for the locations of the talismans. It is imperative that we find them before Duvalle does,' explained Lady Vidjaya. 'We at a disadvantage as he already possesses one of them.'

'The Amber Talisman, also known as the Stone of Wishes,' said Lisandre.

'Yes,' answered Lady Vidjaya, unveiling the scroll. Leo and Lisandre had examined and researched every aspect of the lines of verse each evening with Lady Vidjaya since her return a fortnight before.

'Lady Vidjaya, *why* are they so important? Why is Duvalle after them?' asked Flora as they pondered the lines of the riddle again.

The room then suddenly darkened as clouds gathered outside, and it began to feel like dusk despite it being midday. Lady Vidjaya waved her hand and the crystal lamps began to glow, around the room, bathing the tower in their violet light. A flash of white interrupted their glow as lightning struck in the distance, followed soon after by the rumble of thunder.

'The talismans are said to have extraordinary power over the elements,' explained Lady Vidjaya. 'They were a gift from the dragons — ancient, wise creatures skilled with magic that they were. According to legends and various historical accounts, they imbued the gemstones with powerful runes. Their powers kept Atlantica strong for many centuries until division arose from within.'

'After the Fall of Atlantica, it was decided that the talismans be divided among the races to keep their power hidden and safe, lest they be used against one another or with ill intent. With each talisman Duvalle acquires, he can increase his power. If he finds all of them — well, he would be quite unstoppable,' she finished grimly.

The room fell silent.

'Surely, he has no need for such a thing,' Flora spoke up a few moments later. 'I have heard he is already quite powerful — at least powerful enough to raise the dead.'

'Yes, raising the dead is one thing, but immortality is definitely another,' stated Lady Vidjaya.

'Can the talismans do that? Make him immortal?' asked Leo, intrigued. Flora and Lisandre were likewise curious.

'No. But I suspect he will find a way once he has them,' answered Lady Vidjaya mysteriously, then redirected their attention to the scroll again. 'Now, the Gem of Flowers — that would be the Emerald Talisman. The Stone of Wishes is the

Amber. . . I am yet unsure about the others, there are a few possibilities . . .'

Leo's mind was already racing as he recalled the night he had fled the attack on the Alchemical Court. He brought out his Alchemical Almanac, in which he had been taking notes on the night in question. Flora and Lisandre watched as he flicked quickly through the pages, searching intensely when he suddenly came to the page he had been searching for. He turned the Almanac around and placed it upon the desk, facing towards them.

'This.' Leo pointed at the symbol. The three petals within a circle had been present in his master's notes shortly before his disappearance, also found within the sacred texts of the archives of the fey. 'What is this?' he asked Lady Vidjaya. 'I've never seen anything like it.'

She paused, as if contemplating whether or not to reveal certain information before she answered carefully. 'It is called the Midnight Rose.'

Something clicked in Leo's mind, a memory suddenly emerging. He was sitting in class with Lucien last year, shortly before their master had vanished.

'For centuries the Alchemysts have been in pursuit of the Midnight Rose, a flower that possesses unique healing powers and can bestow immortality,' Duvalle had proclaimed as he stood at the front of the small class. His eyes had glossed over in awe at the mention of such a power.

'Also known as the Alchemical or Sorcerer's Rose, the Midnight Rose grew on the central island of Atlantica,' Lady Vidjaya continued, her voice drawing Leo back to the present. 'He believes it still to be there, but my research indicates it perhaps has not been so in a very long time. You see, in my research, I recently came across a secret manuscript that was hidden in the archives of the Alchemical Library, written in

Ancient Ægyptian, detailing the true history of the rose.'

She produced a book of yellowed papyrus decorated with symbols written in the ancient Ægyptian script.

'It was an ancient document hidden within one of the scrolls. When I translated it, it spoke of the rose and its incredible power, which led to a great division between the inhabitants of Atlantica. To end the feud, it was made into a potion and consumed by two bloodlines, one of the witches and one of the fey.'

She glanced at Flora and Lisandre, noting they were each representatives of such species.

'Over time, the bloodlines were hidden, and all knowledge of the rose as well, until the Midnight Rose became nothing more than a legend, a myth, spoken about in song and poetry.' Lady Vidjaya pointed to the symbol. 'From what I can tell, this rune seems to have been used to secretly communicate about the rose in the centuries since.' She then pointed towards Leo's Almanac. 'See the three petals protected within a sacred circle? It is said they represent the flower protected by the guardians.'

Leo, Lisandre and Flora glanced together in awe at the strange hieroglyphics. The language of the ancient sorcerers of Ægyptia predated even Alcheme itself.

Lisandre's eyes suddenly went wide as she had a realisation. 'These . . .' She pointed at the sets of hieroglyphics depicted in vertical columns within the book. 'I have seen them before. In the oldest scrolls of the fey. Do you think there is a connection?'

'It is thought that many of the inhabitants of Atlantica later went and settled in Ægyptia. Perhaps the language is far older than we know and comes from Atlantica as well,' Lady Vidjaya answered. 'That could explain it, or perhaps members of the fey were in contact with the Ægyptian sorcerers. I would have to research their history more closely to be sure, though,' she mused thoughtfully.

Lisandre continued staring, fascinated with the symbols upon the page. She stumbled over the words as she suddenly revealed, 'I . . . I can read it.'

'You what?' Leo responded, shocked. Flora, too, appeared noticeably surprised.

'Yes, I can understand it quite well,' Lisandre said then turned excitedly towards them. 'It is somewhat similar to our own script, you see. It must share a similar root script with Alcainn.'

'How strange,' Lady Vidjaya commented. 'Your skills may be quite useful to the Alchemical Court, Lisandre.'

Lisandre attempted to hide a shy smile.

'Come. Perhaps we shall find answers in the Alchemical Library,' Lady Vidjaya invited them as the storm outside began to pass, with streams of golden sunlight breaking through the clouds and entering through the stained-glass windows once again.

Leo, Lisandre and Flora followed her, leaving the scroll in her study and continuing downstairs to the ground floor, passing through a courtyard garden as they headed to another part of the castle. Flora watched as Leo and Lady Vidjaya wandered ahead before she firmly pulled Lisandre behind a carved stone pillar.

'Flora, what is it? What couldn't wait — ?'

'My father. I have discovered his identity,' Flora informed her. 'Well, sort of. He is the Leone di Fuschia.'

'And you think he could be the Dark Alchemyst?' questioned Lisandre carefully.

'No, the Leone di Fuschia is his sworn enemy. Though no one knows why. But it is common knowledge. Many in our village and the city talk about them both,' explained Flora as they continued to walk.

'Perhaps you could ask one of them,' Lisandre suggested, 'Someone knowledgeable who may have seen them.'

Flora stopped and turned towards her. 'But we did see them,' she told Lisandre. 'At least one of them. We saw the Leone di Fuschia in the Great Library. All I saw was his eyes. They were green, like mine.'

Eyes that knew not who she was to him. Her own began to well up with tears of frustration as Lisandre wrapped her arm around Flora's.

'It would seem I am no closer to really discovering his identity at all,' Flora lamented.

Lisandre did not know what to say as she tried to comfort her friend.

'And he must despise me now for I have been caught inside the Great Library,' Flora realised to her despair, beginning to feel herself become overwhelmed with shame.

'No, you are his daughter. He will surely understand,' Lisandre reassured her. 'The fate of the realms are at stake; it depends on the talismans being found before the Dark Alchemyst does. A knight as noble as he will understand that.'

Flora glanced towards her with tear-stained eyes. 'Do you truly believe that?' she asked, still unsure.

'Yes,' Lisandre answered her resolutely.

'Thank you,' Flora replied gratuitously as she wiped away her tears. 'Let's find Leo. Perhaps the Alchemical Library will have the knowledge we seek.'

* * *

Chapter Nine

Queen of Alchemy

Blackberry

Prosperity, femininity, earth

Tea brewed from the leaves of the blackberry sends the drinker into a dreamless sleep

Lucien arrived on the edge of a small castle on the coast. The first thing he noticed was the excruciatingly bright sunlight as he exited the other end of the portal. It reflected on the beautiful light-blue Castellean waters under the white cliffs, against which he stood out in stark contrast in his black tunic embellished with silver embroidery. He could smell the sea salt in the air as the wind brushed past his face. The granite sundial in the courtyard read it was late in the afternoon as he walked past along the gravel path towards the castle foyer.

Duvalle immediately addressed him as he entered. 'Where have you been?' he asked curtly, looking up sharply from the book he was reading.

'Following a lead,' Lucien answered evasively.

Duvalle snapped shut his book abruptly and stood up to his full height, towering over Lucien, who was himself by no means short.

'I have been trying to contact you for weeks,' Duvalle growled, evidently displeased. Lucien paused, then attempted to walk past, but Duvalle easily stopped him. 'Never do that again. Do you understand?' he said, his dark tone notably ominous.

Lucien glared slightly, then slowly nodded. 'Do not worry, master. I have not come empty-handed.' He revealed *The Book of Moon.*

Duvalle's eyes lit up ravenously at the presence of the ancient tome, examining the dusky purple cover with its title written in Latinacaec above the crescent moon symbol drawn in silver ink.

'Well done, Lucien,' he congratulated his apprentice as his eyes poured over the book.

It was rare for his master to dole out such praise and yet internally Lucien felt as if he could not accept it, knowing he had betrayed Flora to receive it, even though she was the one that had pushed him away.

Duvalle's voice drew his attention once again. 'Excellent. Now take it to her,' he instructed, his gaze gesturing him along the path to the rose garden. Duvalle then returned to his own book and the comfort of his armchair as Lucien continued outside, moving along the path, passing through the stone archway.

Her. His master's mistress. He could smell her magic as he approached. In all the months he had worked with his former mentor, he had yet to meet her, at least not directly. He had only seen glimpses of their secret conversations through the trees and hedges of the gardens. All he had seen was that she had dark hair and wore beautiful clothes. Up until now.

The sweet perfume of roses mixed with the scents of fresh dirt and crushed blackberries greeted him as he approached.

Arianna DuPoitoires, the Amber Talisman around her neck, had her back toward him as she tended the purple roses. They responded visibly to her touch, their vines floating around her as she worked her magic. Glancing toward a table of potion ingredients that had been assembled in the clearing, she appeared to be working on some kind of spell. Upon the large table rested a small cauldron bubbling away all by itself.

Petite in height and with chestnut-brown hair that fell to her waist, she was wearing a purple cloak over a scarlet dress featuring fine gold stitching and elegant embroidery. Lucien watched as she turned around and peered over the cauldron, checking her potion. A woven cloth bookmark lay beside a pile of small books on the other side of the table.

'Lady Arianna?' he addressed her hesitantly, and she turned around, her sharp falcon-like eyes falling quickly upon him. He was nervous but did not show it, appearing calm and neutral as ever despite her penetrating gaze. He did not have to bare her scrutiny for long, however, as Arianna's eyes were immediately drawn to the purple-covered book he was holding.

'Finally.' She charged over to retrieve the book from Lucien's hands, instantly flipping the cover open and flicking rapidly through its pages. She seemed to be searching for a certain spell as she scanned its contents intensely, scarcely paying mind to the young sorcerer. 'You may go,' she said, barely glancing up from the pages of the book.

As he turned to leave, Lucien paused. 'Oh, the fey girl . . . she's at the Alchemical Court. She has the scroll, if that is of any particular interest to you,' he said, knowing full well this information would capture her attention.

Arianna raised her eyes at the mention of the faerie. 'Thank you . . . ?'

'Lucien.'

'Thank you, Lucien. The scroll and the whereabouts of the

young faerie *are* of particular interest to us,' noted Arianna. 'We have been much concerned since Queen Ivana informed us of her disappearance. It is vital that she be found and returned to the Realm of the Fey. For her safety, of course.'

Lucien nodded silently, casting his eyes toward the ground.

'We appreciate this information, and your loyalty,' she told him, and Lucien glanced up into her eyes. Her features suddenly reminded him of Flora, catching him off-guard, like a ghost determined to haunt his dreams. He recalled Flora's expression of hurt and distrust upon realising what he had kept from her.

He had not known she was not dead, though. Had not realised the very woman currently working with his master was Flora's mother at all. Duvalle had mentioned a Lady Arianna a few times, a Fuschian witch he had worked with in the past. But Lucien had not considered it could possibly be this woman. She was simply too young to be so. Perhaps she truly was a queen of Alchemy, he thought. Another secret, another burden. Would Flora ever forgive him? That he did not know.

He turned on his heel and left, leaving Arianna to return to her spells in the garden.

* * *

Spring had returned in the Realm of the Fey, with flowers blossoming among the bright green leaves on many of the trees, their sweet scent filling the forest air. Queen Ivana sat within the Grand Atrium alone, leaning heavily to one side as she pondered uneasily over many things.

'Fairest one.'

Lady Ivy's voice suddenly interrupted her train of thought and she looked up to see the lady and Lord Rowan were now standing before her.

'You summoned us?' Alaïa asked her expectantly. She glanced sideways at Lord Rowan, wary yet somewhat curious.

The Holly Queen had seemed agitated as they had walked in.

Ivana stood up. Her long, dark hair was tied back in an elegant bun and she wore another sleeveless purple dress, matching her dark purple wings. Her golden eyes reminded Alaïa of Lisandre's.

Alaïa began pacing as she spoke. 'Our spies have informed me the Lady Lisandre has finally emerged. It appears she has been staying at the Alchemical Court, possibly for several weeks now.'

Ivana suddenly turned and focused her fiery gaze upon them. 'Lord Rowan, Lady Ivy. I need you to find her and help her return to our realm, where she belongs, for her safety,' she instructed them.

'Of course, fairest one,' Lord Rowan answered. 'We shall leave at once.' He bowed and together he and Lady Alaïa turned to exit the Atrium.

Once they were out of earshot as they walked along the enormous corridor, Lord Rowan turned his head toward Lady Alaïa.

'Why does she insist so strongly that the Lady of the Vines return? She should be free to visit whichever realms she wishes. As should the rest of us,' he noted.

Alaïa threw him a stern look over her shoulder. 'You know why. She disobeyed a direct order from our queen and ran off with *one-not-of-our-kind*. Her Majesty is rightfully concerned. Lisandre is so young, and naïve.'

'She is not that much younger than you, Lady Alaïa,' he pointed out as they turned the corner.

'And yet I did not run off with some Alchemyst,' she rebuffed him sharply.

'Still bitter I see,' he noted. 'I have a cure for that, or at least I can make you forget him for a few hours . . . '

His hand reached for her waist and she stopped, turning

sharply towards him.

'I am not one of your nymphs, Alistair,' she told him, an edge of warning to her tone. 'And you would do well to remember it.'

Lord Rowan remained undeterred. 'One day you may change your mind, Lady Alaïa. I hope for that day still,' he said, a subtle note of determination lacing his voice.

Her expression remained unreadable as she continued walking swiftly along the corridor, lengthening her stride. Lord Rowan hurried to keep up with her, and was soon alongside her again as they headed toward the portal left by the Alchemyst months before.

* * *

Meanwhile at the Alchemical Court, Leo, Lisandre and Flora were researching once again in the Alchemical Library.

'Beneath ancient springs . . .' Flora muttered to herself as she browsed the shelves of ancient scrolls across from Lisandre and Leo. Together, she and Lisandre had spent each day of the past month in the library, researching every possible mention of springs, while Leo and Lady Vidjaya had resumed their classes as part of the Academy during the day before joining them in the early evenings. The court librarian, Lady Selina, kept a watchful eye from behind her moon-shaped spectacles as they searched the endless shelves of books and scrolls.

They kept searching until a weekend morning in early April, when at last they solved the riddle of the Emerald Talisman.

'Here,' Lisandre suddenly said, drawing their attention to a scroll written in ancient Ægyptian. 'It says the fabled City of the Nymphs was built on top of a series of ancient hot springs that some later cooled to become artesian lakes,' Lisandre read aloud from where she stood on top of the small ladder, towering above them as she had been examining the scrolls hidden away upon the highest shelf.

'City of the Nymphs? I thought that was just a myth?' asked Flora from ground shelves below, perplexed. She glanced questioningly at Leo.

'I can assure you it is no myth,' Leo informed her. 'Duvalle sent us there on missions. Many times. We also passed through there on others.'

'The gem must be buried underneath it somehow,' Lisandre noted, climbing down to join them.

'That's why he sent us to the City of the Nymphs last year.' As the realisation dawned upon Leo he wondered if Lucien had known even back then.

'But how could he have known? That was before we found the scroll,' Flora pointed out.

Even Leo had to admit he did not know the answer to that. When it came to the topic of Duvalle, every clue seemed to provide more questions than answers. 'I am not sure, but he somehow did.'

'Or maybe he was looking for the scroll there, perhaps?' suggested Lisandre.

'Perhaps,' echoed Leo thoughtfully.

'How soon can we go?' asked Flora, excitedly turning toward Leo. They would finally be setting off on an adventure after being stuck in the Alchemical Court for weeks.

Leo retrieved his Alchemical Almanac and opened it, doing some quick calculations. He looked up suddenly from his notes. 'We can travel at the next full moon,' he informed them, a cautiously optimistic smile forming on his lips.

'Excellent,' remarked Flora. 'So about two weeks, then?'

Suddenly, a loud howl-like noise drew the attention of everyone in the library. The three of them rushed outside to the balcony, where they watched as a magnificent purple dragon dawned upon the horizon. The large creature swooped down from the midday blue sky down towards the long bridge – the entrance to the Alchemical Court.

'What is the meaning of this?' Lady Selina cried from behind them. She soon spotted the dragon rapidly approaching the castle. 'Not another attack,' she muttered fearfully, before fainting promptly at the prospect.

'Seriously?' Flora said, glancing behind at her. 'Could she have been any less helpful?'

She followed Leo's gaze as he and Lisandre looked down to see the stone Alchemyst statues stepping off the railing onto the bridge, where they began moving into formation and marching towards the castle, with their heavy, clunky footsteps slowly hitting the stone pathway of the bridge. The three of them watched together, awestruck, as the animated statues came to stand together, turning their elegantly carved stone backs to the large castle doors.

'The statues are said to come alive in times of danger. I was sure it was just a myth,' explained Leo.

'Sounds like an animation spell,' remarked Flora, her eyes shifting to the purple dragon. She had never seen one in real life before, having only read about them. The creature was rather impressive, even more so off the page.

'What do we do now?' Lisandre asked, her eyes wide with concern.

'Come, we must find the Alchemical Council and warn them,' Leo said. He returned into the library with Lisandre and Flora following quickly behind.

They passed the many rows of shelves before reaching the inner corridor of the castle, where they hurried down the circular stairs to the next floor. Lisandre tagged along just behind Flora as they continued through the labyrinth-like interior, struggling to keep pace with the others. Occasionally Flora glanced over her shoulder to make sure she was still with them.

'The Alchemical Council usually meet in the sun chamber at this time of day,' Leo informed them as he led them down another corridor, passing many doors and archways. Sunlight filtered through the high-set stained glass windows, creating a kaleidoscope of colours across the stone walls and ground.

Lisandre had just passed one of the open archways when a pair of fair hands leapt forth from the darkness, pulling her swiftly behind a pillar and out of sight. She struggled, fighting back and tried to scream, but the man already had pulled her several paces down the corridor.

He removed his hand from her mouth. Her eyes widened in shock as he turned around, revealing his identity.

'Lord Rowan! What are you doing here?' Lisandre breathed, barely able to get the words out in her shock at seeing a member of the fey inside the Alchemysts' castle. His iridescent amber wings stood out against the plain cream walls.

'The Holly Queen requests that you return to Na Foraise Síorai, Lady Lisandre. She requests that you return at once,' Lord Rowan told her matter-of-factly.

Lisandre glanced toward the windows overlooking the castle entrance. She caught a glimpse of the dragon's enormous purple form flying in the distance.

'Is this her doing? Is she threatening the Alchemysts if I do not return?' she asked, in disbelief that Ivana would stoop so low.

Lord Rowan followed her line of sight. 'The creature is not with us,' he told her, gaze still fixed upon the dragon. He returned his attention to Lisandre. 'Now come.' He pulled at her arm, dragging her back towards the castle entrance.

'Let go! Please! Stop! Let me go!' she begged as they reached an adjoining corridor.

Flora had caught up to them, having figured out where the

corridors would meet. 'Let her go!' she screamed at the unsuspecting faerie, who glanced up towards her, surprised. Leo also suddenly appeared, rushing up from the corridor behind them.

'Alistair, wait! Listen to me!' Lisandre cried, and he finally paused. 'I cannot return to Na Foraise Síorai until we have found the talismans. Our realm is just as much under threat as theirs until they are found.'

'Let the Alchemysts and this . . . *witch'* — he shot a disapproving glance towards Flora — 'find them. The queen insists upon your immediate return.' He reached for her arm to pull her away, but Lisandre resisted.

'No!'

Lord Rowan seemed caught off guard by her defiance. 'No? Lady Lisandre, are you defying a direct order from our queen?' he questioned her carefully, warningly.

Leo swiftly stepped in front of Lisandre. 'She said no.'

'Out of my way, Alchemyst,' the male faerie responded fiercely with a warning of his own.

'Lisandre is staying with us,' Leo stated calmly.

'Is that so?' Lord Rowan replied tartly. He was beginning find this particular Alchemyst rather irritating.

'Yes,' Leo warned in a soft growl with eyes that dared anyone to so much as challenge him. He too was starting to become annoyed with the faerie's antics.

'Alchemysts, always meddling in others' affairs. No wonder we did away with interacting with your kind a long time ago,' Lord Rowan remarked, reaching into the inside pocket of his tunic. He withdrew a small veridian drawstring pouch, which Leo swiftly recognised from his studies.

'Sleeping dust!' he called to a confused Flora, attempting to warn her. But it was too late.

The powdery substance had no effect on the fey, but was

often used to temporarily send mortals to sleep. In a matter of seconds Lord Rowan had gathered a small amount of the glittering cerulean powder in the palm of his hand, which he then leaned forward and blew into the air. The powder floated through the air, falling upon the witch and heading towards Leo. Leo managed to duck far enough out of the way as the powder fell towards the ground, but Flora was still too close. The dust fell upon her skin and she closed her eyes and fell swiftly to the ground, fast asleep.

Leo glanced back to where Lord Rowan had been standing, but he was now gone. And so was Lisandre.

He quickly turned his attention along the corridor toward the entrance, where he spotted Alistair pulling a resisting Lisandre past the statues, weaving between them before heading towards the end of the bridge, where Alaïa was waiting.

What happened next took place so quickly Leo could scarcely believe his eyes.

Alistair tried to pull Lisandre past the statues, but one of them suddenly moved forward, blocking his path. The purple dragon reappeared from the other side of the castle which it had been circling, and upon seeing the two fey, enormous pillows of steam began to waffle forth from its large nostrils before it opened its wide jaw and a stream of orange fire burst forth towards them.

Lord Rowan and Lisandre both leapt into the air, narrowly avoiding the path of flames, which struck the bridge, pouring over into the chasm beneath, the intense heat of the flames melting some of the statues into a pile of molten granite.

Leo turned on his heel and raced inside the castle, up the stairs of the tallest tower, towards the keep.

Distracted by the dragon as he launched into the air, Lord Rowan lost his grip on Lisandre enough that she managed to slip apart, quickly flying in the opposite direction. She flew out of his reach, and the dragon was forced to choose between going after her or Lord Rowan. He watched for a moment, frightened the giant creature would come after him as he hovered on the spot, only to see the creature turn and take off in the other direction. The dragon had its eyes only on Lisandre, it seemed, charging after her, forcing her to fly at maximum speed to stay just ahead of its grasp.

She dodged and weaved around the castle and its towers, the dragon always following not far behind. Down below, she noticed out of the corner of her eye as the statues in front of the castle began to turn and attack the castle doors, clearly under some kind of enchantment.

Come out princess, let's play.

Somehow the dragon spoke the words tauntingly in her mind, frightening her even more. How could this dragon even know who she was? She had no time to focus on it. Not at the moment while her life and the Alchemical Court were in danger.

The Alchemysts emerged, spilling out from the doors below, battling the statues outside the castle entrance. Lisandre flew higher, spiralling round and round the tower, past the colourful glass windows and up to the keep, struggling to stay out of the dragon's reach as the remaining Alchemysts watched, captivated from within. A faerie flying was a spectacular sight, unheard outside of the histories of the fey.

Not long after she reached the top of the tower, she began to feel tired. She was unused to the heavy weight of her wings, which she had barely used before, and soon felt herself becoming fatigued from the effort. Lisandre landed on the rooftop of the tower, where she finally collapsed, utterly exhausted.

The dragon, having momentarily lost sight of Lisandre, had now found her once again. Its large eyes were now peering at her as she sat with her back against the tiled roof. Her heart raced as she stared up at the dragon with its luminescent green eyes and shimmering purple scales, certain that, despite her best efforts, she was now done for.

Summoning the very last of her strength, she urged herself to move, clambering across the rooftop tiles. She launched herself into the air once again, just as the dragon blew another torrent of flames toward the keep, destroying the upper half of the tower.

Lisandre fell into the now open room, the flames singeing the edge of her dress as they rained past her to the side, pouring down onto the other half of the room. She landed on her elbows and knees upon the wooden floor of the tower. Lisandre trembled as she heard the dragon's wings beat the air around the remnants of the tower. She despaired as the sky grew unnaturally dark around her and the dragon emerged from below, rising before the darkening clouds that were blocking the sun.

She glanced up at the dragon, certain this moment would be her last, when out of the corner of her sight Leo arrived, appearing in the doorway to the stairs of the semi-destroyed keep. He stepped bravely into the centre of the room, pointing his bow and arrow directly at the dragon, blue flames already smouldering around the arrowhead.

'Leave her alone!' he shouted, and let the arrow fly.

The enchanted arrow struck the dragon's shoulder, causing it to let out a thunderous roar and reel back in pain. The dragon responded by swiping Leo with its claw, knocking the bow out of his hands and sending it freefalling to the ground below.

Leo's shoulder ached painfully. Glancing down at the fountain far down below, he quickly had an idea. Muttering the necessary incantation, he closed his eyes, concentrating intensely while summoning the water forth from the fountain.

'*Aquatae aquati animate voli . . .*'

'Leo look out!' Lisandre warned as the dragon took another swipe towards Leo where he stood performing the spell, but it was too late. Leo dove to the side, the dragon's claw just reaching his arm, tearing apart another wound as he retreated behind the nearby bookcase. Across from him, he saw Lisandre hide behind another fallen bookcase.

Their heads then both turned as the spell took effect and the water Leo had called forth from the fountain rose rapidly in a spiral, high up into the air until it was level with the purple dragon, forming into a creature made of water, magic and Alchemy. A water dragon.

The dragons met and locked eyes in the sky above. The water dragon opened its jaw and blew flames of blue Alchemical fire, similar to those Leo had summoned for his arrows, towards the purple dragon. The creature engaged with jets of orange fire in return, their flames combining in hypnotising swirls of blue and orange fire in the sky between them.

A jolt of pain from his wound caused Leo to cry out and clasp his arm, drawing Lisandre's attention. He fell to his knees as he watched the water dragon launch straight toward its fiery opponent.

'Leo!' he had heard Lisandre cry out as the dragons circle one another again. His vision became blurry as the figure of Lisandre came towards him.

The battle continued, each dragon blast forth more bursts of flames as they moved across the sky. The orange flames had little effect upon the enchanted creature, and the purple dragon eventually began to feel more tired as they chased and dodged one another before their flames collided once again. They remained locked upon one another until the intensity of the blue flames gradually wore down those of the orange, and the purple dragon began to retreat, fleeing towards the horizon.

As the dragons had pursued one another above, Lisandre had returned to Leo's side. Quickly stifling her own cries, she noticed the enormous wound to his arm and shoulder extended across his chest, raising her hands to cover her mouth in shock.

Leo barely had time to register Lisandre's reaction before he grew dizzy and collapsed to the floor. At the edges of his vision, he saw Lisandre as she knelt beside him with her long dark hair cascading down the sides of her pale face. She lifted his back so he rested within her arms. Blood stained his white shirt and the black sleeve of his jacket had been shredded, revealing the wound underneath.

Bloodied and losing consciousness fast, he tried to speak the words that came to his mind, raising his hand to touch her cheek.

'Lisandre . . . I need you . . . to know . . .' he whispered to her faintly.

'Hush! No! Do not speak. You must save your energy,' she told him, clasping his hand and gently lowering it. She had to focus on healing him, she reminded herself. She needed to concentrate to get him, and herself, through this.

She recalled her studies of Nádúr and what she had learned about healing magic. Various spells that required leaves and other ingredients she did not have, and the healing crystals she did were in her bag downstairs in her chamber. She glanced at Leo's wounds. He had lost too much blood for her to leave him and fetch them now.

But she couldn't let him die. Not Leo. She had lost so much already. Her father. The queen. Her home. She couldn't lose him too.

Focusing her energy on him, wishing for a miracle, she held him in her arms as she reached out to the cosmos.

Then the words came to her along with an ancient melody, a song of healing. She could feel its power flowing through her. Lisandre closed her eyes and began to sing. She sang words in the faerie language he did not recognise. All he heard was the sound of her voice as he closed his eyes and drifted into unconsciousness.

The air around Lisandre's form then began to shine and shimmer, her aura glowing intensely with brilliant light. She felt the magic working upon his wounds, keeping her eyes closed out of fear whatever magic she had begun working would stop if she dared open them.

The magic she had summoned sewed the edges of his skin back together, restoring the tissue underneath and resetting his shoulder. She felt it as the skin healed, even removing all traces of what would ordinarily have been a scar.

Only when she felt the magic was complete did Lisandre gently open her eyes. She had healed him, surprising even herself.

A few moments later, Leo regained consciousness, opening his eyes to gaze gently upon hers.

'Leo,' she whispered gratefully, and he noticed a teardrop fall from her right eye.

'Lady Lisandre.'

He reached up to touch her face once more and realised his arm was no longer hurting. Glancing down, he saw the wound was no more. His right arm was entirely healed, as if the dragon had never even touched him.

He looked back to Lisandre. 'Did you do this?'

She nodded gently.

'I am so grateful.' He tried to sit up. 'I had no idea you were so gifted with healing magic.'

Lisandre blushed. In truth, for all she had studied so far of the subject, she did not know exactly how she had been able to heal Leo's wounds so quickly. It had been so unusual for her, so instinctive. She was sure if asked she would have no way to truly explain how or why the song came to her. But she was relieved to see that Leo was truly unharmed nonetheless.

'That song . . . I had no idea you could sing like that. It sounded like another language . . . What did it mean?' he asked.

Lisandre did not know what to say. The words did not translate fully to Alcheme in her head. She was not even sure how she knew the words; the song had simply come to her. A song of great power and healing.

'It is difficult to translate. I'm sorry,' she said. The more her mind dwelled upon the strange words, the more she began to realise they were oddly familiar, though more like the ancient runes she had mysteriously been able to read in Lady Vidjaya's study than her own native language of Alcainn.

They sat and rested, watching as the dark clouds above gradually dispersed and blue sky emerged, brilliant golden rays of sunlight falling upon their skin.

'There you are!' Lady Vidjaya called breathlessly, drawing their attention as she appeared in the remnants of the doorway to the tower. A few other members of the Alchemical Court followed not far behind her. 'Leo! Are you alright?'

'I am fine, Lady Vidjaya. Thanks to Lisandre.'

Lady Vidjaya glanced toward her.

'He saved me, Lady Vidjaya. I only wanted to help,' said Lisandre. 'I am sorry—the dragon was after me. I brought it here. I am so sorry.' She began to break down as she realised the extent of the damage around her.

Lady Vidjaya knelt down and looked at her compassionately. 'Do not apologise my dear. I know you did not intend this. The Alchemical Court took great risk protecting you and would do so again. This is not your fault.'

'You are under our protection,' Leo added. He then turned back to face Lady Vidjaya. 'And we must continue our pursuit of the talismans. We may need them to protect Lisandre, if Queen Ivana is willing to align herself with a Dark Alchemyst such as Duvalle.' He returned his gaze to Lisandre. 'She must have heard you were here, and sent Lord Rowan and Lady Alaïa so it would appear she tried to help you return while she contacted Duvalle to make sure you would not.'

Lisandre felt betrayed all over again, reminded of the constant danger she was in.

'Will she never stop?' she uttered, becoming more distressed once again. 'Will I never be safe?'

Leo reached for her hand and she turned to see his eyes upon her.

'You will be, once we find the talismans,' answered Leo. 'She and Duvalle will have no choice but to leave you alone then.'

'I hope you are right,' Lisandre replied.

'As do I,' added Lady Vidjaya. She stood up, glancing over her shoulder at the Alchemysts watching them quietly from the doorway. 'Come. I think it best we continue this discussion in my private study.'

Leo stood and helped Lisandre to her feet. 'Wait, have you seen Flora? Is she okay?' Lisandre asked, suddenly remembering their friend.

'Yes, she is fine,' Lady Vidjaya said. 'Lady Genevieve made sure she was brought inside straight after the faerie —'

'Lord Rowan,' Lisandre supplied.

'Yes, Lord Rowan — used sleeping dust. She is still asleep, but seems otherwise unharmed. Perhaps you could help me, Lady Lisandre — how long does such a substance take to wear off? Is there a tea or tincture that could perhaps help her recover sooner?' Lady Vidjaya asked.

'Lemon water, or some rosemary or nettle tea should help her,' answered Lisandre, recalling her studies.

'Very well. I shall make some as soon as we return to my rooms.'

The three of them headed downstairs as the awaiting Alchemysts quickly set to work repairing the tower keep.

* * *

Flora quickly recovered with the help of Lisandre's tea, and Leo and Lisandre filled her in on the events that transpired after she had fallen under the effects of the sleeping dust. The Alchemical Council held an impromptu meeting in the evening to discuss the events of that day, which they all attended, watching as the Alchemysts argued over who was responsible for the attack and what could be done to prevent another. Leo wished he could simply tell them about the talismans, but many of the Alchemysts still supported Duvalle, and without proof he knew they would not believe him. Lisandre could sense his subtle frustration as she observed the proceedings beside him and Lady Vidjaya, Flora standing by her other side.

' . . . We knew she was being targeted when we agreed to offer Lady Lisandre our protection,' Lady Genevieve curtly reminded them.

'Yes, but a dragon? A dragon!' remarked Master Lumír. 'No one was hurt, thankfully, but Apprentice De La Fontaine almost died!'

'What are you suggesting Master Lumír? That we should abandon the poor girl to the creature?' retorted Lady Genevieve. 'Has the Alchemical Court finally lost all sense of morality and reason?'

'No, of course not. But there must be some solution for this. One that does not put a target on all our backs!' argued Master

Lumír.

'We were already a target—or do you forget the incident of only a few months ago? For all we know, the two are connected and Lady Lisandre is innocent, simply caught in the wrong place at the wrong time,' Lady Selina put forth.

'The creature went straight after her. She was its target. As long as she remains here, we all are too,' said Master Lumír, pointing at Lisandre. She reached for Leo's hand.

'Enough! We swore to give Lady Lisandre our help and protection and the Alchemical Court shall keep its word,' Lady Genevieve thundered. 'If our castle of a hundred Alchemysts cannot withstand whatever ploys the Dark Alchemyst has planned, then perhaps we do not deserve to remain as we are.'

The others fell silent.

She turned towards Leo. 'It is a miracle that Apprentice De La Fontaine and Lady Lisandre were not seriously harmed. We shall re-examine the castle's defences, update the wards and do our best to ensure the Alchemical Court remains a refuge for those in need of protection, as we have always done.'

'Of course,' added Master Lumír.

Leo nodded.

'Very well, I think that is all for now.' Lady Genevieve dismissed the council, and the members of the Alchemical Court began to disperse back to their chambers.

Lisandre glanced toward Leo, who was still watching the council, observing their reactions. They followed Lady Vidjaya back to her study before returning with Flora to their chambers.

That night the dragon still haunted Lisandre in her dreams, chasing her into the wild thicket of trees. She was in the Midnight Forest again. Only this time she stood under a large apple tree in the centre of a clearing. Vines of ivy moved like snakes along the grass towards her, and fire licked the base of the apple tree—sorcerer's fire. The flames glowed a sickly, supernatural green as they crawled upward and devoured the branches.

'Lisandre!'

She turned at the sound of her name to see Leo running towards her, concern in his eyes. Her gaze followed his to see the vines had transformed into emerald-scaled snakes once again, hissing as they snapped forth angrily at her. She stumbled back towards the apple tree as Leo pulled her behind him and retrieved his sword.

The snakes transformed themselves into enchanted vines of poisonous oak leaves that leapt aggressively towards Lisandre as Leo stepped forward. Wielding the sword with notable skill, he cut through the thick vines before they could entangle themselves around her.

Upon waking, she could not help but wonder: had it truly been just a dream?

* * *

Chapter Ten

The City of the Nymphs

Waterlilies:

Sexuality, creation, fertility, rebirth, moon and water magic

Place a waterlily in a pool of water under the full moon to attract a soulmate

A fortnight later they gathered in Leo's chambers once again. They had dressed finely in preparation for travel to the City of the Nymphs, as it was a well-known place where people went to dance and frolic, to escape their troubles and relax for a while. Flora wore a new gown she had created with the finest emerald green silk-like fabric, while Leo had opted for his usual gold-embroidered black Alchemical jacket now that it had been repaired, placing it over the top of his best white shirt. Lisandre wore her usual elegant sleeveless cream-coloured fey dress. Leo quickly reapplied the glamour to conceal her wings so as to draw less attention, and as the evening fell, they were soon ready to travel.

'Aren't you going to draw us a portal?' Flora asked Leo, readjusting her emerald-and-pearl necklace around her neck in the mirror.

'Not here,' he answered, to both her and Lisandre's

surprise.

How else would they get to the City of the Nymphs if not by Alchemical portal? Flora wondered.

Seeing their confusion, Leo turned and offered Lisandre his hand.

'Come. Make sure to follow closely,' he instructed as he led them downstairs. Passing the odd Alchemyst or apprentice wandering the castle, they descended the many stairs to the floor above the entrance hall, where they paused in front of a particular oil painting. It depicted a creature Flora had never seen before, with the brown body of a lion attached to azure wings and featuring a charming female human face with a grin strongly reminiscent of a cat. The creature gazed directly at them from within the painting, standing beneath three bright stars in the night sky above a desert oasis.

'Leo, what is that creature?' Flora asked. Lisandre seemed fascinated as well.

'That, is a sphinx,' Leo answered. He stepped forward and lifted the gold-framed edges of the painting, shifting it upwards. It swung sideways on it hinges, opening very much like a door, revealing a space of empty wall behind it.

A secret passageway, Flora marvelled as she and Lisandre peered over Leo's shoulders. The passageway revealed even more stairs spiralling downwards into the dark below.

As the moon rose outside, they followed Leo downstairs, then through corridors that soon felt like a well-constructed labyrinth before they opened up into an enormous chamber with a spectacularly high ceiling, held up by columns adorned with Ægyptian hieroglyphics.

This place was different. It felt ancient, Lisandre thought as she marvelled at the design. Suddenly Leo's words echoed in her mind. *'The Alchemysts' history goes back a long way, back to the ancient times,'* he had told her. Truly how far back, she now wondered.

In the centre of the cavern, guarded by four stone cat statues, was a large, rectangular moonpool. Its unusually aquamarine waters were of course familiar to the trio. Moonlight entered the chamber through a large circular opening in the ceiling, falling into the centre of the moonpool.

'The Alchemical Court exists on a nexus of ley lines, it is easier to create portals here, working with nature, not against it,' Leo explained. 'But a natural vortex such as a moonpool is always preferred.' He glanced knowingly at Flora.

'An ancient moonpool enhances the energy, strengthening the portal,' she noted.

'Yes,' Leo confirmed. 'I found this place a couple of years ago when Duvalle was away on one of his ventures.'

Lisandre found herself bursting with questions at the implications. 'Incredible. A moonpool right beneath the castle. Do you think that is why they built the Alchemical Court here, right above it? Do other Alchemysts know about this?'

'Only Lucien and I know about it, we think,' Leo told her. 'And quite possibly Duvalle.'

He produced a piece of white chalk and began sketching symbols upon the rocks around the base of the pool: earth and water, the sun and moon, Jupiter, antimony, copper, Venus and various others, first in the five points of a star, then the rest in a continuous circle around the outside edge of the pool. Stepping back, he hid the chalk in the pocket of his jacket and began to speak the necessary incantation in Alcheme. Blue fire danced across the water as the portal ignited, forming a pentagram of flames upon the surface.

Leo turned to Flora and Lisandre, who stood either side of him, waiting for instruction. He nodded gently and stepped forward up onto the edge of the moonpool before stepping completely into the water, a trail of bubbles rising as he fell, sinking to the bottom. One at a time, Flora and Lisandre entered the portal behind him.

Night transformed into day as they passed through the portal and the dark waters above them turned a bright, sparkling turquoise. They rose to the surface, where they were immediately immersed in bright sunlight. They had arrived outside, within the confines of a rock pool on the shores of a mysterious lake. Hanging vines with light purple flowers adorned and grew over the quartz-imbued granite rocks protruding around the edges of the water.

'Come.' Leo led them as if he knew exactly where they were going, and of course, he did.

At the other end of the lake was a waterfall reaching twenty feet tall. They followed him as he approached the rock wall behind the falling water. Behind the waterfall was a series of vines. Leo moved them aside to reveal a secret entrance to a cave. Inside, water dripped from the rocks and onto the floor. More vines covered the wall at the other end.

'Beware the nymphs, they can be . . . tricky,' Leo warned them as he lifted the second curtain of vines and they passed through.

They arrived in a classical paradise. Canal-like streams ran between the lush, grassy green surrounds of the creamy marble-domed buildings. Bridges ran over the larger streams, leading them further into the garden city. Blooms of flowers encircled the buildings, the intoxicating scent of their perfume sweetly overwhelming. An abundance of exotic rainbow roses grew inside the gardens, adding their mix of colours to this strange, otherworldly place.

Then they saw the nymphs. They reminded Leo and Flora of the fey. Their bodies were elegant and slender, even more so than that of the fey, and their feet seem to almost glide along the grass with their lightness of step. They wore chiton dresses of every colour, especially in pastels of blue, purple, green and pink, and garlands of flowers in their long, flowing hair.

Leo and Flora turned their heads to Lisandre then back to stare at the nymphs. Some danced around in circles on the grass, while others gathered flowers, which they put in each other's hair. Some of them had pulled young men into their dances.

'They are indeed my cousins . . . my *distant* cousins,' Lisandre explained warily as they watched.

Leo turned his back on them to face Lisandre and Flora. 'We need to stay together and find the talisman,' he reminded them. 'Nymphs like to play; they like to speak in riddles and play on words. They want you to stay forever.'

'Agreed,' Lisandre confirmed, and glanced over at Flora, who was still gazing at the flowers.

'Hmm?' she muttered dreamily, clearly distracted. Flowers of every shape, colour and design grew together here. Even growing up in Fuschia, she had never seen such flowers as these. Their surreal beauty was a welcome distraction from her melancholy thoughts of late. And the music, such enchanting music, seemed to be coming from somewhere within a distant domed building, luring her away with its melody.

'Flora? Flora?'

Lisandre called her name, but she did not hear. She was already lost in the beautiful music, its melody pulling her away quickly into the gardens, away from Leo and Lisandre.

'We have to find her,' Lisandre said, concerned, as she stared in the direction Flora had disappeared.

'She'll be fine. We'll find her after we retrieve the talisman,' Leo reassured her, and she reluctantly agreed. He took her hand, leading her away from the pairs of cypress trees that lined the path towards the central domed building.

They wandered further along the main path, toward a large

fountain, where many nymphs and their guests had gathered. Lisandre studied the surrounding landscape and gardens as they walked, looking for any clue as to the location of the talisman. Leo quietly examined their surroundings too, though he was soon more occupied by the giggling laughter of a group of nymphs as they approached. Lisandre paid no attention to the nymphs, for a glimmer of something sparkling had caught her eye over the top of the hedges lining the inner gardens.

'Leo, do you see that?' she asked, her voice full of curiosity and hope.

'See what?' he replied as a trio of nymphs approached him. He caught a glimpse of Lisandre's shiny black hair against the abundance of green foliage as she began wandering in the direction of what she'd seen away further into the gardens. 'Lisandre, wait!' he called but she did not hear him, having already passed through the other side of the thick hedge.

He turned back; the circlet of nymphs were now standing before him.

'*Come with us, . . .* ' their enchanting voices spoke a dialect of Ancient Greek but upon realising he was an Alchemyst, they slipped their arms around his shoulders as effortlessly as they slipped into perfect Alcheme.

He heard whispers of 'Trystan' and 'Remember us?' as their musical voices spoke to him in his language, circling him as they pulled him away back into the crowd.

'Lisandre? Lisandre!' he called over the tops of their heads, but she was already out of sight.

* * *

Vines covered the ancient gazebo at the edge of the gardens. It was quiet here, and Lisandre found herself alone aside from the sound of the nearby trickling stream. From the other side, the gazebo overlooked a small lake, upon which floated several white and pink waterlilies. A forgotten part of the gardens, it seemed, for the vines were quite intrusive and thick. *Clearly they were many years old,* she thought, examining them. The vines also covered much of the stairs that spiralled around to the right side of the gazebo.

Lisandre gazed up at the elegantly carved white marble decorating the top of the structure. Sunlight sparkled as it reflected off the surface of a diamond-shaped quartz crystal that was easily the size of the palm of her hand, perhaps bigger even. Lifting the edge of her dress, she approached the steps at the bottom. Carefully, she traversed the spaces between the vines upon the stairs, tiptoeing around the lush plant.

Approaching the entrance, she swept back a curtain of overhanging vines to one side and entered the gazebo. It was dark inside, with so many vines blocking the spaces between the columns through which rays of sunlight would normally enter. Remembering her magic, she reached into the pouch resting around her waist and withdrew a citrine crystal that fit perfectly within the palm of her hand. She whispered over it in Alcainn, activating it, and the crystal began at once to glow from within. The yellow crystal floated in the air to the centre of the domed ceiling, spreading soft, glowing light throughout the gazebo, chasing the shadows away.

Now that she could see more clearly, Lisandre began to examine the chamber more thoroughly. She began by lifting a section of vines from the tiled floor, revealing a detailed mosaic. The arrangement of tiles reminded her of the puzzles of the fey, which made sense, given their shared ancestry. Written around the edge of the circular floor in Alcheme was a distinct phrase which she quickly translated in her mind:

A sacred dance of elements is the key

Only then shall the entrance be revealed to thee

Pondering the riddle, she examined the stylised plants depicted in the mosaic tiles. Each flower was depicted within a circle of its own. Seven circles. Seven plants to choose from. She paused as she considered each of them, recalling their various attributes from her Nádúr studies on the elemental natures of herbs, flowers and trees. She soon surmised the pattern and tapped the stones in order with her feet.

First she placed her foot on the tile depicting a branch of vervain, with its tiny white flowers, for the element of earth. Next was the pine tree to the left, with its branch and cone, representing air. Then bay leaves for fire; she touched her foot to the stone in the bottom right corner of the circle, followed by the apple blossom with its pink and white flowers for water.

She stepped back into the centre of the circle. The four cardinal directions, she realised as she glanced back at the pattern. She had used each plant from the outer circle.

Nothing happened. Perhaps she had performed it wrong, or something else was missing?

Then she recalled the riddle—the sacred dance of the elements was key. The elements were earth, air, fire, water, and spirit. *Of course!* she realised. *But what plant would represent spirit?*

She examined the three remaining flowers in the circles. A red rose, white lilies and violets . . .

Red usually represented passion, she thought, quickly passing to the next flower. White lilies could mean the spirit. But she would have to check the third remaining flower to be sure and so she continued.

Violets. Purple. Purple was often used in candles and spells to represent the element of spirit. It was something Lisandre had learnt from Flora recently when she had been curious about her witchcraft. She had wanted to compare it to her studies of Nádúr, and Flora had been only too happy to tell her about a few basics of the craft as the two of them researched together in the library while Leo had attended his classes.

She gently stretched her leg forward and tapped the stone depicting a bouquet of violets with her right foot. The gazebo pillars suddenly rumbled around her as the mosaic floor sunk into the ground and stairs emerged one by one, heading downwards in a spiral beneath the stone.

Lisandre glanced down into the darkness, and after retrieving her luminescent citrine crystal, she begun the descent.

* * *

The nymphs brought Leo before a large fountain. The fountain itself was shaped like an enormous flower bud, water flowing from its large open petals. Resting across the marble edges was a large group of nymphs surrounding three who sat in the centre. Glancing at their faces, he recognised the trio of nymphs from his travels last year. *Lorelai, Lilianne and Phoebe.*

They wore a chiton dress of turquoise, pastel blue and pink respectively. Each also had beautiful long hair of a different colour; Lorelai's a distinct auburn, Lilianne's chestnut and Phoebe's a sunny blonde. Lorelai sat in the centre, watching Leo warily as Phoebe leapt up and raced to throw her arms around him.

'Trystan, we missed you,' she told him, smiling as she spoke in his ear. 'We knew you would return, Alchemyst. Lilianne had a vision.'

He gently pulled her hands away and Phoebe appeared surprised.

'Look, I'm sorry, Phoebe, but I have to find Lisandre. Did you see where she went?' He kept looking behind her, trying to see if he could spot Lisandre in the gardens in the distance.

'Lisandre? Who is Lisandre?' Phoebe asked, a note of jealousy evident in her voice and her eyes.

'She came here with me. She is a faerie, with long dark hair and beautiful wings,' Leo told her. 'She was here only a moment ago. Please help me find her.'

'The faerie? Why do you need *her*?' Lorelai interrupted. The leader of her sisters, Lorelai was, like many of the nymphs, stunningly beautiful, with large, wide eyes and plush, sensuous lips. Her sirenotic stare was captivating, and Leo was suddenly reminded of how Lucien had fell under its spell when they had visited only last year . . .

* * *

City of the Nymphs

May 1525

A year before

The vines parted behind the waterfall before Leo, though he had barely touched them. He passed through and the vines fell immediately back into place, concealing the entrance to the ancient city, almost hitting Lucien in the face as he followed.

'Strange. I was certain I was the better student,' he remarked dejectedly as he followed Leo through the waterfall.

Leo was just as visibly perplexed as Lucien was. He has barely begun the spell when they had parted for him.

'Relax, have a little fun,' Lucien told him as they entered the city, passing over the first bridge above one of the many canal streams.

'We're not supposed to be relaxing,' Leo swiftly reminded him. 'We're on a mission or have you forgot?'

'I see no reason why we cannot do both,' Lucien replied.

They continued along, heading deeper into the city. Leo came to an unexpected stop at the end of the second bridge. 'Be careful,' he warned Lucien as they observed the beautiful gardens from a distance. 'I read the nymphs can cast spells with their songs.'

Lucien merely gave him a strange look.

They crossed another set of bridges as they wandered through the ancient city, passing over several small canals and lakes. The place seemed eerily quiet to the pair of sixteen-year-old Alchemysts, more a garden than any of the other cities they had ever seen.

'And do not let them draw you into their dances, either. Not if you want to leave,' Leo told Lucien as they encountered a trio of nymphs guarding a large fountain, lounging upon the marble. They each wore a dress of pastel blue, aquamarine and pink respectively. The middle one tossed her auburn tresses over her shoulder and stood to greet them. She wore a diadem of amazonite and silver that matched her dress and eyes perfectly.

'Ignore him,' Lucien told the nymphs nonchalantly. 'He's such a bore anyway.' *They were very beautiful,* he thought, admiring their ethereal beauty, staring as the centre nymph stood before them. He could understand perfectly why many of them were called muses by artists and travellers who passed through their realm.

'Welcome, travellers,' the nymph greeted them in her melodic voice and Leo's spell translated their words perfectly. 'Welcome to Paradisium.'

'Who are you?' Lucien asked boldly. The spell instantly translated his words into their language as they left his tongue.

The centre nymph turned to address him. 'Lorelai. And these are my sisters, Lilianne' — she glanced at the nymph in blue — 'and Phoebe.' She indicated the nymph in pink. 'My sisters and I welcome you to the Rainbow Grove.'

'Who or what are you two?' she asked in return.

Lucien glanced ambivalently at Leo before answering. 'I am Tobias and this is my brother, Trystan,' he answered carefully. 'We are Alchemysts passing through to the Empire.'

'You both seem a little young to be fully-fledged Alchemysts,' noted Lilianne, switching to Alcheme, her otherworldly accent remaining.

'Indeed, we are still both apprentices,' Lucien replied confidently.

'Perhaps you shall like to stay here a while after your journey?' suggested Lorelai.

'It has been so long since we have been visited by an Alchemyst,' noted Lilianne.

'So very long,' added Phoebe.

'Thank you, but we really must be going,' said Leo.

Lucien reached for his arm to prevent him from leaving. 'What my dear brother means is we would love to stay awhile. A few nights would not hurt our cause,' he assured them. He then turned and whispered quietly to Leo, 'We do not want to insult their hospitality. There are strong rumours those who refuse the nymphs can never leave their realm.'

'I believe that is the fey,' Leo replied sharply.

'Do you really want to take the risk?' Lucien answered.

Leo turned back to the nymphs. 'My brother is right. We'd be delighted to stay,' he told them.

'Ἀγαθός!' Phoebe exclaimed in their native tongue, clapping her hands together with joy. *Excellent!*

Lucien addressed the three of them flirtatiously. 'Now tell me, what exactly do nymphs do for fun?'

Lorelai gave him a coy smile.

* * *

Over the next few days Leo and Lucien stayed in the City of the Nymphs. The nymphs thoroughly enjoyed their company, and in turn the Alchemysts observed the arts of the nymphs who performed various songs, dances and poetry. They painted with Phoebe, sang with Lorelai and danced with Lilianne.

One afternoon, Lorelai led Lucien through the surrounding forest of mulberry trees, walking among the vine-like branches and cascading leaves, listening to the sound of running water as they drew closer to their secret destination. The trees parted to reveal a waterfall pouring into a large pool.

Lorelai brought forth a circular golden object that rested perfectly within the palm of her hand. Closer examination revealed ancient Ægyptian runes adorned the shining exterior of the object, Lucien noticed, peering over her shoulder as he caught up to her.

'What an unusual compass,' he commented. He had truly never seen one quite like it.

'It was a gift from an Alchemyst, many, many years ago. Passed down to our mother,' Lorelai explained, staring at the needle.

Lucien began to explore around the edges of the pool. There appeared to be nothing behind this particular waterfall. Still, he examined the various branches of the trees. The area seemed secluded. They were alone and undisturbed except for the sound of the peaceful rushing of the water that filled the clearing.

He returned his attention to Lorelai. Every time he turned around, her eyes were on him. She looked at him with an intense curiosity, as if he were a new kind of creature she had yet to study.

'It has been a long time since we have met an Alchemyst and a sorcerer,' she told him, her wide, sensuous eyes fixed on him. 'A long time since we have met one of your kind.'

'May I ask how it is there are no nymph men?' Lucien asked, flustered. He had been curious about that observation since he had arrived.

'All nymph women are the result of coupling with mortal men. We only give birth to daughters,' she explained, watching Lucien across the pool. 'Most men who visit us are mortals who seek our company or inspiration, they desire us to be their muses.'

Lucien returned to her side. Her voice was enticing, and he suddenly felt himself drawn to it in a way he had never been before. She was also very beautiful.

'You are different,' she said. Placing the compass in Lucien's hand, Lorelai watched as the needle moved to point toward her.

'What are you doing?' he asked, uncertain what was happening, but she did not answer. Instead she retrieved the strange compass, placing it upon a nearby rock before she removed her outer garment, revealing a matching turquoise two-piece of clothing underneath.

Lucien turned away, pretending not to notice her bare skin as she passed him and stepped into the water, swimming towards the shallow centre of the pool. She turned around to lock eyes with Lucien. Her hypnotic stare calling him towards her.

'Come in Tobias, the water is rejuvenating,' she called to him in her enchanting voice, the crystalline waters up to her waist. Lucien felt himself inexplicably drawn to her, stepping into the water, moving himself towards her.

Once he was close enough she reached for him, pulling him closer, her hands searching for his chest before their lips met in a rush of ecstasy as she wrapped herself around his waist. Lucien thought he could drown within her beauty as their bodies moved with pleasure.

* * *

Lisandre's hands felt for the side of the wall as she made her way down the circular staircase. At the bottom was a tunnel that led to the entrance of a cavern, its sandstone walls so smooth it must have been created by magic. Sunlight illuminated the flowers within through an ancient shaft. There was life within this cavern: vines and vibrant crimson roses in bloom covering the walls and rising from the earthy floor. Brightly coloured crystals were dispersed throughout the cavern, their colourful glow adding to the sunlight's luminescence. Coloured light reflected from the crystals upon the walls, creating pleasing patterns and a dazzling rainbow effect across the chamber.

In the centre grew an unusually crystal-like flower, a rose with petals that appeared to be fluid emeralds. Lisandre reached out to touch the flower and the flower unfurled at the mere touch of her fingertip, the emerald petals gently dropping one by one to reveal a single teardrop-shaped green gem.

'The Gem of Flowers,' she breathed. She couldn't believe it. They had found it. They had finally found a talisman. They had succeeded at last.

* * *

'Tell me, Trystan. Why are you and your companions really here?' Lorelai asked, absentmindedly braiding her hair. 'It is not often we are visited by an Alchemyst, a faerie and a witch all in one day.'

'We are here to find the Gem of Flowers. The Dark Alchemyst intends to steal it. Do you know where it is?' Leo asked her directly.

'Really? The Dark Alchemyst . . .' Lorelai raised an

eyebrow. 'Last time you were here, he was your master and you his apprentice.'

Leo paused for a moment, shocked. 'He is no longer my master,' he asserted.

'Isn't he? Has he not manipulated you to find the gem for him? You were so loyal to him last we met,' Lorelai mused, still staring down at her braid.

'I didn't know then who he was,' Leo answered truthfully, then continued determinedly. 'The gem. I can assure you it is not safe here.'

Lorelai's eyes met his as she sung cryptically in response:

'You seek the Gem of Flowers, as many do,

But which none have found

For the sacred Emerald Talisman lies

Far beneath the fertile ground.'

Lorelai stood up. 'The gem is well-hidden, *I assure you,*' she told him resolutely. 'Farewell, Leo.'

She turned and left, Lilianne and Phoebe quickly trailing closely after her along the path into the trees.

* * *

Flora had wandered inside the huge domed building, where she found a number of people and nymphs dancing around a large indoor fountain. More nymphs rested upon the cool marble. Her gaze meandered along the large classical murals depicted on the walls of the corridor, half-heartedly searching for any clues that might lead to the Gem of Flowers. Truthfully, she had many things on her mind already.

'Come away with us Flora.'

'Come dance with us.'

Their words felt like the tide trying to pull her away from where she stood with their enticing melody, their alluring music calling to her like the waves of the ocean.

'Forget Lucien.'

'Forget Lucien's betrayal and his master, the Dark Alchemyst.'

'Forget the pain of never knowing her mother, or father . . .'

She started to move and sway to the enchanting music, closing her eyes as she fell under its spell, feeling as if she could dance for centuries . . .

Until suddenly she noticed the touch of a familiar pair of hands upon her waist.

'Flora? Flora!' a voice called. 'Flora, wake up!'

Her eyes flashed open.

Was that Lucien standing before her, with his eyes full of concern?

The woodnymphs watched on as Flora pushed him away. 'You! How dare you touch me! You betrayed us!' she accused, tears forming around the edges of her eyes as anger rose within her.

'Flora, I can explain,' Lucien pleaded as she walked away.

She paused, and turned around to confront him. 'I loved you!' she said angrily, the tears starting to cascade down her face.

'Harrumph.'

A nymph stomped behind them, followed by a rustle of leaves as she turned swiftly on her heel and began to walk away.

'Lorelai, wait! I can explain . . .' Lucien called to her.

'It's Lilianne!' the nymph shouted angrily over her shoulder.

'Damn it,' Lucien muttered to himself more than anyone, then quickly returned his attention to Flora. 'Flora. I-'

'Spurned by even a nymph, I see,' she noted haughtily. 'And rightly so,' she added, reaching under her skirt.

'Flora, what are you—'

His eyes followed her hand, realising her intent as she suddenly launched at him with her dagger. He quickly raised his arm to block her blow and she tried half-heartedly to strike him again.

'You knew what that book means to me!' she cried, turning and propelling herself at him with another attack.

Lucien quickly spun her by the wrist, turning her back to him and disarming her. 'It's not that simple, Flora,' he told her, speaking in a low voice over her shoulder before releasing her. 'I *owe* him,' he finally confessed. 'He is the one who helped me bring my mother back from the dead.'

'So, he teaches you necromancy and you become his faithful servant!' she accused coldly. 'I bet he was the one who taught you how to turn into a raven too, no doubt!'

'Yes,' Lucien admitted, glancing down at the dagger in his hand. 'He taught me how to raise her from the dead—do you really think that kind of magic doesn't come with a price?' he hissed.

'And when will Duvalle be satisfied such a debt is paid? When you give him your *soul*? He may have bought your loyalty, but he does not deserve it,' Flora told him harshly.

'I am trying to protect the only family I have left. And I would do it again. I would do anything to keep you and her safe,' revealed Lucien.

Flora paused. 'And how many souls will you be putting in danger by giving him that book?' she asked him, searching for the answers in his eyes as he remained silent. 'Where is the book now, Lucien? Where is my mother? She's alive isn't she? That's why the fey said she who *serves*, not she who *served* the Dark Alchemyst isn't it? Have you seen her?''

Lucien seemed torn as he stood silently in front of her. Something caught Lucien's eye over her shoulder, and he suddenly transformed into a raven as Flora cried out to the skies. 'Answer me!!'

She collapsed to her knees, sobbing, as the raven spiralled high into the air and swiftly flew away, carried by the wind.

Leo and Lisandre appeared at the edge of Flora's vision. Lisandre rushed over and knelt beside her friend.

'Flora, are you alright?' She wrapped her arms around Flora's shoulders. It was quite clear that she wasn't. Lisandre raised her hand to her brow against the glare of the sun as she watched the raven disappear in the distance. 'Is that who I think it is?' she asked Flora, who hesitated before nodding.

'I just want to go home,' Flora whispered quietly. She sounded tired.

Lisandre held her hand as they stood up, looking towards Leo. 'Shall we?'

He nodded. 'There's just one more thing I need to do before we go.'

Scanning his surroundings, he quickly recognised the trio of nymphs lounging once again around one of the many fountains. They gazed at him warily as he approached.

'What do you know of Richard Duvalle?' he asked the nymphs.

They hesitated, glancing nervously at one another before they answered.

'There are rumours,' began Phoebe, apprehensively.

'That he is a prince,' added Lilianne.

'A *lost* prince,' said Lorelai.

'*The* lost prince of Brittainnia,' the nymphs finished in a harmonic chorus.

'But that would make him over two hundred years old!' Leo exclaimed in disbelief.

'That's all we know, Alchemyst,' asserted Lorelai, and the three of them left the fountain to go wander somewhere else.

* * *

Chapter Eleven

The Alchemysts' Castle

Blackthorn

Power, darkness, light, balance, clarity, magic, wonders, secrets

Place a blackthorn at each of the four cardinal points for a powerful spell of protection

The three returned quickly to Leo's chambers at the Alchemical Court. Flora remained lost in her thoughts until she heard the familiar groan of metal and clunking of wood as Leo locked the door behind them.

'Wait, what about the talisman?' she asked, remembering their mission once they were safely inside the tower.

Lisandre smiled as she reached into her knapsack and retrieved the flower-shaped gemstone with its five petals, holding it up to the light so Leo and Flora could see.

'The Gem of Flowers—you found it! Magnifiquo!' Flora exclaimed. 'Wherever did you find it?'

'In a cave under the city. It was all very beautiful, but secret, hidden,' Lisandre explained while Flora examined the unique gem.

'It's hard to fathom something so small could turn entire deserts into oases,' she remarked, gazing at its shiny surface.

'We'll take turns hiding it,' suggested Leo, and Flora handed him the gem.

'Now that we know the Dark Alchemyst is also the Lost Prince, we'll need to be more careful who we trust,' he added solemnly.

'I don't understand. Who is the Lost Prince, exactly?' Lisandre asked.

'Come. I'll show you,' Leo said.

He led her and Flora to the Alchemical Library, where he retrieved a large volume bound in vermillion fabric from one of the shelves.

Flora peered around his shoulder at the cover. '*A History of Brittannian Myths & Legends* by Oliver de Oakdene,' she read aloud as Leo opened the book and turned through it, coming to a stop on one particular page.

Lines written in Alcheme decorated the page. A crest featuring an oak leaf accompanied the entry. Even Flora could decipher the Alcheme translation for *Duvalle* among the unfamiliar text.

'*The Lost Prince refers to a prince from the House of Duvalle in the twelfth century. The prince was thought to be the second son of the Brittannian King Lionel III,*' Leo read aloud. '*Records of his name and birth were later lost and are unknown. But legend states that the prince disappeared in 1170 while travelling with his brother in a forest. Unlike his brother, the crown prince, the second son's body was never found. This caused the line to fall to the House of Blackthorn and then more recently to the House of Valiante.*

Rumours emerged that villagers caught sight of the Lost Prince years after his supposed death in the forest. Some believe they saw a ghost; other sightings were simply dismissed due to the age disparity. But it happened enough that the legend grew. As such, the Lost Prince is said to haunt the lower woods of Brittannia, with powers envied of even the most skilled of the Alchemysts.'

Leo turned to face Flora and Lisandre. 'If the nymphs'

knowledge is correct, then he is older and even more powerful than we originally thought. It means he lied when he came to the Alchemical Court. He may have even left and come back to the Court many times, because he simply does not age.' Leo crossed his arms across his chest. It seemed he did not know the man who had been his teacher at all.

'He has been searching for the talismans a long time, then?' Lisandre asked.

'Perhaps. More likely, he only recently discovered about them and the scroll,' Leo mused, moving his hand to his chin, deep in thought. 'Although, now that I think about it, he did send us to find as much information relating to the lost city of Atlantica as we could find. He sent us on missions to find relics, scrolls and books from the lost city scattered across the realm. He kept the missions private. All that we gathered was reported to him and he kept it secret from the other teachers.'

He pulled out his Almanac. 'I was going through his old notes from the information we had collected for him the night of the attack,' he explained, turning to the pages where had copied out his master's notes and searching for any mention of the talismans.

'Hang on. Did it not occur to you he might be related to this royal house when he called himself Duvalle?' Flora interrupted, raising her hand to draw his attention.

Leo glanced up. 'Of course it did, when I was old enough to learn the histories of the kingdoms—but you have to understand, many royals send the occasional family member to become an Alchemyst. Lucien, for example,' he explained. 'It crossed my mind that he was perhaps a descendant, but the house of Duvalle has become so obscure as to almost have dissolved within the branches of the other houses after that. I concluded he was perhaps a distant descendant, a nobody, and that was my mistake.'

'You could not have known what he was, Leo,' Lisandre reassured him.

'We should tell Lady Vidjaya,' suggested Flora. 'He will surely attack the castle again. Lucien saw us, and he knows we were looking for the talisman.'

* * *

'Richard Duvalle is the Lost Prince?' repeated Lady Vidjaya when they told her later in her study. Her violet eyes widened slightly in surprise as she lifted her matching-coloured spectacles, setting down the scroll she had been reading. Beside the scroll on her mahogany desk rested a vase of fresh spring flowers, scenting the surrounding air with their sweet perfume. They were a sprig of exotic pink frangipanis, a flower often found in the tropical gardens of the Australis Empire of Lady Vidjaya's origin. She had taken to growing some of the plants in the shared greenhouse of the Academy downstairs, and now that the days were becoming warmer and longer, the flowers were starting to bloom. Their unusual scent reminded Lisandre of spring in Na Foraise Síorai, and she suddenly felt an unexpected nostalgia for her own realm.

'Yes,' replied Leo.

'But nobody on the council will simply believe the word of a nymph, I'm afraid. Do you have some proof?' Lady Vidjaya asked.

'Not yet,' admitted Leo.

'Then we must keep this knowledge to ourselves for the moment,' she told them sombrely. 'And we must continue to find the talismans. The next, I believe, is the ruby.' She returned to examining her scroll.

Leo, Lisandre and Flora began to file out of the study. Lady Vidjaya looked up and addressed Leo as he reached the doorway.

'Don't forget your classes, Leo. You still have your

penultimate exams coming up soon,' she reminded him kindly.

Leo nodded and left to catch up with the others.

* * *

A fortnight later, the three were heading once again to spend another weekend researching in the Alchemical Library when they unexpectedly passed one of Leo's teachers on the stairs. Lady Irene, who taught mostly about various plants and astronomy, was holding a bunch of opened envelopes as she headed downstairs with an unusually serious expression written upon her face.

Leo immediately paused, Flora and Lisandre watching beside him. 'Lady Irene, what is it?' he asked.

She glanced up anxiously from her letters. 'Oh, Leo! It's you,' she sighed with relief upon recognising one of her favourite students. Her manner then grew serious once again. 'There have been reports, a sighting of the Dark Alchemyst,' she explained in a grave tone. 'An incident in the forest, just north of here. Green flames burning the trees and a strange design on the ground, like an ancient rune of some kind. They said the flames burned in the shape of it. The Alchemical Council is sending a group to investigate. More than that I cannot say. I would stay in the castle if I were you. I fear we may be on the verge of another attack. Perhaps you should send your friends home?' she suggested, glancing nervously at Lisandre and Flora before she continued. 'The Alchemical Council is gathering as we speak to discuss what should be done, and is asking for volunteers. I must go to the meeting and —'

'I'll go,' Leo immediately volunteered.

'How very noble of you. I wish you luck, Leo,' Lady Irene said. The three of them watched as she hurried away downstairs and along the corridor.

'I want to go with you,' said Lisandre once they reached the top of the stairs.

'Lisandre, no. You cannot. It could be a trap. You need to stay here, please, where I know you will be safe,' Leo pleaded, reaching for her hands.

She met his eyes, seeing his concern written clearly in them, and eventually agreed, giving a small nod. She then reached into the small pouch tied around her waist, procuring the Emerald Talisman, which she placed in the palm of Leo's hand. 'Take it. We may not know what his plan is, but if Arianna is there, then he will have the Stone of Wishes and whatever other magic he has . . . If I cannot be there to heal you, then at least take the gem. You may need it.'

Leo nodded, remembering the gem's rejuvenating healing powers.

'I'll stay with Lisandre,' Flora informed them, and Leo returned to his chambers to fetch his cloak before heading to the chamber where the Alchemical Council had gathered.

He stood at the back, quietly listening as the members of the council announced what he had previously heard: that there had been an anomaly in the forest — some kind of unusually enchanted green flames were destroying the woods — and sightings of a man matching the description of the Dark Alchemyst, tall and wearing a distinctive embroidered black cloak detailed with gold runes. None of them had seen his face, though, casting doubt as to whether it was actually him.

Leo stood apprehensively with his arms crossed, his back against the castle wall. It appeared he would be facing his former master sooner rather than later after all. He did not feel ready, but at least he would be accompanied by many skilled Alchemysts and a few other apprentices, including one of the girls from his class. Together they set out later that day to investigate the woods to the north of the Alchemical Court.

Meanwhile, Lisandre stayed at the castle, watching quietly beside Flora from the high tower windows as Leo set off. The party quickly disappeared into the forest, almost as if the pine trees consumed them whole.

After they had disappeared, Lisandre and Flora headed to the Alchemical Library. Together they wiled away the afternoon in the library researching the rich histories of the kingdoms and the ancient legends of Atlantica, which Flora would re-enact for Lisandre, leading to much laughter and not quite so much study. It was too hard to study when the fates of Leo and the others hung in a such a shroud of uncertainty, but she did her best to lift their spirits and keep Lisandre's mind — and her own — off such things.

Leo and the others had still not returned that evening when Lisandre and Flora headed downstairs to the hall for dinner.

'I'm sure they will all return soon,' Flora said, trying to reassure her as they ate, but as Lisandre glanced out the towering glass windows and saw the fading sunlight fall upon the castle, she could not be so sure.

After dinner Flora suggested they play a game of cards in the Alchemical Library. Or rather, she taught Lisandre some basic Fuschian card games in an attempt to distract from her growing gnawing concern for Leo and the others.

An hour or so later, after many rounds, Flora retired to her chamber while Lisandre continued to browse the shelves, eventually settling upon a book of Alyssrian fairytales. It turned out they were, in fact, largely not about faeries at all; indeed some were rather scary stories with tales of curses and strange creatures. She promptly replaced the book back on the shelf and found another book titled *An Introduction to Alchemy*, which she read for a little while before finally returning upstairs. Leo had still not returned, and despite her friend's efforts Lisandre could not help but worry. Perhaps Leo would send a message in the morning with an explanation that would resolve everything.

As she approached the tower, she saw that a messenger stood waiting outside her door, even at this late hour.

'A letter, my lady,' he said and held out the sealed letter upon which her name was clearly scripted in dark blue ink:

Lady Lisandre

'Thank you.' She took the letter and the messenger left.

Lisandre waited until she was safely locked inside her chambers before hurrying to open the letter. *Perhaps it is news from Leo,* she thought, her hopes rising as she opened the seal, only to find the unfamiliar handwriting of another instead.

Lady Lisandre

I know you have the talisman.

Bring the Gem of Flowers to me

Or Leo will face the consequences.

You have until midnight.

Go to the moonpool downstairs

Come alone

Richard Duvalle

Face the consequences . . . Leo was in danger. Lisandre knew at once what she must do.

Fetching her lavender cloak, she set down the letter, did up the buttons over her cream-and-gold dress, and raised the hood. Outside her chamber, where she took one of the glowing torches from its holder on the wall, its vibrant blue flames casting the corridor in a hauntingly luminous shade of blue as she descended the stone steps into the lower floors of the castle. Unnoticed, she headed to the second floor, then into the familiar labyrinth of the dungeons with its many twists and turns, before emerging once again amongst the Ægyptian columns before the moonpool.

She came to a stop, freezing instantly at the sight before her.

A large creature now stood between her and the moonpool. The purple scales covering its body shimmered in the sparse moonlight and tendrils of smoke gusted from its enormous snout as it slowly emerged from the shadows. Lisandre stepped back, releasing a small gasp as she came face to face with the familiar creature.

A dragon. *The* dragon that had attacked the Alchemical Court less than a month ago. The dragon that had chased her, almost killing her in the process.

It lifted its head and its large, hypnotic green eyes met with her own.

Solve my riddle, princess.

The dragon spoke inside her mind again, and Lisandre stood frozen in shock as the dragon then continued.

Present in sun but not in rain,

Disappearing at night, returned at dawn again,

Always following, never leading,

Sometimes growing, sometimes receding,

Never in darkness truly conceding,

That is my game.

Now, what is my name?

Her eyes locked with the dragon's for several moments before she was able to pull herself away from their magnetic gaze and contemplate the riddle.

Her attention was drawn to the light and flickering flame of the torch, the fire dancing with the shadows around it. Shadows fell around the light, like the morning sun falling through the trees of Na Foraise Síorai. And at night there were no shadows, for there was no contrast, only darkness, except for the light of the moon.

Lisandre glanced up at the opening above the moonpool. The full moon under which they had travelled to the City of the Nymphs had been less than two weeks before, and now the new moon was steadily approaching, with its small silver crescent in the sky casting little light upon the waters. She was unsure the portal would even work with such little moonlight to take her to wherever Leo was. Perhaps Duvalle had no intention of letting her rescue him, she despaired. And then she remembered how badly he wanted the talismans as she found her answer.

She turned back to face to the dragon. 'Shadow,' Lisandre answered confidently, and the dragon bowed its head, letting her pass to access the moonpool.

The portal was still glowing, the tendrils of supernatural green light casting fierce shadows as the flames flickered across the surface of the pool. Different symbols marked the spaces between the lines than before, and the reflection of the crescent moon rippled upon the centre of the water. She stepped onto the rocks surrounding the edges of the pool before quietly taking a deep breath to calm herself.

Lisandre stepped forward, plunging into the portal, the green flames still dancing enthusiastically upon the waters around her, burning brightly as they disappeared from sight.

She was instantly engulfed by the familiar feeling of falling before she rose to the surface from within a fountain, emerging in a garden. A gigantic apple tree full of large, ripe red apples hung overhead.

'Salutem, Lady Lisandre,' she heard a strange voice say as she stepped out of the waters.

The man from the portrait, Leo's former teacher, stood before her. *Duvalle.*

He appeared no older than thirty years of age. Tall, handsome and impeccably dressed in a fine black tunic with embroidered details of gold, he stood confidently with his hands clasped behind his back as if waiting for her, which of course he was. He continued to gaze at her intently, his expression unreadable behind his neatly trimmed goatee.

'Mo leithscéal,' he apologised. 'B'fhéidir go mbreadth tú a bheith níos compordaí má.'

My apologies, Perhaps you would be more comfortable if we spoke in your native tongue?

'No, we can speak Alcheme,' she told him, and he gestured for her to sit at the table opposite him. Lisandre warily sat down and lowered her hood.

'Leo has cast an Alchemical languages spell, I see,' noted Duvalle as he reached for the teapot, pouring them each a steaming hot cup of tea.

'Where are we?' asked Lisandre, undeterred as she glanced around. She had never visited a realm quite like this before. There was a strange dreamlike quality to their surroundings, almost as if simply thinking something could make it materialise faster here. And yet it felt as if she had somehow travelled here before, in her dreams perhaps . . .

'The Dreamworld — a parallel realm if you will. Surely as a member of the fey you have been taught about the Dreamworld?' he asked her, but Lisandre remained regretfully silent. The Dreamworld was one of the topics she had not been taught about in her studies.

She changed the subject. If she was to be face to face with the Dark Alchemyst, she may as well find some answers. 'That dragon. The one guarding the moonpool. It was the same one who chased me, the one who attacked the Alchemical Court.' Lisandre held the cup with both hands as she spoke. Steam poured off the rim from the hot liquid inside as she waited for her drink to cool down.

'Ah, yes. Arianna's pet. My apologies — she insisted on leaving it to guard the moonpool to make sure there were no unexpected . . . intrusions to our meeting. She also wanted to test you,' explained Duvalle, drinking calmly from his own cup.

'Why would she want to test me?' Lisandre questioned, attempting to conceal the surprise from her tone before cautiously taking a sip of her tea.

'So many questions. The leaf falls not far from the vine, I see,' Duvalle remarked.

'Excuse me?' replied Lisandre, her hands shaking slightly.

'Your mother. Your *real* mother. Queen Arsinoë I, the Hazel Queen. Hazel is known as the fairest of trees, I believe, is it not?'

Lisandre struggled to hide her shock. How did he know her mother? How did he seem to know so much about *her*? Or the fey? She took another gulp of tea to calm herself.

'How?' she managed to ask. 'The portal only opens every twenty-five of your years. I am only fifteen—how could you possibly know about me?'

'How, precisely,' Duvalle answered, amused. 'How do you think?'

'You have an informant,' Lisandre realised with sudden clarity. Someone at the Court of the Fey was working with the Dark Alchemyst. Her thoughts immediately ran to Queen Ivana.

'Then your father Lord Hawthorn caught on, and I had to have him poisoned. No one knew until your mother figured it out and I had to silence her too. Such a pity. She was truly a great queen, but unfortunately weak; she cared too much. And your sister is scarcely an improvement in that regard.'

Lisandre remained lost in her thoughts at his revelation. Was the informant someone she knew? Could someone she had trusted be working with the Dark Alchemyst?

'What about the gem? Do you promise no harm will come to Leo?' she asked, remembering why she had come here to begin with.

'Of course. And we shall get to that. But first . . .'

Lisandre found herself struggling to concentrate on Duvalle's words. She began to feel dizzy; and her head felt like it was spinning faster and faster. Or was that the ground?

'You are a clever girl, Lisandre,' noted Duvalle, his voice

beginning to echo from somewhere in the background. 'Far cleverer than many realise. And wise for your age.'

He stood up as Lisandre cried, 'Oh no!' She realised what he had done. 'Blackber —'

The cup and saucer clattered to the ground as Lisandre fainted.

Duvalle walked over and picked up the cup and saucer, placing them neatly upon the table.

'Just not clever enough.'

* * *

The clock approached midnight as Leo returned to the castle with the others. Their expedition had been long and drawn-out after they had arrived in the Northern woods. When they had arrived at the forest, it was ablaze with flames in a familiar shade of Duvalle's signature sorcerer's green. In the centre of the clearing the flames formed a large rune upon the ground. The Master Alchemysts immediately began working upon stopping the flames, some using spells to conjure water while others manipulated the air. The enchanted flames continued to burn unabated, but the Alchemysts were undeterred, slowly curbing the edges of the flames' path.

A few of the masters asked the apprentices to spread out and explore the nearby forest, and they obliged, examining the leaves and branches and ground for any sign of the Dark Alchemyst, to no avail. Leo did have time to sketch the mysterious rune of the flames in his Almanac, though. A rune which turned out to be not so mysterious, at least not to him.

Leo was familiar with the symbol of the Midnight Rose, but the other apprentices remained mystified, trying to decipher its meaning, muttering possible explanations amongst themselves. Leo stayed quiet, keeping to himself at the edge of the group. Lost in his own thoughts, he sat with his back against the trunk of a large unscathed oak tree as he tried to figure out the purpose of Duvalle's visit to this part of the forest while he watched the Alchemysts work on the bewitched green flames. It had taken nearly three hours for them to arrive once they had set off from the castle in four enchanted horseless carriages, and more hours had passed since.

He felt for the tiny bulge created by the Gem of Flowers in the pouch underneath his tunic, which he wore beneath his Alchemical jacket. If only he could use its power to restore the trees and plants here in a matter of seconds . . . but he would have to do so another time lest the others start to ask questions.

The sun soon set, and the small crescent moon had begun to rise by the time the Alchemysts had the strange flames truly under control. They had experimented with various different spells and incantations before the flames finally yielded. With the fire finally contained, the Alchemysts conducted an inspection of the damaged forest before preparing at last to return to the castle.

Leo and the other apprentices assisted, examining the forest by the light of their enchanted crystals. Leo could not help but begin to think perhaps the event had been some kind of distraction. He began to worry if the castle was being attacked while half the Alchemysts were absent. He grew concerned about Lisandre. What if Queen Ivana *was* working with the Dark Alchemyst somehow and learned she was there?

He had a sudden strong instinct to return to the castle. Something about this was wrong. An enchanted forest fire only accomplished destruction without purpose, and nothing his former master did was ever without purpose. Leo thought about damning the rules and simply creating a portal back to the castle right now instead of returning in the carriages with the others. He would surely be in trouble for that, abandoning his duties as an apprentice to return to Lisandre and see if she was okay. He liked to think Flora would have contacted him through the ring he'd given her by now if something untowards had truly occurred, and so, feeling slightly less worried, he got into the carriage to head back with the others.

A few hours later they arrived at the Alchemical Court under the deep blue cloak of midnight. Leo was relieved to see the castle appeared to be like any other night as they approached, with its multicoloured glass windows shining brightly against the night sky as they reflected the sources of light within.

Inside the castle, some of the senior Alchemysts met with those who had remained behind, Lady Vidjaya among them. Leo, however, headed straight upstairs to his chambers. He had to tell Lisandre what they had found.

He hoped to gently wake her, so quietly he opened the door and entered — only to find the bed empty and no sign of Lisandre. His heart fell. His instinct had been right; he should have come earlier. He scanned the room, desperately hoping he was wrong. He would never forgive himself if harm had come to her while he had been gone.

He searched the dimly lit room, looking for anything different, anything out of place that may provide a clue as to where Lisandre may have gone. He soon found an unfamiliar piece of paper resting upon the table. Picking it up, Leo quickly realised what had happened as his eyes raced across the page.

He flew across the corridor and began rapping rapidly against the wooden door.

'Flora! Flora, wake up!' he called urgently.

'Leo? Alright! Alright! Amora la Dia, I'm coming!' he heard Flora call sleepily from the other side of the door. She opened it, her purple cloak loosely covering her nightgown. 'What is it, Leo? What happened with your expedition?' She stifled a yawn, still half-asleep. 'It's *late*.'

Leo ignored her, handing her the letter as he passed straight into her chambers. He turned around.

'Lisandre's missing. She's been taken. *He* took her.'

'What? But she was here all day with us. How could he have taken her? Where could he have taken her? And why?' The questions tumbled out of Flora's mouth as she unfolded the piece of paper and started to read Duvalle's message.

'I should have known it was a ruse,' Leo said, pacing aggressively. 'This letter says he wants the talisman.'

'Richard Duvalle . . .' Flora read his name aloud in disbelief. She looked up from the letter. 'But she doesn't have the talisman. You do.'

Leo looked at her gravely. 'I know.'

'Why does he believe she has it then?' Flora asked, confused. 'Was he spying on us at the City of the Nymphs?'

'Perhaps the nymphs told him after we left. I don't know. We can figure it out later. Right now Lisandre is in danger.'

'Well, what are we waiting for? The sun to rise? Let's go!' Flora implored.

Leo glanced questionly at the corner of her white nightdress peeking out from underneath her cloak.

'Oh! Right' she said. Performing a quick spell, she transformed her nightdress into her scarlet day dress underneath her cloak, and fixed her hair. She glanced at her reflection in the nearby oval mirror before they exited her chamber, locking the door behind them, and hurried down the stairs.

* * *

Downstairs by the moonpool, Lucien stood waiting. Scrying in the moonpool, he had watched Leo and Flora's conservation before they hurried along the corridors. Prior to that, he had of course encountered the dragon guarding it.

Go home, warlock, the dragon had spoken inside his mind. Using his knowledge and skill with sorcery, Lucien had managed to solve that particular problem.

He smiled to himself as he spied the now miniature purple dragon glaring down at him angrily from where it sat atop one of the detailed columns. The dragon hissed a tiny puff of smoke amid small orange flames that travelled less than a foot in his direction. Lucien laughed, with his arms crossed. Arianna would not be pleased to see what he had done, but he cared not.

Never mess with a sorcerer, he thought proudly, then resumed scrying in the water of the moonpool.

His gaze was drawn to Flora, the images focusing on her as they reflected his thoughts. She was still as beautiful as she was in his dreams. He noticed her dress under her cloak. The scarlet dress. The one she had worn when they had first met at the Midnight Court.

He looked up as the pair of them approached the chamber. Leo and Flora paused in the doorway. Leo looked displeased to see him. As did she.

'What are you doing here?' she asked him warily.
'I've come to help,' Lucien said sincerely, but Flora tilted her head disbelievingly to the side.

'Oh. You mean like how you were such great help last time. No thanks,' Leo said as Flora retrieved her daggers, pointing them directly toward him at waist level.

'I'll watch him. You go save Lisandre,' she told Leo, who didn't need to be told twice. He walked over to the moonpool and began examining the symbols left upon the surrounding rocks.

Flora swiftly caught a flicker of movement out of the corner of her eye, noticing Lucien's hands as he reached behind his back. She waved at him with her daggers.

'Ah-ah-ah. Show me your hands,' she commanded, and he did . . . revealing *The Book of Moon*. Flora could not conceal her surprise.

'I'm sorry I never should have taken it,' Lucien said as he held the book out to her. Flora eyes were fixed upon the book for a moment before she glanced up at him, reading the expression on his face.

She stepped forward and slapped him.

That's gotta hurt, Leo thought, looking up from his markings.

'I guess I deserve that,' Lucien remarked, gently rubbing his jaw.

Flora cautiously accepted the book from him, enclosing it safely between her arms. 'I do not understand. Why now? Why help us? What about your mother? What about your debt to Duvalle?'

'She is safe from his reach for now,' he said, watching her as she stood before him, her arms wrapped around the book. With his gaze fixed upon her, it felt somehow as if only the two of them were there. 'Besides, it's my fault they knew Lisandre was at the Alchemical Court to begin with. I told them where to find her,' Lucien admitted guiltily, glancing down at his boots.

'Duvalle would have found her anyway,' said Flora.

'But I shouldn't have helped him,' replied Lucien, his eyes meeting hers again.

'Yet you did. Why the change of heart?' she asked, her tone genuinely curious and without accusation.

Lucien looked away again. 'I didn't like the person I was becoming. Micha would have been disappointed in me had I continued down that path,' he admitted. 'So I have chosen another course, to try and make amends.'

There was a pause as Flora seemed to decide whether she should believe him. After a while she seemed to have made up her mind, yet her expression remained unreadable as she spoke.

'Lucien, can I ask you something?'

'Anything,' he answered.

'At the City of the Nymphs, did you really mean what you said?' she asked, her eyes downcast before she glanced up to meet his gaze.

He reached forward and his hand gently touched her cheek. 'Every word.'

Her heart quickened at his words and she felt herself melt a little inside at his touch. Lucien smiled at her and took her hand, suddenly becoming more playful in his manner.

'Now, my dear countess, we have to go assist a certain faerie princess.'

'Oh come on now, you know I'm not really a countess,' Flora protested. 'My aunt is the only *real* lady I know, and besides —'

'Ahem, am I interrupting?' said Leo. Flora blushed as she suddenly remembered they were certainly not alone.

'Yes,' Lucien replied, sounding amused.

Flora dropped his hand and stepped away while he crossed his arms casually against his chest. 'No!' she answered, glaring at Lucien before turning to address Leo. 'Not at all, Leo.' She put on a smile before turning back and whispering to Lucien, 'You're never going to let that go, are you?'

'Never, my lady,' Lucien replied with a small grin, thoroughly enjoying her reaction.

'Shall we?' Leo asked, and the pair returned their attention to him, remembering the urgency of the task at hand. 'Now,' he said mostly talking to himself as he turned to face the portal. 'How exactly do we reactivate the portal?'

He knelt down and checked the symbols on the rocks again, calculating the necessary adjustments to the portal opening spell and making sure they were as accurate as possible. Lisandre was relying on them, so they had to be correct.

As Leo was figuring it out, Lucien and Flora watched him, side by side. And as Lucien stood there, Flora's face profile to his own, he realised he had never wanted anything more in his life than this, to just be with her. To be by her side, forever and always.

A single word, her name, formed on his lips. *Flora.*

Flora turned to face him. 'Did you say something?' she asked, confused. She could almost have sworn she had heard her name spoken in a low reverent whisper.

'What? Uh, no' he replied, awkwardly glancing away, realising he must have been muttering. Flora was still gazing at him questioningly, not entirely convinced, when Leo's voice grabbed their attention.

'There, that should do it.' He stood up, having finished the incantation. The stones in front of the moonpool began to glow a vivid blue once again.

With Flora's attentions firmly diverted as the portal opened, Lucien glanced at her again, capturing another glimpse of her beauty. But it had been more than that. He had missed her company in the weeks they had spent apart since their adventure in the Great Library and visit to the Realm of the Fey. *Perhaps by helping them find Lisandre now, I can begin to finally earn her trust again,* he thought as he watched Leo then Flora leap into the moonpool, before following behind them.

* * *

They arrived in the Enchanted Garden. And then Leo saw her. Lisandre was lying upon a fallen log, underneath a gargantuan apple tree. Skin as pale as snow, lips red as blood, she appeared peaceful as she slept.

'What have you done?!' Leo raced to Lisandre's side, holding her and checking her pulse. She certainly appeared to be sleeping, the steady rise and fall of her chest indicating as such.

Flora picked up and examined the teacup, levitating it with her magic so it was floating just above her palm. 'Blayckberries,' she informed them, setting the cup down. 'In my realm we call them spindlebyrries.'

'Indeed,' a deep male voice interrupted them, and they turned to see Duvalle standing at the other end of the clearing. 'Tea brewed from the leaves of the blayckberry sends the fey into a deep sleep as the poison takes hold. Their bodies have a different constitution from ours, it seems. What is not toxic to us is poisonous to them. I have the antidote, of course, but first you must give me what I need.'

His eyes fell on Lucien, whom he gave a brief look of disgust before continuing.

'The talisman, Leo. I believe that you know –'

'You poisoned her? She never did anything to you!' Leo shouted, unable to keep his composure any longer.

'If anyone is to blame for Lisandre's current predicament, you need look no further than in a mirror,' Duvalle responded sharply. 'You poisoned her with love. She would do anything for you. I wonder Leo, would you do the same?'

Leo glared back at him as Lucien and Flora watched the scene unfold with caution.

'Now. The Gem of Flowers,' Duvalle said bluntly. 'I know she found it, but it was not in her possession. I hope for her sake that you know where it is.' He stepped away from where Lisandre lay sleeping.

'How could you possibly know that?' Leo replied, cautiously following him.

'A nymph named Phoebe told me. She seemed most distressed that you had left her, Leo, and for a faerie no less – a particularly beautiful pale faerie with dark hair, who was at the City of the Nymphs with you recently, looking for the gem.'

They paused at the edge of the grove. Leo glanced over his shoulder and saw that Lucien and Flora remained by Lisandre's side, quietly monitoring her condition. Flora seemed concerned as she watched over her friend.

Leo returned his full attention to Duvalle. For a moment Leo considered telling him neither of them had been successful in finding the gem, but he realised Duvalle would likely see through such a ruse. As he paused, silently contemplating, Duvalle continued.

'Unlike the Amber Talisman, they were not particularly specific about where under the city the Emerald Talisman would be. And that is where you come in, Leo — my talented apprentice, whose own heritage would hold a significant advantage.'

'But I didn't find the talisman,' Leo stated, unsure what Duvalle was implying. 'Lisandre did.'

'Yes, an unexpected outcome. I forgot to take into account the closeness of the fey and their cousins. But her usefulness ends here. The blayckberries will soon see to that. Unless you give me the talisman, of course.' He glanced over at Lisandre's sleeping form. 'Why do you think the portal brought you to their realm, hmm? Some cosmic twist of fate? No. It was by my design, along with the work of my daughter, Alaïa. I left the necessary runes on purpose, knowing you would be curious enough to go through my notes, but it was her spell that drew you into her path. Yet things did not go as I intended and instead you fell for that *Lisandre*.'

Duvalle noted the last with considerable disgust as Alaïa herself emerged from a portal behind him, walking over to join her father.

'Luckily, my plans are adaptable,' he added as she stood beside him.

'Hand over the talisman, Leo,' Alaïa spoke calmly, outstretching her hand towards him.

'The talisman could heal her. Why should I give it to you?' Leo asked.

'Because if you don't, I will end her life before the blayckberry does,' Duvalle stated aggressively, pulling back the edge of his cloak and revealing the sword hanging from his side. 'And I would end each of you as well . . .'

Leo glanced at Lisandre's sleeping form and reached into his jacket, retrieving the Gem of Flowers. He sighed and reluctantly handed the talisman over to Duvalle.

'Now, will you cure her?' he asked as Duvalle gazed at the gem with a self-satisfied smile before tucking it away inside his tunic.

He returned his gaze coldly to Leo. 'Let this be a lesson to you, Leo,' he told him ominously. 'So that next time you make the right choice. Now come. Let us put these events behind us.' He turned around, expecting Leo to follow him and Alaïa back into the trees but Leo had not moved a single step towards them.

'The right choice? You never intended for her to live, did you?' he accused, unable to comprehend Duvalle's actions. 'Why? Because she is a faerie? Or a princess? Or both? Or is it because I love her?'

He was not sure exactly when he had become sure of that. At first he thought her beautiful and enchanting: the more he spent time with her, he realised he found her personality even more so. But she was a faerie—a faerie princess, to be exact, with all the responsibility and danger that brought. And he was an Alchemyst, an Alchemical apprentice, and for as long as he could remember, he thought he would grow up to serve the Alchemical Court.

Meeting Lisandre had changed that. Perhaps his path was not as straightforward now as he would have liked, but in helping her see the truth about her situation, Lisandre had helped him find the courage to do the same for himself. Even so, would she have agreed with what he had done? Giving up the gem to save one person, even if it that person was her or someone she loved? Leo certainly hoped so.

Duvalle's harsh voice returned his thoughts to the present.

'How sweet. Yes, my dear foolish boy. Yes to all those things, but most importantly, it would seem you haven't yet figured it out. With Lisandre gone, *my daughter*, Alaïa Duvalle, remains the rightful heir to the Realm of the Fey. So yes, she *has to* die. Not only the Realm of the Fey but the powers of the Midnight Rose will fall to Lady Alaïa, and no one will be able to find a better queen than she.'

' Daughter of shadows and fairest night

Blooms in the darkest hour

Shine with most brilliant light

Doth this bright and most loveliest flower'

'The Midnight Rose. Are you familiar with the poem?' Duvalle asked Leo after reciting the first verse.

'You think it is her?' Leo glanced toward Lisandre, wondering if it were true. And then he remembered how she healed him when the dragon had attacked. She had seemed capable of truly extraordinary power.

'You do not? At first I believed it to be Alaïa — they are of the same lineage, and it would make sense that her mother, Lady Yaesmin, could also have inherited the powers of the Midnight Rose, given her history. But then I learned about Lisandre, and so I looked into the history of their Queen Arsinoë. I realised that she just as easily could be considered a Midnight Rose as well. For princess Arsinoë grew up in a hidden part of the forest known as The Hollow, where slightly less sunlight reaches through the dense woods. And bloom she did in the darkest hour, ending the civil war of the fey — uniting them all, it seemed.'

He spoke the last few words slowly, as if annoyed by her success, or somehow envious of it.

'And Lisandre's upbringing does rather mirror hers, don't you think, Leo? Hidden for her own protection, and yet she somehow still shines brightly, like an annoying little firefly that just won't go away . . . until now. '

He turned around and looked upon the unconscious faerie.

'Poor Lady Lisandre, destined to sleep for all eternity,' he remarked, then turned back to Leo. 'Listen to me, Leo, my finest apprentice. Love is poison. It has clouded your judgement, distracted you from what is necessary, from who you really are and what together we can achieve.'

Duvalle's words were true. He did consider Leo to be the best he had ever trained. Leo's natural talent for Alchemy was even more advanced than that of Lucien, who was also rather skilled in the art.

But to Leo, the words of his once favourite teacher now seemed like poison, especially in comparison to those of Lisandre. And his love for her could not be further from it, for it was pure, healing and good.

'Come with us, Leo,' Alaïa said again, wrapping her hands around his.

Leo recoiled, taking a step backwards. 'No. Never —'

'Yes, Leo. It is your destiny. After all, did you really think it was a coincidence they left you in front of a fountain outside the Alchemical Court?' said Duvalle.

'What are you talking about?' asked Leo.

'I know that Lady Vidjaya lied to you. I knew your parents, even met them once or twice,' Duvalle continued smoothly.

'Is Leo my real name?' he questioned carefully. *Is this another trick?* he wondered. But part of him was also curious. He knew so little of his family – if even part of what Duvalle said was true, he would want to know.

'That part is true,' Duvalle admitted. 'Your mother, a nymph called Daphne of the Waters – she named you. She too had fair hair. She and Oleander, the second son of the Brittannian king, fell in love during a rather turbulent time in that kingdom's history, during the fall of house Blackthorn. She named you Leopold Trystan Blackthorn shortly before she died. She was very weak after the birth. We believe Trystan may have been her father's name – it is a nymph name, after all.'

'But there are no male nymphs,' Leo corrected him. 'And Trystan Blackwood was an 13th century Alchemyst –'

'And was also part-nymph, as you are. Though he hid it very well,' Duvalle replied. 'Those like you are exceedingly rare, for it is true that the majority of nymph children are born of mortal men and nymph mothers. Those are the female nymphs. But in very rare occasions, an Alchemyst and nymph procreate, and it produces a child with a natural affinity for the arts of Alchemy – a male child born of nymph heritage.'

'Why should I believe you? About anything?' Leo demanded.

'Because I was there. Maybe not always in my usual form, but I had followed the course of their union and Daphne's flight, as I knew she was with child and any child of such a union would possess unique gifts, making them a superiorly gifted Alchemyst. Making them truly worthy of my training and my guidance,' Duvalle explained passionately. 'Worthy of assisting me in implementing my grand vision for uniting the realms. Don't you see? We can make all this better!'

'What?' was all Leo managed to say in response.

Duvalle was growing agitated. 'I wish you would come to

your senses, Leo. You are, after all, my greatest student.'

'You knew who I was all this time and you didn't tell me.' Leo took a step back. 'You manipulated me. Last year, you sent us to the City of the Nymphs—' The realisation dawned upon him. 'You were hoping *I* would find you the talisman . . .'

'I let you discover the truth when you are ready. *I* am your greatest teacher. Now come, enough of this. Let's go, Leo.'

Leo remained where he was.

'No. And you're wrong. Love is necessary, in this world and all the others,' Leo declared. 'It is not poison. It heals, it transforms, it creates. Whatever you are talking about is something else.'

Duvalle's face contorted with sublime anger at Leo's refusal—just as a blinding flash of light suddenly appeared to the side of the clearing in the form of a portal opening.

Leo raised his arm as he looked away, trying to protect his eyes from the searing light. As it faded, he lowered his arm and looked up to see Queen Ivana standing where the portal had been.

'You!' Leo exclaimed, his blood boiling.

'No, Leo it's not what you think!' Ivana raised her hands in surrender.

As they were momentarily distracted, Duvalle and Alaïa swiftly took the opportunity to leap into the endless trees and slip away.

'This is your fault!' Leo proclaimed, returning his attention to Ivana, unable to stop their escape.

'She is my sister,' Ivana revealed, suddenly trembling. 'I do not wish for her to die!'

Leo realised she was speaking the truth. 'I know,' he said quietly.

'Wait. How did you know?' she asked cautiously, a note of surprise in her voice.

'I figured it out from what Lisandre told me of her parents and what I found in the Hall of the Yellow Rose,' Leo explained. 'Turns out Lord Hawthorn's wife Elina died a year before Lisandre was born. Then I learned how close the late queen was with her father, Lord Gwennaël. That, and your efforts to keep Lisandre at court, to keep her from finding out the truth.'

'Does Lisandre know what you have told me?' Ivana asked him.

'Yes.'

'I was just trying to protect her,' she explained, pacing anxiously. 'He came to me, revealed he had killed my mother *and* possessed the Amber Talisman, the very heart of our Crystal Tree. He threatened to use it to destroy the entire faerie race. So I made a deal to protect us, and to protect my sister.'

'The fey should know who she is. They can help protect her,' said Leo, crossing his arms across his chest.

'No. I promised our mother I would keep her secret. I promised to protect Lisandre,' Ivana insisted, shaking her head. 'There may be peace now, but as you can see, there are still some in the other houses who will feel threatened just by Lisandre's existence. Instead of the crown falling back to the House of Duirrose through Alaïa, as determined by the Treaty of the Golden Rose, it would go to her. She is next in line to be queen of our realm. Do you understand? It may be peaceful now, but if they knew of her existence, I assure you it won't be. She will have a target on her back. It would threaten her safety. I cannot allow —'

'She already has a target on her back,' Leo argued. 'Duvalle knows who she is. So do others. Better the fey know now so they can support her and protect her.'

'She'll never be queen if she dies,' Lucien remarked dryly as he and Flora approached them.

'Leo! We don't have time for this!' Flora interrupted. 'What do we do?'

Leo's focus immediately sharpened. Flora was right; they could argue later. Right now they needed to save Lisandre.

'Right. I need my workshop. Lucien, I need you and Flora to help me levitate her back to the castle,' Leo instructed.

Together they levitated Lisandre along the air between them, back through the portal and then upstairs back to Leo's chambers, Ivana following.

'Any ideas on how to save the faerie princess?' Lucien asked, trying to lighten the mood once they were all standing in Leo's chambers.

They laid Lisandre's unconscious form gently down on the bed and Leo rushed over to the bookcase. He knew of a few possible methods to cure her, but suspected only one would prevail. Only a handful of Alchemysts had been able to successfully brew the famous Elixir of Life. Lisandre's life hung in the balance. He hoped that this would be one of those times.

He retrieved a rather large volume as Flora tended to Lisandre. 'Hurry, Leo!' she cried over to him. Lisandre seemed to be becoming even paler than normal, as if the life force were being sucked out of her.

Leo placed the heavy book upon his worktable and opened it. He searched the index of Ancient Scripts before turning to the appropriate page.

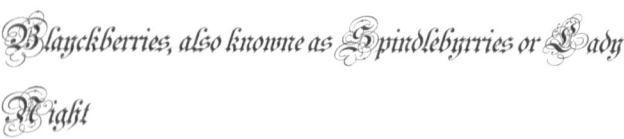

Blayckberries, also knowne as Spindlebyrries or Lady Night

Used to prepare a sleeping draught, these byrries art knowne to be deadly to members of the fey.

Only the glorious Elixir of Life can awaken a faerie from their trance.

The yellowed page confirmed Leo's suspicions. Ivana watched him carefully from across the room as he worked, Lucien and Flora assisting him. Leo turned to another page of the book. The entry was accompanied by an illustration of the elixir and a variety of Alchemical symbols.

The Elixir of Life

The Elixir of Life requires each of the four elements as listed in the forms below:

An additional two forms of each element is also required.

Bottled winds of Zephyr

Water from the Isle de Sabassia of the Mer

Leaves of the sacred vine or bark from the trees of Na Foraise Siorai

Flames of Draconius Rex, or ashes from a rose in their flame

Sands of Time, or a crystal formed from them

He began instructing Lucien and Flora on where to find each ingredient from among the shelves. They hurriedly set to work and began each examining the various little jars, finding those Leo requested and swiftly setting them upon the crowded worktable.

Ablaze with curiousity, Flora lifted the lid of the jar labelled *Flames of Draconius Rex* to see swirling orange flames circling all by themselves inside. She replaced the lid and placed the jar upon the table with the others, wondering just how exactly the Alchemysts had been able to enchant the flames in such a way as to preserve them.

She stood beside Lucien, watching as Leo checked the many tiny different coloured jars before he returned to the open pages of the book, double-checking the list of ingredients until he reached the last line.

and the final ingredient, that which cannot be named

The list ended with a handwritten note.

If you cannot figure out the missing ingredient then you are misusing the noble and sacred art of Alchemy. For those whose intentions are true, remember the greatest alchemy is not magic, nor anything that we do. The greatest Alchemy is the highest expression of **why** *we do what we do.*

Leo paused and reflected. A secret ingredient. But clearly

some Master Alchemysts had been able to decipher it. The Elixir had been created and brewed a few times throughout history. *Typical Alchemysts,* he thought, *writing their secrets in codes and riddles . . .* He pondered the words some more.

The greatest Alchemy . . .

Why we do what we do. What do Alchemysts do?

We protect, we transform and refine, we purify, we collect knowledge, he thought.

And we love.

He thought of Lisandre's laugh and her kindness, and how he admired them both. He thought of the way she cared deeply for all manner of creatures and those around her. Her kindness towards him, even as a stranger. Her caring nature, and her generous heart . . .

Love is the greatest Alchemy, he realised. And that was his answer.

'The elixir can only be used if given out of love,' he whispered to himself. His intentions were pure. He wanted Lisandre to live.

He began preparing the elixir, pouring and mixing the ingredients together as per the instructions. He ground the leaves with a mortar and pestle before adding them to the liquid, distilling the extract and combining it with the remaining ingredients until finally collecting the elixir in a small glass vial.

The Elixir of Life. Or so he hoped. If it worked, he would be one of, if not the youngest to ever prepare it. An honour among the Alchemysts, for sure, but he did not care about any of that at the moment. All he cared about was Lisandre, and whether or not it would save her.

* * *

'And now he has two of them,' Flora commented gloomily, thinking about the talismans as she and Lucien watched Leo carefully poured and weighed the various ingredients for the elixir.

'Not for long,' Lucien told her, standing up. 'We shall see about that.'

'What?' she asked, confused, but he had already gone. Heading down the corridor, she tried following him. 'Lucien? Where are you going? Lucien!'

But he had already slipped away out of sight.

She returned to Leo's workshop, where he was now making the final adjustments to the elixir. 'Do you truly think it will work, Leo?' she asked as she came to stand beside him. Lisandre had become her closest friend, her dearest companion these last few months. Flora did not want to lose her.

Leo glanced at her as she watched over Lisandre fearfully. 'We can only try,' came his grim response.

He held up the small clear vial to the light. Inside was a misty, translucent liquid, swirling around like liquid marble. Flora followed him as he walked over to where Lisandre lay so still, barely breathing, almost statuesque upon the bed. Flora watched as Leo gently poured the mystical liquid between Lisandre's pale lips.

'Now what?' she asked once he had stepped back, holding the now empty vial between his fingers.

'Now we wait. If the elixir works, it could take hours for her to wake,' Leo warned.

'Then we should take turns watching her,' replied Flora. Both of their eyes were still on Lisandre.

'Yes. Return to your rooms and get some sleep, Flora,' Leo instructed. 'I'll come and get you in a few hours.'

'Alright,' Flora conceded, barely stifling the beginning of a yawn. She glanced once more at her friend, then left Leo's chambers.

Leo settled down into the bedside chair to watch over

Lisandre, hoping for her sake that he would be one of the few known Alchemysts to have made the elixir right.

* * *

The falling white hawthorn flowers reminded Lisandre of Beltanes past, spent with her father, Lord Hawthorn. The coming of spring was a huge celebration among the fey. The flowers blossomed from the trees; their sweet scent filled the air.

'They are said to bring love and protection,' her father told her as he bent down, affectionately tucking one of the flowers behind her ear.

She was about seven years old in the dream. She looked up at him as he knelt before her, with his familiar tawny brown hair and hazel eyes. A father's love was clear within those eyes.

'Lisandre.' A female voice affectionately called her name, and she turned around at the sound of the queen's voice.

Queen Arsinoë. She stood there, smiling at Lisandre.

Her mother . . .

As she gazed up into the face of the queen, she recognised some of Arsinoë's features as her own.

'Mother . . . ?'

Queen Arsinoë reached an arm toward her, their hands almost touching.

And she woke up.

* * *

'Lisandre!' Flora cried with relief. 'You're awake!'

Lisandre opened her eyes and saw Flora leap up from where she had been sitting by the window, coming to stand beside the bed.

'Where am I? Where's Leo? Is he alright?' Lisandre asked immediately as she quickly sat up.

'He's fine, you can see him when you are ready,' Flora assured her.

Lisandre rose from the bed. Flora poured her a cup of water

from the jug and handed it to her.

'Here. Drink.'

Lisandre accepted the cup, pouring the water down her dry, scratchy throat.

'Now, what do you remember?' Flora asked her.

'I—I remember the garden . . . and Duvalle . . . and—oh!' Lisandre suddenly exclaimed, almost dropping the cup again as she recalled what had happened. 'The tea—the tea had blayckberries. He tricked me, Flora. I'm so sorry.'

'There is no need to apologise,' Flora told her friend. 'Leo was able to brew the Elixir of Life. He saved you.'

'He did? And the talisman?'

'Leo gave it to Duvalle. He thought he would give an antidote in exchange,' explained Flora. 'Duvalle also threatened all our lives if he did not.'

Lisandre glanced upon the still open book, reading about the elixir. Then she wandered behind the screen and began to change, pulling off her dress.

'Flora, how long was I asleep?'

'Bit longer than a day. Are you sure you are alright?' Flora answered, still slightly concerned.

Lisandre emerged from behind the screen, now in her golden fey dress. 'Yes. Thank you. But I need to find Leo.'

She exited the chamber, searching the corridor for any sign of him. As she wandered her way downstairs, she came across Lucien lurking around an alcove on the second floor. Quickly turning the other way, she continued, but Lucien had already seen her.

'Lady Lisandre,' he addressed her politely.

Lisandre turned around warily, surprised. She hadn't expected him to have the nerve to talk to her after when he had done. She hoped it was not another trap.

He brought forth an object she also had not expected to see.

'I believe this belongs to your people,' he said as he presented her with the Amber Talisman.

'Máith anise,' she thanked him in her native tongue as she reached forth, touching the Amber Talisman, finding herself suddenly engulfed by a vision.

Her surroundings seemed bathed in golden light as she recognised the familiar exterior of the Alchemical Court. She saw the statues leap down from the bridge and march towards the castle below where she, Leo and Flora had stood on the balcony that day only a few weeks ago. The vision then flew north to the forest, deep into the cover of the trees, where a petite woman wearing a purple cloak stood, holding the Amber Talisman around her neck to her lips as she whispered with a wicked smile, 'I wish . . .'

The vision then returned to the castle, and she watched as the statues turned and began attacking the Alchemysts. Then the vision ended, and Lisandre found herself staring down at the gem.

'Are you alright?' Lucien asked her.

'Yes, yes, of course,' she answered, accepting the sacred gem from his hands and placing it around her neck, slipping the piece of amber gently down the front of her dress, hidden from sight.

'I also hope that you will accept my apology for my misdeeds, and that this in some small way makes some amends,' Lucien stated.

She observed him, considering his apology before coming to her decision.

'It is a beginning,' said Lisandre. 'And yes, I do accept your apology.'

Lucien seemed glad, giving her a small smile as he stood with his hands clasped behind his back.

'Have you seen Leo?' she asked abruptly.

'I believe he was waiting in the bluebell woodland, wherever that is,' Lucien answered dismissively.

Confused, she returned to Leo's chambers. Why would he have gone there and left no way for her to get there? That didn't sound like Leo at all. Unless, she thought sadly, he wanted some time to himself away from her . . . but then, why go to the woodland? It didn't make any sense. She paced the room, unsure what to do. She was about to leave when she saw it.

A series of circles had been drawn upon the stone floor. She recognised most of the symbols inside the circles. Including those for air, forest and a pair of bluebells.

A portal.

She smiled, then tapped the centre circle three times and recited the incantation as Leo had told her to activate the portal. Glowing light energy appeared from the centre, following the lines Leo had drawn until all the white circles, including the encompassing outer circle, were glowing. Lisandre could feel the hum of the energy vibrating around her. She took a breath and, for the first time on her own, stepped into the circle.

The walls of Leo's chambers seemed to fall in towards the floor as her surroundings transformed. She stepped out into the forest-guarded woodland. Bluebells formed a sea of flowers at her feet, while the edges of the woodland featured the familiar line of oak trees standing tall and ever watchful. Across the clearing she could see Leo standing with her back to her, peacefully lost in his own thoughts as he quietly observed nature and his surroundings. The sweet melody of birdsong sounded within the trees.

'Leo,' she called out to him, smiling.

He turned around, holding his breath. It was the first time his eyes had met hers since she had been taken by Duvalle, two nights ago. Since then, he and Flora had taken turns watching over her as she recovered while Lisandre remained with her eyes closed, still in her deep sleep.

'Lady Lisandre,' Leo breathed. He couldn't stop staring. She was okay and she was here. He couldn't help himself from smiling, either.

'Leo,' she replied again, also still smiling as she came to stand before him.

'One of the fey here called you the Autumn Princess while you were asleep. It would seem that the Holly Queen recognises you as her heir now,' noted Leo, remembering from his studies the titles given by the fey to the heir depended upon the season of their birth.

'So it would seem,' she replied. 'You saved my life. Thank you.'

'You are welcome,' he answered, and Lisandre felt butterflies rise somewhere within her with his eyes still upon her.

'We seem to keep saving each other . . .' she remarked as she looked away shyly.

'I will always be there for you, Lisandre,' he said, and as she looked up, his steady gaze reminded her of the calm eye in a storm, strong and unstoppable. 'You knew I had the gem and yet you went anyway?' he asked.

She nodded. 'I'm sorry. I was trying to save you. The letter said he would hurt you. He thought I had the gem. He must have talked to the nymphs. It doesn't matter. All I could think of was you, that he would hurt you if I didn't . . . I wasn't thinking clearly.'

Leo calmly took her hands. 'I know, I understand.'

'You do?'

He dropped her hands and walked a few steps away. 'Alchemysts are meant to keep the balance, to remain impartial,' he said, turning towards her once again. 'But that's impossible when it comes to you. My head says one thing . . .'

'And what does your heart say?' she asked, reminding him of his own words from not so long ago.

Leo met her eyes. Despite everything, they still held hope.

'You know what my heart says,' he said, and all of a sudden he rushed towards her, as if a magnet were drawing them together. He placed his lips on hers. He held her as he kissed her passionately, and together they soon fell into the flowers. To him, Lisandre tasted of starlight and strawberries and vanilla. She was everything pure and wholesome and good.

Their union filled one another's hearts with joy, setting both of their souls alight. Lisandre felt as if her back could melt into the ground underneath them as they kissed each other for what felt like hours. Time seemed to stop in their presence. There was only this moment, and within this moment was an untold eternity and timelessness with only each other.

She sat for a while, resting calmly in Leo's arms in the beautiful, serene woodland before together they decided to return to the Alchemysts' castle. They returned through the portal hand in hand, passing Ivana in one of the courtyards.

'I need to speak with her,' Lisandre told Leo.

Still holding her by the waist, he nodded. 'I will see you later,' he promised her, kissing her forehead. They parted and Lisandre went looking for her sister.

She found Ivana still in one of the courtyards near the hall, where she was examining the roses, which were different from those of Na Foraise Síorai in both colour and shape, with their arrangement of intense red petals greater in number than those of her own realm. Ivana did not notice her sister's approach until Lisandre's voice formally addressed her from behind.

'Fairest one.' Lisandre curtseyed.

Ivana turned around, a relieved smile quickly forming on her face. 'Lisandre!' You're alright!' She rushed towards her, wrapping her arms around her and enveloping her in a hug, surprising even Lisandre. 'Oh, Lisandre, I was so worried,' Ivana whispered over her shoulder, struggling to keep the tears from forming in her eyes.

'I am alright. Truly,' Lisandre reassured her calmly.

Ivana stepped back, still holding her dear sister's hands as she looked upon her. She had almost failed. Almost failed to protect her sister and keep the one vow she had made to their mother. Duvalle had wanted Lisandre dead all along, she realised, and if not for the Alchemyst, she would be. Upon arriving in the Dreamworld, she had captured a glimpse of Lady Alaïa by Duvalle's side as he had escaped, and she understood now it had been Lady Ivy behind the attempt on Lisandre's life at the Solstice ball, for she was Duvalle's accomplice. Though she doubted whether the other members of the council would believe her.

Earlier, Leo had informed Ivana that Lady Alaïa was in fact Duvalle's daughter — the daughter of an Alchemyst and a faerie, it seemed. Leo wondered if he believed her heritage would make her a superiorly gifted Alchemyst too, and he remembered her interest in the symbols of his Alchemical Almanac as he told Ivana the truth of her lineage.

Few had known Alaïa's mother at court, for Lady Ash had kept to herself for many years after the triumph of her own mother, Arsinoë, ended the civil war that threatened to divide their realm. Lady Ash had retreated for many centuries, preferring to stay with the faeries of her own region, the Glade. Many of the court of the fey had almost forgotten about her until the unexpected birth of Alaïa, and the news that followed soon after that Lady Yaesmin had died due to unexpected complications resulting from the pregnancy. Many had assumed her lover must have been a faerie from the Glade; it mattered not, after all. Arsinoë had her heir and the many clans and houses had sworn to support her over any children of Lady

Yaesmin and their claim.

But then Arsinoë had passed away, and Ivana had found herself suddenly queen with no husband and no heir, reigniting old rivalries as it dawned upon them all that the then fourteen-year-old Alaïa was in fact now the only successor. Or so it appeared. All that time, Ivana had known the truth: that thirteen-year-old Lisandre was her true heir as her sister, a fact her mother had forbidden her from telling even Lisandre herself until she was older, in the hopes of protecting her from becoming a target the same way Arsinoë herself once was.

Now, Ivana and Lisandre walked together in comfortable silence through the courtyard in the warm morning light of spring.

'You are my sister,' Lisandre said after a few minutes, recapturing Ivana's attention. 'I am heir to the throne. I don't understand. Why didn't you tell me?'

Ivana became noticeably flustered as she began to answer, continuing to look straight ahead, away from Lisandre. Our—our mother forbade me telling you who you really were.' She turned to face Lisandre. 'You are the only family I have left. And Duvalle—he somehow knew who you were, and he had the Amber Talisman. I am so sorry.'

'It was Alaïa. She must have told him. She's his daughter,' Lisandre explained.

'Yes, I know. Leo informed me,' Ivana said with a sigh. 'She was behind the attack on your life, Lisandre. She cannot return to Na Foraise Síorai—not while I am queen, anyway.'

Lisandre's expression became sombre at the thought. She had known Alaïa all her life; they had been friends —perhaps not as close as she was now with Flora, but it still saddened her to know Alaïa would live in exile. 'Such a terrible fate for any member of the fey,' she noted sadly.

Silently Ivana agreed, but she had to protect her sister. The title of Lady Ivy would also be forfeit now. They would have to find another member for their council, it seemed.

Lisandre reached down the front of her dress to procure the talisman. 'And as for the Amber Talisman — I wouldn't worry about that,' she told Ivana as she revealed the gem with a warm smile.

Ivana gazed at it with evident surprise. 'But how?' she asked incredulously. 'I was certain the *amberheart* was in Duvalle's possession. However did you get it back?'

Lisandre paused for a moment, thinking about her answer. 'A friend returned it me. He used to serve the Dark Alchemyst, but has had a change of heart,' she said, admiring the talisman. *The Stone of Wishes*. She wondered what Ivana would wish for.

She looked up at her sister.

'As princess I have to return home now, don't I?' she asked, with notable regret. She liked staying here, seeing the other realms and spending time with Flora and Leo. Besides, someone needed to find the other talismans and stop Duvalle, and the Alchemical Court didn't seem to want to acknowledge who the Dark Alchemyst was, nor the threat they were facing. It seemed Leo would be finding the talismans alone unless she and Flora helped him.

'Not necessarily,' Ivana said, the hint of a smile forming on her lips.

Lisandre's expression was a mixture of surprise and curiosity.

'Now we have resumed formal contact with the Alchemical Court, the fey need someone to represent us,' Ivana explained. 'It can help prepare you in your duties as princess, and no one upon the council is more suited in nature . . . That is only if that is what you choose. Of course, you will still need to return to the Court of the Fey every month or so to provide us with an update on these new relations. And you must continue your

Nádúr studies and—'

Her response was cut short by her sister's sudden embrace.

'Máith agate dialoch—*thank you very much*, Ivana. I am truly so grateful,' Lisandre said over her shoulder.

Ivana gradually relaxed her tenseness, allowing herself to receive the hug.

'Now, I think it is time we went home, don't you?'

* * *

Leo and Flora also chose to accompany the sisters as they returned to Na Foraise Síorai the next day. There was dancing and music and much celebration as they arrived back in time for Beltane, a festival to celebrate the middle of spring and approaching beginning of summer in their realm.

Once they had settled into their rooms, Lisandre changed into her favourite Beltane dress: cream and sunflower yellow, featuring long, flowing sleeves trailing from her arms. After she finished weaving white hawthorn flowers among the crystals in her hair, she glanced at her surroundings, content to be back among the trees once more. They had woven themselves together a long time ago to form the walls and shelves of the room, upon which rested her collection of various crystals and scrolls on the topic of Nádúr.

Glancing at her reflection in the shallow pool of water before her, Lisandre could now see the similarities between herself and the Hazel Queen. She wondered about her destiny. Would Ivana eventually marry and have children of her own? Or would Lisandre someday become queen like her sister and mother? She pondered the many possibilities, each as intriguing as the last. She was officially the Autumn Princess now. But things could change. Leo's entrance into her life had taught her that. And he had reminded her she had some say over her destiny as well.

She paused in the doorway, glancing back. In a few days

she would return to the Alchemical Court with Leo, now as an official ambassador for the fey. Her hands rested upon the tree doorway as her eyes wandered around the room. This was her home, and though she yearned for adventures and to see other places, part of her would always belong in Na Foraise Síorai. The trees and the fey were connected; the Amber Talisman had shown that, she thought, glancing down at the gemstone resting across her chest. Then she left her chamber to rejoin the others and attend the dances.

Jasmine flowers blossomed from the vines upon the trees, their scent filling the air as the fey danced in circles in the clearing beneath them. The fey had adorned Flora's scarlet dress with flowers much like their own and had woven even more flowers and crystals into her hair. Though the fey had been sceptical at first of the witch who had escaped with the warlock, Flora found that, as Lisandre's friend she was now welcome among them. As was Leo.

At first he and Lisandre kept to the edges of the crowd, watching as Flora eagerly partook in the dances, quickly learning the different steps with ease. After a number of dances, she returned to where Leo and Lisandre stood, in need of a rest—at which point Lisandre eagerly took Leo's arm, pulling him into the dance.

Together they joined the other members of the fey, who rapidly formed a large circle to either side of them. With a flurry of flutes, the next song started, and the fey began moving one way before joining their arms to form another circle, crisscrossing their feet in rhythm with the music. Leo made a clumsy effort to match their movements, but was met with limited success that did nothing to lessen his merriment.

The circle then dissolved into groups of four, and a few moments later into pairs, and Leo found himself dancing with only Lisandre again. He held her hand as she twirled, then lifted her up into the air, their eyes locking with one another as he gently set her down again.

'Leo, can I ask you something?' she asked him quietly as the fey continued to dance around them.

He nodded.

'What was it? The missing ingredient?'

He took her hand. 'Love. Love is the greatest Alchemy. It transforms, it creates. Love enables us to heal and to become the greatest version of ourselves,' he explained. 'I deciphered the notes to reveal that the elixir can only be given out of love.'

'Do you love me, Leo? You are still getting to know me,' she warned cautiously.

'That is true,' Leo admitted. 'And yet I love all that I know thus far, and I hope that I will continue to get to know you each and every day from this day forward.'

Lisandre smiled, and they resumed the dance.

* * *

A few hours later, they slipped away and joined Queen Ivana standing underneath the Crystal Tree. The others watched as Lisandre stepped before the imposing tree, the Amber Talisman in her hands an offering to the sacred tree spirit. Leo heard her begin to speak in Alcainn, the language of the fey, addressing the Crystal Tree as she knelt and offered to return the talisman, the *amberheart.*

Lisandre heard the branches of the tree move, and she opened her eyes, concealing her shock much more effectively than Leo as a face formed in the wizened trunk of the ancient trees. In all her life, she had never seen the Crystal Tree act so.

'*Lisandre, daughter of Arsinoë,*' the spirit of the Crystal Tree formally addressed her.

'*We thank you for returning the Amberheart. We are most grateful. We now ask of you to please protect and guard this sacred talisman . . .*'

The tree spoke so all nearby could hear it, yet no lips moved.

'*As long as the Amberheart remains in the hands of the fey, both fey and Crystal Tree will flourish. You are now its guardian and must not misuse its power. The power of wishes is dangerous if used unwisely,*' the spirit warned her.

Lisandre nodded as the tree's features morphed and the face disappeared from the trunk.

She stood, the talisman in her open palm as she turned towards Leo and Flora. She had been asked to protect the Amber Talisman, a great honour among the fey. One that she hoped she would prove worthy of bestowing. She also hoped perhaps the talisman might help them retrieve the others, as there would surely be challenges finding those as well. Glancing at her friends, though, she felt certain now that between the three of them, they could face anything.

* * *

Chapter Twelve

Beneath the Lilac Tree

Lilac

first love, magical, old flame, spirituality, confidence

Wear a garland of lilacs to attract true love

May 1526

*F*lora returned to Rose Cottage from the Alchemical Court a few days later, after Aunt Bellissa sent a letter requesting her to finally come home. Now she was finally back in Fuschia, in her familiar surroundings and her favourite lilac dress, remembering her adventures with Leo and Lisandre fondly until they figured out the location of the next talisman.

She wandered aimlessly around the cottage. Aunt Bellissa had gone out for the afternoon to run some errands, and Flora had asked if she could help, but instead her aunt had insisted she was fine and that Flora should remain at the cottage. Felippe, of course, was away on business, and so she was here again, alone — *almost like before,* she thought sadly.

She wished she could have stayed at the Alchemical Court

with her friends, helping them find out the locations of the talismans, but she knew Aunt Bellissa would not have called her home unless it was important. Or perhaps she had been wrong about that also. She found it strange that Aunt Bellissa had barely spoken to her since she arrived back in Fuschia yesterday morning. Perhaps she was just too busy with the Festival of Flowers currently taking place throughout the country. It was always one of the busiest times of year for many people in Fuschia, especially for florists and those that grew the flowers, artisans, and of course, dressmakers, for many beautiful dresses were required for the number of dances throughout the festival.

Held at the start of May each year, the Festival of Flowers was a sign summer was approaching, and a celebration of everything in Fuschia being in bloom. Flora had hoped to one day attend the dances herself; she had almost done so last year, but Aunt Bellissa had caught her sneaking out of the cottage at the last minute and she had been unable to go anywhere for close to a month after that.

She glanced outside as a speck of brown and white fluttering in the air caught her eye in the distance, growing larger as it came closer. She watched as a beautiful forest owl flew down to settle on a branch on the tree outside her window. Behind her, a scroll appeared on her dresser, only the sound of crinkling paper alerting her to its manifestation. Flora turned around and reached for the tiny scroll, picking it up and opening it to find a note scrawled in the elegant script of Lucien's handwriting:

Meet me by the lilac tree

They had not spoken since the events of the night they had rescued Lisandre, during which he had abruptly left — to go retrieve the Amber Talisman, Lisandre had informed Flora later. He must have taken the opportunity and snuck back to wherever Duvalle resided before he and Alaïa returned. Lucien had returned the talisman to the fey through giving it to Lisandre, and he had returned *The Book of Moon* to Flora. He seemed to be finally making amends, with no promise of anything in return. Perhaps he did share her hope that things between them could finally be different.

Her gaze wandered over the note again, and like a spell, she saw everything flash between them in her mind: every moment, from the moment they had met, to Micha placing her hand in his; the night he'd taken her to the forest, where they had danced in the Dreamworld and he had given her the rose; escaping from the Great Library; standing together before *The Book of Moon*, almost touching; stolen glances at Rose Cottage; the roses blooming around them beneath starlight in the Briar Wood, like an enchanted circle binding them to one another forever . . .

Lucien.

And then she remembered how he had betrayed her — betrayed their friends too. Betrayed them all for the Dark Alchemyst. And Flora had been utterly heartbroken.

But then he had found her at the City of the Nymphs, and he had left her again with more questions than answers, only to reappear at the final hour, returning the book and helping them save Lisandre. Flora was unsure whether to fully trust him just yet, despite his assurances before the moonpool. But she also could not kill the ember of hope that still burned within her since their last meeting.

I would do anything to keep you and her safe

Did you really mean what you said?

Every word

Their past exchanges played over and over in her mind. The way he had looked at her. No one had ever looked at her that way before, not even Mikhail. And now he was an exile, and an Alyssrian, unwelcome in Fuschia, yet he dared to come just to meet with her.

Meet me by the lilac tree . . .

His words called to her from the page. She remembered the large lilac tree from Palazzo Fuschia, the one beside the fountain when they had encountered each other at the New Years Ball — where they saw each other for the first time since leaving the Midnight Court.

Flora set off towards the city, soon approaching the distinguished Palazzo, where she found Lucien at the edge of the grounds, dressed in sapphire blue again, standing beneath the lilac tree, exactly as promised. The tree's branches were now covered with spectacular purple flowers, and the Palazzo behind it had been decorated with flowers to celebrate the middle of spring.

Lucien saw her, and a gentle smile formed upon his lips. She rushed the last few steps towards him, joining him under the shade of the lilac tree. Its heavy, sweet, intoxicating scent filled the air around them as they stared at one another expectantly.

'Why are you here? In Fuschia?' Flora asked breathlessly. 'What if someone sees you?'

'You know why,' he said, keeping his eyes on her as he stepped towards her, closing the distance between them.

She regarded him carefully, crossing her arms nervously across her chest.

'Perhaps I need you to say it,' she said, unconvinced.

'It's the Festival of Flowers, no one will notice me among the crowd today,' he answered nonchalantly.

Flora's expression darkened. 'Ugh. This was a mistake. I shouldn't have come.' She turned to leave, but Lucien grabbed her hand.

'Flora, wait,' he pleaded, his tone now serious as he found his words. She paused. 'I asked you to come here because I wanted . . . I wanted to see you, and I want you to know . . . that I don't care that she is your mother. I care not if you have a title, or no title to your name other than a pair of slippers, or if you called yourself the Countess of Moonshine.'

Flora smiled at that one.

'I would still love you. I do love you, Flora,' he said, all earnestness. 'I will always want to be by your side,' he confessed. 'You have cast a spell upon me no magic can ever undo,' he confessed. 'Please be mine.'

A wide smile, as bright and brilliant as the sun, dawned upon her face in response, and he pulled her suddenly toward him. He kissed her, and it was glorious as they stood entwined together under the purple blossoms of the lilac tree. Flora melted into the kiss, wrapping her arms around Lucien's neck and combing her fingers through his hair. He placed his hands upon her waist, pulling her closer, and then her hips, their touch setting her soul on fire. Flora felt herself glowing with happiness. They were finally together, not as an Alyssrian prince and Castellean countess, or even an exiled prince and a Fuschian maiden, but simply themselves. A sorcerer and a witch. Or perhaps a witch and a warlock. Lucien and Flora.

They pulled breathlessly apart a few moments later, and Lucien offered her his arm to go inside to the dances. Flora accepted, gladly wrapping her arm around his. He stretched his right arm up and made a few motions towards the tree, enchanting four sprigs of lilac into the air, where they fell swirling downwards in a current towards him. A bouquet of freshly conjured indigo lobelias appeared in his awaiting hand as the lilacs came to rest neatly among them. He offered them to her.

Of all species, he had chosen a favourite of the witches, she noted, one that symbolised love, devotion and a strong bond. And of course, lilacs symbolised first love, a magical union, an old flame. She accepted the flowers, feeling almost dizzy as she breathed in their heavenly scent, and they continued happily through the grounds.

As they approached the palazzo, the sounds of music and merriment grew stronger, with a variety of instruments and musicians performing their songs. Some were even outside in the courtyards as the people wandered within.

'Arianna, Arianna,

Only nineteen, suddenly the queen.

Arianna, Arianna,

Caught the king's eye,

'*Won a mighty fine prize . . .*'

A minstrel sang lavishly while playing a violin, catching Flora's attention as they passed by with his song of the mysterious Queen Arianna, who had died many years ago. She knew very little about the former queen who shared her name with her mother. Why was that? she wondered. Why did hardly anyone seem to know anything about the late queen?

Something strange began to knot in the pit of her stomach in response to the thoughts as they took hold. The feeling unsettled her. But Lucien soon drew her attention, and she looked away from the minstrel, allowing him to take her inside.

* * *

Inside the palazzo, the golden staircases had been covered thoroughly with many garlands of bright pink flowers. The entrance to the ballroom was though a square courtyard in the heart of the palazzo, which was surrounded by at least three tall stories of gold balconies, each almost completely covered with the same pink flowers. Lucien realised these were the mysterious Hanging Gardens of Fuschia, which he had read were only allowed to be seen by the public once a year. Flora marvelled at their beauty and tried imagining herself living in such a place.

They followed the sound of the music to the ballroom, where they joined dozens of young couples in the dances as members of the court watched on, entertained. At one end of the ballroom, King Orlando sat alone in his chair, slightly bored as he watched the annual dances being performed once again. They were mostly the same each and every year; after all, the spring dances were a long well-kept tradition of Fuschia.

Lucien, however, had never seen them before, and he found himself impressed by both the array of coordinated dances and the unique Fuschian melodies in the air. Harps were played along with an assortment of flutes and several violins, filling the room with their song. Together, Lucien and Flora danced and danced, unable to keep their glowing smiles off their faces as she taught him the dances, lost in a world of their own. He lifted her by the waist as they spun around in time with the music.

Orlando watched and listened as they sang one of his favourites, a tune popular among the people even two decades ago, known as 'A Dance of Oak and Holly'.

> *'The king saw the queen of shadows,*
>
> *So begins their song so jolly,*
>
> *the fateful prophecy.*
>
> *The sun and the rose,*
>
> *A Tale of Oak and Holly*

> *No longer lost it seems,*
>
> *For now I linger within your melody*
>
> *Weaving a tapestry of dreams*
>
> *A Vision of Oak and Holly*

> *So dry your tears mon amour*
>
> *And let go of your melancholy*

And join me forever more

In a Dance of Oak and Holly'

King Orlando watched, intrigued, as Flora danced. He was suddenly engulfed by a vision of the past. A vision of himself dancing with Arianna. He remembered her warm laughter, the diadem of pearls woven in her dark hair, the way she moved effortlessly in time with the music, her sly little smile that had enchanted him and so many others . . .

'Impossible,' he murmured, unable to take his eyes off the red-haired girl. A *very* familiar arrangement of emeralds and pearls rested around her neck. Bellissa would never have sold that necklace; it had been it her sister's — besides, she had been very successful with her business ventures.

His attention returned to the girl again. This time he examined her features before coming to an unexpected conclusion.

'She is our daughter.'

The realisation dawned upon him, the shock causing him to quickly become lost in his thoughts once again.

He'd been told the child died with Arianna. Had Bellissa lied? His thoughts turned sharp at the implications. He quickly glanced back to the corner of the ballroom he had last seen the girl with her dance partner, only to find they had left.

Or perhaps it had just been a mirage, he told himself, shaking his head.

And then it hit him.

The maiden from the Great Library. The one with red hair who had somehow managed to slip away . . .

The king suddenly rose sharply from his chair, and, with a determined stride, set off down the hall for his chambers.

* * *

'Come! We must tell my aunt!' Flora pulled Lucien by the arm excitedly, racing back to Rose Cottage under the falling twilight of the early evening.

After the dances, they had split the remainder of the afternoon between wandering the city of Florencia, Flora showing Lucien her favourite parts of the city, and the Briar Wood, where they had sat talking and kissing in the ancient forest.

'She'll be so pleased to meet you!' Flora insisted.

'Why? I am not a prince anymore,' Lucien said, allowing Flora to lead him back to the cottage.

'No, silly. Because I am yours and you are mine—and you will always be a prince to me,' she told him playfully, wrapping herself around his arm.

'Well, I suppose there can be no harm in that,' he said, and leaned forward to steal a kiss from her again.

Night was falling swiftly as they arrived back at Rose Cottage. Flora was sure her aunt would be home by now. The glowing candles in the windows indicated someone was already waiting within.

'Aunt Bellissa? Aunt Bellissa!' she called triumphantly as they entered, still holding hands, but the cottage remained eerily quiet. Flora quickly realised they were alone in the parlour. Her gaze fell upon red roses from the garden, standing wilted in a vase upon the table, as she glanced around the cottage for any sign of Aunt Bellissa.

'You have returned.'

She and Lucien both turned at the sound of her aunt's voice coming from upstairs. Aunt Bellissa soon appeared, standing in the shadows at the top of the staircase. Her red lips were in a taut knot, the only indication of the stress she had been wrestling with all day. A letter with a broken gold seal lay open in her left hand. She set it down on the side table at the top of the staircase.

'Flora, who is this?' she asked and smoothed down the front of her dress. She began to descend the stairs as the pair stepped into the candlelight.

'Aunt Bellissa, may I introduce —' Flora began, when her aunt suddenly shouted out as she reached the bottom of the stairs, causing Flora to jump where she stood.

'Lucien Safarov!'

'Yes,' Flora said nervously, clenching his hand. She had not expected such an outburst from her loving aunt, who had also married a foreigner.

'Flora — oh, my darling, this cannot be,' said Aunt Bellissa, her tone full of concern laced with a touch of pity.

'Whyever not?' Flora demanded. 'We are in love. I thought that you would be happy for me, for us.' She tried to hide the hurt her aunt's reaction caused.

Painful lines appeared across Aunt Bellissa's forehead as she attempted to explain. 'Because, darling, dearest, there's something important that you should know.' Aunt Bellissa took Flora's other hand, leading her away from Lucien and over to the window.

'Is it about my mother?' Flora asked once they stood in front of the glass, the garden outside barely visible in the moonlight. 'Aunt Bellissa please, you're scaring me.'

'No, my darling. It's about you. Who you really are,' Aunt Bellissa told her.

'Who I really what?' Flora blurted out, confused.

Aunt Bellissa took a deep breath and answered calmly. 'You are Florencia Yvette DuPoitoires-d'Este, daughter of Orlando d'Este, King of Fuschia and Arianna DuPoitoires, his queen. You are the only living heir to the throne.'

Flora pushed her away. 'No! You are lying. This is some

kind of trick,' she said, even though deep down part of her knew it was true.

To Lucien, it all made sense. Too much sense.

'A princess of Este, the curse . . . *thy mortal enemy*,' he whispered behind her as he took a step backwards in shock.

'Flora . . .'

She turned back to face her aunt as Bellissa reached for her hand.

'My darling, I am sorry, but it is true.'

Flora refused to touch her. 'No.' She shook her head, the tears now spilling down her face.

A principessa, the heir of Fuschia, would never be allowed to be seen with, let alone marry an Alyssrian prince, even one currently in exile. For years she had dreamed of being a noble lady like her aunt, a member of the court — but not like this. Now she did not want it to be so. And her aunt, the one person she had trusted most in this world, had known she was so all this time; had deceived her, hidden her, kept from her the very answers she had desperately been seeking for so long.

'No!' She turned and ran outside, past the garden and into the Briar Wood under the cover of moonlight, tears streaming down her face. She ran through the forest, the frayed lengths of her dress catching on the low branches of the trees. She ran until she came to the moonpool under the rowan tree, where she collapsed to her knees by the water's edge, staring at her reflection on its glassy surface.

Is this true? Am I a daughter of Este?

She had always desired to be a noble lady, though she would have preferred to have been recognised for her talent, like her aunt — but the sole heir to a small kingdom entailed responsibilities she could only dream of. What if she was not good enough? What if her father did not recognise her? Disowned her?

She looked back towards Rose Cottage. She had travelled so many times to the heart of Fuschia, to Florencia, her namesake, that she had developed an honest love for the place and its people. From what she could tell, her country needed her, and soon—for despite King Orlando's robust health and stamina, a kingdom without an heir is always vulnerable to threats. For it was well-known that King Orlando had refused to remarry after the tragic passing of his beloved queen many years before, and so many of the nobles of his own court still squabbled amongst themselves while appealing to the king; it was said Orlando even encouraged it.

Would he even want a daughter? Flora wondered.

From such a position, she could also use her gifts to help her people. The fact that she was a witch in a kingdom that outlawed magic was another issue entirely . . .

Could she really walk away and leave her kingdom behind to potentially fall into chaos?

Nay—it was her duty, when she was ready, to provide guidance and leadership to those who needed it, who asked for it. To help where she could. If the king deemed she could help, she would. And she deserved a chance to know her family.

Flora stood up, took in a deep breath and returned to the cottage.

Rose Cottage was quiet as she entered. Slipping past the foyer, she saw Aunt Bellissa still sitting by the table, bathed in candlelight and shadow. Flora paused, her hand resting cautiously upon the banister.

'Aunt Bellissa . . . What was that letter you were holding earlier?' she asked carefully.

Aunt Bellissa suddenly broke from her thoughts, standing up. 'It was an invitation,' she stated in a manner-of-fact tone.

'An invitation for what?' Flora asked.

'For you to attend the court tomorrow, as per the King's request,' she said, then sighed before she continued. 'It was a reminder, really, that the time for secrets has passed, and I cannot hide who you really are anymore. I am sorry, I really am, that this has been thrust upon you. I just wanted to give you . . . Not necessarily a normal life, but hopefully a happy one,' explained Aunt Bellissa. 'Even if it had to be lived in secret.'

She readjusted her shawl. Picking up the candle, she walked towards Flora.

'Come. Let us go to bed. After all I'm supposed to present you to the king of Fuschia in the morning.'

Together they began to ascend the stairs. Flora wanted to voice her suspicions and point out that it was a bit odd for a maiden such as herself to receive such an invitation if the king truly did not know who was, but she was now quite tired after the evening's events and decided against it. Instead, she followed her aunt quietly upstairs and they each went to bed.

* * *

In the early morning, Flora and Aunt Bellissa set off for court at Palazzo Fuschia, an hour's travel away. Normally such a distance would be only a short ride by coach, but Aunt Bellissa had not wanted to attract attention, and so they left early and walked into the city, as Flora had done so many times before.

As they left Rose Cottage and embarked upon the open road, all seemed as quiet as any other morning. But in the distance, a figure wearing a large, hooded cloak of deep purple trimmed with diamonds stood watching from somewhere just behind the trees. Her face hidden by the cloak's shadow, she watched as they set off towards Florencia.

Soon they approached the familiar high cream walls of the palazzo in the heart of the city. Looking towards the east, Flora saw the Great Library standing boldly at the opposite end of the avenue, where she had been only a few months before. Aunt

327

Bellissa lowered her mystical sapphire-blue hood and spoke discreetly yet assertively with one of the palazzo guards, who opened the gate, allowing them to pass through.

It had been many years since Lady Bellissa had visited the palazzo, but she had once come here often when her sister was queen, always as a guest, and so she knew the place quite well, finding her way around the familiar courtyards again. In the growing morning light, they passed through the entrance courtyard, past the enormous marble fountain, then the smaller one beside the shade of the lilac tree where Flora had met Lucien less than a day ago.

She felt the pain of nostalgia again. They had been so happy for a few hours until destiny had torn them apart once more. But she had little time to dwell on the matter as she attempted to keep pace with Aunt Bellissa.

And so along the main path to the palazzo they continued. To either side, Flora admired the immaculately maintained gardens and the stone stairs leading down to them. A few courtiers were already staring as they made their way across the grounds. Flora was pretty sure they were not staring at her so much as Aunt Bellissa, from whom many had brought beautiful dresses and other fine clothing. With the amount of work Aunt Bellissa had coming in, sometimes it seemed she dressed half the court. Flora was sure at least a few recognised Lady Bellissa DuPoitoires, even though she had long since conducted her business outside the palazzo in another part of the city.

Finally they approached the large main doors of the palazzo, and Flora began to feel nervous. At least four dozen courtiers lay on the other side of those doors, along with the king. Aunt Bellissa too seemed to be almost shaking as she paused nervously at the entrance.

Flora noticed something. No longer hidden by decorative banners, she could now see the embellished emblem of a familiar magnificent bird depicted upon the double doors. The same bird she had seen upon her father's signet ring. In that moment, she knew. She knew what Aunt Bellissa had said was true, even more than she had before.

Aunt Bellissa opened one of the doors, and Flora followed her within.

Inside, she noticed several banners hanging along each side of the room: the orange banners of course depicting the Flower of Fuschia, alternating with the older faded green banners of the phoenix, the air from outside tussling the fabric as a breeze followed them into the hall.

Aunt Bellissa remained quietly hidden in the crowd to one side as Flora gently stepped closer towards the throne — now empty, she realised. She was unaware of his presence, but Lucien watched intently from the shadows in the form of a raven perched upon one of the glass windows high above.

Flora looked nervously to Aunt Bellissa, who nodded back encouragingly. Flora gathered her courage and spoke to the crowd of staring assembled nobles.

'Bonne soli to you all,' she greeted them. 'My name is Florencia Yvette DuPoitoires-d'Este' she informed them, 'I am the daughter of King Orlando d'Este and his queen, Arianna DuPoitoires.' Even saying the words they still felt strange.

There was an unexpected silence as the nobles processed this information. True, Flora resembled her parents, but for nearly seventeen years they had thought their queen and baby princess were dead. For a long time they had watched young King Orlando mourn the loss of his family. Such outlandish claims simply could not be true. And many had since formed strategies to benefit their own claims for the line of succession.

'Imposter!' cried one of the nobles, an elderly gentleman dressed finely in black. 'This is an outrage!'

He swung his arm around in a swift, calculated motion to

direct a pair of guards that stood near the entrance.

'Guards! Remove this ragazza — this *maid girl* — at once!' he instructed, and the guards moved in to surround her.

Flora panicked. This was not going at all how she had hoped. She turned around, preparing to run, when an unexpected voice emerged from the crowd.

'Stop!'

Flora turned and watched as Aunt Bellissa stepped forward, gaining the attention of the court. 'She is indeed Arianna's daughter,' she told them.

'And who are you?' asked a displeased younger nobleman.

Aunt Bellissa conducted herself elegantly as she answered, easily commanding the attention of the court. Flora could see why she was such an impressive businesswoman.

'I am Lady Bellissa DuPoitoires, the late queen's sister,' she stated defiantly. A wave of whispers ran through the court, falling quickly into silence as she continued. 'And I was one of the queen's own council. I was there when my niece was born and my sister died.'

'*I* should like to speak to the maiden in question,' King Orlando's low, husky voice suddenly grumbled behind them.

The entire court, including Flora, turned around to see the king enter the room, wearing his usual orange doublet. He surveyed the reactions of the court before focusing on the mysterious red-haired girl standing in the middle of the hall. *She has returned,* he thought, his eyes the only hint of his shock, which he concealed quickly before he moved forward to observe her more closely.

True, she did share some of Arianna's features, but in examining her now, he found that she also resembled him. His green eyes, for example, characteristic of the Este line; and she was tall, whereas Arianna had been petite. She was also the girl he had seen dancing at the Spring ball . . .

His eyes were then drawn to that necklace around her neck. A familiar arrangement of emeralds and pearls. The pendant depicted a phoenix rising into the air, the old symbol for the House of Este.

It was the one he had given Arianna all those years ago when they first fallen in love. Placing all these pieces together, he realised it was true. She was Arianna's child.

Flora stared at him, uncertain, as he approached. A flare of recognition sparked across his face and in his eyes.

'Daughter. My daughter lives.' He stepped forward, his hand gently touching her cheek as a tear fell from his eye. He lifted her hand.

'Father?' She dared let herself breathe the word.

'Surely you do not believe this obvious charade, my king?' the middle-aged courtier interrupted with a disapproving glare towards Flora.

'I know my daughter when I see her,' Orlando replied firmly.

Aunt Bellissa smiled with tears in her eyes. She had waited so long for this day.

The disgruntled courtier beside her, however, continued. 'But it's impossible. Your daughter has been dead nearly −'

'Seventeen years. I know,' Orlando finished, his gaze remaining fixed upon his daughter.

'I really must insist. You must not listen to this street-maiden, Your Majesty,' the man continued aggressively, becoming more and more agitated. 'She could be anybody. Be reasonable. Don't listen to this lowly *ragazza* −'

'Enough, Lorenzo,' Orlando commanded. 'And do not insult my daughter ever again,' he growled over his shoulder.

The courtier fell silent.

'Come, my dear. It appears we have much to catch up on.'

The king led Flora away from the crowd and through

Palazzo Fuschia. They passed one of the inner garden courtyards, then turned inside along another corridor and another, before reaching a grand tapestry of a lion in a garden. Orlando lifted the tapestry to the side, revealing a large wooden door that opened to his study. He gestured for her to go inside, and Flora entered, staring around the room, taking in her unfamiliar surroundings.

'Wait here. Lady Bellissa and I will return shortly,' he reassured her, and left, closing the door.

* * *

'Lady Bellissa . . . a word,' King Orlando addressed her as she stood anxiously on the outskirts of the crowded court upon his return.

Bellissa passed through the throng of gossiping courtiers and followed him. They walked in an uncomfortable silence until Orlando began airing his grievances.

'You kept her from me—from your king,' he stated coldly. Bellissa had known this was coming. Ever since the night her sister had died—but she had made her choice, to protect Flora for as long as possible.

'She made me promise . . . The two of you were not getting along,' she tried to explain, attempting to keep pace with the king as he began walking faster along the maze of corridors. 'She did not trust you . . . You were having affairs.'

'You kept her from me. You kept me from my daughter for *seventeen years*, Lady Bellissa,' he begrudged, pausing to snap his gaze back at her.

'It was my sister's dying wish! And she was right to do so. You were a mess, if you remember!' Bellissa said. 'The child needed a mother, and you were in no state to be a father. We had both lost Arianna and she thought it best for Flora —'

'That's her name?' he suddenly interrupted. He could not believe he had forgotten to ask for her name.

'Yes, Florencia,' Bellissa answered, and a recognition sparked across his eyes as a small, knowing smile formed briefly upon his face.

'A beautiful name,' he commented simply.

Bellissa resumed as they continued walking again.

'She thought it best Flora be raised away from the court, in secret, for as long as possible,' Bellissa resumed as they continued walking.

'Well, I'd say sixteen years is more than enough,' Orlando remarked. 'It's well past time she returned home.'

Bellissa stopped and turned to confront him. 'How dare you! I am the closest thing that girl has to a mother, and she will only be staying here if she decides to do so,' she snapped harshly at him.

'Don't tell me you still live in — what is it called? Rose Cottage?' Orlando replied with obvious disdain for the home of the DuPoitoires.

'I wish Arianna could hear you now. It makes me glad to have stayed away from court so long,' Bellissa answered, looking away as they approached the study where Flora waited.

'As am I, Lady Bellissa,' said Orlando. 'As am I.'

* * *

After her father had left her to find Aunt Bellissa, Flora found herself alone within the king's study. A desk bearing a vase of purple roses sat before a large window with elegant diamond-shaped glass panes. Large shelves of treasured books rested on each side of an empty fireplace. Above it was a portrait of a young lady. Flora gazed at the painting, quickly realising who this was.

She had never seen a portrait of the queen before. All of them had been removed after her death nearly seventeen years ago. A beautiful brunette stared back at her with deceptive doe-like eyes, wearing a cream-coloured dress with open-cut sleeves from the shoulder. Around her neck was a familiar arrangement of emeralds and pearls. *The* necklace. Her mother's necklace — the one she wore now.

Queen Arianna.

'Welcome home . . . principessa,' a mischievous female voice called from behind her.

Flora spun around to see a petite cloaked woman taking down her deep purple hood, revealing the late queen. She looked as though not a day had passed since her death at the age of five and twenty. An amused smile decorated her face.

'Mother? Queen Arianna? Impossible. You and I are almost the same age!' Flora exclaimed in disbelief.

Arianna glanced dismissively around at the objects in the study, as if she hadn't been here in a truly long time, before her eyes came to rest upon her daughter, drawing her full attention.

'Looks can be deceiving. Surely by now you have learnt this,' Arianna informed her disapprovingly.

Flora began re-examining everything in her head. *The invitation . . . was it magicked? Enchanted to appear in the king's hand, perhaps? Was it all a ruse to get me here? How did she know where I would be otherwise?*

'I don't understand . . .' Flora's voice suddenly became shaky. 'You're . . . you're supposed to be dead, you *were* dead my whole life — why come back now?' She was beginning to feel light-headed with shock now.

'All in good time, my darling, all in good time,' answered Arianna. And Flora's world turned to black.

* * *

Epilogue

An Unlikely Alliance

In a distant realm, on the sequestered shores of the renowned Australis Empire, a classical metropolis nestled amongst a jungle paradise surrounded by peaceful aquamarine waters. Pink frangipani flowers blossomed along the beach, alongside various lush green ferns and plants with enormous thick leaves. Further inward was the capital of the empire, Europa, an island city surrounded by water and many tranquil lagoons.

She emerged among the lily pads near the shoreline, where the lagoon waters rose right before the steps of the nearby palace. Her gaze was quickly drawn to the lone figure outside this part of the structure.

A man with light blonde hair, dressed in a red-and-white tunic, stood upon the tiled patio at the top of the stairs. He did not see her as she hid between the waterlilies, her head barely above water as she watched on silently.

It truly was him, she observed. The young Emperor Cosimo who had succeeded his uncles, despite being in only his early twenties. A master strategist and a well-learned, determined young man, even the nymphs had heard stories of his conquest and mysterious succession.

He turned in her direction and his eyes caught hers. 'And who might you be?' he asked inquisitively as she rose gracefully from the waters. Truthfully, he was somewhat impressed she had managed to circumvent the guards along the riverways to even get this close to his living quarters.

Lorelai raised her chin slightly as she proudly addressed him.

'My name is Lorelai. I approach you on behalf of my sisters, the Daughters of the Emerald Rose.'

She spoke in a voice that reminded him of the sweetest melody. Looking at her he noticed she had a haunting, otherworldly beauty about her, with hypnotic eyes and a face that seemed as if it had been carved in marble by the gods. Her fair skin and slight pointed tips of her ears were clues, but her it was mostly her manner that gave away her true nature. The evasiveness of her watery-like movements and the curiousity in her eyes were most definitely the characteristics of a nymph.

She now stood before him on the patio in her turquoise chiton dress. A matching amazonite-and-silver diadem rested upon the crown of her long auburn tresses, which flowed down to her waist. A warm breeze danced between the tangles of her hair as she watched him calmly observe her.

'A nymph . . . huh,' Cosimo remarked. He had met all kinds of folk, especially in the last two years as he became emperor, but had yet to meet these famous creatures of legend. Now one stood before him of their own free will. He was curious, to say the least. 'And why are you here, Lorelai?' he enquired.

'Something was recently stolen from us. A sacred talisman. We believe you can help us get it back,' she told him, her enchanting eyes fixed upon him.

'The Gem of Flowers, I presume,' he replied.

She nodded.

'And why should I help you?' asked Cosimo, curious to hear her answer.

'Our city rests on the borders of your illustrious empire, and we can be powerful allies. I also possess an unusual compass,' Lorelai stated matter-of-factly.

'Unusual how?' Cosimo's face remained as still as a mask,

yet his voice revealed the true depth of his intrigue.

Lorelai outstretched her palm, in which appeared a gold compass inscribed with a series of ancient Ægyptian runes. *The enchanted compass*, he realised as she weaved herself around his body so that she spoke over his shoulder.

'Ask it the location of anything and it will tell you in which direction to go to obtain it,' Lorelai revealed. 'If you help us recover the Emerald Talisman, you may ask it the location of three things.'

'Anything?' he asked her over his shoulder.

She nodded.

'Very well. We have our resolution, Miss Lorelai. Now perhaps, if you do not mind, you can join me for dinner and inform me more precisely how you managed to escape my guards.'

His tone implied she did not have much choice in the matter, and so, somewhat albeit reluctantly, Lorelai accompanied him into the palace.

* * *

Acknowledgements

Thank you to my family for helping turn my dream into reality.

I also wish to thank my editor, Claire Bradshaw, for helping me find the best version of the book and my friend, Apollo Irvine, for always encouraging and supporting me throughout this adventure and hopefully many more to come.

Catalina Paris

is an Australian writer of Czech, Austrian, English and Scottish heritage, and quite possibly some distant French ancestors. Since she was a young child she has loved books, learning, stories and being creative as well as writing, which allowed her to combine them all together.

The Midnight Rose is her first book.

Thanks for reading!

If you enjoyed this book please consider leaving a review at
Amazon or **Goodreads**.

The Legend of the Midnight Rose continues in

Evening Glory